NUMBER9DREAM

'Mitchell catches the multi-coloured atmosphere of Tokyo **brilliantly** . . . He is a wonderfully amphibious writer, happy in all manner of elements, and seems able to produce an endless parade of interesting characters.'
Robert Macfarlane, *Observer*

'The wonderfully energetic prose is **constantly entertaining**, filled with daring imaginative stunts and the crackling rhythms of the digital age . . . Mitchell's Tokyo is a deliciously confusing virtual reality, a maze of bewildering information. Most impressive of all, though, is the fact that when you reach the end, wondering if it was all just a dream, you don't feel cheated in the least.'
Jerome Boyd Maunsell, *Evening Standard*

'The novel's **imaginative power** re-energises everything it touches'
The Face

'*Ghostwritten*'s range of voices was astonishing. Each narrator revealed anew the author's dexterity and his ability to imagine lives. His second novel is more **ambitious** and more **impressive** . . . the main plot drives one urgently onwards, and Mitchell's delight in his inventiveness is infectious'
Victoria Lane, *Daily Telegraph*

'Generally speaking, the second novel confronts two pitfalls: rehashing the first novel or eliminating all trace of it for fear of rehashing it. In *number9dream*, Mitchell negotiates both dangers, retaining what is best of *Ghostwritten* and creating an **original** and in many ways more complex work.'
Shomit Dutta, *Times Literary Supplement*

'Captures aspects of modern Japan with a **compelling authenticity** and beauty'
Juliet Hindell, *Daily Telegraph*

'The external action of the novel is always engaging. But such is Mitchell's **beautifully precise** style that he can make inaction just as pleasurable . . . The prose bespeaks a kind of observational rapture that offers the smell of Tokyo streets or even the movements of a cockroach as tiny, cherishable shards.'
Steven Poole, *Guardian*

'**Dangerously addictive** . . . Mitchell's writing displays the kind of literary acrobatics and metaphysical depth that won him such huge accolades for his first novel . . . a brave novel, all the more admirable for his ability to push back the boundaries of the imagination.'
Andrew Davies, *Big Issue*

'**Wildly inventive**'
Adam Lively, *The Sunday Times*

'The diversity and sheer pace of the narrative sets it well apart from most contemporary British fiction and Mitchell is an original with a flair for fantasy . . . **oozing panache**, this cosmopolitan and fresh odyssey engages and entertains'
Eileen Battersby, *Irish Times*

'He is a very energised and original sentence architect who elevates the steaming, fizzing city of Tokyo into a city of the imagination . . . a gifted and unusual writer'
Russell Celyn Jones, *The Times*

'**Superlative**'
Sunday Telegraph

'A novel as accomplished as anything being written. **Funny**, tenderhearted and horrifying, often all at once, it refashions the rudiments of the coming-of-age novel into something completely original.'
Malcolm Jones, *Newsweek*

'*number9dream*, with its **propulsive energy**, its Joycean eruption of language and playfulness, represents further confirmation that David Mitchell should be counted among the top young novelists working today . . . [He] writes like a dream, the kind you don't want to end.'
Andrew Rose, *San Francisco Chronicle*

DAVID MITCHELL

Born in 1969, David Mitchell grew up in Worcestershire. After graduating from Kent University, he taught English in Japan, where he wrote his first novel, *Ghostwritten*. Published in 1999, it was awarded the *Mail on Sunday*/John Llewellyn Rhys Prize and shortlisted for the *Guardian* First Book Award. His second novel, *number9dream*, was shortlisted for the Booker and James Tait Black Memorial prizes, and in 2003, he was selected as one of *Granta*'s Best Young British Novelists. His third novel, *Cloud Atlas*, won the Geoffrey Faber Memorial and South Bank Show Literature prizes and the Richard & Judy Best Read of the Year. It was also shortlisted for the Man Booker Prize, and adapted for film in 2012. It was followed by *Black Swan Green*, shortlisted for the Costa Novel of the Year Award, and *The Thousand Autumns of Jacob de Zoet*, which was a No. 1 *Sunday Times* bestseller. Both were also longlisted for the Man Booker Prize.

In 2013, *The Reason I Jump: One Boy's Voice From the Silence of Autism* by Naoki Higashida was published in a translation from the Japanese by David Mitchell and KA Yoshida. David Mitchell's sixth novel is *The Bone Clocks* (Sceptre, 2014).

He now lives with his wife and their two children in Ireland.

David Mitchell

Number 9 Dream

SCEPTRE

First published in Great Britain in 2001 by Hodder & Stoughton

This edition published in 2014 by Sceptre
An imprint of Hodder & Stoughton
An Hachette UK company

30

A CIP catalogue record for this title is available from the British Library

ISBN 978 0 340 74797 1

Printed and bound by CPI Group (UK) Ltd, Croydon, CR0 4YY

Hodder & Stoughton policy is to use papers that are natural, renewable and recyclable products and made from wood grown in sustainable forests. The logging and manufacturing processes are expected to conform to the environmental regulations of the country of origin.

Hodder & Stoughton Ltd
338 Euston Road
London NW1 3BH

www.sceptrebooks.com

for Keiko

ACKNOWLEDGEMENTS

Jocasta Brownlee, A. S. Byatt, Emma Garman, James Hofman, Jan Montefiore, Lawrence Norfolk, Ian Paten, Alasdair Oliver, Jonathan Pegg, Mike Shaw, Carole Welch, Ian Willey, Hiroaki Yoshida.

Noburu Ogawa, curator of Kaiten Memorial Museum at Tokuyama, provided valuable information regarding kaiten torpedos and their pilots. For technical data I also consulted *Suicide Squads* by Richard O'Neill (Salamander Books 1999). Any errors are my own handiwork.

‘It is so much simpler to bury reality than it is to dispose of dreams.’

Don Delillo, *Americana*

One

□

Panopticon

'It is a simple matter. I know your name, and you knew mine, once upon a time: Eiji Miyake. Yes, *that* Eiji Miyake. We are both busy people, Ms Katō, so why not cut the small talk? I am in Tokyo to find my father. You know his name and you know his address. And you are going to give me both. Right *now*.' Or something like that. A galaxy of cream unribbons in my coffee cup, and the background chatter pulls into focus. My first morning in Tokyo, and I am already getting ahead of myself. The Jupiter Café sloshes with lunch-hour laughter, Friday plottings, clinking saucers. Drones bark into mobile phones. She-drones hitch up sagging voices to sound more feminine. Coffee, seafood sandwiches, detergent, steam. I have an across-the-street view of the PanOpticon's main entrance. Quite a sight, this zirconium gothic skyscraper. Its upper floors are hidden by clouds. Under its tight-fitting lid Tokyo steams – 34°C with 86% humidity. A big Panasonic display says so. Tokyo is so close up you cannot always see it. No distances. Everything is over your head – dentists, kindergartens, dance studios. Even the roads and walkways are up on murky stilts. Venice with the water drained away. Reflected airplanes climb over mirrored buildings. I always thought Kagoshima was huge, but you could lose it down a side alley in Shinjuku. I light a cigarette – Kool, the brand chosen by a biker ahead of me in the queue – and watch the traffic and passers-by on the intersection between Ōmekaidō Avenue and Kita Street. Pin-striped drones, a lip-pierced hairdresser, midday drunks, child-laden housewives. Not a single person is standing still. Rivers, snowstorms, traffic, bytes, generations, a thousand faces per minute. Yakushima is a thousand minutes per face. All of these people with their boxes of memories labelled 'Parents'. Good shots, bad shots, frightening figures, tender pictures, fuzzy angles, scratched negatives – it doesn't matter, they know who ushered them on to Earth. Akiko Katō, I am waiting. Jupiter Café is the nearest lunch place to PanOpticon. It would be so much simpler if you would just drop by here for a sandwich and a coffee. I will recognize you, introduce myself, and persuade you that natural justice is on my side. How do daydreams translate into reality? I sigh. Not very well, not every often. I will have to storm your fortress in order to get what I want. Not good. A building as huge as the PanOpticon probably has other exits, and its own restaurants. You are probably an empress by now with slaves to fetch your meals. Who says you even eat lunch? Maybe a human heart for breakfast tides you over until suppertime. I entomb my Kool in the remains of its ancestors, and resolve to end my stake-out when I finish this coffee. I'm coming in to get you, Akiko Katō. Three waitresses staff Jupiter Café. One – the boss – is as brittle as an imperial dowager who poisoned her husband with misery, one has a braying donkey voice, and the third is turned away from me, but she has the most perfect neck in all creation. Dowager is telling Donkey about her hairdresser's latest failed marriage. 'When his wife fails to measure up to his fantasies, he throws her overboard.' The waitress with the perfect neck is serving a life sentence at the sink. Are Dowager and Donkey cold-shouldering her, or is she cold-shouldering them? Level by level, the PanOpticon disappears – the clouds are down to the eighteenth floor. The fog descends farther when I look away. I calculate the number of days I have been alive on a paper serviette – 7,290, including four leap years. The clock says five to one, and the drones drain away from Jupiter Café. I guess they are afraid they'll get restructured if one o'clock finds them anywhere but their striplit cubicles. My coffee cup stands empty in a moat of slops. Right. When the hour hand touches one, I'm going into the PanOpticon. I admit I'm nervous. Nervous is cool. A recruitment officer for the Self-Defence Forces came to my high school last year, and said that no fighting unit wants people who are immune to fear – soldiers who don't feel fear get their platoon killed in the first five minutes on the battlefield. A good soldier controls and uses his fear to sharpen his senses. One more coffee? No. One more Kool, to sharpen my senses.

The clock touches half-past one – my deadline died. My ashtray is brimming over. I shake my cigarette box – down to my last one. The clouds are down to the PanOpticon's ninth floor. Akiko Katō gazes through her air-conned office suite window into fog. Can she sense me, as I sense her? Can she tell that today is one of those life-changing days? One final, final, final cigarette: then my assault begins before 'nervous' becomes 'spineless'. An old man was in Jupiter Café when I arrived. He hasn't stopped playing his vidboy. He is identical to Lao Tzu from my school textbook – bald, nutty, bearded. Other customers arrive, order, drink and eat up, and leave within minutes. Decades' worth. But Lao Tzu stays put. The waitresses must imagine my girlfriend has stood me up, or else I am a psycho waiting to stalk them home. A muzak version of 'Imagine' comes on and John Lennon wakes up in his tomb, appalled. It is vile beyond belief. Even the traitors who recorded this horror hated it. Two pregnant women enter and order iced lemon teas. Lao Tzu coughs a cough of no return, and dabs phlegm off his vidboy screen with his shirtsleeve. I drag smoke down deep and trickle it out through my nostrils. What Tokyo needs is a good flooding to clean it up. Mandolineering gondoliers punting down Ginza. 'Mind you,' continues Dowager to Donkey, 'his wives are such grasping, mincing little creatures, they deserve everything they get. When *you* marry be sure to select a husband whose dreams are exactly the same size as your own.' I sip my coffee foam. My mug rim has traces of lipstick. I construct a legal case to argue that sipping from this part of the bowl constitutes a kiss with a stranger. That would increase my tally of kissed girls to three, still less than the national average. I look around the Jupiter Café for a potential kissee, and settle on the waitress of the living, wise, moonlit viola neck. A tendril of hair has fallen loose, and brushes her nape. It tickles. I compare the fuchsia pink on the mug with the pink of her lipstick. Circumstantial evidence, at any distance. Who knows how many times the cup has been dishwashed, fusing the lipstick atoms with the porcelain molecules? And a sophisticated Tokyoite like her has enough admirers to fill a pocket computer. Case dismissed. Lao Tzu growls at his vidboy. 'Blasted, blasted, *blasted* bioborgs. Every blasted time.' I sup my dregs and put on my baseball cap. Time to go and find my maker.

□

PanOpticon's lobby – cavernous as the belly of a stone whale – swallows me whole. Arrows in the floorpads sense my feet, and guide me to a vacant reception booth. A door hisses shut behind me, sealing subterranean blackness. A tracer light scans me from head to foot, blipping over the barcode on my ID panel. An amber spotlight comes on, and my reflection stares back. I certainly look the part. Overalls, baseball cap, toolbox and clipboard. An ice maiden appears on the screen before me. She is blemishlessly, symmetrically beautiful. SECURITY glows on her lapel badge. 'State your name,' she intones, 'and business.' I wonder how human she is. These are days when computers humanize and humans computerize. I play the overawed yokel. 'Afternoon. My name is Ran Sogabe. I'm a Goldfish Pal.'

She frowns. Excellent. She's only human. 'Goldfish Pal?'

'Not seen our ad, ma'am?' I sing a jingle. 'We cater for our finny friends—'

'Why are you requesting access to PanOpticon?'

I act puzzled. 'I service Osugi and Kosugi's aquarium, ma'am.'

'Osugi and *Bo*sugi.'

I check my clipboard. 'That's the badger.'

'I'm scanning some curious objects in your toolbox.'

'Newly imported from Germany, ma'am. May I present the ionic flurocarb pellet popper – doubtless you know how crucial pH stability is for the optimum aquarium environment? We believe we are the first aquaculturists in the country to utilize this little wonder. Perhaps I could offer a brief—'

'Place your right hand on the access scanner, Mr Sogabe.'

'I hope this is going to tickle.'

'That is your left hand.'

'Beg pardon.'

A brief eternity elapses before a green AUTHORIZED blinks.

'And your access code?'

She is vigilant. I scrunch my eyes. 'Let me see: 313 – 636 – 969.'

The eyes of the ice maiden flicker. 'Your access code is valid.' So it should be. I paid the finest freelance master hacker in Tokyo a fortune for those nine numbers. 'For the month of July. I must remind you we are now in August.'

Cheapskate bum jet-trash hackers. 'Uh, how peculiar.' I scratch my crotch to buy myself a moment. 'That was the access code I was given by Ms' – a doleful glance at my clipboard – 'Akiko Katō, associate lawyer at Osugi and Kosugi.'

'*B*osugi.'

'Whatever. Oh well. If my access code isn't valid I can't very well enter, can I? Pity. When Ms Katō wants to know why her priceless Okinawan silverspines died from excrement poisoning, I can refer her to you. What did you say your name was?'

Ice Maiden hardens. Zealous ones are bluff-susceptible. 'Return tomorrow after rechecking your access codes.'

I huff and shake my head. 'Impossible! Do you know how many fish I got on my turf? In the old days, we had a bit more give and take, but since total quality management got hold of us we operate within an hour-by-hour timeframe. One missed appointment, and our finny friends are phosphate feed. Even while I stand here nitpicking with you, I got ninety angel-fish at the Metropolitan City Office in danger of asphyxiation. No hard feelings, ma'am, but I have to insist on your name for our legal waiver form.' I do my dramatic pen-poise pause.

Ice Maiden flickers.

I relent. 'Why not call Ms Katō's secretary? She'll confirm my appointment.'

'I already did.' Now I'm worried. If my hacker got my alias

wrong too, I am already burger-meat. 'But your appointment appears to be for tomorrow.'

'True. Quite true. My appointment was for tomorrow. But the Fish Ministry issued an industry-wide warning last night. An epidemic of silverspine, uh, ebola has come in from a contaminated Taiwanese batch. It travels down air conduits, lodges itself in the gills, and . . . a disgusting sight to behold. Fish literally swelling until their entrails pop out. The boffins are working on a cure, but between you and me—'

Ice Maiden cracks. 'Anciliary authorization is granted for two hours. From the reception booth proceed to the turbo elevator. Do not stray from the sensor floor arrows, or you will trigger alarms and illegal entry recriminations. The elevator will automatically proceed to Osugi and Bosugi on level eighty-one.'

'Level eighty-one, Mr Sogabe,' announces the elevator. 'I look forward to serving you again.' The doors open on to a virtual rainforest of pot plants and ferns. An aviary of telephones trill. Behind an ebony desk, a young woman removes her glasses and puts down a spray-mister. 'Security said Mr Sogabe was coming.'

'Let me guess! Kazuyo, Kazuyo, am I right?'

'Yes, but—'

'No wonder Ran calls you his PanOpticon Angel!'

The receptionist isn't falling for it. 'Your name is?'

'Ran's apprentice! Jōji. Don't tell me he's never mentioned me! I do Harajuku normally, but I'm covering his Shinjuku clients this month on account of his, uh, genital malaria.'

Her face falls. 'I beg your pardon?'

'Ran never mentioned it? Well, who can blame him? The boss thinks it's just a heavy cold, that's why Ran didn't actually cancel his name from his clients' books . . . All hush-hush!' I smile gingerly and look around for video cameras. None visible. I kneel, open my toolbox with the lid blocking her view, and begin assembling my secret weapon. 'Had a hell of time getting in here, y'know.

Artificial intelligence! Artificial stupidity. Ms Katō's office is down this corridor, is it?'

'Yes, but, look, Mr Jōji, I have to ask you for a retinal scan.'

'Does it tickle?' Finished. I close the toolbox and approach her desk with my hands behind my back and a gormless grin. 'Where do I look?'

She turns a scanner towards me. 'Into this eyepiece.'

'Kazuyo.' I check we are alone. 'Ran told me, about, y'know – is it true?'

'Is what true?'

'Your eleventh toe?'

'My eleventh *what*?' The moment she looks at her feet I pepper her neck with enough instant-action tranquillizer micro-pellets to knock out the entire Chinese Army. She slumps on her blotter. I make a witty pun in the manner of James Bond for my own amusement.

I knock three times. 'Goldfish Pal, Ms Katō!'

A mysterious pause. 'Enter.'

I check that the corridor is empty of witnesses, and slip in. The actual lair of Akiko Katō matches closely the version in my imagination. A chequered carpet. A curved window of troubled cloud. A wall of old-fashioned filing cabinets. A wall of paintings too tasteful to trap the eye. Between two half-moon sofas sits a huge spherical tank where a fleet of Okinawan silverspines haunt a coral palace and a sunken battleship. Nine years have passed since I last saw Akiko Katō, but she has not aged a single day. Her beauty is as cold and callous as ever. She glances up from behind her desk. 'You are not the ordinary fish man.'

I lock the door, and drop the key in my pocket with my gun.

She looks me up and down.

'I am no fish man at all.'

She puts down her pen. 'What the *hell* do you—'

'It is a simple matter. I know your name, and you knew mine, once upon a time: Eiji Miyake. Yes, *that* Eiji Miyake. True. It has been many years. Look. We are both busy people, so why not cut the small talk? I am in Tokyo to find my father. You know his name and you know his address. And you are going to give me both. Right *now*.'

Akiko Katō blinks, to verify the facts. Then she laughs. 'Eiji Miyake?'

'I fail to see the funny side.'

'Not Luke Skywalker? Not Zax Omega? Do you seriously expect to reduce me to a state of awed obedience by your pathetic spiel? "One island boy embarks on a perilous mission to discover the father he has never met." Do you know what happens to island boys once they leave their fantasies?' She shakes her head in mock pity. 'Even my friends call me the most poisonous lawyer in Tokyo. And you burst in here, expecting to intimidate me into passing on classified client information? *Please!*'

'Ms Katō.' I produce my Walther PK 7.65mm, spin it nattily and aim it at her. 'You have a file on my father in this room. Give it to me. *Please*.'

She fakes outrage. 'Are you threatening me?'

I release the safety catch. 'I hope so. Hands up where I can see them.'

'You got hold of the wrong script, child.' She picks up her telephone, which explodes in a plastic supernova. The bullet pings off the bulletproof glass and slashes into a picture of lurid sunflowers. Akiko Katō bulges her eyes at the rip. 'You heathen! You damaged my Van Gogh! You are going to pay for that!'

'Which is more than you ever did. The file. Now.'

Akiko Katō snarls. 'Security will be here within thirty seconds.'

'I know the electronic blueprint of your office. Spyproofed and soundproofed. No messages in, none out. Stop blustering and give me the *file*.'

'Such a nice life you could have had, picking oranges on Yakushima with your uncles and grandmother.'

'I don't want to ask you again.'

'If only matters were so simple. But you see, your father has too much to lose. Were news of his whored bastard offspring brat – you, that is – to leak out, it would cause red faces in high places. This is why we have a modest secrecy retainer arrangement.'

'So?'

'So, this is a cosy little boat you are attempting to rock.'

'Ah. I see. If I meet my father you won't be able to blackmail him.'

'"Blackmail" is a litigable word for someone still in search of the perfect acne lotion. Being your father's lawyer calls for discretion. Ever heard of discretion? It sets decent citizens apart from criminals with handguns.'

'I am not leaving this office without the file.'

'You have a long wait ahead. I would order some sandwiches, but you shot my telephone.'

I don't have time for this. 'Okay, okay, maybe we can discuss this in a more adult way.' I lower my gun, and Akiko Katō allows herself a pert smile of victory. The tranquillizers embed themselves in her neck. She slumps back on to her chair, as unconscious as the deep blue sea.

Speed is everything. I peel the Akiko Katō fingerpads over the Ran Sogabe ones, and access her computer. I wheel her body into the corner. Not nice – I keep thinking she's going to come back to life. The deeper computer files are passworded, but I can override the locks on the filing cabinets. MI for MIYAKE. My name appears on the menu. Double-click. EIJI. Double-click. I hear a promising mechanical *clunk*, and a drawer telescopes open halfway down the wall. I leaf through the slim metal carrier cases. MIYAKE – EIJI – PATERNITY. The case shines gold.

'Drop it.'

Akiko Katō closes the door with her ankle, and levels a Zuvre Lone Eagle .440 at the spot between my eyebrows. Dumbly, I look at the Akiko Katō still slumped in her chair. The doorway Katō laughs, a grin twisted and broad. Emeralds and rubies are set in her teeth. 'A bioborg, dummy! A replicant! You never watched

Bladerunner? We saw you coming! Our spy picked you up in Jupiter Café – the old man you bought cigarettes for? His vidboy is an eye-cam linked to PanOpticon central computer. Now kneel down – slowly – and slide your gun across the floor. *Slowly*. Don't make me nervous. A Zuvre at this range will scramble your face so badly your own mother wouldn't recognize you. But then, that never was her strong point, was it?'

I ignore the taunt. 'Unwise to approach an intruder without back-up.'

'Your father's file is a highly sensitive issue.'

'So your bioborg was telling the truth. You want to keep the hush money my father pays you all for yourself.'

'Your main concern should not be practical ethics, but to dissuade me from omeletteing you.' Keeping her eyes trained on me, she bends over to retrieve my Walther. I aim the carrier case at her face and open the switchclips. The lid-mounted incandescent booby trap explodes in her eyes. She screams, I roll-dive, her Zuvre fires, glass cracks, I leap through the air, kick her head, wrench the pistol from her grip – it fires again – spin her around and uppercut her over the half-moon sofa. Silverspines gush and thrash on the carpet. The real Akiko Katō lies motionless. I stuff the sealed folder on my father down my overalls, load up my toolbox and exit. I close the door quietly over the slow stain already gathering on the corridor carpet. I stroll down to the elevator, casually whistling 'Imagine'. That was the easy part. Now I have to get out of PanOpticon alive.

Drones fuss around the receptionist still slumped in her rainforest. Weird. I leave a trail of unconscious women wherever I go. I summon the elevator, and show appropriate concern. 'Sick building syndrome, my uncle calls it. Fish are affected in the same way, believe it or not.' The elevator arrives and an old nurse barges out, tossing onlookers aside. I step in and press the close button to whisk me away before anyone else can enter.

'Not so fast!' A polished boot wedges itself between the closing doors, and a security guard muscles them apart. He has the mass and nostrils of a minotaur. 'Ground Zero, son.'

I press the button and we begin our descent.

'So,' says Minotaur. 'You an industrial spy, or what?'

Blood and adrenalin swish through my body in strange ways. 'Huh?'

Minotaur keeps a straight face. 'You're trying to make a quick getaway, right? That's why you nearly closed me in the elevator doors up there.'

Oh. A joke. 'Yep.' I rap my toolbox. 'Full of goldfish espionage data.'

Minotaur snorts a laugh.

The elevator slows and the doors open. 'After you,' I say, even though Minotaur shows no signs of letting me go first. He disappears through a side door. Floorpad arrows return me to a security booth. I beam at Ice Maiden. 'I get to have you on the way in and on the way out? This is the hand of destiny.'

Her eyes dart over a scanner. 'Standard procedure.'

'Oh.'

'You have discharged your duties?'

'Fully, thank you. You know, ma'am, we at Goldfish Pal are proud to say that we have *never* lost a fish due to negligence in eighteen years of business. We give each a post-mortem, to establish cause of death. Old age, every time. Or client-sourced alcohol poisoning, during the end-of-year party season. If you are free I could tell you more about it over dinner.'

Ice Maiden glaciates me. 'We have nothing whatsoever in common.'

'We're both carbon-based. You can't take that for granted these days.'

'If you are trying to disgust me out of asking why you have a Zuvre .440 in your toolbox, I must tell you that your efforts are wasted.'

I am a professional. Fear must wait. How, *how*, could I have been so stupid? 'That is absolutely impossible.'

'The gun is registered under Akiko Katō's name.'

'Oooh!' I chuckle, open the box and take out the gun. 'Do you mean this?'

'I do mean that.'

'This?'

'That.'

'This is, uh, for—'

'Yes?' Ice Maiden reaches for an alarm.

'—*this*!' The glass flowers with the first shot – alarms scream – the glass mazes with the second shot – I hear gas hiss – the glass cracks with the third shot, and I throw my body through the window – shouting and running – I land tumbling over the floor of the lobby, flashing with arrows. Men and women crouch, terrified. Everywhere is noise and jaggedness. Down an access corridor guards' boots pound this way. I engage the double safety catch, switch the Zuvre to continuous plasma fire, toss it into the path of the guards, and dive for the entrance. Three seconds to overload doesn't give me enough time, and the explosion lifts me off my feet, slams me into the revolving door, and literally spins me down the steps outside. A gun that can blow up its user – no wonder Zuvres were withdrawn from production nine weeks after their launch. Behind me all is chaos, smoke and sprinklers. Around me is consternation, traffic collisions, and what I need most – frightened crowds. 'A madman!' I rave. 'Madman on the loose! Grenades! He's got grenades! Call the cops! We need helicopters! Helicopters everywhere! More helicopters!' I hobble away into the nearest department store.

I take my father's file from my new briefcase, still in its plastic seal, and mentally record the moment for posterity. August 24th, twenty-five minutes past two, in the back of a bioborg taxi, rounding the west side of Yoyogi Park, under a sky as stained as a bachelor's underfuton, less than twenty-four hours after arriving in Tokyo, I discover my father's true identity. Not bad going. I straighten my tie. I imagine Anju swinging her legs on the seat beside me. 'See?' I tell her, tapping the file. 'Here he is. His name, his face, his house, who he is, what he is. I did it. For both of us.' The taxi swerves to one side as an ambulance blue-shifts towards us. I slit open the seal with my thumbnail, and extract the card file. EIJI MIYAKE. IDENTITY OF FATHER. I take a deep breath, and far things feel near.

Page one.

The air-reactive ink is already melting into white.

Lao Tzu growls at his vidboy. '*Blasted* bioborgs. Every *blasted* time.' I sup my dregs, put on my baseball cap, and mentally limber up. 'Say, Captain,' Lao Tzu croaks, 'you wouldn't have a spare ciggie there, by any chance?' I show him the empty carton of Mild Seven. He gives me a doleful look. I need some more anyway. I have a stressful meeting ahead. 'Is there a machine in here?' 'Over there' – he nods – 'in all those plants. I smoke Carlton.' I have to break open yet another one-thousand-yen note. Money evaporates in Tokyo. I may as well order another coffee to build up my adrenalin before facing the real Akiko Katō. In lieu of a fantasy Walther PK. I deploy my telepathy – 'Waitress! You with the most perfect neck in all creation! Stop unloading the glasswasher, come to the counter and serve me!' My telepathy fails me today. I get Dowager instead. This close up I notice Dowager's nostrils are hairdryer-plug compatible – pinched little slits. She nods gracelessly when I thank her for the coffee, as though she is the customer, not me. I walk slowly back to my window seat, trying not to spill my drink, open the box of Carltons, and fail to coax a flame from my disposable lighter. Lao Tzu slides a box of courtesy matches from a bar called Mitty's. I light my cigarette, then his – he is concentrating on a new game. He takes it – his fingers are as tough as crocodile skin – drags, and gives a grateful sigh that only smokers understand. 'Thanks a million, Captain. My daughter-in-law nags at me to give up, but I tell her, I'm dying anyway, why interfere with nature?' I make a vague noise of sympathy. Those ferns look too perfect to be real. Too lush and feathery. Nothing prospers in Tokyo but pigeons, crows, rats, roaches and lawyers. I sugarize my coffee, rest my teaspoon on the meniscus, and slooooowly dribble the cream on to the bowl of the spoon. Pangaea rotates, floating unruptured before splitting into subcontinents. Playing with coffee is the only pleasure I can afford in Tokyo. The first three months' rent on my capsule wiped out all the money I saved working for Uncle Orange and Uncle Pachinko, leaving me with a chicken-and-egg problem: if I don't work, I can't stay in Tokyo and look for my father; but if I work, when do I look for my father? *Work*. A slag-heap word that blots out the sun. My two saleable talents are picking oranges and my guitar. I must be five hundred kilometres from the nearest orange tree, and I have never, ever played my guitar for anyone. Now I understand what fuels dronehood. This: you work or you drown. Tokyo turns you into a bank account balance with a carcass in tow. The size of this single number dictates where the carcass may live, what it drives, how it dresses, who it sucks up to, who it may date and marry, whether it cleans itself in a gutter or a jacuzzi. If my landlord, the honourable Buntarō Ōgiso, stiffs me, I have no safety net. He doesn't seem to be a con man, but con men never do. When I meet my father – at most a couple of weeks away – I want to prove I am standing on my own two feet, and that I am not looking for handouts. Dowager heaves out a drama-queen sigh. 'You mean to tell me this is the very last box of coffee filters?'

The waitress with the perfect neck nods.

Donkey joins in. 'The very last?'

'The very, very last,' my waitress confirms.

Dowager shakes her head at heaven. 'How can this be?'

Donkey manoeuvres. 'I sent a purchase order off on Thursday.'

The waitress with the perfect neck shrugs. 'Deliveries take three days.'

'I hope,' warns Dowager, 'you aren't blaming Eriko-san for this crisis?'

'And I hope you aren't blaming me for pointing out that we are going to run out of filters by five o'clock. I just thought I should say something.' Stalemate. 'Why don't I take some petty cash and go and buy some more?'

Dowager glowers. 'I am the shift supervisor. *I* make that sort of decision.'

'I can't go,' whines Donkey. 'I had my hair permed this morning, see, and it's going to bucket down any minute.'

Dowager turns back to the waitress with the perfect neck. 'I want you to go and buy a box of filters.' She pings the till open and removes a five-thousand-yen note. 'Keep the receipt, and bring back the exact change. The receipt is crucial, or you'll wreck my bookkeeping.'

The waitress with the perfect neck removes her rubber gloves and apron, takes an umbrella, and leaves without a word.

Dowager narrows her eyes. 'That missy has an attitude problem.'

'Rubber gloves indeed!' Donkey tuts. 'As if she's a handcream model.'

'Students today are just too coddled. What is it she studies, anyway?'

'Snobology.'

'She thinks she lives above the clouds.'

I watch her wait at the lights to cross Ōmekaidō Avenue. This Tokyo weather is extraplanetary. Still oven-hot, but a dark roof of cloud, ready to buckle under the weight of rain, at any moment. The pedestrians waiting on the island in the middle of Kita Street sense it. The two young women taking in the sandwich board outside Nero's Pizza Emporium sense it. The battalion of the elderly sense it. Hemlock, nightingales, E-minor – thunnnnnnnnnder! Bellyflopping thunnnnnnnnnder, twanging a loose bass. Anju loved thunder, our birthday, treetops, the sea and me. Her goblin grin flashed when it thundered. Raindrops are heard – shhhhhhhhh – before raindrops are seen – shhhhhhhhh – quivering ghost-leaves – dappling the pavements, smacking car roofs, drumming tarpaulins. My waitress opens up a big blue, red and yellow umbrella. The lights turn green and the pedestrians dash for cover, sheltering under ineffective tents of jackets or newspapers. 'She'll get drenched,' says Donkey, almost gleefully. The furious rain erases the far side of Ōmekaidō Avenue. 'Drenched or undrenched, we need coffee filters,' replies Dowager. My waitress disappears. I hope she finds somewhere dry. Jupiter Café fills with holiday refugees being nice to one another. Lightning zickers, and the lights of Jupiter Café dip in counterpoint. The refugees all go 'Woooooooooo!' I help myself to a match and light another Carlton. I can't go and confront Akiko Katō until this storm passes. Dripping in her office, I would be as formidable as a drenched gerbil. Lao Tzu chuckles, chokes, and gasps for air. 'My, my, I ain't seen rain like this since 1971. Must be the end of the world. I seen it coming on the telly.'

□

One hour later and the Kita Street/Ōmekaidō Avenue intersection is a churning confluence of lawless rivers. The rain is incredible. Even on Yakushima, we never get rain this heavy. The holiday atmosphere has died, and the customers are doom-laden. The floor of the Jupiter Café is, in fact, underwater – we are all sitting on stools, counters and tables. Outside, traffic stalls, and begins to disappear under the foaming water. A family of six huddles on a taxi roof. A baby wails and will not shut up. Group dynamics organize the customers, and there is talk of moving to a higher floor, staying put, navy helicopters, El Niño, tree-climbing, an invasion force from North Korea. I smoke another Carlton and say nothing: too many captains pilot the ship up the mountain. The taxi family is down to three. Objects swirl by that have no business being water-borne. Somebody has a radio, but can tune it to nothing beyond torrential static. The flood creeps up the window – now it is up to the halfway mark. Submerged mailboxes, motorbikes, traffic signals. A crocodile cruises up to the window and snout-butts the glass. Nobody screams. I wish somebody would. Something is twitching in the corner of its mouth

– a hand. Its eye surveys us all, and settles on me. I know that eye. It gleams, and the animal sidles away with a twitch of its tail. 'Tokyo, Tokyo,' cackles Lao Tzu. 'If it ain't fire, it's earthquake. If it ain't earthquake, it's bombs. If it ain't bombs, it's floods.' Dowager crows from her perch, 'The time has come to evacuate. Ladies and babies first.' 'Evacuate to where?' asks a man in a dirty mac. 'One step outside, the current'll sweep you clean past Guam!' Donkey calls from the safest place of all, the coffee-filter shelf. 'Stay inside and we'll drown!' The pregnant woman touches her bump, and whispers, 'Oh no, not now, not now.' A priest remembers his drinking problem and swigs from his hip flask. Lao Tzu hums a sea shanty. The wailing baby will not shut up. I see an umbrella shoot down the fiercest artery of the flood, a red, blue and yellow umbrella, followed by my waitress, rising, falling, flailing and gasping. I don't think. I jump up on the window counter and unfasten the top window, which is still above the water level. 'Don't do it,' chorus the refugees, 'it's certain death!' I frisbee my baseball cap to Lao Tzu. 'I'll be back for this.' I kick off my trainers, lever myself through the window, and – the torrent is a mythical force walloping, submerging and buoying me at a cruel velocity. Lit by lightning, I recognize Tokyo Tower, in floodwater up to its middle. Lesser buildings sink as I am swept by. The death toll must be in the millions. Only PanOpticon appears safe, rising into the heart of the tornado. The sea slants and peaks, the wind howls, an orchestra of the insane. Sometimes the waitress and the umbrella are near, sometimes far away. Just when I don't think I can stay afloat any longer, I see the waitress paddling towards me on her umbrella coracle. 'Some rescuer you turned out to be,' she says, gripping my hand. She smiles, glances behind me, and unspeakable horror is reflected in her face. I turn around and see the gullet of the crocodile closing in. I whip my hand out of hers and shove the umbrella away as hard as I can, turn around, and face my death. 'No!' screams my waitress appropriately. I am strong and silent. The crocodile rears and dives, its fat body feeding into the water until its tail vanishes. Was it only trying to scare me?

'Quick,' calls my waitress, but barbed teeth mesh my right foot and yank me under. I pound the crocodile but I might as well be attacking a cedar. Down, down, down, I kick and struggle, but only succeed in thickening the clouds of blood spewing from my punctured calf. We reach the floor of the Pacific. It is heavily urbanized – then I realize the crocodile has chosen to drown me outside Jupiter Café, proving that amphibians have a sense of irony. The customers and refugees look on in helpless terror. The storm must have passed, because everywhere is swimming-pool blue and tap-dancing light and I swear I can hear 'Lucy in the Sky with Diamonds'. The crocodile watches me with Akiko Katō eyes, suggesting I see the funny side of having my bloated corpse stowed in a lair and being snacked on over the upcoming weeks. I lighten as I weaken. I watch Lao Tzu help himself to my final Carlton and doff my cap. Then he mimes stabbing himself in the eye and points to the crocodile. A thought unsilts itself. Yesterday my landlord gave me my keys – the one for the shopfront shutter is three inches long and might serve as a mini-dagger. Twisting into striking range is no easy feat, but the crocodile is taking a nap, so he doesn't notice me fit the key between its eyelids and ram the sharp point home. Squeeze, squelch, squirt. Crocodiles scream, even underwater. The jaws unscissor and the monster thrashes off in spirals. Lao Tzu mimes applause, but I have already gone three minutes without air and the surface is impossibly distant. I kick feebly upwards. Nitrogen fizzes in my brain. Sluggishly I fly, and the ocean sings. Face submerged, searching for me from the stone whale, is my waitress, loyal to the last, hair streaming in the shallows. Our eyes meet for a final time, and then, overcome by the beauty of my own death, I sink in slow, sad circles.

As the first red ray of light picks the lock of dawn, the priests of Yasukuni shrine light my sandalwood funeral pyre. My funeral is the most majestic within living memory, and the whole nation is united in mourning. Traffic is diverted around Kudanshita to allow the tens of thousands to come and pay their respects. The flames lick my body. Ambassadors, various relatives, heads of state, Yoko Ono in black. My body blazes as the sun cracks the day wide open. His Imperial Majesty wished to thank my parents, so they are reunited for the first time in nearly twenty years. The journalists ask them how they feel, but they are both too choked with emotion to reply. I never wanted such an ostentatious ceremony, but, well, heroism is heroism. My soul rises with my ashes and hovers among the television helicopters and pigeons. I rest on the giant torī gate, wide enough to drive a battleship under, enjoying the new perspective of human hearts that death grants.

'I should never have abandoned those two,' thinks my mother.

'I should never have abandoned those three,' thinks my father.

'I wonder if I can keep his deposit,' thinks Buntarō Ōgiso.

'I never even asked him his name,' thinks my waitress.

'I wish John were here today,' thinks Yoko Ono. 'He would write a requiem.'

'Brat,' thinks Akiko Katō. 'A lifelong earner comes to a premature end.'

Lao Tzu chuckles, chokes, and gasps for air. 'My, my, it ain't rained like this since 1971. Must be the end of the world. I seen it coming on the telly.' But no sooner has he spoken than the downpour turns itself off. The pregnant women laugh. I think about their babies. During those nine pouched-up months, what do babies imagine? Gills, swamps, battlefields? To people in wombs, what is imagined and what is real must be one and the same. Outside, pedestrians peer upwards suspiciously, testing the rain with the flats of their hands. Umbrellas close. Theatre-backdrop clouds unscroll. Jupiter Café's doors grind open and my waitress comes back, swinging a bag. 'Took your time,' grumbles Dowager. My waitress puts the box of filters on the counter. 'Queues in the supermarket. It took for ever.' 'Did you hear the thunder?' asks Donkey, and I suspect that she is not such a bad person, just a weak one under the influence of Dowager. 'Of course she heard it!' snorts Dowager.

'My Aunt Otane heard *that* thunder, and she's been dead for nine years.' My money says Dowager tampered with the will and shoved Aunt Otane down the stairs. 'Receipt and change, if you please. I am known by head office as an exemplary bookkeeper, and I intend to keep my reputation untarnished.' My waitress gives her the receipt and a pile of coins. Indifference is a powerful weapon in her hands. The clock says two-thirty. I draw pentagrams in my ashtray with a toothpick. The thought occurs to me that I should at least check that Akiko Katō is in the PanOpticon before I go up to her office – if I barge past her secretary only to find a 'Back Thursday' Post-It sticker on her computer screen I will look a total fool. I carry Ms Katō's name card in my wallet. I borrowed it from my grandmother's fireproof box when I was eleven, intending to study voodoo and use it as a totem. AKIKO KATŌ. ATTORNEY. OSUGI & BOSUGI. This Shinjuku address and telephone number. My heartbeat is already quickening. I make a deal with myself – one iced coffee, one last Carlton, then I call. I wait until my waitress is at the counter and go up to receive my coffee and her blessings. 'Glasses!' calls Dowager so sharply I mistakenly believe she's talking to me. Donkey comes to the counter and my girl goes back to the sink. I'm in danger of ODing on caffeine, but I'll look stupid if I change my mind now. 'One iced coffee, please.' I wait until Lao Tzu gets rekilled by the bioborgs and swap a Carlton for another match. I try to bisect an almond flake, but it wedges itself up my fingernail.

'Good afternoon. Osugi and Bosugi.'

I try to inject a shot of authority into my voice. 'Ye-es—' My voice squeaks as though my balls are still in puberty freefall. I blush, fake a cough, and restart five octaves down. 'Is Akiko Katō working today, please?'

'Do you want to speak with her?'

'No. I want to know if . . . yes. Yes, please.'

'Yes what, sir?'

'Could you please put me through to Ms Akiko Katō. Please.'

'And may I ask who's calling, sir?'

'Is she, uh, in the office, then?'

'May I ask who's calling, sir?'

'This is a' – disaster – 'confidential call.'

'You can count on the utmost confidence, sir, but I must ask who is calling.'

'My name, uh, is Tarō Tanaka.' The duddest of dud names. Idiot.

'Mr Tarō Tanaka. I see. May I ask what your call is concerning?'

'Certain legal, uh, matters.'

'You can't be any more specific, Mr Tanaka?'

'Uh. No. Actually.'

A slow sigh. 'Ms Katō is in a meeting with the senior partners at the moment, so I can't ask her to speak with you right now. But if I could ask for your number and company, and some outline of your business, I could ask her to return your call later today.'

'Naturally.'

'So, your company, Mr Tanaka?'

'Uh . . .'

'Mr Tanaka?'

I drown and hang up.

A D-minus for style. But now I know that Akiko Katō lurks in her web. I count twenty-seven floors up the PanOpticon before touching cloud. I blow smoke at you, Akiko Katō. You have less than thirty minutes to live with Eiji Miyake as nothing but a foggy memory from a foggy mountain island off the southern foot of Kyūshū. Do you ever daydream about meeting me? Or am I just a name on certain documents? The icebergs in my coffee fuse and chink. I pour in the juglets of syrup and cream and watch the liquids swirl and bleed. The pregnant women are comparing baby magazines. My girl is going from table to table emptying ashtrays into a bucket. *Come this way, empty mine.* She doesn't. Dowager is on the telephone, all smiles. A man crossing Kita Street catches my attention: I swear I saw this same man cross this same street a minute ago. I focus on him, tracking his progress among the puddle-hopping masses. He crosses over, then waits for the man to turn green. He crosses over Ōmekaidō Avenue, waits for the man to turn green. Then he crosses back over Kita Street. He waits, and crosses back over Ōmekaidō Avenue. I watch him complete one, two, three circuits. A private detective, a bioborg, a lunatic? The sun will rub through the cloud cover any minute now. I prod my straw down through the ice, and suck. My bladder will no longer be ignored. I get up, walk to the toilet door, turn the handle – locked. I scratch the back of my head and go back to my seat, embarrassed. When the occupant leaves – an office lady – I avert my gaze so she doesn't suspect me of rattling her toilet knob, and so lose my turn to a demure high-school girl in uniform, who emerges fifteen minutes later as a boob-banded, candy-striped, miniskirted wet dream. I get up, but this time a mother and her little kid dash in ahead of me. 'Emergency!' giggles the mother at me, and I smile understandingly. Am I in one of those dreams where the closer you get the farther away you are? 'Look,' shrieks my bladder, 'get your act together, and soon, or I won't be held responsible!' I stand by the door and try to think of sand dunes. Another of Tokyo's vicious circles – to use a toilet you have to buy a drink that fills your bladder. On Yakushima I just find a tree to piss behind. Finally the mother and kid come out and I get to go in. I hold my breath and fight the lock shut. I lift the lid and piss three coffees. I run out of breath and have to breathe in – not too smelly, considering. Urine, margarine, chemical lavender. I think better of wiping the rim. A sink, a mirror, an empty soap canister. I squeeze a couple of blackheads, and try on my reflection from various angles: I, Eiji Miyake, Tokyoite. Do I fool anybody, or is every laugh, meeow and muffled stare directed at me, as I suspect? A good acne day. Is my Kyūshū tan pasting over already? My reflection plays the staring game. It wins and I look away first. I start work on a volcanic chain of blackheads. Somebody on the outside knocks and turns the toilet handle. I ruffle back my gelled hair, and fumble the door open.

□

It is Lao Tzu. I mutter an apology for making him wait, and decide to attack the PanOpticon without further delay. Then, cutting across the foreground, strides Akiko Katō. In the flesh, right here, right now, only five millimetres of glass and a metre of air, max, between us. My wished-for coincidence has come about just as I have given up hope. In slo-mo she turns her head, looks straight at me, and carries on walking. Temporary disbelief catches me off balance. Akiko Katō strides to the intersection where the men turn green on her approach. In my fantasy she hadn't aged; in reality she has, but my memory is surprisingly accurate. Lidded cunning, aquiline nose, wintry beauty. *Go!* I wait for the doors to grind open, run out, and—

Baseball cap, you idiot!

I dart back into Jupiter Café, get my cap, and race over to the crossing, where the green men are already flashing. After two hours in air-con I can feel my skin crackle and pop in the afternoon heat. Akiko Katō has already reached the far shore – I risk it and run, leaping over the stripes and puddles. The donorcycles rev and nudge forward, the traffic-crossing man is red, I get an angry blast from a bus, but I leap to the far bank without bouncing off a bonnet. My quarry is already at the PanOpticon steps. I dodge upstream through the crowd, clipping insults out of people and scattering apologies – if she gets inside I'll lose my chance to meet her on neutral territory. But Akiko Katō does not enter PanOpticon. She carries on walking towards Shinjuku station – I should catch her up and detain her, but I suddenly feel that accosting her on the street would make her less sympathetic, not more, to my cause. After all, I am asking her the favour. She would think I was stalking her – she would be right. What if she misunderstands before I can explain? What if she starts screaming 'Rapist!'? However, I can't just let her melt into the crowds either. So I follow her at a safe distance, reminding myself that she doesn't know the face of the adult Eiji Miyake. She never turns around, not once – why should she? We pass under a row of scraggy trees dripping dry. Akiko Katō flicks her long hair and puts on sunglasses. An underpass takes us beneath rail tracks, and we emerge into strong sunshine down traffic-and-people-crammed Yasukuni Street, lined with bistros and mobile phone shops blaring guitar riffs. Following people is difficult in real life. I clang my shin on a bicycle. The sun steam-irons the street through its rain-washed lens. Sweat gums my T-shirt to my skin. Past a shop that sells ninety-nine different flavours of ice cream, Akiko Katō turns and ducks down a side street. I hack through a jungle of women outside a boutique, and follow her. No sun, bins on wheels, fire escapes. A Chicago film set. She stops outside what appears to be a cinema, and turns around to make sure she isn't being followed – I increase my stride, as if in a tearing hurry. I avoid her eyes and swivel my baseball cap as I pass to hide my face. When I double back, Akiko Katō has vanished into the Ganymede Cinema. The place has seen much better days. Today's presentation is a movie called *PanOpticon*. The poster – a row of screaming Russian dolls – tells me nothing about the movie. I hesitate. I want a cigarette, but I left my packet at Jupiter Café, so I make do with a champagne candy. The film starts in under ten minutes. I go in, at first pulling the door instead of pushing. The deserted lobby swarms with psychedelic carpet. I don't notice the step, trip and nearly twist my ankle. All is tatty glitz and putty-odoured. A sorry chandelier glows brownly. A woman in the ticket box puts down her needlepoint embroidery with obvious annoyance. '*Yes?*'

'Is this the, uh, cinema?'

'No. This is the Battleship Yamato.'

'I'm a customer.'

'How pleasant for you.'

'Uh. The film? What is it, uh, about?'

She feeds a thread through a needle's eye. 'Do you see a sign on my desk that reads "Plot Synopses Sold Here"?'

'I only—'

She sighs, as if dealing with a moron. 'Do you, or do you not, see a sign on my desk that reads "Plot Synopses Sold Here"?'

'No.'

'And why, pray tell, do you suppose no such sign exists?'

I would shoot her but I left my Walther PK in my last fantasy. I would walk out but I know Akiko Katō is somewhere in this building. 'One ticket, please.'

'One thousand yen.'

There goes my budget for the day. She gives me a raffle ticket. Lumps of plaster lie here and there. By rights this place should have gone out of business decades ago. She returns to her embroidery, leaving me to the tender mercies of a sign reading ☞ SCREEN THIS WAY – THE MANAGEMENT ARE NOT LIABLE FOR ACCIDENTS ON THE STAIRWELL ☞. The steep stairs descend at right angles. Posters of films line the glossed walls. I don't recognize a single one. Each flight of stairs I expect to be the last, but it never is. In the event of fire, the audience is kindly requested to blacken quietly. Is it getting warmer? Suddenly I have got to the bottom. I smell bitter almonds. A woman with the shaven, bruised skull of a chemotherapy patient blocks my way. When I meet her eyes I see that her sockets are perfect voids. I clear my throat. She doesn't move. I try to squeeze past her, but her hand shoots out. Her fore and middle fingers and her ring and little fingers have fused into trotters. I try not to look. She takes my ticket and shreds it. 'Popcorn?'

'I'll give it a miss, thank you.'

'Don't you like popcorn?'

'I, uh, don't feel strongly about popcorn.'

She weighs my statement. 'So you refuse to admit you dislike popcorn.'

'Popcorn isn't something I like or dislike.'

'Why do you play these games with me?'

'I'm not playing games. I just had a big lunch. I don't want to eat anything.'

'I hate it when you lie.'

'You must be mistaking me for somebody else.'

She shakes her head. 'Mistakes never make it this far down.'

'Okay, okay, I'll buy some popcorn.'

'Impossible. There is none.'

I'm missing something. 'Then why did you offer to sell me some?'

'Look back. I never did. Do you want to see the film or not?'

'Yes.' This is getting irritating. 'I want to see the film.'

'Then why are you wasting my time?' She holds open the curtain. The steeply sloping cinema has a population of exactly three. In the front row I recognize Akiko Katō. A man is next to her. Down the far aisle a third man is in a wheelchair, apparently dead: his neck is bent back brokenly, his jaw gapes, his head is unhinged, and he is quite motionless. I follow his gaze to the night sky painted on the roof of the cinema. I creep down the centre aisle, hoping I can get close enough to the couple to eavesdrop. A loud bang goes off in the projectionist's room and I hunker down to hide. A shotgun, or an inexpertly opened bag of potato chips. Neither Akiko Katō nor her companion turn around – I creep down to within a couple of rows behind them. The lights fall and the curtain rises on a rectangle of flickering light. An advert for a driving school: the advert is either very old or the driving school only accepts learners with a 1970s bent in clothes and hair. The soundtrack is the 'YMCA' song. Next, an advert for a plastic surgeon called Apollo Shigenobo who grafts permanent grins on to all his customers. They sing about facial correction. I enjoy the 'Coming Soon' trailers at the Kagoshima cinema – it saves the bother of watching the film – but here there are none. A titanium voice announces the film, *PanOpticon*, by a director I could never pronounce, winner of a film festival award in a city I could not even pinpoint to the nearest continent. No titles, no music. Straight in.

In a black-and-white city of winter an omnibus shoulders through crowds. A middle-aged passenger watches. Busy snow, wartime newspaper vendors, policemen beating a black marketeer, hollow faces in empty shops, a burnt skeletal bridge. Getting off, the man asks the driver for directions – he receives a nod at the enormous wall obscuring the sky. The man walks along its foot, looking for the door. Craters, broken things, wild dogs. Circular ruins where a hairy lunatic talks to a fire. Finally the man finds a wooden door. He stoops and knocks. No reply. He sees a tin can hanging from a piece of string vanishing into the masonry, and speaks into it. 'Is anybody there?' The subtitles are Japanese, the language is all hisses, slushes and cracks. 'I am Dr Polonski. Warden Bentham is expecting me.' He puts the can to his ear and hears drowning sailors. The door opens by itself on to a bleak forecourt. The doctor stoops through. A strange chanting echoes with the wind. 'Toadling at your service, Doctor.' A very short man unbows, and Dr Polonski jumps back. 'This way, if you will.' Snow is gravelly. Incantations whirl and die and rise again. Keys jangle on Toadling's belt. Past card-playing guards, through a maze of cages. 'Your destination,' he croaks. The doctor gives a stiff bow, knocks, and enters a scruffy office.

'Doctor!' The warden is decrepit and drunk. 'Take a seat, do.'

'Thank you.' Dr Polonski steps gingerly – the floors are not only bare, but half the floorboards have been removed. The doctor sits on a schoolchild's chair. The warden is photographing a peanut in a tall glass of liquid. Warden Bentham explains. 'I am penning a treatise on the behaviour of bar snacks in brandy soda.'

'Indeed?'

The warden checks his stopwatch. 'What's your poison, Doc?'

'Not while I'm on duty. Thank you.'

The warden empties the last drop from his brandy bottle into an eggcup and disposes of the bottle by dropping it between floorboards. A distant scream and tinkle. 'Chin chin!' The warden knocks back his eggcup. 'Dear doctor, permit me to cut to the quack. The quick, I mean, the quick. Our own Dr Koenig died of consumption before Christmas, and what with the war in the East and whatnot we still have no replacement. Prisons are not priorities in wartime, except to house politicals. We had such high hopes. A Utopian prison, to raise the inmates' mental faculties, to allow their imaginations to set them free. To—'

'Mr Bentham,' interrupts Dr Polonski. 'The quick?'

'The quick is' – the warden leans forward – 'the Voorman problem.'

Polonski shifts on his tiny chair, afraid of joining the brandy bottle. 'Voorman is a prisoner here?'

'Quite so, Doctor. Voorman is the prisoner who maintains he is God.'

'God.'

'Each to his own, I say, but he has persuaded the prison population to share his delusion. We isolated him, but to no avail. The singing you heard coming in? The psalm of Voorman. I fear disturbances, Doctor. Riots.'

'I see you have a problem, but how—'

'I am asking you to examine Voorman. Ascertain whether his madness is feigned, or whether his tapirs run amok. If you decide he is clinically insane, I can parcel him off to the asylum, and we can all go home for tea and fairy cakes.'

'Of what crime was Voorman convicted?'

Warden Bentham shrugs. 'We burned the files last winter for fuel.'

'How do you know when to release the prisoners?'

The warden is flummoxed. '"Release"? "The prisoners"?'

Akiko Katō looks behind her. I duck down, in time, I think. At the end of the row a rat stands upright in a pool of silver screenlight. It looks at me before climbing into the upholstery. 'I only hope,' Akiko Katō's companion speaks softly, 'this is urgent.'

'An apparition appeared in Tokyo yesterday.'

'You summoned me from the defence department to tell me a ghost story?'

'The ghost was your son, Congressman.'

My father is as thunderstruck as I am.

Akiko Katō flicks her hair. 'And I assure you he is a ghost who is very much alive. In Tokyo and looking for you.'

My father says nothing for the longest time. 'Does he want money?'

'Blood.' I opt to bide my time while Akiko Katō cuts more rope to hang herself later. 'I can't dress up what I have to say. Your son is a crack addict who vowed to me that he would kill you for his stolen childhood. I've come across many a damaged young man in my time, but I'm afraid your son is salivating psychosis on two legs. And it isn't only you he wants. He says he wants to destroy your family first, to punish you for what happened to his sister.'

Voorman's cell is a palace of filth. 'So, Mr Voorman . . .' Dr Polonski paces over faeces and flies. 'How long have you believed yourself to be a god?'

Voorman is in a straitjacket. 'Let me ask you the same question.'

'I do not believe I am a god.' Something crunches under his shoe.

'But you believe yourself to be a psychiatrist.'

'Correct. I have been a psychiatrist since I graduated from medical college – with first-class honours – and entered my practice.' The doctor lifts his foot – a twitching cockroach is glued to his sole. He scrapes it off on fallen masonry.

Voorman nods. 'I have been God since I began practising *my* profession.'

'I see.' The doctor stops to take notes. 'What does your profession involve?'

'Chiefly, on-going maintenance. Of my universe.'

'So you created our universe?'

'Quite. Nine days ago.'

Polonski weighs this up. 'A considerable body of evidence suggests that the universe is somewhat older than nine days.'

'I know. I created the evidence, too.'

The doctor sits on a shelf-cot opposite. 'I am forty-five years of age, Mr Voorman. How do you account for my memories of last spring, or my childhood?'

'I created your memories when I created you.'

'So everything in this universe is a figment of your imagination?'

'Precisely. You, this prison, gooseberries, the Horsehead Nebula.'

Polonski finishes the sentence he is writing. 'Must be quite a workload.'

'Greater than your puny hippocampus – no offence – could ever conceive. Worse still, I have to keep imagining every last atom, or it all goes "poof"! "Solipsist" only has one *l*, Doctor.' Polonski frowns and changes the position of his notebook. Voorman sighs. 'I know you are sceptical, Doctor. I made you that way. May I propose an objective experiment to verify my claims?'

'What do you have in mind?'

'Belgium.'

'Belgium?'

'I don't suppose even the Belgians would miss it, do you?'

My father says nothing. His head is bowed. He has a full head of hair – I don't need to worry about baldness. This is a dark, delicious, unexpected turn of events. I will announce my presence any moment now, and expose Akiko Katō as a lying viper – I want to keep my advantage a little longer, and build up my arsenal for the battle ahead. Akiko Katō's mobile phone rings. She gets it out of her handbag, snaps 'Call back later, I'm busy,' and puts it back. 'Congressman. The general election is four weeks from now. Your face is going to be plastered over every candidate board in Tokyo. You will be on television daily. This is not a time to keep a low profile.'

'If I could only meet my son—'

'If he knows who you are, you are doomed.'

'Everybody has a reasonable side.'

'He has a criminal record – GBH, burglary, drugs – as long as your wife's fur rack. He has a very nasty cocaine habit. Imagine what the opposition would do. "Abandoned Ministerial Love-Child Criminal Swears 'I *will* kill him!'"'

My father sighs in the flickering darkness. 'What do you suggest?'

'Liquidate the problem before it turns into your political death.'

My father quarter-turns. 'Surely you're not suggesting violence?'

Akiko Katō chooses her words carefully. 'I foresaw this day. Plans are in place. Accidents happen in the city, and I know people who know people who can make accidents happen sooner rather than later.'

I wait for my father's reply.

The Polonskis live in a third-floor apartment in an old city house with a gate and courtyard. She hasn't eaten or slept properly in months. Pale fire shudders in the shade. A convoy of tanks rumbles by. Mrs Polonski slices iron bread with a blunt knife and ladles thin broth. 'Are you still fretting about that Boorman prisoner?'

'Voorman. I am still fretting, yes.'

'Forcing you to do the job of a court judge, it's so unreasonable.'

'That doesn't worry me. In this city there is little difference between the prison and the asylum.' He captures the tip of a carrot in the bowl of his spoon.

'Then what is it?'

'Is he the slave, or the master, of his imagination? He swore to make Belgium disappear by teatime.'

'Is Belgium another prisoner?'

Polonski chews. 'Belgium.'

'A new cheese?'

'Belgium. The country. Between France and Holland. Belgium.'

Mrs Polonski shakes her head doubtfully.

Her husband smiles to hide his annoyance. 'Bel-gi-um.'

'Is this a joke, dear?'

'You know I never joke about my patients.'

'"Belgium." A shire or village of Luxembourg, perhaps?'

'Bring me my atlas!' The doctor turns to the general map of Europe and his face stiffens. Between France and Holland is a feature called the Walloon Lagoon. Polonski gazes, thunderstruck. 'This cannot be. This cannot be. This cannot be.'

'I refuse to believe,' insists my father, 'that any son of mine could be capable of murder. His temper must have flared when he met you – your imagination is rewriting what he says and means.'

'I am a lawyer,' replies Akiko Katō. 'I am not paid to imagine.'

'If I could only meet my son, and explain—'

'How many times must I say it, Minister? He will kill you.'

'And so I have to rubber-stamp his death?'

'Do you love your real family?'

'What kind of a question is that?'

'Then the steps you must take to protect them are obvious.'

My father shakes his head. 'This is sheer insanity!' He combs his hair with his fingers. 'May I ask a direct question?'

'You are the boss,' says Akiko Katō in the tone of the boss.

'Is our privacy retention agreement a factor in your calculations?'

Akiko Katō's offence is razor-sharp. 'I resent that insinuation.'

'You must admit—'

'I resent that insinuation so much that the price of my silence is doubled.'

My father nearly shouts. 'Remember who I am, Ms Katō!'

'I do remember who you are, Minister. A man with a kingdom to lose.'

The time has come. I stand up two rows behind my father and the snakewoman who manipulates his life. 'Excuse me.' They turn around – guilty, surprised, alert. 'What?' hisses Akiko Katō. I look from her, to my father, to her, to my father. Neither of them recognizes me. 'Well? What the hell do you want?' I swallow. 'It is a simple matter. I know your name, and you knew mine, once upon a time: Eiji Miyake. Yes, *that* Eiji Miyake. True. It has been many years . . .'

Icicles fang the window of Voorman's cell. Voorman's eyelids open very, very slowly. Bombers drone across nearby airspace. 'Good morning, Doctor. Will Belgium figure in your session notes today?' The guard with the cattle prod slams the door shut. Polonski pretends to ignore this. His eyes are dark and baggy.

'Sleep badly last night, Doctor?'

Polonski opens his bag with practised calm.

'Wicked thoughts!' Voorman licks his lips. 'Is that your medical opinion, Doctor? I am not a lunatic, not a malingerer, but a demon? Am I to be exorcised?'

Polonski looks at the prisoner sharply. 'Do you believe you should be?'

Voorman shrugs. 'Demons are merely humans with demonic enough imaginations.'

The doctor sits down. The chair scrapes. 'Just supposing you do possess . . . powers—'

Voorman smiles. 'Say it, Doctor, say it.'

'What is God doing straitjacketed in this prison?'

Voorman yawns in a well-fed way. 'What would you do if you were God? Spend your days playing golf on Hawaii? I think not. Golf is so tedious when holes-in-one are dead certs. Existence drags so . . . non-existently.'

Polonski is not taking notes now. 'So what do you do with your time?'

'I seek amusement in you. Take this war. Slapstick comedy.'

'I am not a religious man, Mr Voorman—'

'That is why I chose you.'

'—but what kind of a god finds wars amusing?'

'A bored one. Yes. Humans are equipped with imaginations so you can dream up new ways to entertain me.'

'Which you choose to observe from the luxury of your cell?'

Gunfire crackles in a neighbouring precinct. 'Luxury, poverty, who cares when you are immortal? I am rather fond of prisons. I see them as open-cast irony mines. And the prisoners are more fun than well-fed congregations. You also amuse me, good doctor. Your remit is to prove me either a faker or a lunatic, and yet you end up proving my omnipotent divinity.'

'Nothing of the sort has been proven.'

'True, Dr Diehard, true. But fear not, I bear glad tidings. We're going to change places. *You* can juggle time, gravity, waves and particles. *You* can sift through the dreckbin of human endeavour for tiny specks of originality. *You* can watch the sparrows fall and continents pillaged in your name. Now. I'm going to make your wife smile in a most involuntary way and partake of the chief warden's brandy.'

'You are a sick man, Mr Voorman. The Belgian trick stymies me, but—'

Dr Polonski freezes.

Voorman whistles the national anthem of France.

The frame jumps.

'Time has flown,' says the doctor. 'I must be leaving.'

The prisoner chokes. 'What—'

The doctor flexes his new muscles.

The prisoner screams. '*What have you done to me*?'

'If you can't discuss things like a rational adult I'll terminate this interview.'

'*Put me back, you monster*!'

'You'll soon learn the ropes.' The doctor clips his bag shut. 'Watch the Balkans. Hot spot.'

The prisoner bellows. '*Guards! Guards*!' The door scrapes open and the doctor shakes his head sadly. Cattle prods buzzing, the guards approach the hysterical prisoner. 'Arrest that impostor! *I'm* the real Dr Polonski! He's an infernal agent who made Belgium disappear overnight!' The prisoner shrieks and twists as the guards wham 5,000 volts through his body. '*Stop that abomination*! He's going to molest my wife!' His shackled feet bang the floor. Knock, knock, knock.

I should have left my blackheads alone – I have the complexion of a winged crab attack victim. Somebody on the outside knocks and turns the toilet door handle. I ruffle back my gelled hair, and fumble the door open. It is Lao Tzu. 'Took your time in there, Captain.' I apologize, and decide that the PanOpticon assault hour is nigh. Right after one last Carlton. I watch workmen erect a giant TV screen against the side of PanOpticon's neighbour. The waitress with the perfect neck has finished her shift – the clock says six minutes to three – and changed out of her uniform. She is wearing a purple sweater and white jeans. She looks drop-dead cool. Dowager is giving her a talking-to over by the cigarette machine when Donkey rings the help-me bell – Dowager drops my waitress in mid-sentence and goes over to bestow order upon the sudden throng of customers. The girl with the perfect neck glances at the clock anxiously. She feels her mobile phone vibrate and turns in my direction to talk, cupping her mouth so nobody can hear. Her face lights up, and I am piqued by jealousy. Before I know it I am choosing another brand of cigarettes from the cigarette machine next to her. Eavesdropping is wrong, but who can blame me if I innocently overhear? 'Yeah, yeah. Put Nao on, would you?' Naoki a boy or Naoko a girl? 'I'll be a little late, so start without me.' Start what? 'Amazing rain, wasn't it?' She practises piano movements with her free hand. 'Yes, I remember how to get there.' Where? 'Room 162. I *know* we only have two weeks left.' Until what? Then she looks at me and sees me looking at her. I remember I am supposed to be choosing cigarettes and study the range on offer. On an advert a lawyer-type woman smokes Salem. 'You let your imagination run away with you again. See you in twenty minutes. 'Bye.' She pockets her phone and clears her throat. 'Did you catch all of that, or would you like me to go over any bits you missed?' To my horror I realize she is talking to me. My blush is so hot I smell smoke. I look up at her – I am still crouching to take my Salems from the dispenser. The girl is not angry as such, but she is as tough as a drill-bit. I search for words to defuse her contempt while keeping my dignity intact. I come up with 'Uh'. Her stare is merciless. '*Uh*,' she repeats. I swallow hard, and touch the leaves of the rubber plant. 'I was wondering,' I flounder, 'if these plants were, uh, artificial. Are. I mean.' Her stare is a death ray. 'Some are real. Some are fake. Some are full of shit.' The Dowager returns to finish her sentence. I cockroach back to my coffee. I want to run out under a heavy truck, but I also want to smoke a Salem to calm down before I go and ask my father's lawyer for her client's name and address. Lao Tzu returns, posturing his behind. 'Eat big, shit big, live big, dream small. Say, Captain, you wouldn't have a spare ciggie there?' I light two sticks with one match. The girl with the perfect neck has finally escaped from Jupiter Café. She gazelles across the puddles over Ōmekaidō Avenue. I should have been honest. One lie and your credibility is bankrupt. Forget her. She is way out of my class. She is a musician at a Tokyo university with a conductor boyfriend called Naoki. I am unemployed and only graduated from high school because the teachers gave me a sympathy vote due to my background. She is from a good family and sleeps in a bedroom with real oil paintings and CD-ROM encyclopaedias. Her film director father allows Naoki to sleep over, on account of his money, talent and immaculate teeth. I am from a non-family, I sleep in a capsule the size of a packing case in Kita Senju with my guitar, and my teeth are not wonky but not straight. 'What a beautiful young creature,' sighs Lao Tzu. 'If only I were your age, Captain . . .'

I surprise myself by not chickening out and heading straight back to Shinjuku station, although I do nearly get killed by an ambulance crossing Kita Street. The handful of traffic lights on Yakushima are just there for effect – here they are life and death. When I got off the coach yesterday I noticed that Tokyo air smells of the insides of pockets. I haven't noticed today. I guess I smell of the insides of pockets too. I walk up the steps of the PanOpticon. It props up the sky. Over the last seven years I have imagined this moment so often I cannot believe it is actually here. But it is here. The revolving door creeps around slowly. The refrigerated air makes the hairs on my arm stand up – when it gets this cold in winter they put on the heating. The marble floor is the white of bleached bone. Palm trees sit in bronze urns. A one-legged man crutches across the polished floor. Rubber squeaks, metal clinks. Trombone-flowers loom, big enough to eat babies. My left baseball boot makes a stupid eeky sound. A row of nine interviewees wait in identical leather armchairs. They are my age, and may very well be clones. Drone clones. 'What a stupid eeky sound,' they are all thinking. I reach the elevators and look up and down the signboard for Osugi and Bosugi, Legal. Concentrate on the prize. I could be ringing the doorbell at my father's house by suppertime today. 'Where do you think you're going, kiddo?'

I turn around.

The guard at the reception desk glowers. The drone clones' eighteen eyes swivel this way. 'Didn't they teach you to read?' He raps his knuckles on a sign. VISITORS *MUST* REPORT TO RECEPTION. I backtrack and bow apologetically. He folds his arms. 'So?'

'I have business with Osugi and Bosugi. The lawyers.'

PANOPTICON SECURITY is embroidered into his cap. 'How swanky for you. And your appointment is with *whom* exactly?'

'Appointment?'

'Appointment. As in "appointment".'

Eighteen drone clone noses scent humiliation upwind.

'I was, uh, hoping to see Ms Akiko Katō.'

'And is Ms Katō aware of this honour?'

'Not exactly, because—'

'So you have no appointment.'

'Look—'

'No, you look. This is not a supermarket. This is a private building where business of a sensitive nature is regularly transacted. You cannot just breeze in. Nobody enters those elevators unless they are employees of the companies housed in here or unless they have an appointment, or a valid reason for being here. See?'

Eighteen drone clone ears tune into my boondock accent.

'Could I make an appointment through you, then?'

Way wrong. The guard gears up and one clone pours fuel on the fire by snickering. 'You didn't hear me. I am a security guard. I am not a receptionist. I am employed to keep time-wasters, salesmen and assorted scum *out*. Not to usher them *in*.'

Damage control. 'I didn't want to offend you, I just—'

Too late for damage control. 'Listen, kiddo.' The guard removes his glasses, and polishes the lenses. 'Your accent tells me you aren't from round here, so listen while I explain to you how we work in Tokyo. You scuttle away before I get really irritated. You get your appointment with Ms Kato. You come back on the right day five minutes before your time. You report to me and tell me your name. I confirm your appointment with the Osugi and Bosugi receptionist. Then, and only then, do I let you step into one of those elevators. Am I understood?'

I take a deep breath.

The guard opens his newspaper with a snap.

Post-rain sweat and grime regunge Tokyo. The puddles are steaming dry in the magnified heat. A busker sings so off key that passers-by have a moral responsibility to steal his change and smash his guitar on his head. I head back towards Shinjuku submarine station. The crowds march out of step, beaten senseless by the heat. My father's doorbell is lost at an unknown grid reference in my Tokyo street guide. A tiny nugget of earwax deep inside my ear where I can't dig it out is driving me crazy. I hate this city. I pass a kendō hall – bone-splintering bamboo-sword screams escape through the window grille. On the pavement is a pair of shoes – as if their owner suddenly turned to vapour and blew away. I feel a boiling frustration and a sort of tired guilt. I have broken some kind of unseen contract. Who with? Buses and trucks clog the arteries, pedestrians squeeze through the gaps. When I was going through my dinosaur phase I read a theory claiming that the great extinction occurred because the dinosaurs gagged to death on mountains of their own dung. Trying to get from A to Z in Tokyo, the theory no longer seems so ridiculous. I hate its wallpaper adverts, its capsules, tunnels, tap water, submarines, air, its NO RIGHT OF WAY on every corner and MEMBERS ONLY above every door. I swear. I want to turn into a nuclear warhead and incinerate this dung-heap city from the surface of the world.

Two

Lost Property

Sawing the head off a thunder god with a rusty hacksaw is not easy when you are eleven years old. The hacksaw keeps jamming. I rejiggle, and nearly slip from the thunder god's shoulders. If I fall backwards from this height I snap my spine. Outside the shrine a blackbird sings in dark purples. I wrap my legs around the god's muscled torso, the same as when Uncle Tarmac gives me a piggy-back. I drag the blade across his throat. Again, again, again. The wood is stone hard, but the nick deepens to a slit, the slit becomes a groove. My eyes sting with sweat. The quicker the better. This must be done, but there is no point getting caught. They put you in prison for this, surely. The blade slips and cuts my thumb. I wipe my eyes on my T-shirt and wait. Here comes the pain, in pulses. The flap of skin pinkens, reddens, and blood wells up. I lick it and taste ten-yen coins. Fair payment. Just as I am paying the thunder god back, for what he has done to Anju. I carry on sawing. I cannot see his face from where I am, but when I cut through his windpipe both our bodies judder.

Saturday, 2nd September is already one hour old. One week since my Jupiter Café stake-out. On the main thoroughfare through Kita Senju the traffic is at low tide. I can see the Tokyo moon down a crack between the opposite apartment buildings. Zinc, industrial, skid-marked. My capsule is as stifling as the inside of a boxing glove. The fan stirs the heat. I am not going to contact her. No way. Who does she think she is, after all this time? Across the road is a photo developer's with two Fujifilm clocks – the left clock shows the actual time, the right shows when the photos will be ready, forty-five minutes into the future. In the sodium glow my skimpy half-curtain is dungish. Girders crank, cables buzz. I wonder if this building gives me insomnia. Sick building syndrome, Uncle Bank calls it. Below me, Shooting Star is shuttered up and waiting for the night to pass. In the last week I have learned the routine: ten to midnight, Buntarō drags in the sandwich board and takes out the trash; five to midnight, the TV goes off, and he washes up his mug and plate; around now a customer may come sprinting down the street to return a video; at midnight on the nail, Buntarō pings open the till and cashes up. Three minutes later the shutters roll down, he kicks his scooter into life, and off he goes. A cockroach tries to flap free of the glue trap. My muscles ache from my new job. I should chuck out Cat's bowl, I suppose. Keeping it is morbid, now I know the truth. And the extra milk, and the two tins of quality cat food. Is it edible, if I mix it into a soup or something? Did Cat die instantly, or did she lie on the roadside thinking about it? Did a passer-by whack her on the head with a shovel to put her out of her misery? Cats seem too transdimensional to get hit by traffic, but it happens all the time. All the time. Thinking I could keep her was crazy in the first place. My grandmother hates cats. Yakushima islanders keep chained-up dogs as guards. Cats take their own chances. I know nothing about litter trays, when you bring cats in, when you take them out, what injections they need. And look what happened to it when it dossed down with me: the Miyake curse strikes again. Anju climbed trees like a cat. A summer puma.

'You are so, so, slow!'

I shout back up through the early mist and floppy leaves. 'I'm snagged!'

'You're scared!'

'I am not!'

Anju laughs her wild zither when she knows she is right. The forest floor is a long way down. I worry about rotted-through branches snapping. Anju never worries because I always do her worrying for her. She skip-reads her way up trees. She finds fingerholds in coarse bark and toeholds in smooth bark. Last week was our eleventh birthday, but already Anju can climb the gym ropes faster than any of the boys in our class, and, when she is in the mood, multiply fractions, read second-year texts and recite most Zax Omega adventures word for word. Wheatie says this is because she grabbed most of the brain cells when we were growing inside our mother. I finally unpick my T-shirt and climb after my sister, swift as a three-toed sloth with vertigo. Minutes later I find her on the top branch. Copper-skinned, willow-limbed, moss-stained, thorn-scored, dungareed, ponytail knotted back. Waves of spring sea wind break on the woods. 'Welcome to my tree,' she says. 'Not bad,' I admit, but it is better than 'not bad'. I have never climbed so high before. We have already trekked up the razor escarpment to get here, so the view is awesome. The fortress-grey mountain-faces, the green river snaking out of the gorge, the hanging bridge, mishmash of roofs and power lines, port, timber yards, school soccer ground, gravel pit, Uncle Orange's tea-fields, our secret beach, its foot rock, waves breaking on the shoals around the whalestone, the long island of Tanegashima where they launch satellites, glockenspiel clouds, the envelope where the sea seals the sky. Having bombed as tree-climber-in-chief, I appoint myself head cartographer. 'Kagoshima is over there . . .' I am afraid to let go and point, so I nod. Anju is squinting inland. 'I think I can see Wheatie airing the futons.' I can't see our grandmother but I know Anju wants me to ask 'Where?' so I don't. The mountains rise towards the interior. Miyanoura Peak props up the sky. Hill tribes live in the rainshadow – they decapitate the lost tourists and make the skulls into drinking bowls. And there is a pool where a real webby, scaly kappa lives – it catches swimmers, rams its fist up through their bum-holes and pulls out their hearts to eat. Yakushima islanders never go up into the mountains, except for the tourist guides. I feel a lump in my pocket and remember. 'Want a champagne bomb?'

'Sure.'

Anju suddenly monkey-shrieks, swings, and dangles down in front of me, giggling at my panic. Scared birds beat away near by. Her legs grip the branch above.

'Don't!' is all I can blurt.

Anju bares her front teeth and chicken-wings her arms. 'Anju the bat.'

'Anju! Don't!'

She swings to and fro. 'I vant to suckkk your bluddd!' Her hair clasp falls away and her ponytail streams earthward. 'Bother. That was my last one.'

'Don't dangle like that! Stop it!'

'Eiji's a jellyfish, Eiji's a jellyfish!'

I imagine her falling, ricocheting from branch to branch. '*Stop it!*'

'You're even uglier upside down. I can see your bogies. Hold the tube steady.'

'Swing back up first!'

'No. I was born first so you have to do what I say. Hold the pack steady.' She extracts a sweet, unpeels the wrapper and watches it flutter away into the sea-greens. Watching me, she puts the sweet in her mouth, and lazily swings herself back upright. 'You really are such a wuss!'

'If you fell Wheatie would murder me.'

'Wuss.'

My heartbeat gradually calms down.

'What happens to you when you die?' So Anju.

I don't care as long as she stays upright. 'How should I know?'

'Nobody says the same thing. Wheatie says you go to the pure land and walk in gardens with your ancestors. Boooring. Mr Endō at school says you turn into soil. Father Kakimoto says it depends what you were like in this life – I'd get changed into an angel or a unicorn, but you'd come back as a maggot or toadstool.'

'So what do you think?'

'When you die they burn you, right?'

'Right.'

'So you turn into smoke, right?'

'I guess.'

'So you go there.' Anju lets go of the tree and shoots the sun with both hands. 'Up, up and away. I want to fly.'

A careworn buzzard rises on a thermal.

'In an airplane?'

'Who wants to fly in a pongy airplane?'

I suck my champagne bomb. 'How do you know airplanes pong?'

Anju crunches her champagne bomb. 'Airplanes must pong. All those people breathing the same air. Like the boys' changing room in the rainy season, but a hundred times worse. No, I mean proper flying.'

'Like with a jetpack?'

'No such things as jetpacks.'

'Zax Omega has a jetpack.'

Anju airs her recently acquired sigh. 'No such thing as Zax Omega.'

'Zax Omega opened the new building at the port!'

'And did he arrive by jetpack?'

'No,' I admit, 'by taxi. But you're too heavy to fly.'

'Sky Castle Laputa flies, and that's made of rock.'

'If I can't have Zax Omega, no way are you having Sky Castle Laputa.'

'Condors, then. Condors weigh more than me. They fly.'

'Condors have wings. I don't see any wings on you.'

'Ghosts fly without wings.'

'Ghosts are dead.'

Anju picks champagne bomb shrapnel from her teeth. She is in one of those moods when I have no idea what she is thinking. Leaf shadows hide my twin sister. Parts of Anju are too bright, parts of Anju are so dark she isn't even here.

Jerking off usually sends me to sleep. Am I normal? I never heard of a nineteen-year-old insomniac. I am no war criminal, no poet or scientist, I'm not even lovelorn. Lustlorn, yes. Here I am, in a city of five million women, cruising into my sexual prime, when females should be posting themselves to me naked in padded envelopes, single as a leper. Let me see. Who is riding the caravan of love tonight? Zizzi Hikaru, wet-suited as per the lager ad; the glam-rock mother of Yuki Chiyo; the waitress from Jupiter Café; Insectoid-woman from *Zax Omega and Red Plague Moon*. Back to good old Zizzi, I guess. I ferret around for some tissues.

I ferret around for matches to light my post-coital Mild Seven, but end up having to use my gas stove. One throttled Godzilla, and I am wider awake than ever. Zizzi was disappointing tonight. No sense of timing. Is she getting too young for me? Fujifilm says 01:49. What now? Clean myself up? Practise my guitar? Write an answer to one of the two epoch-shifting letters I received this week? Which one? Let's stick with the simpler: Akiko Katō's reply to the letter I wrote after failing to see her. The single sheet of paper is still in the plastic bag in the freezebox with The Other. I put it on the shelf next to Anju but it kept laughing at me. It came . . . when was it? Tuesday. Buntarō read the envelope as he handed it to me. 'Osugi and Bosugi, Legal. Chasing lawyer ladies? Be careful, lad, you could end up with injunctions slapped on where it hurts. Want to hear my lawyer joke? What's the difference between a catfish and a lawyer? Guess – go on. No? One is a scaly, bottom-dwelling scum-sucker, and the other is a catfish.' I tell him I've already heard it and dash up the videobox-stacked stairs to my capsule. I tell myself I am expecting a negative answer, but I wasn't expecting that Akiko Katō's 'No' would pack such a slap. I already know the letter by heart. Its greatest hits include: *Disclosure of a client's personal data constitutes a betrayal of trust which no responsible attorney could consider*. Pretty final. *Furthermore I feel obliged to refuse your request that I forward mail which my client has stated categorically he does not wish to receive*. Not much room for doubt there. Not much room for a reply, either. *Finally, in the event that legal proceedings are initiated to force data regarding your patrimony to be released, assisting your enquiries at this early stage represents a clear conflict of interest. I urge you not to pursue this matter, and trust that this letter clarifies our position.* Perfectly. Plan A is dead on arrival.

Mr Aoyama, sub-station-master of Ueno, is bald as a rivet-head and has a perfect Adolf Hitler moustache. This is Tuesday, on my first working day at Ueno station lost property office. 'I am far busier than you can imagine' – he speaks without taking his eyes off his paperwork – 'but I make a point of addressing new intake on an individual basis.' Mile-wide silences open up between his sentences. 'You know who I am.' His pen scratches. 'You are' – he checks a sheet – 'Eiji Miyake.' He looks at me, waiting for a nod. I nod. 'Miyake.' He pronounces my name as if it were a food additive. 'Previously employed on an orange farm' – he shuffles sheets, and I recognize my writing – 'on an island of no importance south of Kyūshū. Most bucolic.' Above Aoyama are portraits of his distinguished forebears. I imagine them bickering over who will come alive every morning to pilot the office through another tiresome day. His office smells of sun-faded card files. A computer buzzes. Golf clubs shine. 'Who hired you? The Sasaki woman?' I nod. A knock on the door, and his secretary appears with a tray of tea. 'I am addressing a trainee, Mrs Marui!' Aoyama speaks in an appalled hiss. 'My ten-thirty-five tea becomes my ten-forty-five tea, does it not?' Stressed Mrs Marui bobs an apology and withdraws. 'Go over to that window, Miyake, look out, and tell me what you see.'

I do as he says. 'A window cleaner, sir.'

The man is immune to irony. '*Below* the window cleaner.'

Trains pulling in and pulling out in the shadow of Terminus Hotel. Mid-morning passengers. Luggage haulers. The milling, the lost, the late, the meeters, the met, the platform-cleaning machines. 'Ueno station, sir.'

'Tell me this, Miyake. What *is* Ueno station?'

I am foxed by this question.

'Ueno station – Aoyama replays his grave spiel – 'an extra*ordinary* machine. One of the finest-tuned timepieces in the land. In the world. And this fireproof, thiefproof office is one of the nerve centres. From this console I can access . . . nearly everything. Ueno station is our lives, Miyake. You serve it, it serves you. It affords a timetabled career. You have the privilege to be a minute cog in this machine. Even I began in a position as lowly as yours: but with punctuality, hard work, integrity—' The phone rings and I stop existing. Aoyama's face switches to a higher-watt glow. His voice beams. '*Sir!* What a pleasure . . . yes . . . indeed . . . indeed . . . quite. A superb proposal. And may I venture to add . . . yes, sir. Absolutely . . . at the membership brokerage? Priceless . . . superb . . . and may I propose . . . indeed, sir. Rescheduled for Friday? How true . . . we're all very much looking forward to hearing how we performed, sir. Thank you, sir . . . quite . . . And may I—' Aoyama replaces the receiver and gazes at it.

After some seconds I cough politely.

Aoyama looks up. 'Where was I?'

'Minute cogs and integrity, sir.'

'Integrity.' But his mind is no longer here. He closes his eyes and pinches the bridge of his nose. 'Your probationary period is six months. You will have the chance to sit the Japan Railways examinations in March. So, the Sasaki woman hired you. Not my ideal role model. She is one of these men-women. Never quit work, even after marriage. Her husband died – sad, of course, but people die all the time, and she expects a man's job by way of compensation. So, Miyake. Rectify your accent problem. Listen to NHK radio announcers. Dump the junk that stuffs your head. In my day high schools trained tigers. Now they turn out peacocks. You are dismissed.'

I give him a bow as I close the door, but he is watching vacant space. The office outside is empty. The tray is on the side. To my own surprise, I lift the teapot lid and spit into it. This must be work-related stress.

*

The lost property office is an okay place to work. I have to wear uncool Japan Railways overalls, but I finish at six sharp and Ueno station is only a few stops down the Kita Senju line from Umejima, near Shooting Star. During my six-month probation period I get paid weekly, which suits me fine. I am lucky. Buntarō got me the job. When I got back from PanOpticon a week ago last Friday, he said he had heard from a contact that there might be a job going there, and would I be interested? You bet, I said. Before I knew it I had an interview with Mrs Sasaki. She is a stern old bird, a Tokyo version of my grandmother, but after talking for about half an hour she offered me the job. I spend the mornings cataloguing – writing date/time/train labels on the items collected by conductors and cleaners when the trains terminate, and housing them on the right metal rack. Mrs Sasaki runs the lost property office and deals with the high-value items in the side office – wallets, cash cards, jewellery – which have to be registered with the police. Suga trains me to do the low-value ones, stored in the back office. 'Not much natural light in here, right?' says Suga. 'But you can tell the month from what gets handed in. November to February, skis and snowboards. March – diplomas. June is all wedding gifts. Swimsuits pile up in July. A decent rain will bring hundreds of umbrellas. Not the most inspiring job, but it beats leaping around a garage forecourt or delivering pizzas, imho.' Afternoons I spend on the counter, waiting for claimants, or answering the phone. Rush hours are busiest, of course, but during mid-afternoon my job is almost relaxing. My memory is the most regular visitor.

The leaves are so green they are blue. Me and Anju play our staring game: we stare at one another and the first one to make the other smile and look away wins. I pull stupid faces but they bounce off her. Her Cleopatra eyes are sparked with bronze. She wins – she always does – by bringing her eyes close to mine and opening wide. Anju returns to her higher branch and looks at the sun through a leaf. Then she hides the sun with her hand. The webby bit between her thumb and forefinger glows ruby. She looks out to sea. 'The tide is coming in.'

'Going out.'

'Coming in. Your whalestone is diving.'

My mind is on miraculous soccer exploits.

'I really used to believe what you told me about the whalestone.'

Bicycle kicks and diving headers.

'You spouted such rubbish.'

'Uh?'

'About it being magic.'

'What being magic?'

'The whalestone, deaf-aid!'

'I never said it was magic.'

'You did. You said it was a real whale that the thunder god had turned into stone, and that one day when we were older we would swim out to it, and once we set foot on it the spell would be broken, and it would be so grateful that it would take us anywhere we wanted to go, even to Mother and Father. I used to imagine it happening so hard that I could see it sometimes, like down a telescope. Mother putting on her pearls, and Father washing his car.'

'I never said all of that.'

'Did, too. One of these days I'll swim out to it.'

'No way could you *ever* swim that far. Girls can't swim as well as boys.'

Anju aims a lazy kick at my head. 'I could swim there, *easy*!'

'In your dreams. Way too far.'

'In *your* dreams.' Waves break at the foot of the grey humpback.

'Maybe it really is a whalestone,' I suggest. 'A fossil one.'

Anju snorts. 'It's just a stupid rock. It doesn't even look like a whale. And next time we go to the secret beach I'm going to show you and swim out there, me, and stand on it and laugh at you.'

The Kagoshima ferry crawls across the horizon.

'This time tomorrow—' I begin.

'Yeah, yeah, this time tomorrow you'll be in Kagoshima. You'll get up really early to catch the ferry, arrive at Kagoshima junior high school at ten o'clock. The third years, the second years, then your match. Then you go to the restaurant of a hotel with nine floors and eat while you listen to Mr Ikeda tell you why you lost. Then you come back on Sunday morning. You already told me a zillion times, Eiji.'

'I can't help it if you're jealous.'

'Jealous? Eleven smelly boys kicking a bag of air on a pitch of muck?'

'You used to like soccer.'

'You used to wet our futon.'

Ouch. 'You're jealous because I'm going to Kagoshima and you're not.'

Anju stays aloof.

The tree creaks. I didn't expect Anju to lose interest in our argument so soon. 'Watch,' she says. She stands up, feet apart, steadies herself, takes her hands away—

'Stop it,' I say.

And my sister jumps into empty air

My lungs wallop out a scream

Anju flashes by me

and lands laughing on a branch below, swinging down to a lower branch. I hear her laughter long after she has vanished in the leaves.

Fujifilm says two o'clock has come and gone. A single night is stuffed with minutes, but they leak out, one by one. My capsule is stuffed with Stuff. Look up 'stuff' in a dictionary, and you get a picture of my capsule above Shooting Star. A shabby colony in the empire of stuff. An old TV, a rice-cracker futon, a camping table, a tray of cast-off kitchen utensils courtesy of Buntarō's wife, cups containing fungal experiments, a roaring fridge with chrome trimmings. The fan. A pile of *Screen* magazines, offloaded by Buntarō. All I brought from Yakushima was a backpack of clothes, my Discman, my Lennon CDs and my guitar. Buntarō looked at my guitar doubtfully the day I arrived. 'You don't intend to plug that thing in anywhere, do you?' 'No,' I answer. 'Stay acoustic,' he warns. 'Go electric on me, and you're out. It's in your contract.' I am not going to contact her. No way. She will try to talk me out of looking for my father. I wonder how long it will take for Cockroach to die. The glue trap is called a 'cockroach motel', and has windows, doors and flowers printed on the side. Traitor cockroaches wave six arms – 'Come in, come in!' It has an onion-flavoured bait-sachet – curry, prawn salad and beef jerky are also available at all good Tokyo supermarkets. Cockroach greeted me when I moved in. It didn't even bother pretending to be scared. Cockroach grinned. Who has the last laugh now? I have! No. It has. I can't sleep. In Yakushima night means sleep. Not much else to do. Night does not mean sleep in Tokyo. Punks slalom down shopping malls. Hostesses stifle yawns and glance at their patrons' Rolexes. Yakuza gangsters fight on deserted building sites. High-schoolers way younger than me engage in gymnastic love-hotel sex-bouts. In an apartment high above, a fellow insomniac flushes a toilet. A pipe behind my head chunders.

Last Wednesday, my second day as a drone at Ueno station. I am taking a good solid dump during my lunch break, smoking a Salem in the cubicle. I hear the door open, a zipper scratch, and the chime of urine against porcelain urinal. Then the voice begins – it is Suga, the computer nerd whose part-time job I am taking over from the end of the week when he goes back to college. Obviously he thinks he is alone in here. 'Excuse me, are you Suga? Are you responsible for this?' His voice isn't his real voice – it is a cartoon voice, and it must scrape the lining off his vocal chords to produce it. 'I don't *wanna* remember, I don't *wanna* remember, I don't *wanna* remember. Don't make me. Can't make me. Won't make me. *Forget* it! *Forget* it! *Forget* it!' His voice reverts to its bland, nasal calm. 'It wasn't my fault. Could have happened to anyone. To anyone. Don't listen to them.'

I am in a fix. If I leave now we'll both be embarrassed as all hell. I feel as though I have heard him mutter a secret in his sleep. But if I stay here, what might he reveal next? How he chopped up the corpse in his bath and put it out with the garbage bit by bit? If he finds me listening, it will look like I was eavesdropping. I cough, flush the toilet, and take a long time to pull my trousers up. When I emerge from my cubicle Suga has disappeared. I wash my hands and walk the roundabout way back to the office, via the magazine stands. Mrs Sasaki is dealing with a customer. Suga is in the back eating his lunch, and I offer him a Salem. He says no, he doesn't smoke. I forgot, he told me that yesterday. I go to the mirror and pretend to have something in my eye. If I show him too much kindness he may twig it was me who heard him being memory-whipped.

Later, back at the claims counter, Suga perches on his stool reading a magazine called *MasterHacker*. Suga has a weird physique – he is overweight around his belly, but he has no bottom. Long dangly ET arms. He suffers from eczema. His face has been medicated into submission, but the backs of his hands flake, and even in this heat he wears long-sleeved shirts to hide his forearms. A trolley of lost items from the afternoon trains is in the back office waiting for me. Suga smirks. 'So you already had the Assistant Station-Master Aoyama experience?' I nod. Suga puts down his magazine. 'Don't let him intimidate you. He isn't as big time as he makes out. The man is losing it, imho. A big shake-up is being announced, Mrs Sasaki was saying last week. Not that I care. Next week I'm doing my IBM internship. Week after, back to uni. I'm getting my own postgrad research room. You can come and see me when I'm not supervising. Imperial Uni, ninth floor. Near Ochanomizu. I'll draw you a map. You can get the front desk to ring up for me. My masters is in computer systems, but between you, me and the lost property, all that academic crap is a cover for this—' He waves

MasterHacker. 'I'm one of the five best hackers currently working in Japan. We all know each other. We swap info. We break into systems and leave our tags. Like graffiti artists. There is *nowhere*, right, in Japan I can't hack into. There's a secret website in the Pentagon – you know what the Pentagon is, right, the American defence nerve centre – called Holy Grail. This site is protected by their top computer brains, right. If you hack into Holy Grail it proves that you are better than they are, and men in black appear to offer you a job. That is what I'm going to do. Imperial Uni has the fastest modems this side of the twenty-fifth century. Once I get access to those babies, I am in. Then, whoosh, I am out of this shithole commonly known as Tokyo. Deep joy. You suckers won't see me for dust.'

I watch Suga read *MasterHacker* while I work. His eyebrows twitch up every time he reaches the bottom of a column of text. I wonder what Suga wouldn't call a shithole. What would make Suga happy? Weird, but when I remember that I'll only be here until I find my father, I almost like Tokyo. I feel I'm on holiday on another planet, passing myself off as a native alien. I might even stay on. I like flashing my JR travel pass to the train man at the barrier. I like the way nobody pokes their nose into your business. I like the way the adverts change every week – on Yakushima they change every ten years. I like riding the train every day from Kita Senju to Ueno: I like the incline where it dives below the ground and becomes a submarine. I like the way submarines pass by at different speeds, so you can fool yourself you are going backwards. I like the glimpses of commuters in parallel windows – two stories being remembered at the same time. Kita Senju to Ueno is crammed beyond belief in the morning. Us drones all swing and lurch in droozy unison as the train changes speed. Normally only lovers and twins get this close to other people. I like the way nothing needs to be decided on submarines. I like the muffled clunking. Tokyo is one massive machine made of smaller components. The drones only know what their own minute component is for. I wonder what

Tokyo is for. I wonder what it does. I already know the names of the stations between here and Ueno. I know where to stand so I can get off nearest the exit. Do not ride in the first compartment, says Uncle Tarmac – if the train collides, this is the crumple zone – and be extra alert on the platform as the train pulls in, in case a hand in the small of your back shoves you over the edge. I like the brew of sweat, perfume, crushed food, grime, cosmetics. I like how you can study reflected faces, so deeply you can almost leaf through their memories. Submarines carry drones, skulls carry memories, and one man's shithole may be another man's paradise.

'Eiji!' Anju, of course. Moonlight bright as a UFO abduction, air heady with the mosquito incense which my grandmother uses to fumigate the lived-in rooms. Anju whispers so as not to wake her. 'Eiji!' She perches on the high windowsill, hugging her knees. Bamboo shadows sway and shoo on the tatami and faded fusuma. 'Eiji! Are you awake?'

'No.'

'I was watching you. You are a boy-me. But you snore.'

She wants to wake me up by getting me angry. 'I do not.'

'You snore like a piggy puking. Guess where I've been.'

Let me sleep. 'Down the toilet.'

'Out on the roof! You can climb up the balcony pole. I found the way. So warm out there. If you stare at the moon long enough you can see it move. I couldn't sleep. A pesky mosquito woke me up.'

'A pesky sister woke me up. My soccer match is tomorrow. I need sleep.'

'So you need a midnight snack to build you up. Look.'

On the side is a tray. Omochi, soy, daikon pickles, peanut cookies, tea. I see trouble ahead. 'When Wheatie finds out she'll—'

Anju scrunches up her face and voice for a Wheatie impression. 'Your mother may have made your bones, young missy, but inside that head of yours is going to be all *my* handiwork!'

As always, I laugh. 'You went down to the kitchen on your own?'

'I told the ghosts I was one of them and they believed me.' Anju jumps and lands at my feet without a sound. I know resistance is pointless so I sit up and bite into a squeaky pickle. Anju slides under my futon and dunks an omochi into a saucer of soy. 'I had my flying dream again. Only I had to keep flapping *really* hard to stay above the ground. I could see lots of people moving about, and there was this big stripy circus tent where Mum lived. I was about to swoop down on it when the mosquito woke me up.'

'Be careful about falling.'

Anju chews. 'What?'

'If you dream about falling and hit the ground you really die in your bed.'

Anju chews some more. 'Who says so?'

'Scientists say so.'

'Rubbish.'

'Scientists proved it!'

'If you dreamed of falling, hit the ground, and died, how could anyone know that you were dreaming of falling in the first place?' I think this through. Anju enjoys her victory in silence. Frogs start up and die down, a million marimbas. In the distance the sea is asleep. We chomp one omochi after another. Suddenly Anju speaks in a voice I don't remember her using. 'I never see her face any more, Eiji.'

'Whose face?'

'Mum's. Can you?'

'She's ill. She's in a special hospital.'

Anju's voice wavers. 'What if that isn't true?'

Huh? 'Sure it's true!' I feel as if I've swallowed a knife. 'She looks like how she looks in the photographs.'

'The photographs are old.' Why now? Anju wipes her eyes on her nightshirt and looks away. I hear her jaw and throat sort of clench. 'Wheatie sent me to buy a box of washing powder at Mrs Tanaka's while you were at soccer practice this afternoon. Mrs Oki and her sister from Kagoshima were there. They were at the back of the shop and they didn't notice me at first, so I heard everything.'

The knife reaches my gut. 'Heard what?'

'Mrs Oki said, "Of course the Miyake girl hasn't shown her face here." Mrs Tanaka said, "Of course, she has no right to." Mrs Oki said, "She wouldn't dare. Dumping her two kiddies on their grandmother and uncles while she lives it up in Tokyo with her fancy men and fancy apartments and fancy cars." Then she saw me.' The knife turns itself. Anju gasps between tight chains of snivels.

'What happened?'

'She dropped her eggs, and hurried out.'

A moth drowns in the moonlight.

I wipe Anju's tears. They are so warm. Then she brushes me away and hunches up in a stubborn crouch. 'Look,' I say, wondering what to say. 'Mrs Oki and her sister from Kagoshima and Mrs Tanaka are all witches who drink their own piss.'

Anju shakes her head at the daikon pickle I offer her. She just mumbles. 'Broken eggs. Everywhere.'

Fujifilm says 02:34. Sleep. Sleep. You are feeling sleepy. Your eyelids are veeeeeerrry heavy. I don't think so. Let me sleep. Please. I have to work tomorrow. Today. I close my eyes but see a body falling through space. Cartwheeling. Cockroach is still fighting the glue. Cockroaches have sensors that start the legs running even before the brain registers the danger. How do scientists find these things out? Cockroaches even eat books if nothing juicier comes along. Cat would have kicked Cockroach's butt. Cat. Cat knows the secret of life and death. Wednesday evening, I get home from work. 'Good day at the office, dear?' asks Buntarō, drinking iced coffee from a can. 'Not bad,' I say. Buntarō drains the last drops. 'What are your co-workers like?' 'I haven't met many. Suga, the guy I'm replacing, believes he is a sort of arch cybercriminal. Mrs Sasaki, my boss, doesn't seem to like me much but I sort of like her anyway. Mr Aoyama, her boss, is so uptight I'm surprised he can walk without squeaking.' Buntarō lobs his can into a bin, and a customer comes in with a stack of videos to return. I climb up to my capsule, slump on my futon and read Akiko Katō's letter for the hundredth time. I practise my guitar as the room fills with suburban dusk. I can't afford any light fittings yet, so all I have is a knackered lamp that the previous tenant stowed in the back of the closet. I suddenly decide to admit to myself that the vague hope I have entertained all my life, that by coming to Tokyo I would bump into my father sooner or later, is laughable. Lamentable. Instead of setting me free, the truth makes me too depressed to play the guitar, so I fold my futon into a chair and switch on the TV, salvaged from the trash last week. This TV is a pile of crap. Its greens are mauves and its blues pink. I can find five channels, plus one in a blizzard. All the programmes are crap, too. I watch the governor of Tokyo announce that in the event of an earthquake all the blacks, Hispanics and Koreans will run amok, loot, rape and pillage. I change channel. A farmer explains how a pig gets fat by eating its own shit. I change channel. Tokyo Giants trounce Hiroshima Carp. I get the box of discount sushi from the fridge. I change channel. A memory game comes on where contestants are posed questions about tiny details in a film section they have just watched. I imagine a shadow crouching in the corner of my eye. It launches itself at me and I half-drop my dinner.

'Gaaah!'

A black cat lands at my feet. It yawns a mouth of hooks. Its tail is dunked in white. It has a tartan collar. 'Cat,' I blurt pointlessly, as my pulse tries to calm itself. It must have jumped on to my balcony from a ledge and entered through the gash in the mosquito netting. 'Get lost!' Cat is the coolest customer. I do the sudden stomp people do to intimidate animals, but Cat has seen it all before. Cat looks at my sushi and licks its lips. 'Look,' I say to it, 'go and find a housewife with a freezer full of leftovers.' Cat is too cool to reply. 'One saucer of milk,' I tell it, 'then you go away.' Cat downs it as I pour. More. 'This is your last saucer, okay?' As Cat laps more genteelly, I wonder when I started talking to animals. It watches me blow the fluff off the last of my sushi. So I end up eating a box of crackers while Cat chews on fresh yellowtail, octopus and cod roe.

Leave Ueno station through the park entrance, go past the concert hall and museums, skirt around the fountain, and you come to a sort of tree shrubbery. Homeless people live here, in tents made of sky-blue plastic sheeting and wooden poles. The best tents even have doors. I guess Picture Lady lives there. She appeared at the claims counter just before my lunch break on Thursday. It was the hottest day this week. Tarmac was as soft as cooking chocolate. She wore a headscarf tied tight, a long skirt of no clear colour or pattern, and battered gym shoes. Forty, fifty, sixty years old – hard to tell beneath the weathering and engrained grime. Suga saw her coming, did his smirk, announced it was his lunch break, and slipped away to flagellate himself in the toilet. The homeless woman reminds me of the farming wives on Yakushima, but she's more spaced out. Her eyes don't focus properly. Her voice is cracked and hissed. 'I lost 'em.'

'What have you lost?'

She mumbles to her feet. 'Has anyone given 'em to you yet?'

My hands reach for the claim pad. 'What is it you lost?'

She shoots a glance at me. 'My pictures.'

'You lost some pictures?'

She takes an onion out of her pocket and unpeels the crispy brown skin. Her fingers are scabby and dark.

I try again. 'Did you lose the pictures on a train or in the station?'

She keeps flinching. 'I got the old ones back . . .'

'It would help me if you could tell me a little more about—'

She licks the onion. 'But I ain't got the new ones back.'

'Were the pictures valuable?'

She bites. It crunches.

Mrs Sasaki appears from the side office, and nods at the picture lady. 'Roasting weather we're having, isn't it?'

Picture Lady talks through onion cud. 'I need 'em to cover up the clocks.'

'We don't have your pictures today, I'm afraid. Maybe tomorrow you'll come across them. Have you looked around Shinobazu pond?'

Picture Lady scowls. 'What would me pictures be doing there?'

Mrs Sasaki shrugs. 'Who knows? It's a cool spot on a hot day.'

She nods. 'Who knows . . .'

I watch her wander away. 'Is she a regular customer?'

Mrs Sasaki straightens up the desk. 'We're a part of her schedule. It costs nothing to be civil to her. Did you work out what her "pictures" are?'

'Some sort of family albums, I figured.'

'I took her literally at first, too.' Mrs Sasaki speaks carefully, the way she does. 'But I think she's talking about her memories.' We watch her disappear in the shimmer. Cicadas wind up and wind down. 'All we are is our memories.'

The moon has moved. Anju sips her tea, calm again. I am between sleeping and waking. I am doing my best to remember our mother's face. I think I remember a perfume she wore, but I can't be sure. I feel Anju settle inside my sleeping curl. She is still thinking. 'The last time we saw her was at Uncle Money's in Kagoshima. The last time we left Yakushima.'

'The secret beach birthday. Two years ago?'

'Three. Two years ago was the rubber dinghy birthday.'

'She left suddenly. She was staying all week, then she just wasn't there.'

'Want to know a secret?'

I am awake again. 'A real one?'

'I'm not a little kid any more. 'Course it's a real one.'

'Go on, then.'

'Wheatie told me never to tell anyone, not even you.'

'What about?'

'When she left that day. Mum, I mean.'

'You kept a secret for three years? I thought she left because she was ill.'

Anju yawns, indifferent to what I think or thought.

'Tell me.'

'I was sick that day. You were at soccer practice. I was doing homework on the downstairs table. Mum started making tempura.' Anju's voice has gone sort of limp. I prefer it when she blubs. 'She dipped weird stuff into the batter.'

'What weird stuff?'

'Stuff you can't eat. Her watch, a candle, a teabag, a light bulb. The light bulb popped when she put it in the oil and she laughed funny. Her ring. Then she arranged everything on a dish with miso leaves and put it in front of me.'

'What did you say?'

'Nothing.'

'What did she say?'

'She said she was playing. I said, "You've been drinking." She said, "It's all Yakushima's fault." I asked her why she couldn't play without drinking. She asked me why I didn't like her cooking. She said to eat my dinner up like a good girl. I said, "I can't eat those things." So she got angry. You remember how scary she got on her visits sometimes? I can't remember what she looks like but I remember that.'

'What happened then?'

'Auntie Money came and led her to the bedroom. I heard her.' Anju swallowed. 'She was *crying.*'

'Mum was crying?'

'Auntie Money came back and told me that if I told anyone what had happened, even you, a bad doctor might take Mum away.' Anju frowns. 'So I kind of made myself forget it. But not really.'

An owl hoots.

I must go to sleep.

Anju rocks herself, slowly, slowly.

A dog in the distance barks at something, real or remembered.

'Don't go to Kagoshima tomorrow, Eiji.'

'I have to go. I'm in defence.'

'*Don't go.*'

I don't understand. 'Why not?'

'Go, then. I don't care.'

'It's only two days.'

Anju snaps at me. 'You're not the only one who can do grown-up things!'

'What do you mean by that?'

'Me to know and you to guess!'

'What are you going to do?'

'You'll find out when you get back from your soccer game!'

'Tell me!'

'I can't hear you! You're in Kagoshima!'

'Tell me!' I'm worried.

Her voice turns spiteful. 'You'll see. You'll see.'

'Who cares what you do anyway?'

'I saw the pearly snake this morning!'

Now I know my sister is lying. The pearly snake is a stupid tale our grandmother tells to scare us. She says it has lived out in the Miyake storehouse since before she was born, and that it only ever appears to warn of a coming death. Anju and I stopped believing her ages ago, only our grandmother never noticed. I am offended that Anju thinks she can awe me into submission with the pearly snake. I listen to the March midnight bird trying to remember the words to its song. It is always losing track and starting again. Every year I re-remember this bird, but by the rainy season I forget it again. Much later, I try to make friends with my sister, but she is asleep, or pretending to be.

Fujifilm smuggled three o'clock over the border without me noticing. Two more hours to dawn. This sticky web of a night is three-quarters spun. I am going to be exhausted all day at work. Mrs Sasaki warned me Saturday is busier, not quieter, than weekdays, because commuters are more careful with their baggage than weekend shoppers and Friday-nighters, and because a lot of people wait until Saturday before coming in to claim lost items. I guess the media people will be snooping around for follow-up stories about Mr Aoyama. Poor guy. Sudden and rude as a bullet through a drumskin, the telephone riiiiiiiiings. That noise drills me with guilt and dread. The telephone riiiiiiiiings. Weird. I only got my number last week. Nobody knows it. The telephone riiiiiiiiings. Suppose a pervert is out there, trawling for kicks at random? I answer, and before I know it I have a psycho in my shower. No way am I answering. The telephone riiiiiiiiings. Buntarō? Some kind of emergency? What kind of emergency? The telephone riiiiiiiiiings. Wait. Someone at Osugi and Bosugi knows my number – suppose a co-worker of Akiko Katō read my letter before she shredded it, and felt an unaccountable empathy with my plight? She contacts my father, who has to wait until his wife is asleep before daring to contact me. He is whispering coarsely, fiercely, in a closed-off part of his house. 'Answer!' The telephone riiiiiiiiings. I have to decide now. No. Let it die. Answer it! I dive off my futon, trap my foot in a folding peg-frame, stub my toe on my guitar case and lunge for the receiver. 'Hello?'

'Never fear-o, 'tis a Nero!' A singing man.

'Hello?'

'Never fear-o, 'tis a Nero.' A mildly irritated man.

'Yes, I thought you said that.'

'I never wrote that stupid jingle!' A buttered voice.

'Me neither.'

'Look here, young man – you delivered some fliers to our office, which promise that the first two hundred people to phone up off-peak and sing "Never fear-o, 'tis a Nero!" are entitled to one free medium-size pizza of their choice. That is what I just did. I'll plump for my regular Kamikaze: mozzarella crust, banana, quail's eggs, scallops, treble chilli, octopus ink. Don't chop the chilli. I like to suck them. Helps me concentrate. So – am I one of the first two hundred or am I not?'

'Is this a joke?'

'It had better not be. All-night overtime makes me ravenous.'

'I think you misdialled.'

'Impossible. This is Nero's Pizzeria, right?'

'Wrong.'

'Are you quite sure?'

'Yep.'

'So I called a private residence after three in the morning?'

'Uh-huh.'

'I am so, so dreadfully sorry. I don't know what to say.'

'Not to worry. I have insomnia tonight, anyway.'

'But I was so patronizing! I thought you were a numbskull pizza boy.'

'No problem, really. But you have one weird taste in pizzas.'

He chuckles with devious pride. He is older than I thought. 'I invented it. At Nero's they nickname it the Kamikaze – I heard the telephone girl tell the chef. The secret is the banana. It glues all the other tastes together. Anyway, I mustn't take up any more of your time. Once more – my sincerest apologies. What I did is inexcusable. Inexcusable.' He hangs up.

I wake up alone. A window of summer stars melted to nearly nothing. Anju's futon is a discarded pile. So Anju. Could she be out on the roof? I slide the mosquito net across. 'Anju? Anju!' The wind sifts the bamboo, and the frogs start up. Fine. She wants to sulk, let her. Fifteen minutes later, I am dressed, breakfasted and walking down the track to Anbō harbour with my sports bag and my new baseball cap which Anju bought me with her pocket money from Uncle Tarmac. I catch sight of the Kagoshima ferry lit up like a starship on its launch pad and feel a vhirrr of excitement. This day is finally here. I am leaving for Kagoshima, on my own, and

I refuse to let my stupid jealous sister make me feel guilty about leaving her for one night. I refuse. How can I even be sure the stuff she said last night about our mother was true? She's been acting weird lately. A meteor scratches the dark purple. The dark purple unscratches the meteor. And then a fantastic idea comes to me. It is the greatest idea of my life. I am going to train, train, and train, and become such a brilliant soccer player that I will play for Japan on my twentieth birthday against Brazil in the World Cup final. Japan will be eight–nil down in the sixtieth minute, then I will be called on as a substitute and score three hat tricks by the end of injury time. I will be in newspapers and on TV all over the world. Our mother is so proud that she gives up drinking, but better still our father sees me, recognizes me, and drives to the airport to meet the team jet. Of course, Anju is waiting there too, and our mother, and we are reunited with the world watching. How perfect. How obvious. I am burning with genius and hope. A light is on in Anbō, and crossing the hanging bridge I see a flash. A salmon leaps.

Where the river widens into an estuary, the valley is steep and narrow. Wheatie and the Anbō old people call it the Neck. It is the most haunted place, but I'm not afraid. I half-fear and half-hope Anju will ambush me. The faces between the pine trees are not really there. Where the water floods the track in the rainy season, a torī gate marks the beginning of the path that winds up the hill to the shrine of the thunder god. Wheatie warns us not to play there. She says that apart from the Jōmon cedars themselves, the thunder god is the oldest living thing on Yakushima. Show any disrespect to him, and the next time you cross water a tsunami will come and drown you. Anju wanted to ask if that was what happened to our grandfather, our mother's father, but I made her promise not to. Mrs Oki told a kid in our class that he drowned face down in a ditch, drunk. Anyway, the villagers never bother the thunder god with small-fry favours like exams, money or weddings – they go to Father Kakimoto's new temple next to the bank for that. But for babies, and blessings for fishing boats, solace for dead relatives, they climb the steps to the shrine of the thunder god. Always alone.

I check my Zax Omega watch. Plenty of time. The road to the World Cup starts today in Kagoshima, and I will need all the help I can get. Finding our father is big fry. No fry is bigger for Anju and me. Without another thought I sling my sports bag behind a mossy rock and, fuelled by energy from my awesome brainwave, start running up the muddy steps.

I replace the receiver. Weird guy, the way he kept apologizing. Maybe the telephone call will break the insomnia spell. Maybe my body will realize how tired it is, and finally shut down. I lie on my back and stare upwards doing chess knight-moves on the ceiling tiles until I forget which ones I've already landed on. Then I begin again. On the third attempt I am overwhelmed by the pointlessness of the exercise. If I can't sleep I may as well think about the letter. The Other Letter. The Big Letter. It came – when? – Thursday. Yesterday. Well, the day before yesterday. I get back to Shooting Star utterly exhausted. Thirty-six bowling balls were left on platform nine, the farthest platform from the lost property office. Suga had performed his disappearing act so I had to lug them over one by one. They were claimed later by a team who were waiting for them at Tokyo Central station. I am learning that laws of probability work differently in the field of lost property. Mrs Sasaki once had a human skeleton wind up on her trolley, stuffed inside a backpack. A medical student left it on the train after his professor's leaving party. Anyway, I get back to Shooting Star, dripping sweat, and Buntarō is perched on his stool behind the counter spooning down green tea ice cream, studying a sheet of paper with a magnifying glass. 'Hey, lad,' he says. 'Want to see my son?' This is weird because Buntarō told me that he hasn't got any kids. Then he shows me a page of inky fuzz. I frown at my proud landlord. 'The miracles of ultrasound scans!' he says. 'Inside the womb!' I look at Buntarō's belly, and he glares. 'Very funny. We decided on his name. Actually, my wife decided. But I agree. Want to know what name we decided?'

'Sure,' I say.

'"Kōdai". "Kō" as in "voyage", "dai" as in great. Great Voyage.'

'That is a really cool name,' I tell him, meaning it.

Buntarō admires Kōdai from various angles. 'See his nose? This is his foot. Cute, huh?'

'The cutest. What's this shrimpy thing?'

'How do you think we know he's a he, genius?'

'Oh. Sorry.'

'Another letter arrived for you. I would rig up a special mailbox for you, but then I'd miss out on the fun of steaming open my tenants' private letters. Here you go.' He hands me a plain white envelope, originally postmarked in Miyazaki, and forwarded by Uncle Money in Kagoshima. I slit it open and unfold three sheets of crumpled paper. On the video screen helicopters collide and buildings explode. Bruce Willis takes off his sunglasses and squints at the inferno. I read the first line and realize who the letter is from. I shove it into my jacket pocket and climb the stairs – I don't want Buntarō to see the shock on my face.

On the steps to the thunder god shrine, spider webs tug, tear and stick to my face. Boiled-candy spiders. I trip and muddy up my knees. I try to forget the ghost stories I've heard about how dead children live on these steps, but once you try to forget something you already remember it. Colossal ferns tower over me. Freshwater crabs skitter into rooty cracks. A deer thuds and disappears into thicket. I focus on the ultimate reunion with our father once my ultimate plan bears fruit, and run, and run, and suddenly I am standing in the shrine clearing right at the top. I can see for miles. Inland mountains heave and lurch towards the breaking sky. Light smooths the sea over. I can see the windows on the Yakushima ferry. I approach the bell nervously and look around for an adult to ask permission. I've never woken a god up before. Wheatie takes Anju and me to the harbour shrine every New Year's Day to change our zodiac amulet, but that is a jolly affair of relatives, neighbours and having our heads patted. This is the real thing. This is sober magic. Only me and the god of all thunder in his mildewed drowse. I grip the rope that swings the bell-hammer—

The first gong is to slosh through the forest, scaring pheasants.

The second gong is to make swing-wing fighters wobble in turbulence.

The third gong is to slam shut for ever the iron doors.

I wonder if Anju heard the bell in her sulking-place. When I get back tomorrow I'll tell her it was me. She'll never admit to it, but she'll be impressed by my daring. This is like something she normally dreams up. I approach the shrine itself. The thunder god scowls. His face is hatred, typhoon and nightmare all knotted up. I can't back out now. He's awake. My coin clatters into the donation box, I clap three times and close my eyes. 'Good morning, uh, God of Thunder. My name is Eiji Miyake. I live with Anju and Wheatie in the last house up the valley track, past the big Kawakami farmhouse. But you probably know that. I woke you up to ask for your help. I want to become the greatest soccer player in Japan. This is a big, big thing, so please don't give me piles like you did the taxi driver.'

'And in return?' asks the silence.

'When I'm a famous soccer player I'll, uh, come back and rebuild your shrine and stuff. Until then, anything that I can give you, you can have. Take it. You don't have to ask me, just take it.'

The silence sighs. 'Anything?'

'Anything.'

'Anything? Are you sure?'

'I said "anything", and I mean it.'

The silence lasts nine days and nine nights. 'Done.'

I open my eyes. The fin of an airliner trails rose and gold. Doves spin predictions. Down in Anbō harbour the Kagoshima ferry sounds a solitary horn, and I can see cars arriving. The million and one clocks of the forest flutter, dart, shriek and howl into life. I rush off, flying down the muddy steps where the ghosts of the dead children are dissolving in the first sunlight.

◆

Miyazaki Mountain Clinic
25th August

Hello Eiji,

How do I begin this? I already wrote a stroppy letter, then a moaning one, then a witty one that began, 'Hello, I am your mother, nice to meet you.' Then one that began with 'Sorry'. They are scrunched up, near the bin on the other side of my room. I am a lousy shot.

Hot summer, isn't it? I knew it would be when the rainy season didn't happen. (I suppose it is still raining in Yakushima, though. When doesn't it?) So, you're nearly twenty now. Twenty. Where do all the years go? Want to know how old I'll be next month? Too old to tell anyone. I'm at this place receiving treatment for nerves/drinking. I never wanted to come back to Kyūshū, but at least the mountain air here is cool. My therapist has advised that I write to you. I didn't want to at first, but she is even more persistent than me. That looks wrong – I want to write to you, but after all this time it's so, so much easier not to. But I have this story (more a serial memory). My therapist says I can only stop it hurting me by telling you about it. So if you like, I'm writing out of selfishness. But here goes.

Once upon a time I was a young mother living in Tokyo with infant you and infant Anju. The apartment was paid for by your father, but this story isn't about him, or even Anju. This is about you and me. In those days, it looked like I was on to a good thing – a ninth-floor split-level apartment in a fashionable quarter of the big city, flower boxes on the balcony, a very rich lover with his own wife to wash his shirts. You and Anju, I have to admit, were not part of the plan when I left Yakushima, but it seemed that the life I led twenty years ago was better than the life of orange farming and island gossip that my mother (your grandmother) had arranged (behind my back, as usual) with Shintaro Baba's people to marry me into. Believe me, he was every bit as much a slob and a yob a quarter of a century ago as I'm quite sure he is now.

This isn't easy to write.

I was miserable. I was twenty-three, and everyone told me I was beautiful. The only company young mothers have is other young mothers. Young mothers are the most vicious tribe in the world if you don't fit in. When they found out I was a 'second wife' they decided I was an immoral influence and petitioned the building manager to have me removed. Your father was powerful enough to block that, but none of them ever spoke to me afterwards. As you know, nobody on Yakushima knew about you (yet), and the thought of living with all the knowing glances was too much.

Around that time your father began seeing a newer-model mistress. A baby is not a sexy accessory on a woman. Twins are twice as unsexy. It was an ugly ending – you don't want the details, believe me. (Maybe you do, but I don't want to remember them.) When I was pregnant, he swore he'd take care of everything. Naïve young petal that I was, I didn't realize he was only talking about money. Like all weak men, he acted all confused and presumed everyone would forgive him. His lawyers took over and I never saw him again. (Never wanted to.) I was allowed to live in the apartment, but not to sell it – it was during the bubble economy, and the value of the place doubled every six months. This was shortly after your first birthday.

I was not a well woman. (I've never been a very well woman, but at least now I know it.) Some women take to motherhood like they were mothers even before they were mothers – I was never cut out to be a mother, even when I was one. I still hate little children. All the money your father's lawyer sent for your maintenance I spent on an illegal Filipina nanny so I could escape the apartment. I used to sit in coffee shops watching people walk by. Young women my age, working in banks, doing flower arranging, shopping. All the little ordinary things I had looked down on before I became pregnant.

Two years passed. I got a job in another hostess bar, but I was jaded. I'd already caught my rich patron, and every time I went home you and Anju reminded me where rich patrons leave you. (Nappies and bawling and sleepless nights.) One morning you and I were alone in the house – you'd had a fever, so the nanny took Anju to kindergarten. Not the local one – the young-mother mafia had threatened to boycott them if they admitted you – so we had to take you to another neighbourhood. You were bawling. Maybe because of the fever, maybe because there was no Anju. I'd been working all night so I washed down some pills with vodka and left you to it. Next thing I knew you were rattling my door – you were walking by this time, of course. My migraine wouldn't let me sleep. I lost it. I screamed at you to go away. So of course you bawled some more. I screamed. Then silence. Then I heard you say the word. You must have got it from kindergarten.

'Daddy.'

Something broke in me.

Quite calmly, I decided to throw you over the balcony.

New ink, new pen. Pretty dramatic point for my pen to die. So. Quite calmly. *I decided to throw you over the balcony.* Those eight words explain our lives since. I'm not saying they justify what I did, not at all. I don't mean I wanted to throw you over the balcony. I mean I was going to. Really. It is so hard to write this.

This is what happened. I flung open my bedroom door – it opened outwards – and slid you clean across the polished wooden landing, over the lip of the stairs and out of sight. I froze, but I couldn't have stopped your fall, not even if I was superhuman. You didn't cry as you fell. I heard you. Imagine a sack of books falling downstairs. You sounded like that. I waited for you to start screaming, and waited, and waited. Suddenly time moved three times as fast, to catch up with itself. You were lying at the bottom, with blood squirting out of your ear. I can still see you. (I still do, every time I go down any stairs anywhere.) I was hysterical. The ambulance people had to shout at me to stop me jabbering. Then, when I put down the phone, guess what I saw? You were sitting up, licking the blood on your fingers.

The ambulanceman said that children go limp sometimes, like rag dolls. That saved you from major damage. The doctor said you were a lucky boy, but he meant I was a lucky woman. The vodka on my breath pretty much shot down my story about you climbing over the stair guard. Actually, we were all of us lucky. I know I was going to kill you, and could have spent the rest of my life in prison. I can't believe I'm finally writing this. Three days later I paid the nanny a month's money and told her I was taking you to see your grandmother. I was mentally unfit to raise you and Anju. The rest, you know.

I'm not writing this for your sympathy or forgiveness. This story is beyond all that. But the memories even now keep me awake, and showing you them is the only way I know to ease them. I want to get well. I mean—

—you can tell from the creases, can't you, I just scrunched this up and threw it at the bin. I didn't even bother aiming. And guess what? It fell straight in, didn't even touch the sides. Who knows? Maybe this is one of those times when superstition pays. I'll go and slip this under Dr Suzuki's door, before I change my mind again. If you want to call me, phone the number on the letterhead. Up to you. I wish—

Fujifilm is pushing four o'clock. What is the proper way to react to the news that your mother wanted to kill you? After three years of non-communication. I'm used to my mother being out there, somewhere; but not too near. Things are painless that way. If I move anything, I'm afraid it will all start all over again. The only plan I can think of is Do Nothing. If this is a cop-out then, okay, a rubber-stamped 'Cop-Out' is my official response. It is my father's 'nowhere' that I can't handle, not my mother's 'somewhere'. I know what I mean even if I can't put it into words. Cockroach is still struggling. I want to see it. I crawl over to the fridge – so humid tonight. The motel starts vibrating as I pick it up. Cockroach panics. A part of me wants to free it, a part of me wishes it instant death. I force myself to peer in. Bicycling feelers and furious wings! So revolting I drop the motel – it lands on its roof. Now Cockroach is dying upside down, poor shiny bastard, but I don't want to touch the motel. I look for something to flip it over. I fish in the bin – gingerly, in case Brother of Cockroach is in there – and find the squashed box Cat's biscuits came in. On Thursday, after I read the letter, I put it down and did nothing for I don't know how long. I'm about to re-read it when Cat appears. She jumps on my lap and shows me her shoulder. Clotted blood and soft skin shows where a gobbet of fur has been gouged off. 'You've been fighting?' I forget about the letter for a moment. I don't know anything about first aid, especially cat first aid, but I think I should disinfect the wound. Of course, I don't have anything as practical as antiseptic fluid, so I go downstairs and ask Buntarō.

Buntarō pauses the video at the moment the *Titanic* up-ends and people fall down the mile-long deck. He takes a cigarette from his box of Caster and lights it without offering me one. 'Don't tell me. Upon receiving another letter from his mysterious lawyer lady, telling our hero it was all over, he becomes so depressed that he decides to disembowel himself, but all he has is a pair of nail scissors, so—'

'I have a wounded cat on my hands.'

Buntarō clouds over. 'A what, lad?'

'A wounded cat.'

'You're keeping pets in my apartment?'

'No. It just wanders in when it's hungry.'

'Or when it wants medical attention?'

'It's just a scratch. I want to dab some disinfectant on it.'

'Eiji Miyake, animal doctor.'

'Please, Buntarō.'

He grumbles and sifts under the till for a while. He pulls out a dusty red box, causing a landslide of junk around his feet, and hands it to me. 'It better not be bleeding on my tatami.'

'You tight-arsed, whinging parasite, you've fleeced every outgoing tenant for replacement tatami, but you haven't actually replaced it since 1969, have you?' is not how I respond to my landlord and job benefactor. Instead I just shake my head meekly. 'She isn't bleeding now. She just has this sort of gammy place that needs seeing to.'

'What's this cat look like? My wife might know the owner.'

'Black, white paws and tail, and a tartan collar with a silver bell.'

'No owner, no name?'

I shake my head. 'Thanks for this.' I tap the box and begin my getaway.

'Don't get too attached,' Buntarō calls up the stairs after me. 'Remember the "Thou shalt not have pets except cactuses" clause in your contract.'

I turn around and peer down at him. 'What contract?'

Buntarō grins sort of nastily and taps his forehead.

I seal up my capsule and attend to Cat. The witch-hazel must sting her – it always stung me and Anju when Wheatie doused our cuts with it – but Cat doesn't even flinch. 'Girls shouldn't get into fights,' I tell her. I chuck the cotton wool away and return the first-aid box to Buntarō. Cat makes herself comfortable in my yukata. Weird. Cat trusts me to look after her, me of all people.

A head appears on the claims counter. Its owner is a spindly girl of maybe eleven, in a Mickey and Donald jogging suit with red ribbons in her hair. Her eyes are enormous. 'Good afternoon,' she says. 'I followed the signs. Is this the lost property office?'

'Yes,' I answer. 'Have you lost anything?'

'Mummy,' she says. 'She forever wanders off without my permission.'

I tut. 'I can relate to that.' What do I do? Suga skipped the 'lost child' chapter, and now he is collecting the trolley from Ueno annexe. Mrs Sasaki is on her lunch-hour. Somewhere a mummy is running around in hysterics, imagining train wheels and organ-harvesting child kidnappers. I flap. 'Why don't you sit on the counter,' I tell the girl. She clambers up. Right. What do I do? 'Aren't you going to ask me my name?' asks the girl.

'Of course I am. What's your name?'

'Yuki Chiyo. Aren't you going to call Mummy on the big speaker?'

'Of course I am.'

I go into the side office. Mrs Sasaki mentioned the PA system on my first day, but Suga never showed me how to use it. Turn this key, flick this switch. I hope. A green light flashes under 'Speak'. I clear my throat and lean into the microphone. The sound of me clearing my throat fills Ueno. When Yuki Chiyo hears her name she hugs herself.

I'm broiling with embarrassment. Yuki Chiyo studies me.

'So, Yuki. How old are you?'

'Ten. But Mummy tells me not to speak to strangers.'

'You already spoke to me.'

'Only because I needed you to call Mummy.'

'You ungrateful tadpole.'

I hear Aoyama marching this way before I see him. His shoes, his keys. 'You! Miyake!'

Obviously I am in deep shit. 'Good afternoon—'

'Do *not* "Good afternoon" me! Since when have you had the authority to make a general override announcement?'

My throat is dry. 'I didn't realize that—'

'Suppose a train were hurtling into Ueno with a snapped brake cable!' His eyes froth. 'Suppose I were making an evacuation announcement!' Veins bulge. 'Suppose we receive a bomb warning!' Is he going to fire me? 'And you, *you*, blanket out my warning with a request for a lost girl's mother to proceed to the lost property office on the second floor!' He pauses to restock air. 'You, *you*, pollute the order with your teenage chaos!'

'Tra-la-la!' A leopardskinned woman pads up to the counter.

'Mummy!' Yuki Chiyo waves.

'Dearest, you know it upsets Mummy when you go off like this! Have you been making trouble for this handsome young stripling?' She nudges Aoyama aside and deposits her designer bags on the counter. A perky vixen smile. 'I am so frightfully sorry, young man. What can I say? Yuki plays this little game whenever we go shopping, don't you, dearest? My husband says it's just a stage she's going through. Do I have to sign anywhere?'

'No, madam.'

Aoyama smoulders.

'Let me give you a little something for your trouble.'

'Really, madam, no need.'

'You are a darling.' She turns to Aoyama. 'Jolly good! A porter!'

I kill my snicker a fraction too late. Aoyama radiates nuclear fury. 'No, madam, I am the assistant station-master.'

'Oh. Well, you look like a porter in that get-up. Come on, Yuki.'

Yuki turns to me as her mother leads her away. 'Sorry I got you bollocked.'

Aoyama is too furious to bollock me further. 'You, Miyake, *you*, I am *not* going to forget this! I am going to file a report about this *outrage* to the disciplinary committee this very afternoon!' Off he storms. I wonder if I still have a job. Suga steps out from the back office. 'Quite a talent you have there for annoying people, Miyake.'

'You were there all along?'

'You seemed in control of the situation.'

I want to kill Suga so I say nothing.

I am on the ferry! So many times Anju and I have watched it; now I am actually on it! The deck slopes side to side, and the wind is strong enough to lean back into. Yakushima, the enormous country I live in, is slowly but surely growing smaller. Mr Ikeda is scanning the shoreline with his army binoculars. Seabirds follow the boat, just hanging there. The second-graders are arguing about what will happen when the ferry sinks and we have to fight for the lifeboats. Others are watching the TV, or being chucked out of places you're not allowed. One kid is vomming in the toilets. The engine booms. I smell engine fumes. I watch the hull slice through the spray-chopped waves. If I hadn't already decided on being a soccer star I would become a sailor. I look for the shrine of the thunder god, but it is already hidden in the morning haze. I wish Anju were here. I wonder what she'll do today. I try to remember the last day we weren't together. I go back as far as I can, but no such day ever was. Yakushima is now the size of a barn. I watch new islands rise ahead and fall behind. I can fit Yakushima inside the 'O' of my thumb and first finger. A tooth is wobbling loose. Mr Ikeda is on the deck too. 'Sakurajima,' he shouts at me above the wind and the engine, pointing ahead. I watch the volcano grow and take up a third of the sky. The torn crater belches graceful solid clouds of smoke over another third. 'You can taste the ash,' shouts Mr Ikeda, 'on your tongue! And over there, that's Kagoshima!' Already? The voyage is supposed to take three hours. I consult my Zax Omega watch and find that nearly three hours have passed. Here comes Kagoshima. Huge! You could fit the whole of Anbō, our village, between two jetties in the harbour. Enormous buildings, vast cranes, huge freighters marked with place names I mostly haven't heard of. I guess when I was here last my memory was switched off. Or maybe it was night? This is the where the world starts. Wait until I tell Anju. She'll be amazed. Amazed.

According to Fujifilm, four o'clock slipped by fifteen minutes ago. The best I can hope for now is a couple of hours of sleep, so I can be dead at work instead of buried. Yesterday was the last day of Suga, so I'll be on my own all afternoon. I can still see the body falling. Cockroach is quiet. Has he escaped? Is he plotting revenge? Is he asleep, dreaming of nubile cockroach thighs and stewing garbage? They say that for every single cockroach you see, there are ninety relatives out of sight. Under the floor, in cavities, behind cupboards. Under futons. 'Poor Mum,' she is hoping I'll think. 'Okay, she dumped us at our uncle's when we were three, but let bygones be bygones. I'll phone her this very morning.' No *way*! Forget it! I imagine I can hear Tokyo stir. My neck itches. I scratch. My back itches. I scratch. My crotch itches. I scratch. Once Tokyo itself wakes, all hope of sleep is doomed. The fan stirs the heat. How dare she write me a letter like that. I was tired when I went to bed. What happened?

'My final Friday,' says Suga. 'Deep joy. Tomorrow, freedom. Imho, you should go back to college, Miyake. It beats earning a living for a living.' I am not really listening – this is the morning after I discover that when I was three years old my mother decided to throw me off a ninth-floor balcony – but when he says that word again I give in. 'Why do you keep using that word?'

Suga acts puzzled. 'What word?'

'"Imho".'

'Oh, sorry,' Suga says, not sounding at all sorry, 'I forgot.'

'Forgot what?'

'Most of my friends are e-friends. Other hackers. We use our own language, right. "Imho" stands for the English "in my humble opinion". Like, "*I* think that . . ." Cool word, or what?'

The telephone rings. Suga looks – I answer.

'Pleased with ourselves, Miyake?' A voice I know, simmering with malice.

'Mr Aoyama?'

'You work for them, don't you?'

'For Ueno station, you mean, sir?'

'Drop the act! I mean what I mean! I know you work for the consultants!'

'Which consultants, sir?'

'I told you to drop it! I see right through you! You were in my office to snoop. To filch. To assess. I know your little game. Then there was your provocation the day before yesterday. That was to get me out of my office, while my files were copied. It all adds up now. Oh yes. Deny it! I dare you to deny it!'

'I swear, Mr Aoyama, there has been some mistake here . . .'

'A mistake?' Aoyama shouts. 'How right you are! The biggest mistake of your treacherous life! I have served Ueno since before you were born! I have friends at the transport ministry! I went to an influential university!' I can't believe his voice can get any louder, but it does. 'If your masters believe *I* can be "restructured" to an end-of-the-line deep freeze in Akita with two platforms and a company dormitory made of paper, they are greviously mistaken! My lackey years are long behind me!' He breaks, pants, and launches his final assault. 'Ueno has standards! Ueno has systems! Your scumbag parasite know-nothing poking masters want war, I will give them war and you, you, *you*, will get blasted by crossfire!'

He hangs up.

Suga looks at me. 'What was that about?'

Why me? Why is it always me? 'I have no idea.'

'How can I say this tactfully?' Mr Ikeda paces to and fro during our half-time peptalk. 'Boys. You are utterly, utterly crap. Shambolic. Subhuman. In fact, submammalian. A disgrace. A sickening waste of shipping fuel. A non-team of myopic crippled sloths. We have a *miracle* to thank that the enemy are not nine goals up, and the name of this miracle is Mitsui.' Mitsui chews gum, enjoying the taste of despotic favour. He is a gifted and aggressive goalkeeper – it is lucky he lacks the imagination to expand into playground bullying. Mitsui's father is Yakushima's most notorious alcoholic, so our goalkeeper has been calculating the flight paths of projectiles from an early age. Ikeda goes on. 'In a more civillized century, I could have insisted that the rest of you commit seppuku. You will, however, shave your heads in shame if we lose. Defenders. Despite Mr Mitsui's valiant work, how many times have the enemy hit the crossbar? Nakamori?'

'Three times, sir.'

'And the post?'

I suck my warm orange, readjust my shin pads, watch the enemy team having their pep talk – their coach is laughing. The stale smell of boys and soccer kits. The afternoon has clouded over. The volcano puffs. 'Miyake? The post?'

'Uh, twice, sir,' I guess.

'Uh, twice, sir. Uh, yes. Uh, Nakayama, midfield means "middle of the pitch", not "middle of the penalty area". Attack means we attack the enemy goal. How many times has their goalkeeper had to touch the ball? Nakamura?'

'Not very often, sir.'

Ikeda massages his temples. 'Not once, *actually*, sir! Not once! He has made three – separate – dates with three – separate – cheerleaders! Listen to me! I am videoing the match! Boys. It is my birthday tomorrow. If you do not give me a goalless draw you will remember my displeasure until your deaths. In the second half the wind is on our side. Your orders are to dig in and hold out. One more thing. Do not give away a penalty. I got the enemy coach drunk last night, and he boasted that their penalty-taker has never missed. Ever. And remember, if you feel your poor little limbs flagging, my videocam is watching and will extract retribution on a man-by-man basis.'

*

The referee blows his whistle for the second half. We lose possession of the ball three seconds later. Briefly I remember my deal with the god. Fat lot of use he turned out to be. I do my best to look good for Ikeda's videocam – running around, shouting 'Pass', groaning, and generally avoiding the ball as cleverly as I can. 'Possess and push!' screams Ikeda. Our 4-3-3 formation buckles into 10-0-0, and our penalty area becomes a pinball zone of kicks, screams and curses. I fake a spectacular injury but nobody is watching. Time after time Mitsui pulls off a brilliant save, a daring pounce, a midair punch. 'Positions!' screams Ikeda. If only I could be as good as Mitsui. I would make the national sports papers tomorrow. Time after time the enemy launches an attack, but the mass of defenders reinforces our luck. The breeze rises to a wind. I make a daring aerial challenge – and win – but the ball hits the top of my head – squashing it – and carries on deeper into our half. I have to do a throw-in at one point, but the referee blows his whistle for a foul throw – I don't know why, but Ikeda will make me pay anyway. Nakatani and Nakamura, our star strikers, are both given a yellow card for punching each other. I turn around and the ball bounces off my face. A corner. 'Cretins!' screams Ikeda. Elbow fights with a mutant boy twice my height with a killer's eyes. A tooth that is coming loose suddenly becomes very loose. Mitsui pulls off a diving save. An enemy supporter throws a rice-ball at Nakata, our winger, who drop-kicks the offender. Nakayama takes a flying kick, boots the ball up the field – the wind picks it up – and we all banzai-charge after it. 'Positions!' screams Ikeda. My tooth is hanging on by a strand of gum. The enemy appears to be falling back. We surge. I hear military bands. A wall of enemy strikers is surging this way – they have the ball – a trap? A trap! 'Sphincters!' screams Ikeda. I have no breath left but I run back, hoping to salvage an iota of mercy from the post-goal trial. Mitsui is sprinting out to narrow the angle, roaring like a Zero bomber. The enemy striker toe-pokes the ball under his nemesis a moment before impact – I hear the bones crunch – unable to brake in time I springboard over the bodies – my boot clips a scalp – momentum rockets me forward, and without thinking I dive, skimming over the empty goalmouth of grit, and hand-grapple the ball to a halt just this side of the goal line.

Rushing silence.

The referee's whistle drills through my head. Red card for Mitsui, yellow one for me, a stretcher and a drive to hospital for the striker, a verbal sewer from Ikeda, a penalty to the enemy, and yet another problem for our team. We have no goalkeeper. Ikeda arrives in a whirlwind of abuse and snarls down from his chariot of ire. 'You looked pretty useful with your hands just then, Miyake. *You* go in goal.' My team-mates adopt the proposal at bushfire speed. Sacrificial lambs cannot answer back. I traipse to the goalmouth. The skin is sandpapered off my knees and thighs. The enemy wall in the penalty area. Fathoms yawn either side of me. The enemy kicker gloats, curling his rat's-tail lock of hair around his little finger. Moments drum. The drumming slows. The whistle blows. The world sets. Here he comes. God of Thunder. Remember me? We had a deal.

Suga empties the contents of his locker into his shoulder bag. I hear police sirens. This is when? Only yesterday. The long corridor that passes the lost property office links two sides of Ueno, so it is always quite busy – but we hear a special commotion approach and lean out over the counter to see. A TV crew stream past – a presenter, an NHK cameraman bristling with lenses, a sound-pole carrier and a young man heaving a trolley thing. They are not the usual local station film-the-fuzzy-duck crew. Their sense of mission clears a way through the oncoming commuters. 'Looks worthy of further investigation,' says Suga. 'Hold the fort, Miyake. I can sniff scandal.' He bolts off and the telephone rings – 'Lost property? I'm calling about a friend's wig.' I groan. We have hundreds of wigs.

Luckily it is a glam-rock wig with sequinned spangles, so I can identify it in the five minutes it takes Suga to return. 'Aoyama's flipped!' Suga is feverish with gossip. 'Deep-fried his circuitry! On my last day, too!'

'Aoyama?' I remember the telephone call.

'A report was published today. The top Tokyo JR people decided to kick him sideways. All the big Tokyo stations are being shaken up by the new governor, and Aoyama is a symbol of the old school of untouchables. The consultant – this guy who spent ten years teaching at Harvard Business School – gave him the news in front of a gang of junior managers. It was like a 'how to demote somebody' seminar.'

'Grim.'

'Not as grim as what happens next. Aoyama gets out a crossbow, right—'

'A crossbow?'

'A crossbow, and aims it at the consultant's chest, right. He must have seen the news coming. He tells all but one of the juniors to leave if they don't want to witness a bolt puncturing a human heart. Deep madness. Aoyama then throws a reel of mountaineering rope to the remaining junior, and orders him to tie the consultant to the chair. Then he tells the junior to leave. Before Security can get there, Aoyama locks the door from the inside.'

'What does he want?'

'Nobody knows yet. The police were called, so the TV people came too. The director was up there, trying to fight the journos away, but we're going to be on the evening news whatever happens! Deep thrill. I guess the SWAT teams will be here soon, and negotiators in bulletproof jackets. Nothing this exciting ever happens in Ueno. National news!'

I dive left and I know the ball is veering right. The ground whacks the breath from my body, my skeleton crunches, and the enemy roars. I spit out my tooth. It lies there, no longer a part of me. White, a speck of blood. Why bother getting up? Ever. I have lost the match, my friends, my soccer, my fame, my hopes of meeting my father – everything except Anju. I should never have left Yakushima. The islanders will remember my shame for all time. How can I go back now? I lie in the goalmouth dirt – if I begin to sob here, how can I—

'Get up, Miyake!' Nakamori, the team captain.

I look up. The rat's-tail kid is holding his head in his hands. The enemy are stalking away. The referee is pointing to the twelve-yard box. I look in our goal. Empty. Where is the ball? I realize what has happened. *The ball went wide*. The thunder god musses my hair. Thank you. Oh, thank you. I place the ball for the goal kick. Can my supernatural protector save my luck for another twenty-five minutes? Please. 'Nice save,' sneers an enemy supporter. 'Positions!' screams Ikeda. 'Go, go, go!' I look for a friendly face on our team, but nobody will make eye contact in case I kick the ball to them. What do I do? The wind increases. 'Look,' I vow to the thunder god, 'let me be as great a goalkeeper as Matsui, just for this game, and my future is yours. I know you saved me just now. Don't turn your back on me now. Please. Please.' I run back a few paces, turn, take three deep breaths, sprint at the ball and . . . it is a perfect, clean, powerful, rocket-fuelled, divine kick. The thunder god intercepts the ball at house height and volleys it over the pitch. The ball soars over the enemy strikers. Their defenders are still jogging back into their half, unaware that the goal kick has been taken. Some spectators gawp. Some players look around, wondering where the ball has gone. The enemy goalkeeper is having his photo taken with a girl, and the ball falls to earth before he realizes his services are needed. He dashes out in panic. The ball bounces over the goalkeeper, and the south wind nods it back down into the net.

The walk back from Kita Senju station to Shooting Star usually clears my head, but it is impossible not to think of Aoyama holed up in his office with a crossbow bolt aimed at the head of an executive with red braces and pin-stripes. Suga stayed around after work, but I wanted to get away. I didn't even say goodbye to Suga. At Shooting Star, Buntarō is glued to the TV, spooning macadamia ice cream. 'My, my, Miyake. You are a harbinger of doom.' 'What do you mean?' 'Look at the TV! Nothing like this happened at Ueno until you started working there.' I fan myself with my baseball cap and watch the screen. The camera shows an outside zoomed-in view of Aoyama's office, taken, I guess, from Terminus Hotel. The blinds are drawn. *Ueno Station Under Siege*. 'There is absolutely no question,' a policeman assures a cluster of interviewers, 'of a forced entry operation at this present moment in time.' 'Lull him into a false sense of security,' says Buntarō. 'What do you make of this Aoyama character? Does he seem like a man on the edge of grand lunacy? Or does he seem like a publicity stunter?'

'Dunno . . . just unhappy.' And I spat into his teapot. I traipse upstairs.

'Aren't you going to watch?'

'No.'

'Oh, by the way. About your cat. The cat.'

I peer down. 'You found her owner?'

Buntarō keeps one eye on the TV. 'No, lad, but she found her maker. Unless she has a secret twin she never told you about. Real coincidence. I was cycling here this morning and what did I see by the drainage channel down the side of Lawson's? One dead cat, flies buzzing. Black, white paws and tail, a tartan collar with a silver bell, just like you described. I did my civic bit and rang the council when I got here, but someone had already reported it. They can't let things like that lie around in this heat.'

This is the worst day on record.

'Sorry to be the bearer of ill tidings and all.'

The second worst, I mean.

'Only a cat,' I mumble. I enter my capsule, sit down, and appear to lack the will to do anything except smoke the rest of my Dunhills. I don't want to watch TV. I bought a cup noodle and a punnet of mushy strawberries walking back from Kita Senju, but my appetite has vanished. I listen to the street fill up with evening.

❖

Yakushima never returns to its full size when the ferry takes us back the following morning. The day is glossy with sunshine, but heightens the illusion that this boundless island is a scale model. I look out for Anju on the sea wall – and when I can't find her I have to admit that my elation is dented. Anju is a gifted sulker, but a thirty-six-hour sulk is a long haul, even for my sister. I zip open my sports bag – the man of the match trophy glints back. I look for the thunder god's shrine on its cliff – and this time I find it. The passengers pour down the gangplank, my team-mates disappearing into waiting cars. I wave goodbye. Mr Ikeda claps me on the shoulder and actually smiles. 'Want a lift?'

'No, thanks, sir, my sister'll be walking down to meet me.'

'Okay. Training first thing tomorrow. And well done again, Miyake. You turned the game around. Three–nil! Three–nil!' Ikeda is still glowing with revenge. 'That wiped the snotty, shitty sneer off the fat face of their cretin coach! I caught his despair on camera!'

I kick the same stone from the harbour up the main street, over the old bridge, and all the way up to the valley neck. The stone obeys my every wish. Sun mirrors off the rice-fields. I see the first dragonflies. This is the beginning of a long road. At the end is the World Cup. The abandoned house stares with empty sockets. I pass the torī gate, and think about running up to thank the thunder god right now – but I want to see Anju first. The hanging bridge trembles under my footsteps. Tiny fish cloud the leeward sides. Anju will be at home, helping our grandmother make lunch. Nothing to worry about. I slide open the front door – 'I'm back!'

Anju's foot-thump—

No, it was only the old house. I can tell from the shoes that my grandmother is out too. They must have gone to see Uncle Tarmac, but somehow missed me around the new harbour building while Mr Ikeda was talking to me. I pour myself a glass of milk, and dive on to the sofa. On the insides of my eyelids I watch the exact parabola of the soccer ball curving over a volcano and under a distant crossbar.

'Miyake!' Buntarō, of course. I lift my head too quickly and yank my neck cords. A hammering on my capsule door. 'Come quick! Quick! Now!' I clatter downstairs where customers cluster around Buntarō's TV. The outside of Aoyama's office, high above the tracks. *Live from Ueno Station Hostage Crisis Centre*. The picture is being taken with a night camera – light is orange and dark is brown. I don't need to ask what is happening because the commentator is telling us. 'The blind is up! The window is being opened and . . . a figure, Mr Aoyama has . . . yes, that is him, I can confirm that, the figure climbing out of the window is Mr Aoyama . . . he is on the ledge . . . the light is going on behind . . . please wait while . . . I'm receiving . . .' Background radio scratchings. The consultant . . . is unharmed! The police have taken the office! Whether they broke down the door or . . . now, Aoyama appears to have honoured his promise not to . . . but the question now is . . . Oh, oh, he surely isn't thinking of jumping . . . The face at the window, I can confirm that is a police officer, attempting to talk Aoyama out . . . he is dealing with a very disturbed man at this moment in time . . . he will be saying that . . .'

Aoyama jumps from the ledge.

Aoyama is no longer alive but not yet dead.

His body cartwheels, and falls for a long, long time.

Footsteps in the hallway wake me up. I open my eyes – my trophy shines on the table, proof that I didn't dream the whole glorious afternoon. Evening lights the worn wooden room where my uncles and mother spent their childhoods. And here are my grandmother and Mr Kirin, one of Yakushima's four police officers. 'I'm back,' I say, worried. 'We won.'

My grandmother doesn't care. 'Did Anju say she was going anywhere?'

'No. Where is she?'

'If you're lying I'll, I'll, I'll—'

Mr Kirin gently sits my grandmother down and turns to me. 'Eiji—'

I want to be sick. 'What happened to Anju?'

'Anju seems to have run away—'

He knows more.

'She wouldn't, not without telling me. Never.'

My grandmother's voice is broken. 'So what did she tell you? She told me she was going to Uncle Tarmac's yesterday evening. He called me this lunch-time to find out why she had changed her mind. If this is a game you two cooked up, you are in a sackload of trouble!' Mr Kirin sits down on the other end of the sofa. 'I want you to think, Eiji. Is there a secret place where she might have gone?'

First I think of trees. Then, with sickening certainty, I think of the whalestone. To get even with me. Her swimming costume . . . I run upstairs. I open our drawer. I was right – it's gone. I remember my promise with the thunder god. *Anything that I can give you, you can have. Take it.* Mr Kirin fills the bedroom doorframe. 'What is it, Eiji-kun?' I get the words out before everything crashes down. 'Look in the sea.'

Nearly five o'clock, says Fujifilm. I get up and piss. In my toilet cube mirror a drone looks back at me in mild surprise. I need a cigarette. The packet of Dunhills is empty, but I find one rolled under the ironing board. I light it on the gas stove, and go on to the balcony to smoke it. Dawn sketches outlines and colours them in. Tokyo roars, far off and near. So, that is the end of Mr Aoyama. He ran out of minutes, so he jumped. I sloosh the fungus out of a mug and make myself a cup of instant coffee. I take Anju's photograph out to the balcony, and drink my coffee in her company. I think about the letter from my mother, and a deal presents itself. Should I? I must do my washing up today. I look in the cockroach motel – I look again. Cockroach escaped. A leg and a smear of cockroach shit remain. I take in my washing and fold it into a neat pile. I tune my guitar and run through some bossa nova chords, but all those sunlit breezes are not how I feel. Very well, Mother. You are my Plan B. I'll give you what you want, if you tell me how to find our father. Nearly six o'clock. Early, but people at clinics get up early. That's the point. Before I change my mind I dial.

'Good morning. Miyazaki Mountain Clinic.'

'Morning. Could you put me through to Mariko Miyake's room, please.'

'Not possible, I'm afraid.'

'Is it too early?'

'Too late. Mrs Miyake checked herself out yesterday evening.'

Oh, no. 'Are you sure?'

'Quite sure. She even took our towels as a souvenir.'

'Look, this is her son. I need to contact her. It's urgent.'

'I'm sure it is, but once our guests decide to leave us they never hang around.'

'Did she leave a forwarding address?'

She doesn't bother to pretend to check. 'No.'

'How was she?'

'You'd need to talk to her counsellor—'

'What time does he start work?'

'She. But Dr Suzuki would never discuss a patient with anyone. Even her son.'

If only I had called yesterday, if only, if only. 'Did you meet her?'

'Mrs Miyake? Of course. I'm a staff nurse.'

'Can you tell me if she was . . . okay?'

'It depends what you mean by okay.'

'Well, you've been really helpful. Thanks so much.'

She uppercuts my irony. 'It was my pleasure, sir.'

Click, buzz, click, purrrrrrrr.........

*

Plan B down the pan. The submarines are running, and I feel wide awake, but it is still too early to leave for work. What a night. It mauled me, not refreshed me. Buntarō called me down for a smoke later, in the quiet hour between eleven and midnight. We talked for a little while. I nearly forgot he is my bloodsucking landlord. I put *Plastic Ono Band* into my Discman and lie down on my futon, just for a moment. Deep bells and beat boxes.

Plastic Ono Band is long over when a pattering sound pads into my dreams. At first I think it is a pipe dripping splashes, but then I feel her settling inside the curl of my body. I open my eyes. 'Hey.' My voice is a croak. 'I thought you were supposed to be dead.' She yawns, indifferent to what I think or thought. She regards me with her bronze-spark Cleopatra eyes.

The fibres in the neck of the thunder god tear, snap and scream. I am still gripping it – I never expected it to come loose so soon. It comes away, the saw goes clattering down, I reshift my weight too far, lose my balance and slide down between his back and the shrine wall. I seem to be falling for the longest time. The floor of the shrine whacks the breath out of my body. I don't break my back, but within an hour I will have turned into the incredible walking bruise. My enemy's head rolls away, wood on wood, and comes to a rest on its side, looking right this way. Hatred, revenge, jealousy, rage – all twisted into the same contortions, and pulled tight. A smear of my blood over one nostril. The woods are too quiet. No adult, no police car, no grandmother. The blackbird has gone. Only the cannon boom of the ocean against the rocks a long way down. The gods are all related, and from this day on they are going to be in conspiracy against me. I will live a life without luck. So be it. I get to my feet. I pick up the head, cradling it like an infant, and take it outside to the edge of the rock face. The sea breaks over the whalestone's humpback, and the spray flies. One, two, three – I watch the severed head of the thunder god, all the way down. It vanishes in a white crown. Now I must vanish too.

Three

♋

Video Games

I catch a glimpse of my father being bundled into an unmarked van parked across the baseball field. I would recognize him anywhere. He hammers on the back window, but the van is already through the gates and disappearing into the smoking rubble of Tokyo. I leap onto our patrol stratobike, take off my baseball cap and rest it on the console. Zizzi flashes me a peppermint smile and off we zoom. Lavender clouds slide by. I train my gun on a chillipepper schoolboy, but for once things are exactly as they appear. The sunroof of a midnight Cadillac flips open, and out pops a lobster-mobster*Bang*! Shell and claws everywhere. I drill the rear window and the vehicle explodes in paintbox flames. The van swerves down the road to the airport. In the underpass an ambulance cuts us up – a scalpel-slashing medic leaps on to our bonnet, eyeballs afroth with plague*Bang*! In the nuts! *Bang*! Vomit on the bonnet*Bang*! The mutant staggers, but refuses to die*Bang*! Blasted through a billboard. *Reload*. 'You're my top gun,' croons Zizzi. We get to the airport just in time to see my father dragged into a vanilla Cessna aircraft. I daren't shoot his kidnappers at this range in case I miss. A mighty chokmakopter eclipses the sun, and zombie spawn abseil to earth. I pulp dozens in midair, but the semolina army of death sludges up too quickly. 'Zax, honey!' says Zizzi. 'Megaweapon in McDonald's!' I fire the golden arches and collect the twenty-third-century rapid-fire bazooka. It purrs as I scythe – soon the runway is a spill of twitching limbs. I pepper the chokmakopter until it nosedives into the fuel trucks. Octane fuchsia explosions light the world. 'Way to go, Zax! Now to follow your father's abductors to their laboratory!' We soar in pursuit of the Cessna – I click my trigger to skip the preamble. We enter the underworld. The sewers are quiet. Too quiet. A gigahydra erupts, nine heads dripping lime slime from nine lassooing necks*Bang*! Cleft like a cabbage. *Reload*. But from the stump two new heads are born. 'Deep-fry the freak!' screams Zizzi, so I aim at the beast's trunk and activate my flamethrower. *Whoooooorrrsh*! It shrivels away in my swathe of unlooping strawberry fire. A lily-white Lilith one*Bang*! and she's history. A swarm of cyberwasps – *bangabangabanga* – *reload*. My hand is killing me. The tunnel narrows to a dead end. An unseen iron door creaks open – a scientist in silhouette. 'My son! You found me! At long last!' I relax and flex my gun hand. 'You are in time' – he rips off his false beard, his briefcase morphs into a grenade launcher – 'to die!' The gritty gloom swarms with intelligent missiles, homing in on my body heat. *Bangabangabanga*! I miss most of them, and can't even take aim at the impostor. Scarlet pixels of life-blood splatter the screen. 'Zax,' begs my sister, 'don't leave me here – insert a coin to continue. Honey, don't quit now.'

'Honey,' mimics a voice over my shoulder, 'don't quit now!' I replace my gun and turn around to face my spectator and his slow applause. My first thought is that he is way too cool to be hanging out in games centres. Older than me, a sleek ponytail, an earring. Pop star good looks. 'First time in the underworld, right?' His real voice is tailored Tokyoite.

I nod. The real world fades in.

'It was the same for me, my first time in the underworld.'

Laser zaps, vampire howls, coin rattles, cyclical video game music. 'Oh.'

You see your father, so you let your guard down. A dirty trick! Next time, shoot the egghead on sight. It takes about nine shots to kill him.'

'Well. Sorry I died and spoilt your fun.'

The most casual of shrugs. 'You're doomed from the first coin. You pay to postpone the ending, but the video game will always win in the long run.'

My last half-Marlboro died in the ashtray. 'Very deep.'

'Actually, I was waiting for my date in the pool hall upstairs. Looks like she's playing the be-late-keep-him-on-tenterhooks game. So I came down to make sure she hadn't fucked up and was waiting outside. I saw you, wrapped up in *Zax Omega and Red Plague Moon*, and had to stay to watch. Did you know your tongue pokes out when you concentrate?'

'No.'

'It's a two-player game, really. It even took me a fortnight to polish it off.'

'That must have cost you a fortune.'

'No. My father owns a man who owns a distributor.'

No reply presents itself. 'Well, hope your date shows up soon.'

'The bitch had better. Or I'll flay her alive.'

Saturday night in Shibuya bubbles and sweats. One week since my sleepless night, I decided to come exploring. The pleasure quarter is so hot, one more struck match could ignite the place. Uncle Bank took me out last year to his bar in Kagoshima, but that is nothing compared to this. Neither are the prices. Drones drink in squadrons, ties loose, collars undone. She-drones, office uniforms stuffed into shoulder bags. I damn drones too much, considering I am one now. But I only pretend to be one. Maybe we all start out that way. Same as Mr Aoyama. Couples on dates. Americans and beautiful women in moonglasses. I bet the waitress with the perfect neck has a whole phone book of boyfriends like my spectator in the games centre. A giant DRINK COCA-COLA cascade, magma maroons and holy whites. I suck a champagne bomb and walk on. Hostesses wave geriatric company presidents into taxis. In an amber-lit restaurant everyone knows one another. A giant Mongol warrior scooters past, flanked by bunny girls handing out leaflets advertising a new shopping complex somewhere. Girls in cellophane waistcoats, panties and tights sit in glass booths outside clubs, offering chit-chat and ten-per-cent-off coupons. I imagine scything through the crowds with the twenty-third-century megaweapon. The clouds are candy-coloured from the lights and lasers. Outside Aphrodite's Soapworld, a bouncer runs through the girls pinned up on the board. 'Number one is Russian – classy, accommodating. Two, Filipina – attentive, well trained. The French girl – well, need I say more. The Brazilian, dark chocolate, plenty of bite. Number five, English, white chocolate. Six is German, home of the wiener. Not an ounce of flab on the Koreans. Number eight are our exotic black twins, and number nine – ah, number nine is beyond the grasp of ordinary mortals—' He catches me gawping and cackles. 'Come back in a decade or so, sonny, with your summer bonus.' I wander past an electronics shop, and on TV see someone familiar walking past an electronics shop. He stops, examines the TV, amazed and semi-appalled at how he must appear to other people. I buy a new pack of Marlboro. As I pass by the red lanterns of a noodle shop and smell the kitchen vapours pumped out, I suddenly remember how hungry I am. I peer through the window – it looks greasy enough to be affordable, even for me. I slide open the door and enter through the strings of beads. A steamy hole with a roaring kitchen. I order fried tōfu noodles with green onions and sit by the window, watching the crowds wash by. My noodles arrive. I help myself to a glass of iced water. Happy twentieth birthday, Eiji Miyake. Buntarō handed me a fine crop of cards this evening – one from each of my four aunts. The fifth envelope was another one from the ministry of unwelcome letters, still operating its Get Miyake campaign. I light up a Marlboro and take out the letter again to reread, trying to figure out whether it is a step forward, backward or sideward.

Tokyo
8 September

Eiji Miyake,

I am your father's wife. His <u>first</u> wife, his <u>real</u> wife, his <u>only</u> wife. Well, well. My informant at Osugi & Bosugi tells me

> you have been trying to contact my husband. How dare you? Was your upbringing so primitive you were never taught shame? Yet somehow I always suspected this day would come. So, you have learned of your father's influential status and are seeking quick cash. Blackmail is an ugly word, done by ugly people. But blackmail demands panache and pliable victims. You possess neither. Presumably, you believe you are clever, but in Tokyo you are a greedy boy from the countryside with a mind mired in manure. I will protect my daughters and my husband. We have paid enough, more than enough, for what your mother did. Perhaps this is her idea? She is a leech. You are a boil. My message to you is simple: if you dare to attempt to intimidate my husband, to show your face to any of our family, or to request a single yen, then, as a boil, you will be lanced.

I drain the puddle of soup from my noodles. A dragon chases its tail around the world. So. For my coming-of-age birthday I also received a paranoid stepmother who underlines too much, and two or more stepsisters. Unfortunately the letter itself won't help me find my father – it was unsigned, unaddressed, and posted in the northern ward of Tokyo, which narrows down the search to about three million people, assuming it was even written there. My stepmother is no fool. Her negative attitude is yet another hurdle. On the other hand, to be pushed away, I have to be touched. Also, my father didn't write the letter himself – so at worst, this means he still isn't sure about meeting me. At best, it means he hasn't actually been told I am trying to contact him. It is at this moment that I realize I don't have my baseball cap. This is the worst unbirthday present I could receive. That cap was a present from Anju. I think back – I had it in the games centre just now. I leave, and backtrack through the currents of pleasure seekers.

*

Zax Omega and Red Plague Moon is still plying for trade, but my baseball cap has gone. I search the rows of students pummelling the offspring of *Street Fighter*, a crowd of kids gathered around *2084*; the booths of girls digitalizing their faces with those of the famous; the alleys of salarymen playing mah-jong with video stripstresses. Weird. All these people like my mother paying counsellors and clinics to reattach them to reality: all these people like me paying Sony and Sega to reattach us to unreality. I identify the jowly supervisor by the way he jangles his keys. I have to yell into his ear. I smell the wax. 'Anyone handed in a cap?'

'Wha'?'

'I left a baseball cap here, thirty minutes ago.'

'Why?'

'I forgot it!'

Please wait – transaction being processed. 'You forgot why you left it?'

'Never mind.'

I remember my spectator. In the upstairs pool room, he said. I find the back stairs and go up. The sudden quietness and gloom are subaquatic. Three rows by six of ocean-blue tables. I see him on the far side, playing alone, and on his head is my baseball cap. His ponytail is fed through the strap-gap. He pockets a ball, looks up, and gestures me over. 'I figured you'd be back. That's why I didn't chase you. Want to win it off my head?'

'I'd rather you just took it off your head.'

'Where's the fun in that?'

'There isn't any. But it is my cap.'

He sizes me up. 'True.' He presents my cap with a courtier flourish. 'No offence meant. I'm not really myself tonight.'

'No worries. Thanks for rescuing my cap.'

He smiles an honest smile. 'You're welcome.'

My move. 'So, uh, how late is she now?'

'When does "late" become "stood up"?'

'I dunno. Ninety minutes?'

'Then the bitch has well and truly stood me up. And I had to pay for this table until ten.' He gestures with his cue. 'Play a few frames, if you're not busy.'

'I'm unbusy. But I'm too broke to bet.'

'Can you afford one cigarette per game?'

I am sort of flattered that he takes me seriously enough to offer me a game of pool. All I have had in the way of company since I got to Tokyo has been Cat, Cockroach and Suga. 'Okay.'

Yuzu Daimon is a final-year law student, a native of Tokyo, and the finest pool player I have ever met. He is brilliant, truly. I watched *The Hustler* last week. Daimon could whip the Paul Newman character into coffee froth. He lets me win a couple of frames out of politeness, but by ten o'clock he's mopped up seven more in U-turn-spinning, jump-shotting, unerring style. We hand in the cues and sit down to smoke our winnings. My plastic lighter is buggered: a flame flicks from Daimon's thumb. It is a beautiful object. 'Platinum,' says Daimon.

'Must be worth a fortune.'

'It was my twentieth birthday present. You should practise more.' Daimon nods at the table. 'You have a good eye.'

'You sound like my sports teacher at high school.'

'Oh, please. Say, Miyake, I've decided Saturday owes me compensation for being stood up. What say we go to a bar and find a pair of girls.'

'Uh, thanks. I'd better pass.'

'Your girlfriend will never find out. Tokyo's too big.'

'No, it's nothing that—'

'So you don't have a woman waiting anywhere?'

'Not a non-imaginary one, no, but—'

'You're trying to tell me you're gay?'

'Not as far as I know, no, but—'

'Then you took a vow of celibacy? You're a member of a cult?'

I show him the contents of my wallet.

'So? I'm offering to foot the bill.'

'I can't scav off you. You already paid for the table.'

'You won't be scavving off me. I told you, I'm going to be a lawyer. Lawyers never spend their own money. My father has a hospitality account of a quarter of a million yen to get through, or his department will face a budgetary reassessment. So you see, by refusing you put our family in a difficult position.'

That's quite a lot of money. 'Every year?'

Daimon sees I am serious, and laughs. 'Every *month*, dolt!'

'Scavving off your father is even worse than scavving off you.'

'Look, Miyake, I'm only talking about a couple of beers. Five at most. I'm not trying to buy your soul. C'mon. When's your birthday?'

'Next month,' I lie.

'Then consider it a premature birthday present.'

Santa Claus works behind the bar, Rudolf the Red-nosed Reindeer emerges from the toilets holding a mop, and elves in floppy hats wait on the tables. I watch snowflakes dance on the ceiling, smoking a Marlboro lit by the Virgin Mary. Yuzu Daimon drums along to psychedelic Christmas carols. 'It's called the Merry Christmas Bar.'

'But it's September ninth.'

'It's December twenty-fifth every night, in here. It is what we call a chick magnet.'

'I might be being naïve, but could your girlfriend have just been held up?'

'You are being whatever lies beyond naïve. What decade is this Yakushima place trapped in? The bitch stood me up. I know it. We had an arrangement. If she wanted to be there, she would have been, and I am now as single as a newborn babe, and she is jet-trash to me. Jet-trash. And don't turn around right now, but I believe our feminine solace has just arrived. Over in the nook between the fireplace and the tree. The one in the coffee leather, the other in the cherry velvet.'

'They look like models.'

'Model whats?'

'They wouldn't look at me twice. Once.'

'I said I'll buy your drinks, not massage your ego.'

'I mean it.'

'Crap.'

'Look at how I'm dressed.'

'We'll say you work as a roadie.'

'I'm not even smart enough to be a roadie.'

'We'll say you work as a roadie for Metallica.'

'But we've never met them.'

Daimon buries his face in his hands and chuckles. 'Ah, Miyake, Miyake. What do you think bars are for? Do you think all these people enjoy paying exorbitant prices for pissy cocktails? Finish your beer. We need whisky to penetrate the enemy interior. No more buts! Look at the one in velvet. Imagine yourself untying the cords of that bodice thing she's wearing with your front teeth. A simple yes or no will do: do you want her?'

'Who wouldn't? But—'

'Santa! Santa! Two double Kilmagoons! On the rocks!'

'So, after the rape,' Daimon says in a loud voice as we take the adjacent table, 'their world is bulldozed. Razed. She stops eating. She rips out the telephone. The only thing she shows any interest in is her dead son's video games. When my friend leaves home for work in the mornings she is already there, hunched over the pistol, wasting men on the sixteen-inch Sony. When he gets back, she hasn't moved a muscle. Kitchen pots still on the table – she doesn't care. *Bangabangabang! Reload.* Back in the real world, the police drop the case – sexual assault during a night on the bare mountain? Forget it. Most men just can't begin to understand what an experience like that . . . I despair of our sex, sometimes, Miyake. So. Nine months pass this way. She doesn't leave the house once. Not a single time. He is going frantic with worry – you remember what a mess he was when you got back from your Beatles reunion gig. Finally he asks a psychiatrist for advice. Somehow, the shrink concludes, she has to be reintegrated into society or risk sinking into a state of self-willed autism. Now, they originally met in their university orchestra – she was a xylophonist, he was a trombonist. So he buys two tickets for *Pictures at an Exhibition*, and day by day erodes her resistance until she agrees to come. Cigarette?'

I could swear there was an ashtray when we sat down.

'Excuse me?' Daimon leans over to Coffee. 'May I?'

'Sure.'

'Thanks so much. The night of the concert, she takes sedatives, they get dressed up, have a candlelit dinner somewhere high up, and take their seats in the front row. The trumpet starts. You know . . .' Daimon hums the opening bars. 'And she freezes. Her eyes are *ice*. Her fingernails sink into his thigh until they draw blood. She starts trembling. Forget the embarrassment, he has to get her out of there before she gets hysterical. Out in the foyer she tells him. The cymbal clasher – in the orchestra – she swears on her ancestor's tomb that he was the man who raped her.'

I notice that Coffee and Velvet are tuned in.

'I know what you're thinking. Why not go to the cops? Nine cases out of ten, the judge tells the woman she was asking for it by wearing her skirt too high, and the rapist gets away with signing an apology form. She tells him that unless he avenges her honour she'll throw herself from the top of the Tokyo Hilton. Now. You met him. He's no mug. He does his homework, and gets an unregistered gun with a silencer, surgical gloves. One evening, while the orchestra are performing Beethoven's Fifth, he breaks into the cymbalist's apartment – he lives alone with his pet crystals. What he finds backs up his wife's story. Internet porn print-outs, S&M gear, manacles hanging from the ceiling, a seriously worn and torn inflatable Marilyn Monroe. He hides under the bed. After midnight the cymbalist gets back, listens to his answering machine, has a shower, and gets into bed. My friend has a sense of the dramatic. "Even a monster should check under his mattress." *Bangabangabanga!*'

'Quite a story.'

'Not over yet. My damn lighter isn't working. One moment . . .' Daimon leans over to Coffee, who is already opening her designer handbag. 'I'm terribly sorry to trouble you – thanks so much.' She even lights it for him, and then one for me. I nod shyly. 'Revenge is the purest medicine. You probably remember the local rags – "Who Banged the Cymbal?" – but a successful murder is only a question of planning, and the police have no clues. His wife recovers in a matter of *days*. She starts teaching at her school for the blind again. Chucks out the video games. And come spring, when the Saitō Kinen Orchestra go to Yokohama, this time *she* insists that they buy front-row tickets. Like before, but happier. He can live with his conscience – he only dispensed the same natural justice as the state would have done if it had sharper cops. They get dressed up, have the candlelit dinner somewhere high up, and take their seats in the front row. The string section start in – and she freezes. Her eyes are *ice*. Her breathing changes. He thinks she's having some sort of attack, and manages to get her out into the lobby. "What?" he asks. "The second cellist! It's him! The man who raped me!" "*What?* How about the cymbal clasher I killed last year?" She shakes her head like he's crazy. "What are you talking about? The second cellist is the rapist, I swear on my ancestor's grave, and if you don't avenge my honour I'll electrocute myself.'

'Unbelievable!' gasps Coffee. 'Like, what did he do next?'

Daimon rotates, Coffee crosses her legs, and we become a foursome. 'Went to the cops. Confessed to the cymbal player's murder. By the time he was brought to trial, his wife had accused nine different men of raping her, including the minister for fish.'

Velvet is aghast. 'Did all that really happen?'

'I swear' – Daimon blows a wobbly smoke ring – 'every word is true.'

When I get back to the table after placing my order with Santa, Daimon's arm is around Coffee's chair. 'Like, aha' – Coffee pokes out her tongue between her white lips – 'Santa's little helper.' Her face is marshmallowed with cosmetics. Velvet swivels towards me. Her tights whisper and Godzilla wakes up. 'Yuzu-kun tells me you're in the music biz.' I smell her perfume, moistened and salted with sweat. 'I'm modelling at the moment, doing a series of shoots for Tokyo's biggest chain of body correction clinics.' She leans towards me, her Lark Slim awaiting a flame, and Godzilla rears his fearsome head. Daimon spins his lighter across the table. Velvet's face glows. A whole evening without thinking of Anju, until now.

Velvet wraps her arms around my chest as we lean into the first corner, less than a second behind Daimon's Suzuki 950. My Yamaha 1000 bucks and growls down a gear. The sun-buckled stadium, the golden trumpets, the giant Bridgestone airship: the touch of Velvet's hands makes it hard to concentrate. Daimon clips a row of dancing police cones, and above the din I hear Coffee puppy-squeal. 'C'mon!' Velvet whispers in my ear, just for me, and her whisper is a ghost writhing naked in the curves of my inner ear. I feel as hard and full as the Yamaha fuel tank. Coffee whoops. 'Better than the real thing! Giddyup!' Daimon leans into the chicane. 'Realer than the real thing,' I hear him murmur. I follow his driveline, and down the long straight I nearly pass him, but Coffee watches my screen and tells Daimon when to block me – 'Gotcha!' she laughs. I skid through a patch of oil, at 180 kph – Velvet's fingers dig into me, the rear wheel overtakes the front, but I keep my bike on the road. We scissor through the zoo – I glimpse zebras streaming, manes flowing. Coffee retrieves her mobile phone, beeping 'Star Spangled Banner', answers it and proceeds to have a conversation about where she is and how totally unbelievable her night is. Recklessly I frape my Yamaha around the long, banking curve – I cut inside Daimon and we are neck and neck. 'Say, Miyake, this is as valid or as stupid a test of masculinity as anything else, don't you agree?' I risk a side glance. 'I guess' – he flashes a dangerous grin. 'Like, a twenty-first-century duel,' comments Coffee, putting her phone back in her bag. 'For sure!' replies Velvet. 'Miyake is going to make you eat grit, right, Miyake?' I say nothing but her little finger mines my navel and threatens to worm farther down until I say, 'Okay.' 'Settled, then,' replies Daimon, and veers into me. Velvet screams as I lose control and slam into an oncoming JOMO fuel tanker. *Baaannnnnngggggggg!* When the fun-size nuclear explosion dies down, Daimon and Coffee are disappearing into the distance, small as a full stop. 'Nasty accident,' tuts Daimon. My Yamaha stutters into second gear. 'Like, ruthless!' laughs Coffee. 'No way he'll catch up now.' Daimon glances over at me. 'Poor Miyake. Remember, it's only a video game.' Velvet's grip loosens. An absurd idea comes to me that owes more to two whiskies on two beers than original thinking. I skid the Yamaha through a U-turn, and discover that, yes, I can drive counter-clockwise. The 'Seconds Elapsed' tick down. The zebras in the zoo stream backwards. A programmer as nutty as Suga must have written the software. Velvet's hands tweak my nipples to show approval. We pass the start line – 'Laps Completed' reads '-1'. I tear up the swing-bridge – the bike flips up as we leap through space, and shudders as we land on the far ramp. Here comes Daimon on his Suzuki. 'Like, what?' Daimon begins a sentence with 'You sneaky fucking—' I mirror his evasive swerve, and skid straight into his headlamp, as round as the moon on a bright day. No explosion. Our bikes freeze in mid-tilt, the music stops and the screens die.

'I am not used to not winning.' Daimon gives me a look that would worry me if we weren't friends. 'Deep down, you are one devious sonofabitch, Miyake.'

'Poor Daimon. Remember, it's only a video game.'

'Advice.' Daimon does not smile. 'Never punch above your weight class.'

Coffee makes a confused noise. 'Like, where'd the velocodrome go?'

'I think' – Velvet dismounts – 'Miyake busted the video machine, big time.'

Daimon swings off his Yamaha. 'Let's go.'

'Like, where?' Coffee slips off the bike.

'A quiet little place where they know me.'

'Did you know,' asks Coffee, 'if you pluck your nasal hair instead of trimming it you can burst a blood vessel and die?' Daimon leads us through the pleasure quarter as if he created it. I am lost, and hope I won't need to find my own way back to Shinjuku metro. The crowds have thinned a little from before, the pleasure-seekers all harder core now. A sports car nudges by, throbbing with bass. 'Lotus Elise 111S,' says Daimon. Coffee's mobile phone beeps 'Auld Lang Syne', but she can't hear the caller despite shouting 'Hello?' a dozen times. Jazz brays through an open door. A queue of the hippest people wait outside. I enjoy the envious stares we earn. I would die to hold Velvet's hand. I would die if she slapped my hand away. I would die if she wanted me to take it and I never realized. Daimon tells us a long story about misunderstandings with drag-queens in Los Angeles that make the girls shriek with laughter. 'But, like, LA is really dangerous,' says Coffee. 'Everyone has guns. Singapore's the only really safe place abroad.' 'Ever been to LA?' asks Daimon. 'No,' says Coffee. 'Ever been to Singapore?' asks Daimon. 'No,' says Coffee. 'So somewhere you have never been is less dangerous than somewhere else you have never been?' Coffee rolls her eyes. 'Like, who says you need to go a place to know about it? What do you think TV is for?' Daimon defers. 'Hear that, Miyake? This must be feminine logic.' Coffee waves her arms in the air. 'Like, long live girl power!' We walk down a passageway lit with signs for stand bars, where an elevator is waiting. Coffee hiccoughs. 'Which floor?' The elevator doors close. I shudder with cold. Daimon adjusts his reflection, and decides to switch on his good humour. 'Ninth. Queen of Spades. I have a great idea. Let's get married.' Coffee giggles and presses '9'. 'I accept! Queen of Spades. Like, freaky name for a bar.'

The elevator's movement is imperceptible, but for the changing floor numbers. Coffee picks some fluff off Daimon's collar. 'Nice jacket.' 'Armani. I'm very choosy about what comes into contact with my skin. That's why I chose you, oh my divinity.' Coffee rolls her eyes and looks at me. 'Is he always like this, Miyake?' 'You can't ask him,' smiles Daimon. 'Miyake's too good a friend of mine to be honest with you.' I look at the four reflections of our four reflections. Spaceship-humming silence. 'Stay in here too long,' I say, 'and you'd forget which one was you.' A gong bronzes, and the elevator doors open. Me, Velvet and Coffee nearly fall over. We are on the roof of a building so high Tokyo has disappeared. Higher than clouds, higher than the wind. The stars are near enough to prod. A meteor arcs around. I see a curtain in the night behind Orion and the illusion is obvious – we are in miniature planetarium, less than ten metres across. A gong bronzes again, and a grapefruit dawn blushes up the sides of the dome from the floor. 'Like,' gasps Coffee, 'totally unbelievable.' Velvet looks quietly impressed. Daimon claps. 'Miriam! As you can see, I couldn't keep myself away.'

A woman in an opal kimono and full geisha make-up slips through the curtain. She bows exquisitely. She *is* exquisite, from her lacquer hairclip to her sunset slippers. 'Good evening, Mr Daimon.' A pillow-hushed voice. Her cosmetics conceal whatever is beneath, but from the way she moves I put her in her mid-twenties. 'This is an unexpected pleasure.'

'I know it is, Miriam, I know it is. I heard you were due to be going on an exotic holiday tonight – but here you are, still. Well, well. Meet my new bride.' He kisses Coffee, who giggles but squirms closer. 'Do tell me Dirty Daddy isn't on the premises.'

'Would you be referring to . . . whom, Mr Daimon?'

'Hear that diplomacy, Miyake? Miriam is a pro. A bona fide pro.'

The woman glances at me.

'Mr Daimon senior isn't here tonight, Mr Daimon.'

Daimon sighs. 'That father of mine. Off rutting Chizumi *again*?

At his age? Has anyone else around here noticed how fat he's grown? Talk about excess baggage. Does Chizumi dish you the dirt on Mr Daimon senior, Miriam? Is the trysting wig on or wig off? . . . Ah, I can see you're not going to answer. Well, if he isn't here, I can entertain my tinkywinky wifey' – he encircles Coffee's waist – 'in the Daimon clan's private room. Naturally, the evening's festivities go on Father Ratfuck's bill.'

'Naturally, Mr Daimon, Mama-san will invoice Mr Daimon senior.'

'Why so formal, Miriam? What happened to "Yuzu-chan"?'

'I'll have to ask you to sign the guest book, Mr Daimon.'

Daimon waves his hand. 'Whatever.'

I ignore a voice advising me to get in the elevator and leave right now, because I lack any kind of excuse or explanation. I am still buzzing with alcohol, but I see something dangerous in Daimon. The moment passes. Daimon sweeps us on, in Daimon we trust. 'The enchanted land awaits.'

Miriam leads us through a series of curtained anterooms – I forget which way we faced when we came in. Each curtain is embroidered with a kanji too ancient to read. Finally we enter a quilted chamber, unchanged since the 1930s. Tapestries of ancient cities hang on the windowless walls. Stiff leather chairs, an unattended mahogany and brass bar, a pendulum swinging too slowly, a dying chandelier. A rusty cage with an open door. The parrot inside opens its wings as we pass. Coffee squeals like a rubber sole on varnish. A number of older men sit around in clusters, discussing secrets in low voices and slow gestures. Smoke at dusk. Girls and women fill glasses and occupy the arms of the chairs. They are here to serve, not to entertain. Alchemy has distilled all colour into the girls' kimonos. Persimmon golds, cathode indigos, ladybird scarlets, tundra olives. A rotary fan hanging from the ceiling paddles the thick heat. In the shadow of a nightmarish aspidistra a piano plays a nocturne to itself, at half-speed.

'Wow,' says Velvet.

'Like, freaky,' says Coffee.

A powerful odour similar to my grandmother's hair lacquer makes me sneeze. 'Mr Daimon!' A thickly rouged woman appears behind the bar. 'And companions! My!' She wears a headdress of peacock feathers and sequinned evening gloves, and flutters a faded actress's wave. 'How green and growing you all look! That's young blood for you!'

'Good evening, Mama-san. Quiet, for a Saturday?'

'Saturday already? The days don't find their way up this far.'

Daimon cocks a smile. Coffee and Velvet are welcome wherever there are men's imaginations to strip them, but in my jeans, T-shirt, baseball cap and sneakers, I feel as out of place as a shit-shoveller at an imperial wedding. Daimon clasps my shoulder. 'I want to take my brother-in-arms here – and our imperial consorts – to my father's room.'

'Sayu-chan can show you—'

Daimon cuts in. His smile is nearly vicious. 'But Miriam is free.'

Messages pass between Daimon and Mama-san. Miriam looks away miserably. Mama-san nods, and sort of hoicks up her face. 'Miriam?' Miriam turns back and smiles. 'What joy that would bring me, Mr Daimon.'

'I mostly drive my Prussian blue Porsche Carrera 4 cabriolet. I have a weakness for Porsches. Their curves, if you look closely, are *exactly* those of a kneeling woman, bent over submissively.' Daimon watches Miriam pour the champagne. Velvet kneels. 'What about you, Eiji?' Wonderful. We are on 'Eiji' terms. 'I'm, uh, more of a two-wheel sort of person.' Velvet bubbles – 'Oh, *don't* tell me you drive a Harley?' Daimon barks a laugh. 'However did you guess? Miyake's Harley is his, how can I put it, his pelvic thrust of freedom between gigs, right? You get so much shit in a rock star's entourage, you wouldn't believe it. Groupies, smackheads, drummers, Miyake's been through it all. Splendid, Miriam, you didn't spill a drop. I suppose you get a lot of practice. Tell me, how long have you been holed up here as a waitressImeana hostess?' Miriam is ghostly but dignified in the lamplight. The room is intimate and warm. I smell the girls' perfume and cosmetics and recently laid tatami. 'Come now, Mr Daimon. Ladies never discuss years.'

Daimon undoes his ponytail. 'Years, is it? My, my. You must be very happy here. Well, everyone, now the champagne has been poured, I wish to propose two toasts.'

'What are we, like, drinking to?' asks Coffee.

'One: as Miyake here knows, I recently broke free of a sewer woman who peels promises like a whore – a fair description – peels condoms on and off.'

'I know exactly the sort of woman you mean.' Coffee nods.

'We understand each other so deeply.' Daimon sighs. 'Shall we get married in Waikiki, Lisbon or Pusan?'

Coffee toys with Daimon's earring. 'Pusan? The toilet of Korea?'

'Poisonous little country,' agrees Daimon. 'You can have that earring.'

'Like, great. Here's to freedom.' We chime our flutes.

'What's your second toast?' asks Velvet, stroking the chrysanthemum.

Daimon gestures at Coffee and Velvet. 'Why – a toast to the flower of true Japanese womanhood. Miriam, you're a woman, you know about these things. What qualities should I look for in a wife?'

Miriam considers. 'In your case, Mr Daimon, blindness.'

Daimon places his hands over his heart to stop the bleeding. 'Oh, Miriam! Where is your compassion tonight? Miriam is the duck-feeding type, Miyake. She treats her waterfowl with more compassion than her lovers, I hear.'

Miriam smiles slightly. 'Waterfowl are more dependable, I hear.'

'Dependable, did you say? Or dependent? No matter. Don't you agree that Miyake and I are the two luckiest men in Tokyo?'

She regards me for a moment. I glance away. I wonder what her real name might be. 'Only you know how lucky you are,' she says. 'Will that be all, Mr Daimon?'

'No, Miriam, that will not be all. I want some grass. Instant-karma mix. And you know how peckish drugs make me, so bring something peckable in half an hour or so.'

The room has a fusuma screen that opens on to a balcony. Tokyo rises from the floor of the night. Four weeks ago I was helping my cousin repair Uncle Orange's tea plantation Rotavator. Now look. A six-storey can of KIRIN LAGER BEER pours dandelion neon, over and over. Across the unlit lake of the Imperial Palace I can see aircraft warning lights pulse on the crown of PanOpticon. Altair and Vega pulse either side of the Milky Way. Traffic noises ebb up. Velvet leans out. 'Miles and miles,' she says to herself. Her hair shifts in the hot breeze. Her body is made of curves I can feel just by looking. 'I do declare,' says Daimon, the friend who is giving me all this on a plate, 'I have rolled the most perfect joint this side of the whorehouses of Bogotá.'

'And just how would you know?' Coffee bends down to light it.

'I own a dozen.' He wriggles out of his jacket and slings it into the room. His T-shirt reads *We don't see things as they are, we see things as we are*, which I have heard somewhere before.

Velvet leans out farther. 'Are those islands or ships? That loop of lights.'

Daimon peers through the railings. 'Reclaimed land. New airport.'

Coffee looks. 'Let's go out there and see how fast your Porsche runs.'

'Let's not.' Daimon puckers the joint into life, holds the smoke down, and exhales an aaaaaaaaa . . . Coffee kneels, and Daimon holds the joint to her lips. Uncle Money gave me a stern lecture about drugs and Tokyo which I know from one glance at Velvet I shall ignore. Coffee purses her lips as dragon smoke uncurls from her nostrils. 'Did I tell you' – Daimon gazes into the flame of his lighter – that this lighter is a piece of history? It used to belong to General Douglas MacArthur during the Occupation.' 'Like, sure it did, if you say so,' scoffs Coffee. 'I say so, but never mind. Get me a zabuton, my coffeecreamyhoneyhole, let your lungs soak up this beauty, we'll drive to Tierra del Fuego and repopulate Patagonia . . .' While Coffee is fetching a cushion from the tatami room the mobile phone in her bag beeps the Moonlight Sonata. Daimon heaves a mighty sigh – 'Irritating!' – and passes the joint to me. I give it to Velvet. Daimon answers the mobile in a fair imitation of the royal crown prince. 'I bid you a splendid evening.' Coffee dives, giggling. 'Mine!' Daimon scissors her to the floor between his legs. She writhes, giggling, mantrapped. 'No, I'm terribly sorry, but you can't speak with her. Her boyfriend? Really? That's what she told you? How awful. I'm fucking her later tonight, you see, so go and hire a naughty video, you sad fuck. But first, listen very carefully to this – this is how your death sounds.' And he tosses the phone over the balcony.

Coffee's giggle has its plug pulled.

Daimon smiles wide as a stoned toad.

'You just threw my mobile over the railing!'

Daimon dribbles giggles. 'I know I just threw your mobile over the railing.'

'It might hit somebody on the head.'

'Well, scientists warn us that mobile phones can harm the brain.'

'My mobile!'

'Oh, I'll buy you another one. I'll buy you another ten.'

Coffee weighs up various factors. 'The most up-to-date model?'

Daimon grabs the zabuton, lies back and does a gangster impression. 'I'll buy ya da factory, shweetie.' Coffee does a little-girl pout and holds the champagne glass to her ear. 'I can hear bubbles.' Velvet takes my earlobes in a thumbpinch, seals my mouth with hers and marijuana smoke rushes in. Stolen chocolate, smeared and soft. 'Ohohohohohohohoho,' observes Daimon, 'do that inside, you two. It looks like I – and my newlywed – have been overtaken by the young upstart once again.' I open my eyes, and gasp, and cough. Velvet prods me in the chest, so I go inside.

'You sit there,' she says, pointing to the far side of the low table. A monk on heat, a dog in a cassock. Her forearms glisten with sweat. She blows out the candle. We take solemn turns with the joint and say nothing. Our fingertips might brush. Hers contain an electric current. Bioborg. I make out her outline in the glow of the night city, even filtered through the paper. She doesn't actually touch me, and her demeanour warns me against touching her until she tells me to. The bright tip of the joint travels through the turfy air. Sometimes I am me, sometimes I am not quite. Pearls, moonstone, teeth enamel. A time/space irregularity explores my limbs. Onto the dark, I identikit in her breasts, her hair, her face. If I sneezed right now Godzilla would probably explode in my boxer shorts. 'You smoke this all the time?' Her words are twists in the smoke. 'Ever since my twentieth birthday.' A scroll, doll, droll troll, a bowing chrysanthemum in a vase. 'So how old are you, roadie?' I even hear her lush hair hush. 'Twenty-three. You?' Bitter snowflakes flurry. 'I am one million today.' One spanky whoop from Velvet and a grrrrrrrr from Daimon, and Velvet and I are laughing hard enough to fracture ribs, even though no sound comes out. Then I forget why I'm laughing, and I sit up again. 'Keep your hands on the table,' she warns me severely, 'I hate boys whose hands get everywhere.' After a couple of attempts our mouths meet and we kiss for nine days and nine nights.

The fusuma to the balcony slides open. Velvet and I jump apart. Daimon stands in the moonlight, his torso stripped, with a sort of vampire Miffy the rabbit painted across his chest in lipstick. His nipples are Miffy's greedy pupils. 'Miyake! Stoned or boned? Want to swap yet?' The shōji to the outer corridor slides open. Miriam stands in the entrance, holding a tray of sticky pearls and cubes of watermelon and naked lychees. I glimpse shock, anger and hatred before professional indifference regains control. 'Miriam!

Bearing nibblies! Caviare, no less? One of her assets, Miyake, is her sense of timing.' She removes her slippers, steps up, and sets the tray on the table. 'Pardon me.' She withdraws. 'Oh, Miriam, you don't need me to pardon you, not with your powerful and influential patrons to take care of you.' Pigletty Coffee appears, doing herself up, supporting the fusuma frame to stop it collapsing. She sees Miriam. She is used to ordering domestics. 'Show us to the powder room!'

Daimon speaks to Eiji, but Eiji finds it hard to concentrate because his head keeps unscrewing itself and rolling into the corner. Coffee and Velvet have been in the ladies' room since time began. 'I use a quiet East Shinjuku love hotel near the park, attached to a four-star place so you can order up decent food from the kitchen.' Eiji is somehow uneasy. Daimon peers in. 'Not still worried about money?' Eiji tries to shake his head but nods it by accident. 'Money is only this stuff my father has too much of.' 'The girls,' thinks Eiji, 'is it all right, just to—' Daimon hears his friend's thoughts, buttons up his shirt and wags a finger. 'These two are strictly a double act, Miyake. Either both get laid, or they both go home to their lavender-scented bedrooms. You back out on me now and I'll be left with the most expensive wank on my hands since Michael Jackson last played at the Budōkan. And yours has at least evolved problem-solving intelligence. Mine has a fashion sense where her brain should be.' Eiji is about to say something but forgets what he was going to say the moment before he begins. 'Girls are like video games, Miyake. You pay, you play, you leave.' Eiji is all gratitude. He tries to express this, but his words are flowing out like endless rain into a paper cup, they slither wildly as they make their way across the universe, so he gives up. Another hostess brings the coffee. 'Who the *fuck* are you?' Daimon demands. The hostess bows. 'Aya-chan, Mr Daimon. Miriam-san has come over unwell.' Daimon begins to get angry. 'Trot back to Mama-san and remind Daimon who my father is, and what a stroppy fuck I can be if I—' But his sentence trails off. He pinches the head off the chrysanthemum, and pulls off the petals. 'Forget I said that, Aya-chan. Give this to the ghost of Miriam, with my profoundest respects,' and he hands her the flower-stump, which Eiji thinks is sort of cute. Eiji sits in the front of the taxi. Daimon sits in the back with his two concubines. The streets clear, they go over a wide bridge. Atlas holds up his globe in the foyer, Daimon gazes up at the screen showing rooms lit and unlit and prices and presses panels and gets keys. Another elevator ride. Daimon kisses Eiji on the lips and jump-shots him into the room behind. A ten-second shower and uncurious porn on Pay TV. Nine different types of condom. A pink 'H' flashes on and off outside. Heads on stalks, sunflower heads. Coffee comes in, a lemon towel around her lozenge honey skin, sort of numb somehow now, rather factually the legendary swimming pool of sex laps, she draws the curtain, close your eyes, she says, and slips into bed, her skin slides out, berries swell, yeah okay you can but you are *not* to touch me there, snagged on a twig, yeah okay, does he normally swap over like this? Your friend? Yuzu Daimon? What a name, *Yuzu*, like the fruit? I guess. Shush. Waxy chocolate, cheap and teeth biting midriff, mossy nooks, nervous push, no I said you are *not* to touch me there, Godzilla retreats, nervous tricklets of sweats down our back, hoisting, lowering, raising, all technical stuff, *that's it there*, Godzilla changes his mind again, roots dig in harder, boughs thrash back and forth, her fingers grasp, her toes find leverage, swimming in the blue, the sheets of blue, billowing and grunty and lethargic, she gasps for air, she dives, winces, and *yes* is this all there is *no* and surface and *yes* and under and *no* and surface and *yes* and under and surface and under *coming* and *coming* if *coming* you – don't – wake – up – before – you – hit – the – ground – you

I wake up in a round bed, alone as a chucked-away toy. This love hotel room is a temple of pink. Not flower pink – offal pink. The curtains are soiled with morning. I hear jackhammers, traffic crossings and crows. Husky sunflowers bend in their vase. My head is corkscrewed from temple to temple. My tongue has been salted and sun-dried and shat on by desert weasels. My throat has been attacked by geologists' hammers. My elbows and knees have been friction-burned raw. My groin smells of prawn. The bedsheets are twisted, and the undersheet is dashed with crusty blood. So, two virgins defrocked one another. *That* groin sneeze was sex? That was no Golden Gate bridge to a promised land. It was a wobbly plank across a soggy bog. Nobody even gives you a badge to sew on. This room is a public tissue – love hotels must have the highest sex-per-cubic-metre ratios this side of . . . where? Paris. I grope for a cigarette – empty. Still. All things considered, I got off lightly. The telephone riiiiiiiiings. Daimon calling from the room next door, I bet.

'Good morning, sir, this is reception.' A man, brisk and breezy.

'Uh, g'morning.'

'This is just to remind you that your suite is booked until seven . . .'

My watch is on the bedside: 6:45. 'Okay.'

'After seven, hourly charges reapply.'

'Okay, I'll be right out.'

'Will you be paying cash or credit, sir?'

'*What?*'

'When your lady friends left just now they didn't know if you were paying cash or credit. Two rooms for all night comes to fifty-five thousand yen, provided nothing is taken from the minibar, and that you vacate the room in the next fifteen minutes.'

Cold shock squeezes down my colon.

Still brisk, less breezy. 'So I'm calling up to ensure there has been no kind of unpleasant misunderstanding.'

Would vomiting help?

'No kind of problem, is there, sir?' Veiled menace.

'No, none at all. Uh, I'll pay cash, I think. I'll be right down.'

'We'll be waiting for you in the entrance lobby, sir.'

*

I get dressed in my gummy clothes and dart into Daimon's room. Nobody. Identical to mine, only on the mirror, scrawled in some sort of jelly, are the characters – 'ONLY A VIDEO GAME'. Daimon, you primetime bastard. Miyake, you idiot. I turn out my jeans pockets and find 630 yen, in small change. This isn't happening. I try to wake up. I fail. This is definitely happening. I am 54,370 yen short. I need a fantastic plan in the next nine minutes. I sit on the toilet and shit as I run through my alternatives. One: 'You see, the guy I was with, he promised he would pay for everything on his, uh, father's expense account.' The Yakuza king places his fingertips together. 'Eiji Miyake, employed in a lost property office? A position of trust. How fascinated your employers would be to learn how you spend your weekends. I feel it is my civic duty to report this matter unless you are willing to compensate us with certain *duties*, not all of which, I must warn you, could be described as *pleasant*.' Two: 'Buntarō! Help! I need you to bring me fifty-five thousand yen to a love hotel right now or you'll have to find another tenant.' Not a choice that poses him much difficulty. Three: 'The Yakuza king licks his razor blade. So, *this* is the thief who attempted to escape from my hotel without paying for services consumed.' I raise my bloodied head and swollen eyelids. My tongue lies in his shaving bowl.

If only crises could be flushed away down toilet bowls too.

In movies people escape along rooftops. I try to open the window, but it isn't designed to open, and anyway, I can't crawl down the sides of buildings. I see people in the littered streets and envy every single one of them. Could I start a fire? Trigger alarms and sprinklers? I follow the fire alarms to the end of the corridor, just so I feel I'm doing something. 'In the event of fire, smoke alarms will automatically unlock this door.' Uncle Tarmac says love hotels are designed to stop people doing runners – the elevator always takes you straight to reception. What else do people do in movies? 'Out the back way,' they hiss. Where is this 'back way'? I try the other end of the corridor. 'Emergency stairs. No way out.' Back ways are through kitchens. I dimly remember Daimon, may his bollocks fester, telling me there was a kitchen. Hotel kitchens are in the basement. I slip through the door and start down the stairs. Stupidly, I look over the handrail. The distant floor is the size of a stamp. The Aoyama escape route. I go as fast and quietly as I can. What will I say if they catch me here? That I get claustrophobic in lifts. Shut up. I get down to the ground floor. A large glass door opens into reception. A huge male receptionist is standing there. An ex-sumō wrestler, waiting for me. The stairs continue down one more floor. I can beg for mercy, or up the stakes and continue down. The receptionist narrows his eyes, running his finger down a ledger. Him and mercy do not sleep in the same bed. I slip by the glass door – a statue of Atlas and the globe blocks his line of sight – and creep down the stairs to a door marked STAFF ONLY. Please let it be open. It doesn't open. I barge it. It judders open. Thank you. Beyond is a stuffy corridor of pipes and fuse boxes. At the end mops are stacked against another door. I turn the handle and push. Nothing doing. I barge it. The door is locked. Worse still I hear the glass door opening one floor above – and I didn't close the STAFF ONLY door behind me. 'Hey? Anyone there?' Mr Sumō. Doom pisses hot dread on my head. What can I do? Desperate, I knock on the locked door. I hear Mr Sumō's shoes on the steps. I knock again. And suddenly a bolt slides, the door is yanked open and a chef is glaring at me – behind him a striplit kitchen chops and bubbles. '*You*,' he snarls, 'had *better*' – his eyes belong to Satan – 'be the new mousseboy.'

Huh?

'Tell me you're the new mousseboy!'

Mr Sumō is nearly here.

'Yes, I'm the new mousseboy.'

'Get in here!' He pulls me through, slams the door behind me and, giving me my first lucky break of the morning, bolts it shut. *Head Chef Bonki* is sewn into his hat. 'What the *hell* are you doing turning up for your first morning *forty-five minutes late*, looking like a vagabond? *Take off that baseball cap in my kitchen!*' Behind him, junior chefs and kitchen hands watch the human sacrifice. I take off my cap and bow. 'I'm very sorry.' Cream, steam, mutton and gas. I see no windows and no doors. How do I get out of here? Head Chef Bonki snarls. 'Master is *disappointed.* And when Master is disappointed, *we* are disappointed. We run *a very* – tight – ship!' He suddenly yells at the top of his voice and blasts what are left of my nerves away. 'And what do we do to members of the crew who let the ship down?' The kitchen staff chant back in one air-punching chorus. 'To the sharks! To the sharks! To the sharks!' I seriously consider giving myself up to Mr Sumō, after all. 'Follow me, mousseboy. Master will conduct his inspection.' I am hustled between shining counters and racks of pans, past a rack of punch-cards. A door. Please let there be a door. 'This is where you check in, if Master forgives your disgraceful start.' Mr Sumō must be at the bolted door by now. All these knives worry me. A boy with a sunken nose scrubs floor tiles with a toothbrush – the chef deals him a powerful kick for no apparent reason. We come to a poky office full of the chug, grind and kiss of a knife-sharpening lathe. On the far side is an open door – steps lead up to a yard of rubbish bags. The chef raps on the door frame, and shouts. 'The new mousseboy has reported for active duty, Master.' The lathe dies.

'Finale*mente*.' Master does not turn around. 'Show the scoundrel in.' His voice is far too high for his bulk. The head chef stands aside and prods me forward. Master turns around. He is wearing a blowtorcher's mask that reveals a petite mouth. He holds a cleaver sharp enough to castrate a bull. 'Leave us, Head Chef Bonki. Hang the sign on the door.' The office door clicks shut. Master tests the blade on his tongue. 'Why prolong your little deception?'

'Sir?'

'You are not the mousseboy who served me so *amply* at Jeremiah the Bullfrog's, are you?'

Lie, quick! 'Uh, true. I'm his brother. He got sick. But he didn't want to let down the crew, so he sent me instead.' Not bad.

'How sup*rem*ely sacri*fic*ial.' Master advances. Not good.

The door touches my back. 'My pleasure,' I say. Do I hear banging?

'*My* pleasure. *Mine*, I tell you. Touch it. Mousse is springy.'

I see my face in the black glass of his mask wondering what the mousseboy is supposed to do exactly. 'You are the best in the business, Master.' Sudden commotion is loose in the kitchen. No way around him to the yard door. Master pants. I smell liver pâté on his breath. 'Tweak it. Mousse is delicate. Slice it. Oh yes. Mousse is soft. So soft. Sniff it. Mousse will yield. Oh yes. Mousse *will* yield.' Four fat fingers swim towards my face.

A shout. *'Oy!'*

'Irksome. Irksome.' Master lifts up a tiny curtain next to my head that covers a peep-hole. His mouth stiffens. He picks up his cleaver, knocks me aside, flings the door open, and barges through. 'Whorehouse vermin!' he screams. 'You have been warned!' I glimpse Mr Sumō throwing assistant chefs over counters. 'You have been warned!' shouts Master. 'You have been warned what happens to pimps from the dark side who bring herpes and syphilis on to my spotless ship!' He hurls his cleaver. No point hanging around to examine the damage – I am out through the door, running up the steps, leaping over the plastic garbage bags, scattering through the crows, sprinting across the back yard, down a side street, and I don't stop zigzagging and checking behind me until seven-thirty.

At seven-forty I suddenly know where I am. Ōmekaidō Avenue. That zirconium skyscraper is PanOpticon. I walk a little farther towards Shinjuku and get to the intersection with Kita Street. Jupiter Café. The morning is already shallow-frying. I check my money. If walk back to Ueno, I can afford my submarine back to Kita Senju and buy a light breakfast. So light it would blow away if I sneezed.

Jupiter Café is air-conned soggy cool. I buy coffee and a pineapple muffin, sit at my window seat and examine my ghostly reflection in the window: a twenty-year-old Eiji Miyake, hair matted with sweat, smelling of dope and shrimpish sex, and sporting – I see to my horror – a lovebite the size of Africa over my Adam's apple. My complexion has completed its metamorphosis from Kyūshū tan to drone-paste. The waitress with the most perfect neck isn't working this morning – if she saw me in this condition, I would give a howl, age nine centuries and desiccate into a mound of dandruff and fingernails. The only other customer is a woman studying a fashion magazine with a toolbox of make-up. I vow never to mentally stroke another woman again, ever. I savour my pineapple muffin and watch the media screen on the NHK building. Missile launchers recoil, cities on fire. A new Nokia cellphone. Foreign affairs minister announces putative WW2 Nanking excesses are left-wing plots to destroy patriotism. Zizzi Hikaru washes her hair in Pearl River shampoo. Fly-draped skeletons stalk an African city. Nintendo proudly presents *Universal Soldiers*. The kid who hijacked a coach and slit three throats says he did it to stand out. I watch the passing traffic, until I hear a hacking cough. I never noticed Lao Tzu appear. He takes out a pack of Parliament cigarettes, but has lost his lighter. 'Hello again, Captain.' I lend him my lighter. 'Morning.' He notices my lovebite, but says nothing. In front of him is a flip-up video game screen, book-sized but designed in the twenty-third century. 'Brand-new vidboy3 – ten thou by ten thou res, four gigabytes, wraparound sonics, Socrates artifical intelligence chip. Software was only launched last week: *Virtua Sapiens*. A present from my daughter-in-law.' Lao Tzu shifts on his stool. 'On doctor's orders, to stave off senility.' I slide the ashtray between us. 'That's nice of her.' Lao Tzu flicks ash. 'You call getting my cretin son to sell off my rice-fields to a supermarket owner *nice*? So much for filial duty! I let the brat have the land to stop the tax wolves attacking when I die and *this*' – he prods the machine – 'is how I get repaid. I got to go shake the hose – you get leaky at my age. Care for a test drive while I'm gone?' He slides his vidboy3 over the counter towards me, and wanders off to the bathroom. I take off my baseball cap, plug myself in and press RUN. The screen clears.

♋

Welcome to *Virtua Sapiens*

[all rights reserved]

I see you are a new user. What is your on-line title?

>eiji miyake

Congrats for registering with *Virtua Sapiens*, Eiji Miyake. You will never be lonely again. Please select a relationship category. Friend, Enemy, Stranger, Lover, Relative.

>relative

Okay, Eiji. Which relative would you like to meet today?

>my father, of course

Well, excuse me. Please hold still for three seconds while I digitalize your face. An eye icon blinks and a microlens built into the screen frame blinks red. Okay ☟ now hold extra still while I register your retina. One wall, a floor and a ceiling appear. A whirlpool carpet bitmaps the floor. Pin-stripes unroll up the walls. A window appears, with a view of plum blossoms tossing in a spring storm. Curtains of rain blur the glass. I even hear the raindrops, ever so faint. The room is gloomy. A lamp appears on the left and glows cosy yellow. A see-through sofa appears under the window. The sofa is inked in with zigzags. And in the centre of the sofa appears my father, right foot folded on left knee, which looks cool but cannot be comfortable. The program has given him my nose and mouth, but made him jowlier and thinned his hair. His eyes are those of a mad scientist on the eve of world domination. His wrinkles are symmetrical. He is wearing a black dressing gown – he sort of glows, as if he got out of the bath five minutes ago. My father leans over to screen right, where a wine-bucket appears – he slides the bottle out and reads the label. 'Chablis, 1993.' A crisp, clear, even voice, perfect for weather forecasting. He pours himself a glass, makes a great show of savouring the bouquet, and sort of snorts it through his lips. He winks. An enamel smile flashes. 'Welcome home, son. Refresh my memory, will you – how long has it been?'

`> never, actually`

His eyebrows shoot up. 'Such a long time? Time flies like an arrow! What a lot of news we have to catch up. But you and I will get on like a house on fire. So tell me about school, son.'

`> I left.i am 20`

He sips his wine, slooshing it around his tongue, and runs a hand back through his hair. 'Is that so, son?' He leans towards the screen between us. The resolution is amazing – I flinch back. 'So you must be at university, right? Is that a cafeteria I see in the background?'

`> I didn't bother applying for university. no parents to pay and no money.`

My father reclines, and lounges a lazy arm over the back of the sofa. 'Is that so, son? That strikes me as a pity. Education is a wonderful thing. So how do you spend your time exactly?'

`> I am a rock star`

His eyebrows shoot up. 'Is that a fact, son? Tell me. Are you a successful rock star, with fame and fortune, or are you one of the unwashed millions still waiting for your lucky break to come along?'

`> very successful.all over the world`

He winks and flashes and enamel smile. 'I know meeting your old man after all this time is tough, son, but honesty is always the best policy. If you are such a big noise in the entertainment world, how come I never heard of you from *Time* magazine?'

`> I perform under an alias to protect my privacy`

He knocks back the rest of his wine. 'It isn't that I don't believe you, son, but could you tell me your alias? I want to boast about my rock star son to my buddies – and bank manager!'

`> john lennon`

My father slaps his knee. 'The real John Lennon was assassinated by Mark Chapman in 1980, therefore I know you are pulling my leg!'

`> mind if I change the subject?`

He comes over all serious, and puts down his glass. 'Time for a father and son heart-to-heart, is it? We don't have to be afraid of our feelings any more. Tell me what's on your mind.'

`> who are you exactly?`

'Your father, son!'

`> but as a human, who are you?`

My father refills his glass. Lightning fuses the sky, the plum blossom scratches the window pane, and the purple on grey is transformed to black on titanium white. I guess the program needs more time to respond to unlikely or general questions. My father chuckles and places his feet together. 'Well, son, that is one big question. Where would you like me to begin?'

`> what sort of man are you?`

My father rests his left foot on his right knee. 'Let me see. I'm Japanese, fifty next birthday. By profession I am an actor. My hobbies are snorkelling and wine appreciation. But fear not – all these details will come to light as our relationship unfolds, and I trust you'll be visiting again soon! I would like to introduce you to a special person. What do you say?'

`> okay`

The screen scrolls to the right, past the wine bucket. A woman – in her late thirties? – sits on the floor, smoking, humming snatches of 'Norwegian Wood' between drags. She is wrapped in a man's shirt, and black leggings hug her shapely legs. Long hair flows down to her waist. She has my eyes. 'Hi, Eiji.' Her voice is tender and pleased to see me. 'Can you guess whom I might be?'

`> snow white?`

She smiles at my father and puts out her cigarette. 'I see you have your father's sense of humour. I'm your mother.'

`> but mummy dear, you haven't seen daddy for 17 years`

The program processes this unexpected input while the storm head-butts the window. My mum lights another cigarette. 'Well, we had a few fences to mend, I admit. But now we get on like a house on fire.'

`> so you finally ran out of suckers to give you money?`

'That hurts, Eiji.' My virtual mother turns away and sobs alarmingly like my real one, a sort of dry, hidden quaking. I am typing in an apology, but my father responds first. He speaks in a slow and threatening thespian lilt. 'This is a home, young man, not a hotel! If you can't keep a civil tongue in your head, you know where the door is!' What a pair of virtual parents the program generated for me! They are thinking, what a virtual son reality generated for us. The plum blossoms suffer wear and tear in the unseasonal weather.

'Hello? Wakey! Anybody home?' A man in Jupiter Café shouts so loudly he drowns out the sound of the virtual rainstorm. 'Wrong change, girlie!' I unplug myself and turn around to see what the fuss is about. A grizzly drone in a stained shirt snarls at the girl with the most perfect neck in creation – when did she get here? She stares back, surprised but unfazed. Donkey is washing dishes, staying out of trouble, while my girl struggles to be polite with this human hog. 'You only gave me a five-thousand-yen note, sir.'

'Listen to me, girlie! I gave you a ten-thousand-yen note! Not five! Ten!'

'Sir, I am quite sure—'

He rears up on his two hind legs. 'You accusing me of lying, girlie?'

'No, sir, but I am saying you are mistaken.'

'You a feminist? Short-changing 'cos you're frigid?'

The queue of customers ruffles uneasily, but nobody says anything.

'Sir, I—'

'I gave you a ten-thousand, you abortion bucket! Correct change! *Now!*'

She pings open the till. 'Sir, there isn't even a ten-thousand note in here.'

Hog slavers and twitches his tusks. 'So! You steal from the till as well!'

Maybe I am still semi-stoned from the hash, or maybe *Virtua Sapiens* reshuffled my sense of reality, but I find myself walking over and tapping the guy on his shoulder. He turns around. His mouth is one bent sneer. Hog is larger than I thought, but it is too late to back out so I attack first and hardest. I douse his face with coffee and head-butt his nose, really, *really* hard. Christmas lights flicker in my eyes – Hog backs off, leaking a bubbly 'Aaaaaaaa' noise. Blood trickles from his nose through his fingers. I steady myself and my hand gropes for something to brandish. The pain in my forehead crushes my voice jagged. 'Get out *right now* or I'll *smash* your *fricking teeth* into *tiny fricking splinters* with' – I look at what I'm holding – 'this ashtray!' I must look deranged enough to mean business – after wheezing about police and assault in a beaky voice, Hog retreats. The customers look on. Lao Tzu pats my shoulder. 'Neat work, Captain.' Donkey comes over to her co-worker, all concern. 'Are you okay? I didn't know what was going on . . .' The waitress with the perfect neck slams shut the till, and glares at me. 'I could have handled him.'

'I know,' I reply. The Christmas tree lights fizz dangerously.

'But thank you anyway.' She gives me a cautious smile, so when the Christmas lights fuse I have something to take my mind off the pain. I sit back down and pain takes over my head for a while.

I wonder if my mother drank at Jupiter Café during her time in Tokyo. Maybe after Anju and I were born, maybe in this very seat, waiting for a summons from Akiko Katō. PanOpticon drones work Sundays too. A steady stream files in and out of the building. Nearly two weeks have passed since my abortive stake-out, and my father is still lost in Tokyo. Could be a distant suburb, could be that guy reading the sports pages on the next table. Lao Tzu is two stools along, plugged into his nutty game.

'Hi.' The waitress with the most perfect neck holds a coffee jug. 'Refill?'

'No more money, I'm afraid.'

'On the house. Payment in kind for security services rendered.'

'Then I would love a refill. Thank you.'

She pours. I watch. She asks, 'How is your head?'

I lean on my elbow and cover my throat to hide my lovebite. 'Fine.'

'Anything else?'

'Anything else?'

'Another muffin? I'll pay for it.'

'What I would love, if you wouldn't, uh, mind' – my pain makes me braver than I would normally dream of being – 'is your name.'

Her cautious smile takes a moment to arrive. 'Ai Imajō.'

'Ai Imajō.' What a cool name.

'And yours?'

'Eiji Miyake.' Not so cool.

'Eiji Miyake,' says Ai Imajō, and I feel loads, loads better. She studies the bash on my forehead. 'Doesn't it hurt like crazy when you head-butt somebody?'

'Not if you know what you're doing. Apparently.'

'So you don't go around head-butting people every day?'

'That was my first head-butt.'

'An historic occasion.' The intersection lights go green and the traffic buzzes and swarms into the haze. 'Where else have I seen you, Eiji Miyake?'

'The day of the storm. Two weeks ago. You thought I was – well, I was, I suppose – listening in to your phone call. At the end of your shift. I was sitting here for a couple of hours.'

'Yeah.' Ai Imajō thinks back, nodding. 'I remember.'

'Blasted, blasted, *blasted* bioborgs!' Lao Tzu swears at the vidboy3.

'I'm on my break. Mind if I sit here?'

Do I mind? 'Sure.' And to my joy and mortification – I am so cacked up from a night with a stranger in a love hotel – the girl with the most perfect neck in creation is sitting beside me. 'So,' she says. 'Did you meet up with whoever?'

'Who?'

'Whoever you were waiting for, on the day of the storm.'

'No. Not yet.'

'Girlfriend?'

I work from the abridged version and leapfrog Akiko Katō. 'Relative.'

'How long have you been looking?'

'Three weeks . . .'

'Three weeks since you arrived in Tokyo?'

'How do you know?'

Her cheeks dome and her eyes crescent. I love smiles like this. 'Your accent. You'll lose it in six months. Where are you from?'

'You won't have heard of where I'm from.'

'Try me.'

'Yakushima. An island off—'

'—Southern Kyūshū where the Jomōn cedars grow, the oldest living things in the eastern hemisphere. So how are you finding Tokyo, this difficult town?'

Tokyo, this difficult town. How cool is that? 'Full of surprises. Sometimes lonely. Mostly weird. I can't walk in a straight line. I keep bumping into people.'

'You have to stop thinking about walking. Like catching food in your mouth – think about it, you miss. How do you know your relative passes by here?'

'I don't, really. I don't even know what he looks like.'

'Is he a distant relative?'

'I wouldn't want to bore you.'

'Do I sound bored? Why not look in the telephone book?'

'Dunno his name, even.'

Ai Imajō frowns. 'And does he know your name?'

'Yes.'

'Place an ad in the personal columns. "Relatives of Eiji Miyake

– please contact this PO box." That kind of thing. Most Tokyoites read the same three or four newspapers. Your relative might not read it himself, but somebody else might. You're looking dubious.'

I think hard.

Ai Imajō studies me. 'What?'

Oh, I love being studied by Ai Imajō. 'I have no idea.'

That smile again, mixed with confusion. 'I have no idea what?'

'No idea why am I so stupid I never thought of that. Which newspapers?'

'O Wild Man of Kyūshū,' says Buntarō back at Shooting Star, 'your eyes are a pair of piss-holes in the snow.' My landlord is eating a blueberry-blooded ice lolly. On the video screen a man in a black suit walks through a desert. A bottleneck guitar swirls with the tumbleweed. The black suit needs a dry clean and the man needs a shave and a shower. 'Morning. What's the movie?'

'*Paris, Texas*, by Wim Wenders.' Buntarō piles in the last of the ice lolly before it collapses down his hand. I watch for a while longer. Not much happens in Paris, Texas. 'Sort of slow, isn't it?'

Buntarō licks his hand. 'This, lad, is an existentialist classic. Man with no memory meets woman with huge hooters. So. How was your night? No memory or huge hooters? You can't fool me, y'know. I was young myself, once. You are a quick worker, though, I got to grant you that. Two weeks in the big bad city and already chasing the more fragrant sex.'

'I sort of ran into friends.'

'Yeah, yeah. Speaking of friends, I saw a monster cockroach earlier.'

'Take it up with my landlord.'

'Seriously, I thought it was a hairless rat. Then it twitched its antlers. I tried to splat it, but it took off and flew up the stairs. Vanished under your door quicker than you could say "In the name of all that is holy, what *is* that thing?" Maybe your starving moggy ate it. Maybe it ate your starving moggy.'

'I fed my starving moggy before I went out.' Good to see Buntarō getting used to the idea of Cat living in my capsule.

'Aha! So your tryst was planned!'

My head throbs. 'Leave me alone,' I beg. 'Please.'

'Was I knocking you? Empty what's full, fill what's empty, scratch what itches. The three keys to harmony. But what *is* that unidentified red patch covering your throat?'

Attack is defence. 'Your trouser flies are way open.'

'Who cares? The dead bird does not leave the nest.'

'The bird can't be that dead. Look at your wife.'

'The bird is dead. Look at my wife.'

'Huh?'

'You'll see what I mean one day, my boy.'

I'm about to go upstairs when three high-school boys march in. The leader asks me: 'You got *Virtua Sapiens*?'

'Never heard of it,' says Buntarō. 'The sequel of *Homo*?'

'You what?'

'It's a video game,' I explain. 'Out last week.'

The second-in-command ignores me. 'Got *Broadsword of Zyqorum*, then?'

'No software. All videos.'

'Told yer!' says the leader, and they troop out.

'You're welcome, lads.' Buntarō watches them go. 'Y'know, Miyake, I have it on reliable authority – *Baby and You*, no less – that the average Japanese father spends seventeen minutes per day with his sprog. The average schoolboy spends ninety-five minutes per day inside video games. A new generation of electronic daddies. When Kōdai is born, he is getting his bedtime stories from his parents, not from sicko druggo psycho freako programmers. I'm already getting my big fat "No" for when Kōdai comes running for a video game machine thing.'

'What if he comes running in tears because none of the kids in his class will talk to him because his daddy's too mean to buy him a game system?'

'I—' Buntarō frowns. 'I never thought of that. What did your dad do?'

'He was in another part of the country.'

'What about your mum, then?'

One little lie leads to another. 'I had my soccer club. Anyway, I need to, uh, get cleaned up.' I climb up to my capsule, shower – by the time I towel myself dry I am sweaty enough for another shower – and unroll my futon. Sleep is not coming. Ai Imajō keeps floating up. Her supple neck, her smile. She says my name. I get up and try to do some bottleneck guitar chords, but my fingers are rusty. I check the cockroach motel. Only one guest – a baby. Cockroach has spread the word about motel hospitality. Cat comes back and laps her water dish dry. I fill it up, but she laps that dry too.

Later I go out to buy the *Tokyo Evening Mail*. I take the submarine into Ueno, and find a quiet place in the park to fill out the classified ad box. I make several false starts – it is crucial that I don't write anything that will provoke my stepmother or make it look like I want money. Finally I'm satisfied with Plan C: a short, simple message. I'll post it tomorrow during my lunch break. I suck a champagne bomb. Ueno park is full of families, kids, couples, old people, rings of foreigners – Brazilians maybe, Chinese, each nationality on its own patch of territory. Museum-goers, photographers, skateboarders. Cicadas in the trees, babies under the trees, a funfair through the trees. Oily pigeons. Velocodrome motorbikes rip around the far perimeter. The air is candy floss, incense, zoo and octopus-dumpling-flavoured. I walk down to Shinobazu pond to watch people feed the ducks. I lie down against a tree and put *Mind Games* on my Discman. It is the hottest afternoon in the history of September. I watch clouds. Here comes Picture Lady, arguing with an invisible companion. I wonder if I will ever find the guts to ask Ai Imajō out on a date. I watch a young woman feeding the ducks bread crusts from a paper bag. She has a stack of library books on her bench. I drowse. The woman wheels her bicycle over, as if she wants to talk to me. She studies my face. I press 'Stop' on my Discman and park noises flood back. 'No,' she finally says, 'this is not just one of those coincidences.'

'I'm sorry?'

She shakes her head in disgusted disbelief. 'Daimon is spying on me.'

I prop myself up. 'Who are you?'

She sets her face hard. 'I do not need this shit.'

Uh?

Her finger curses me as she hisses. 'Tell him to go fuck himself! Tell him to sell his elopement fantasies to his squeaky schoolgirls! Tell him he is worth nothing! Tell him my country stopped being a Japanese colony at the end of the last war! Tell him if he tries to call I'll change my number! Tell him that if he shows his face at my apartment I'll drive a fork into it! Tell Yuzu Daimon to slime away and die! And all of this applies to you, too.'

Ducks honk.

All at once I understand. This woman is Miriam, the hostess at Queen of Spades. The woman who didn't meet Yuzu Daimon at the games centre yesterday evening. The woman I helped Daimon get even with. This is awful. 'I swear,' I begin, 'I . . . I had no idea, I wasn't spying on you just now, I' – ducks flap by – 'I never realized, I mean, this is all a mistake, I had no idea you would be here – how could I? I mean, I don't even know Daimon really—'

First, the sycamore tree blips spokes. Second, it sinks in that she kicked me hard and straight and true, in the balls. Third, I writhe on the ground as acorns of agony shower down around me. Fourth, I hear her voice, cold enough to freeze the pond. 'I know *exactly* who you are, Eiji Miyake. You are a leech who tells lies for a living. Exactly like your father.' She walks to her bike. I try to ignore the pain and replay her last line. 'Wait!' She is already cycling away. I wobble to my feet. 'Wait!' She is pedalling away, over the causeway between the duck-pond and the boating lake. I try to run but the pain takes my breath away. 'Miriam! Wait!' Mothers with pushchairs turn to look, a bunch of motorbike kids watch and laugh. Even the ducks laugh. '*Miriam!*' I crouch down, defeated, and watch her disappear into mirages and spray from the fountains. She knows my father! I want to feel hope but I want to bawl with frustration. I hobble back to my stuff, where I find one thing more, lying in the dust between the roots of the sycamore. A library book which fell when Miriam crippled me. What book is it? I can't read a word – it is in Korean.

In the Shibuya back streets I am lost in no time. Yesterday and this afternoon seem weeks apart. This grid of narrow streets and bright shadows, and the pink quarter of last night, seem to be different cities. Cats and crows pick through piles of trash. Brewery trucks reverse around corners. Water spatters from overflow pipes. Shibuya's night zone is drowsing, like a hackneyed comedian between acts. My eyes begin to get lost in the signboards – Wild Orchid, Yamato Nadeshiko, Mac's, Dickens, Yumi-chan's. Even if I happened to find Queen of Spades, search fatigue would probably stop me seeing. I left Shooting Star without my watch, and I have no idea how fast the afternoon is passing. My feet are aching and I taste dust. So hot. I fan myself with my baseball cap. It makes no difference. An old mama-san waters marigolds in her third-storey window box. When I look back at her she is still watching me, absently.

The phone booth is a safari of porn and smells of never-washed trousers. You don't need to buy sex mangas in Tokyo – just find the nearest callbox. Me and my cousins would have saved a fortune. All the shapes and sizes I ever imagined, and lots of others, too. Threesomes, foursomes, S&M, high-school revue, special silver service for octogenarians. 'Directory enquiries,' answers a woman. 'What city, please?'

'Tokyo.'

'What area, please?'

'Shibuya.'

'And the name, please?'

Miss Manilla Sunrise pouts over two beachballs. No, surely—

'Name, please?'

—they *can't* actually be her actual—

'Name, please!'

'Uh, sorry. I'm trying to track down a bar. Queen of Spades.'

'Queen of Spades . . . one moment, please.' Keyboard taps.

Miss Whippy Cream licks the froth off her stilettos.

Keyboard taps. 'Queens of England . . . Queer Sauna . . . sorry. Nothing.'

'Are you sure? It was there last night. Could it be a new number?'

Mrs Mop rides a broom, speech ballooning: 'In! Out! Shake it all about!'

'New numbers are added to the computer as they are registered.'

'So if Queen of Spades isn't on your computer . . .'

'Then it must be ex-directory.'

Weird. 'What kind of bar wants to hide its telephone number?'

'A very exclusive one, I imagine. Sorry, but I can't help you.'

'Oh well. Thanks for trying.'

I hang up. One big card is handwritten in childish letters. It has no telephone number. 'If you want sex with me, I'm standing outside.' I look around. She looks right at me through the glass. Sixteen? Fifteen? Fourteen? Her eyes have a damaged look. She presses her lips softly against the glass. I scuttle away, faster than Cockroach.

The police box door is stiff. I have to grind it open. Ancient Aum Shinrikyō wanted posters, Dial 110 posters, Join-the-Police-and-Serve-Japan posters. I'll pass, thanks. Filing cabinets. The same black-and-white clock with the gliding second hand you get in all government buildings. A CitiBank calendar, rustling in the breeze from the paddling fan. The cop is tilted back with his hands behind his head, deep in meditation. One eyelid rises. 'Son?'

'Excuse me. I'm looking for a bar.'

'You're looking for a bar?' His words leak from the side of his mouth.

'Yes.'

'Will any bar do? Or does it have to be one bar in particular?'

'I'm looking for one bar in particular.'

'You're looking for one bar in particular.'

'Yes.'

A sigh as long as the end of the world. The other eyelid rises. Two bloodshot eyeballs. A long silence. He leans forward, his chair screeches, and he slowly unfolds a map on the desk. Upside down. 'Name?'

'Eiji Miyake.'

A long stare. 'Not your name, genius. The name of the bar.'

'Uh, sorry. Queen of Spades.'

The cop focuses and darkens. 'You are a member of this bar?'

I swallow. 'Not exactly. I went there last night.'

He frowns as if I am being evasive. 'Somebody took you?'

I nod. 'Yeah.'

He peers at me from another angle. 'And you want to go back? Why?'

'I need to speak to a sort of . . . friend who works there.'

'You need to speak to a sort of friend who works there. How old exactly did you say you are?'

'I, uh, didn't.'

'I know you didn't, genius. That is why I asked. How old are you?'

What is this about? 'I'm twenty.'

'ID.'

Nervously, I open my wallet and hand over my driving licence. The cop scrutinizes it. 'Eiji Miyake, resident of Kagoshima prefecture. In Tokyo to work?' I nod. He reads. 'Date of birth, 9th September. You were twenty yesterday, correct?'

'Correct.'

'So upon visiting said bar you were under the minimum drinking age. Correct?'

'I went to Queen of Spades yesterday. On my birthday.'

'You went to said bar yesterday. On your birthday.'

'All I want is the address of this place, Officer.'

He searches my face for clues for a long time. Eventually he hands back my licence. 'Then all I can suggest is you obtain said address by calling said sort of friend. Queen of Spades is not listed on any map of mine.' The end. I bow and leave, struggling to slide the door shut as he memorizes my face.

I admit defeat. My legs are about to unscrew and fall off. I explored every street and alley in Shibuya, twice at least, but Queen of Spades is no longer here. I buy a can of Calpis and a packet of Seven Stars and sit down on a step. Could I find Daimon back at the pool hall? No. He will avoid the place for a long time, to avoid me. If only Miriam had said she knew my father last night. How did she know my name? Because Daimon mentioned it several times. 'Miyake' is pretty common, though. Daimon signed me in, and she must have seen the weird kanji for 'Eiji'. My father must have talked about me. I swig from my can and light a Seven Star. My father moves in these exclusive club circles – about the only thing I know about him is his wealth. I imagine smoke swirling in my lungs, dust in sunny mine shafts. Bumping into Miriam at Shinobazu pond – not so outlandish, really. She feeds ducks – how many places are there where you can feed ducks in Tokyo? I balance my cigarette on the lip of the can and flick through Miriam's dropped library book. Wow. Being kicked in the balls by the same woman who hostesses my father. No. Something is too wrong. All these coincidences are too weird. Even so. Finding where they join into an explanation is a sort of Plan D. I wonder if my father is a womanizer, like Daimon's father seems to be. I always imagined him as a sort of faithful adulterer. Still, I am here to meet him, not judge him. The cigarette rolls off the can, which, all on its own, has begun to vibrate, wobble, and . . .

. . . fall over, the ground groans, windows sing, buildings shake, shit, *I* shake, adrenalin seeps, a million sentences drop dead, elevators die, millions more Tokyoites dive under tables and into doorways – I curl into a sort of ball, already flinching under the mass of the falling masonry – and the whole city and I hurl up shining prayers to anyone – *anyone* – God, gods, kami, ancestors – who might be listening: stop this stop this stop this *now*, please, please, please, don't let this be the big one, not the big one, not today, not now, not another Kobe, not another 1923, not today, not here. Calpis runs in a delta over the thirsty sidewalk. Buntarō told me you get vertically oscillating earthquakes and horizontally oscillating ones. Horizontal ones are okay. Vertical ones floor cities. But how do you tell one from the other? Who cares – just *stop*!

The earthquake stops.

I uncrouch, newborn and dumb, not believing it quite yet. Silence. Breathe. Relief rains down from heaven. People switch on their radios to find out if it was just a local snore or if Yokohama or Nagoya has been rubbled off the map of Japan. I right my can and light another cigarette. Then I see something else I can't trust myself to believe quite yet. Across the road from my step is the entrance to a passageway. The passageway runs into the building and ends at an elevator. Next to the elevator is a signboard. On the signboard, next to #9, two trapezoid eyes stare straight back at me. I know those eyes. The eyes of the queen of spades.

The elevator doors open with a bronze gong. A bucket of soapy water stands beside the projector. A woman in dungarees is cleaning tiny holes in the planetarium with a cocktail stick. She glances at me from her stepladder. 'We open at nine, I'm afraid, sir.' Then she sees how scuzzy my clothes are. 'Not another mobile phone sales geek, *please*.' So I skip the pleasantries too. 'I was hoping I could have a quick word with Miriam.'

I am scanned. 'Who are you exactly?'

'My name is Miyake. I was here last night with Yuzu Daimon.

Miriam was our hostess. I just need to ask her one question. Then I'll go.'

The woman shakes her head. 'I think you'll go right now, actually.'

'Please. I'm not a psycho or anything. Please.'

'Miriam isn't working tonight, anyway.'

'Could I just have her telephone number?'

She cocktail-sticks a hole. 'What is this question of yours?'

'A personal one.'

I have never been so looked at until today. She jerks her thumb towards the curtain door. 'You'd better ask Shiyori.'

I thank her and make my way through to the smoking chamber. The tapestries are rolled up and sunlight leans against the windows in solid bars. Women in T-shirts and jeans sit around slurping sōmen. A mechanical parrot is being operated upon by a fragile lady. When I enter, all conversation stops. 'Yeah?' asks one of the girls.

'The girl in the entrance told me to ask for Shiyori.'

'That's me.' She pours herself some oolong tea. 'What do you want?'

'I need to speak with Miriam.'

'She isn't working today.'

Another girl rearranges her chopsticks. 'You were here last night. One of Yuzu Daimon's guests.'

'Yes.'

The vibes go from indifference to hostility. Shiyori washes out her mouth with tea. 'So he sent you over to see how his little prank went down, did he?' 'I don't understand,' says another, 'how he gets a kick out of the way he treats her.' Another girl chews a chopstick blunt. 'The way I see it, if you think Miriam is going to want to be in the same room as you, you are demented.'

'I had no idea there was anything between them.'

'Then you are blind as well as demented.'

'Fine. I am blind as well as demented. But please, I have to speak to Miriam about something.'

'What is so urgent exactly?'

'I can't talk about it. Something she said.'

The women fall quiet as the parrot woman puts down a tiny screwdriver. 'If you wish to speak with Miriam, you need to become a member of this club.' I realize she is the mama-san from last night. 'Prospective members must collect nine nominations from existing members, excluding Yuzu Daimon, who is now barred. The application fee is three million yen – non-returnable. If the selection committee approves your application, the first annual payment is nine million yen. Upon receipt of this, you are free to ask Miriam anything you wish. In the meantime, tell Yuzu Daimon he would be wise to leave the city for a long time. Mr Morino is most displeased.'

'Could I just leave a note for—'

'No. You can just leave.'

I open my mouth—

'I said, you can just leave.'

Now what?

'Masanobu Suga?' The receptionist at Imperial University looks blank. 'A student? But it's four in the afternoon on Sunday! He'll probably be having breakfast.'

'He's a postgraduate. Computers.'

'In that case he won't have got out of bed yet.'

'I think he has a room on the ninth floor.'

I see her colleague lean over and mouth, 'Flaky.'

'Oh! Him. Yeah. Go on up. Nine-eighteen.'

Another elevator. The doors open at the third floor, and some students get in. I feel as though I am an enemy intruder. They carry on their conversation. I imagined students only ever talked about philosophy, engineering and whether love is something sacred or merely sexual programming: they are discussing the best way of getting past the hydra on *Zax Omega and Red Plague Moon*. So this is where the top stream in my high school were bound. I summon the courage to tell the students to attack the hydra with the flamethrower, but the doors open for the ninth floor. I always thought universities were wide and flat. In Tokyo they are tall and thin. The corridor is deserted. I walk up and down a few times, trying to work out how the room numbers work. Perhaps this is a part of the entrance examination. Finally I see 'Masanobu Suga. Abandon hope, all Microsofters who enter here.' I knock. 'Enter!' I push the door open. The air pongs of armpit, and the Doraemon bedspread over the window keeps the room as dank and dark as one. Bongo drums, manuals, magazines, computer equipment, the boxes they came in, a Zizzi Hikaru poster, a pot containing a stump, a complete set of manga entitled 'Vulvavaders from Cloud Nine', a pile of dead cup ramen packs, and a mountain range of paper files. At Ueno lost property Suga was forever harping on about paperless offices. The man himself is in the corner, hunched over his keyboard. Tappety-tap-tap-tap-tappety-beepety-beep-beep-beep. 'Shit!' He swivels around and peers at his visitor. Then he tries to access my face and name, even though only nine days have passed since Suga quit Ueno. 'Miyake!'

'You said I could come and see you some time.'

Suga frowns. 'But I never thought you actually would . . . How is the lost property business? Mrs Sasaki still freezing the ground beneath her feet? And did you see Aoyama's final dive on TV? It was all over the news until that high-school kid busjacked the holiday coach. See that? Cut the passengers' throats. Goes to show, if you're going to perform a dramatic suicide like Aoyama, schedule it clear of any major news stories.'

'Suga, I came to—'

'You're lucky I'm in. Pull up a chair. You might find one under . . . never mind, sit on that box. I got back from my week at IBM yesterday. You should see their labs! They put me on the helpdesk to wipe the arses of the great unwashed. Deep grief. I wanted to be in R&D to check out the new stuff, right. It took me a few minutes to hatch my escape plan. My first call comes in, this bumpkin from Akita with an accent even thicker than yours, no offence. "Oim having some bovver with my 'puter. Screen went blank." "Oh dear, sir. Can you see the cursor?" "You wot?" "The little arrow, sir, that tells you where you are." "Don't see no arrow. Don't see nuffin. Screen went blank, I tell yer." "I see, sir. Is there a power indicator on your monitor?" "On me wot?" "On your monitor, sir. The TV. Does it have a little 'On' light?" "No light, no nuffin." "Sir, is the TV plugged into the wall?" "No idea, can't see nuffin, I tell yer." "Not even if you crane your head around, sir?" "How could I? It be as black as night in here, oim tellin yer." "Maybe it would help if you turned the lights on, sir?" "Oi tried, but they won't come on – the electric company are testing the wotsits, and there won't be no power until three o'clock." "I see, sir. Well, I have good news." "You do?" "Yes, sir. Do you still have the boxes the computer came in?" "Oi never throw nuffin away." "Splendid, sir. I want you to pack your computer up and take it back to the shop you bought it from." "Is the problem that serious, then?" "I'm afraid it is, sir." "Wot do I tell 'em at the shop, then?" "Are you listening carefully, sir?" "Oi am." "*Tell them you're too much of a shit-for-brains to own a computer!*" And then I hang up.'

'That was your escape plan?'

'I know my calls are monitored by the drongo in charge of me, right. Plus, I know they know I'm too valuable to chop. So the supervisor agreed my talents might be more profitably employed in another department. I suggested R&D, and off I went. Miyake, what is that thing you're carrying?'

'A pineapple.'

'I thought so. Why are you carrying a pineapple?'

'This is a present.'

'I thought they came in cans. Who are you giving a live pineapple to?'

'You.'

'Me?' Suga is mystified. 'What do you do with them?'

'People slice them into chunks with a knife, and, uh . . . eat them.'

Suga suddenly beams. 'Hey, thanks. I forgot lunch. Guess where

I am?' He nods at his computer, and pulls a beer free from its six-pack – I shake my head. 'French Nuclear Energy. Their anti-hacking tech is Iron Age.'

'I thought your Holy Grail was in the Pentagon.'

'Oh, shit.' Suga hiss-pisses beer everywhere. 'It is. The French are zombies.'

'Zombies? I know their Pacific nuclear tests suck, but—'

Suga shakes his head. 'Zombies. No hacker worth his silicon ever hacks directly. We hack into a zombie computer, and go fishing from there. Often, we zombify another zombie via the first. The hotter the target, the longer the zombie conga.'

Time to get to the point. 'I have a favour to ask. A delicate one.'

'What do you want me to hack into?'

He looks at me as he swigs his beer. I realize there is a whole lot more to Suga than I judged. I judge people too fast. I get out the library book that Miriam dropped in the park. 'This might be a tall order, Suga, but could you get into a Tokyo library computer and look up the address of the person who is borrowing this book?'

Suga wipes away the beer froth. 'You must be joking.'

'Can you do it?'

'Can I piss straight when I waz?'

Miriam's Korean name is Kang Hyo Yeoun. She is twenty-five, and has three books on loan from the library service. I take an overland train to her apartment in Funabashi. It is a run-down neighbourhood, but sort of friendly. Everything needs a new coat of paint. I ask a woman who works in a cake shop next to the station where I can find Miriam's address, and she draws me a map and says goodbye with a crafty wink. I walk past a long row of bicycle stalls, turn a corner and there is the sea, for the first time in a month. Tokyo bay sea air has a petrol tang. Cargo ships lie berthed, loaded and unloaded by cranes with four legs and llama necks. Fiery weeds sprout from wrinkled tarmac. A yakiniku restaurant smokes the evening with meat and charcoal. A garage band rehearse a song called 'Sonic Genocide'. A taxi driver stands in a corner of the quay, rehearsing his golf swing, watching imaginary holes-in-one land in the calm evening. A window-grilled pawnshop, a bright curry shop, a laundromat, a liquor store, a gateball ground, and Miriam's apartment building. It is an old three-storey affair. I smoke a Seven Star in a record few drags. The first floor has already been abandoned. The metal stairs jangle as I climb up. One decent typhoon and the whole structure would be blown clean across Hokkaido. Here it is: 303.

Her face appears in the gloom above the door chain.

She slams the door.

I hammer, embarrassed. I crouch down to speak through the letterbox. 'I brought your library book. You dropped it in the park. This is nothing to do with Daimon. Miriam, I don't even know him! Please.' No reply. A dog with its head in a lampshade walks past. Its overweight owner is several paces behind, panting. He scowls, daring me to laugh. 'Bob had his bollocks lopped off. The restraint is to stop him licking where he shouldn't.' He unlocks the apartment next to Miriam's and disappears. Miriam's door opens. She is smoking. I am still crouched down. The door chain is still on. 'Here is your book.'

She takes it. Then she silently judges me.

'You gave Daimon my message?'

'I tried to tell you, I don't know Daimon.'

She shakes her head in frustration. 'Why do you keep saying that? If Daimon didn't send you, how did you know where to come?'

'I got your address from the library.'

She accepts this without me needing to explain the illegal part. 'And so you returned my book from the kindness of your heart?'

'No.'

'So what do you want now?'

She shifts, and reflected amber light catches the side of her face. I understand why Daimon fell in love with her. I don't understand anything else. 'Do you really know who my father is?'

'What?'

'In Ueno park, you talked about my father as if you know him.'

'He's a regular at the club! Of course I know him.'

I swallow. 'What is his name?'

She is half irritated, half confused. 'Your father is Yuzu Daimon's father.'

Plan C buckles right down its crumple zone. 'He told you that?' Oh, it all falls into place now. 'Plan' was a fat name for a skinny little lie.

'He signed you into Queen of Spades as his stepbrother. His father – your father – keeps a couple of mistresses at any one time, so you aren't the first one.'

I look away, hardly able to believe this. No, this is all too easy to believe.

Miriam probes. 'Was that all Daimon bullshit?' My father rejoins the unknown millions. I don't answer her. She sort of yowls. 'That selfish, stupid jerk. Just to get back at me . . . Listen, Eiji Miyake. Look at me!' She stubs out her cigarette. 'Queen of Spades is not . . . an ordinary place. If you ever go back there, bad things could happen to you. Oh, hell. This could be very bad. By admitting you, Daimon . . . well, he broke a pretty major rule. Normally, male guests are blood relatives only. Listen to me. Do not go back there, and do not come back here, ever. Steer clear of Shibuya, in fact. This is fair warning. Understand?'

No, I don't really understand, but she closes the door anyway. It is the last moment of the day. The sunset would be beautiful, if I were in the mood. A dying SF movie sun sits on a Warner Cinema multiplex. I wonder what metro line takes you to that sort of sunset, and what station you need to get off at. I amble back the way I came and find a games centre. Inside are a whole row of full-sized *2084* machines, doing brisk business with schoolkids. Today has been a bad day. I change a thousand-yen note into hundred-yen coins.

♋

Photon fire bursts around me, and my final comrade falls. I get the prison guard in my sights and fricassé him. The last echo dies. Eerie silence. Is the shooting finally over? Eight stages since the red door. The metal walkway clanks as I walk over the pile of guards and fallen rebels. It is down to me. Here is the prison door. 'Prisoner Ned Ludd. Crime: Cyber-Terrorism. Sentence: Life Incarceration. Security Access: Orange.' Inside is my father, the man who will free humanity from the tyranny of OuterNet. The revolution to reverse reality starts now. I fire the 'Open' pad, and the door slides sideways. I enter the cell. Darkness. The door slides shut and the lights come on. OuterNet intelligence officers! With old-fashioned revolvers? I open fire, but my photon gun is dead. The whole cell is a dampening field. Somewhere I took the wrong turn. Somewhere I failed to read the sign. Before my eyes, my 'Energy' bar shrinks to .01. I cannot move. I cannot even stand. A man – I recognize him, he is the farmer from the soya farm during my waking hours – walks over, loosening his tie. 'My name Agent K00996363E. The revelation is this, Player I8192727I. Ned Ludd is a project created by OuterNet to detect antiGame tendencies among players, and assess their potential danger to OuterNet. Your susceptibility to indoctrination by our provocateurs is evidence of defective wetprogramming. The very idea that ideology can ever defeat the image is itself insanity. OuterNet will reprocess your wetware, in accordance with Propagation of Game Law 972HIJ. This grieves me, I81, but it is for your own good.' He brings his face up close. It is not hateful. It is tender and forgiving. 'Game over.'

Four

Reclaimed Land

So this is how I die, minutes after midnight on reclaimed land somewhere south of Tokyo bay. I sneeze, and the swelling in my right eye throbs and nearly ruptures. Sunday, 17th September. I cannot call my death unexpected. Not after the last twelve hours. Since Anju showed me what death was, I have glimpsed it waiting in trains, in elevators, on pharmacist's shelves. Growing up, I saw it booming off the ocean rocks on Yakushima. Always at some distance. Now it has thrown off its disguise, as it does in nightmares. I am here, this is real. A waking nightmare from which I will never wake up. Splayed on my back, far from anyone who knows me, my life bar at zero. My body is racked and I am running a temperature as high as this bridge. The sky is spilling with stars, night flights and satellites. What a murky, gritty, pointless, unlikely, premature, snot-sprayed way to die it has been. One bad, sad gamble that was rigged from the beginning. Very nearly my last thought is that if this whole aimless story is to go on, God the vivisectionist is going to need a new monkey for his experiments. So many stars. What are they for?

Wednesday afternoon, I go to the bank near Ueno station to pay for my ads in the personal columns. The bank is a ten-minute walk down Asakusa Avenue, so I borrow an orphaned bike – the company car of the lost property office. It is too decrepit for anybody to ever want to steal, but saves my lunch break nearly a quarter-of-an-hour walk down a busy road hot with fumes and the dying summer. No shade in Tokyo, and all the concrete stores the heat. I park the bike outside and go in – the bank is busy with lunch-time, and burbling with a million bank noises. Drones, telephones, computer printers, paper, automatic doors, murmurs, a bored baby. Using an ATM to pay for Plan D is cheaper as long as I don't make a single mistake typing in the long string of digits, otherwise my money will go flying into the wrong account. I am taking my time. A virtual bank teller on the screen bows, hands clasped over her skirt. 'Please wait. Transaction being processed.' I wait, and read the stuff about lost cards and cheap credit. When I next look at the virtual bank teller she is saying something new. I gag on disbelief. 'Father will see you shortly, Eiji Miyake.' I treble-check – the message is still there. I look around. Somebody must own this practical joke. A bank teller stands at the head of the row of machines to help people in difficulty, and she sees the look on my face and hurries over. She has the same uniform and expression as her virtual co-worker. I just point dumbly at the screen. She traces her finger across the screen. 'Yes, sir. The transaction is now processed. This is your card, and don't forget to keep your receipt safe and sound.'

'But look at the message!'

She has a Minnie Mouse voice. '"Transaction completed. Please take your card and receipt." No problem here, sir.'

I look at the screen. She is right. 'There was another message,' I insist. I look around for a practical joker. 'A message with my name on it.'

Her smile tightens. 'That would be most irregular, sir.'

People in the queue are tuning in. I flap. 'I know how irregular it is! Why else do you think I . . .' A uniform in a yellow armband arrives on the scene. He is only a couple of years older than me but he is already Captain Smug, Samurai of Corporate Finance. 'Thank you, Mrs Wakayama.' He dismisses his underling. 'I am the duty manager, sir. What seems to be the trouble?'

'I just transferred some money—'

'Did the machine malfunction in any way?'

'A message flashed up on the screen. A personal message. For me.'

'What leads you to conclude the message was for you, may I ask, sir?'

'It had my name.'

Captain Smug puts on this troubled frown from a training seminar. 'What did this "message" say exactly, "sir"?'

'It told me my father wanted to see me.'

I feel housewives in the queue bristle with curiosity and turn to one another. Captain Smug does a passable imitation of a doctor humouring a lunatic. 'I think it might be more than possible that our machine uses characters that may be somewhat tricky to read.'

'I don't work in a bank but I can read, thank you.'

'But of course.' Captain Smug eyes my work overalls. He scratches the back of his neck to show he is embarrassed. He glances at his watch to show I am embarrassing. 'All I am saying is that either some misunderstanding has occurred here, or you just witnessed a phenonemon which has never before occurred in the history of Tokyo Bank, nor, so far as I am aware, in the history of Japanese banking.'

I put my card back into my wallet and cycle back to Ueno station. I am so on edge all afternoon that Mrs Sasaki asks what the matter is. I lie about feeling feverish, so she gives me some medicine. During my tea break I use the ATM in the station which gives balance statements but which does not take payments. Nothing unusual happens. I search the faces of lost property customers for knowing glints. Nothing. I wonder if Suga did it. But Suga doesn't know about my father. Nobody in Tokyo knows about my father. Except my father.

Riding the submarine back to Kita Senju, I look around. Paranoia, but. No drone catches my eye, only a little girl. Walking back from the station, I catch myself looking in the road mirrors for stalkers. In the supermarket I buy a fifty-per-cent-off okonomiyaki and some milk for Cat. 'Buntarō,' I think while I queue. I got my capsule because a relative of my guitar teacher in Kagoshima knows a friend of Buntarō's wife – could he have found out about my father? But what sort of video shop owner is powerful enough to use ATM screens as a personal telegram system? Some sort of unholy alliance between Suga and Buntarō? I get back to Shooting Star to find my suspect on the phone to his wife, running his hand through his thinning hair. They are talking about kindergartens for Kōdai. He nods at me and makes a nagging goose with his hand. I watch a scene or two from a horror movie called *You Go to My Head*. A cop is on the trail of a psychic killer who discovers his victims' darkest fear, and murders by trapping them in appropriate nightmares. 'I know what you're thinking, lad,' Buntarō says, putting down the receiver. 'Kōdai isn't even born yet. But these places have waiting lists longer than Grateful Dead guitar solos. Get into the right kindergarten, and the conveyor belt goes all the way up to the right university.' He shakes his head, sighing. 'Listen to me. Education Papa. How was your day? You look like you had your bone marrow sucked out.' Buntarō offers me a cigarette and strikes himself off my list of suspects. Unlikely as it seems, the sole remaining candidate is now the likeliest: my father. What are we up to now? Plan E.

On Thursday lunch-time I go back to the same branch of the same bank to try out the ATM again. The same woman is on duty – she avoids eye contact the moment she recognizes me. I insert my card, type in my PIN, and the virtual bank teller bows. Look! '`What dark room has no exits, but only entrances into rooms darker than the one before? Father waits for your answer.`' I search for meaning – is this some sort of warning? I look around for Minnie Mouse, but Captain Smug has been lying in wait for me. 'Another inexplicable message, sir?'

'If this isn't an inexplicable message' – you sarcastic bastard; I rap the screen with my knuckles – 'then give me another name for it.'

'Oh dear, sir, not exactly Bill Gates, are we? Perhaps the message was telling you that you lack the funds necessary to complete your transaction?' Of course, the screen has returned to normal: my pitiful bank balance. I look around – is somebody watching? Erasing the message when a witness comes up? How? 'I know this looks weird,' I begin, not sure how to continue. Captain Smug just raises his eyebrows. 'But somebody is using your ATM to mess your customers around.' Captain Smug waits for me to go on. 'Shouldn't that worry you?' Captain Smug folds his arms and tilts his head at an I-went-to-a-top-Tokyo-university angle. I storm off without another word. I cycle back to the lost property office, as suspicious of parked cars and half-open windows as yesterday. My father was influential enough to have his name left off my and Anju's birth certificates, but surely this is in another league. I spend the rest of the afternoon attaching labels to forgotten umbrellas, and weeding out the ones we have held for twenty-eight days for destruction. Might my stepmother be somehow trying to intimidate me? If it is my father, why is he playing these pranks instead of just calling me? Nothing makes sense.

Friday is pay-day for us probationary employees recruited in the middle of the year. The bank is packed – I have to wait several minutes to get to a machine. Captain Smug hovers in the wings. I pull my baseball cap down low. A woman with ostrich feathers in her hat keeps sneezing over me, and groaning. I insert my card and ask for 14,000 yen. The virtual bank teller smiles, bows, and asks me to wait. So far so normal. `'Father warns you that your breathing space is all used up.'` I am expecting this: from under the visor of my cap I study the queue of impatient people. Who? No clue, no idea. The machine shuttles my money. The virtual bank teller bows again. `'Father is coming for you.'` Come on, then! What else do you think I am in the city for? I drum the the virtual teller with the bases of my fists. 'You aren't from Tokyo, are you, sir?' Captain Smug is at my shoulder. 'I can tell because our Tokyo customers usually have the manners to refrain from assaulting our machines.' 'Look at this! Look!' I show him the screen and curse. What did I expect?

`'Please take your money and remove your card.'` It beeps. I know if I say anything to Captain Smug, or even look at the guy, I will be seized by an urgent desire to make him hurt, and I don't think my cranium could take another head-butt less than seven days since the last. I ignore his vexed sigh, take my money, card and receipt, and walk around the bank lobby for a while, trying to meet stares. Queues, marble floors, number chimes. Nobody looks at anyone in banks. Then I notice Captain Smug talking to a security man, and glancing in my direction. I slink off.

Between the bank and Ueno is the seediest noodle shop in all of Tokyo. As Tokyo has the seediest noodle shops in Japan, this is probably the seediest noodle shop in the world. It is too seedy even to have a name or a definite colour. Suga told me about it – it is as cheap as it should be and you can drink as much iced water as you want, and they have comic book collections going back twenty years. I park my bike in the alley around the side, smell burnt tar through the fan outlet, and walk in through the strings of beads. Inside is murky and fly-blown. Four builders sit around four greasy bowls in silence. The cook is an old man who died several days ago. The single round light is dappled with the bodies of dead insects, and the walls are decorated with spatters and dribbles of grease. A TV runs an old black-and-white Yakuza movie, but nobody watches it. A gangster is chucked into a concrete mixer. Fans turn their heads, this way and that. With a shudder, the cook reanimates his corpse and sits up. 'What can I do for you, son?' I order a tempura-egg-onion soba, and take a stool at the counter. Today, the message said. This time tomorrow I will know everything – whether this Plan E is the true lead, or whether it is yet another dud. I must keep a lid firmly on my hopes. My hopes boil over. Who else could it be, but my father? My noodles come. I sprinkle on some chilli pepper and watch it spread among the jellyfish of grease. Tasted better, tasted worse.

Outside in the glare, the bike is missing. A black Cadillac takes up the side alley, the sort that the FBI use for presidential missions. The passenger door inches open and a lizard pokes his head out – short, spiky, white hair, eyes too far apart that can do 270-degree vision. 'Looking for anything?' I turn my baseball cap around to shade my eyes. Lizard leans on the Cadillac roof. He is about my age. A dragon tail disappears up one arm of his short-sleeved snakeskin shirt, and a dragon head twists out of the other.

'My bike.'

Lizard says something to somebody in the Cadillac. The driver's door opens, and a man in sunglasses with a Frankenstein scar down the side of his face gets out, walks around the back of the Cadillac and picks up a mangle of metal. He brings it around to me and hands it to me. 'Is this your bike?' His forearms are more thickly muscled than my legs and his knuckles are chunky with gold. He is so big he blocks out the sun. In shock, I hold the metal for a moment before dropping it.

'It was, yeah.'

Lizard tuts. 'People are such mindless vandals, ain't they?' Frankenstein shunts my ex-bike aside with his foot. 'Get in.' He jerks his thumb at the Cadillac. 'Father sent us to pick you up.'

'*You* came from my father?'

Frankenstein and Lizard find this funny. 'Who else?'

'And did my father tell you to trash my bike?'

Lizard hoicks and spits. 'Get in the car, yer lippy cock-wart, or I'll break both yer fucking arms right here, right now.' Traffic drags its heat and din to the next red light. What choice do I have?

The Cadillac purrs over the Sumida river bridge on air cushions. The tinted windows retune the bright afternoon, and the air-con chills the inside to fridge-beer temperature. I get goose bumps. Frankenstein drives, Lizard is in the back with me, sprawled pop star fashion. I could almost enjoy the ride if I weren't being abducted by Yakuza and if I weren't going to lose my job. Maybe I could find a phone and call Mrs Sasaki to say . . . what? The last thing I want to do is lie to her. Mrs Sasaki is okay. I tell myself these things are trifles – my father has sent for me. This is it. Why am I unable to get excited? Northside Tokyo slides by, block after block after block. Better to be a car than a human. Highways, flyovers, slip roads. A petrochemical plant runs pipes for kilometres, lined by those corkscrewing conifers. A massive car plant. Acre upon acre of white body shells. So my father is some kind of Yakuza man. Makes sense, sort of. Money, power and influence. The white lines and billowing trees and industrial chimneys are dreamlike. The dashboard clock reads 13:23. Mrs Sasaki will be wondering why I am late. 'Any chance I could make a phone call?' Lizard gives me the finger. I push my luck – 'All I—' but Frankenstein turns around and says, 'Shut the fuck up, Miyake! I cannot *stand* whinging children.' My father gives me no status. I should stop guessing, sit back and wait. We pass through a toll-gate. Frankenstein moves into top gear and the Cadillac eats the expressway up: 13:41. The buildings get more residential, and densely pyloned mountains shuffle this way. On the right the sea pencils in the horizon. Lizard yawns and lights a cigarette. He smokes Hope. 'Travelling in style, or what?' says Frankenstein, not to me. 'Know how much one of these babies costs?' Lizard toys with a death-head ring. 'Fuck of a lot.' Frankenstein wets his lips. 'Quarter of a million dollars.' Lizard: 'What's that in real money?' Frankenstein thinks. 'Twenty-two million yen.' Lizard looks at me. 'Hear that, Miyake? If yer pass yer entry exams, slave in an office all yer life, save your bonuses, get reincarnated nine times, yer'll be able to zip around in a Cadillac too.' I stare ahead. 'Miyake! I'm talking to yer!' 'Sorry. I thought I had to shut the fuck up.' Lizard whistles and a switchblade knife hisses open. 'Watch yer lippyliplip' – the knife flashes at my wrist; the blade slices through the casing of my wristwatch and scrapes through its innards – 'fuckhead.' The knife is spinning back in his fingers. Lizard's eyes flare, daring me to open my mouth. He wins his dare and laughs this scratchy, staccato laugh.

*

Xanadu, way out beyond Tokyo bay, is having its grand opening today. Bunting flutters over the expressway exit, a giant Bridgestone airship floats above the enormous dome. The glands in my throat start to throb. Valhalla opens in the new year, and Nirvana and its new airport monorail terminus are still under construction. The traffic slugs to a crawl. Coaches, family wagons, jeeps, sports cars, coaches queue bumper to bumper through the toll-gate. Flags of the world hang limp. An enormous banner reads 'Xanadu Open Today! Family Paradise Here on Earth! Nine-Screen Multiplex! Olympic Pool! Krypton Dance Emporium! Karaoke Beehive! Cuisine Cosmos! California Lido! Neptune Sea Park! Pluto Pachinko! Parking space for 10,000 – yes, 10,000! – automobiles.' A motorbike cop waves us into an access road. 'Cadillacs get you in anywhere.' Lizard stubs out another Hope. 'One of ours,' says Frankenstein as the window slides down. 'The good old days are back. Before your time every fucking cop in the fucking city recognized us.' The Cadillac veers up a slope straight into the sun, tinted by the windscreen into a dark star. Over the top we enter a building site, walled off from Xanadu by a great screen of metal sheeting. Gravel piles, slab stacks, concrete mixers, unplanted trees with roots in sacks. 'Where are all the happy workers?' asks Lizard. 'Holiday for the Grand Opening,' says Frankenstein. Rounding a block of Portakabins comes Valhalla. This is a dazzling black glass pyramid built of triangles rising from building rubble. The Cadillac drives down a ramp into shadow, surfing to a halt in front of a barrier arm. A porter slides open the window of his box. He is about ninety and is either drunk or has Parkinson's disease. Frankenstein's window lowers and Frankenstein glowers. The porter repeatedly salutes and bows. 'Open,' growls Frankenstein, 'fucking sesame.' The arm rises and the porter bows out of sight. 'Where did they dig him up?' asks Lizard. 'The pet sematary?' The Cadillac cruises into the black, reverses and halts. I feel a lurch of excitement. Am I really in the same building as my father?

*

'Out,' says Lizard.

We are in a basement carpark smelling of oil, petrol and breeze blocks. Two Cadillacs are parked alongside ours. My eyes need more time to adjust – it is too dark to see the walls, or anything. Frankenstein pokes me in the small of my back. 'March, cub scout.' I follow him – a ball of dim light flickers on and off. A round window in a swing-door. Beyond is a gloomy service corridor smelling of fresh paint and echoing with our footsteps. 'Hasn't even been built yet and the lighting's already fucked,' notes Lizard. Other corridors run off from this. It occurs to me to be afraid. Nobody knows I am here. Wrong: my father knows. I try to fix landmarks in my memory – right at this fire hose, straight on past this notice-board. Frankenstein halts by a men's toilet. Lizard unlocks it. 'In you go.'

'I don't need the toilet.'

'It wasn't a fucking question.'

'When do I meet my father?'

Lizard smirks. 'We'll tell him how eager yer are.' Frankenstein foots the door open, Lizard clamps my nose and shoves me in – the door is locked before I regain my balance. I am in a white bathroom. The floor tiles, wall tiles, ceiling, fittings, sinks, urinals, cubicle doors – everything is snowblindingly white. No windows, no other exits. The door is metal and unkickdownable. I bang on it a couple of times. 'Hey! How long are you going to leave me in here?'

Behind me a toilet flushes.

'Who's there?'

A cubicle door unbolts and swings open. 'Thought I recognized that voice,' says Yuzu Daimon, doing up his belt. 'What timing. You caught me in mid-dump. So what are you doing in a bad dream like this?'

Yuzu Daimon washes his hands, watching me in the mirror. 'Are you going to answer my question or am I going to get the silent treatment until our prison guard comes along to take me away?'

'You have a nerve.'

He shakes his hands under the dryer but nothing happens, so he dries them on his T-shirt. Its picture shows a cartoon schoolgirl lowering a smoking gun; her speech bubble reads *So that's what it feels like to kill . . . I like it.* 'I get it. You're still sulking about the love hotel.'

'You are going to make one great lawyer.'

'Thanks for the non-compliment.' He turns round. 'Are we going to keep up this period of mourning or are you going to tell me why you are here?'

'My father brought me.'

'And your father is whom?'

'I dunno yet.'

'That seems rather careless of you.'

'Why are you here?'

'To have the shit kicked out of me. You may get to watch.'

'Why? Did you maroon them in a love hotel?'

'Pretty funny, Miyake. It's a long story.'

I look at the door.

'Okay.' Daimon perches on the washbasin. 'Sit on any chair you like.'

There are no chairs. 'I'll stand.'

The toilet cistern stops filling and the silence sighs loudly.

'This is an old-fashioned war of succession tale. Once upon a time there was an ancient despot called Kōnosuke Tsuru. His empire had its roots way back in the Occupation days, in outdoor markets and siphoned-off cigarettes. You don't happen to . . . ?' I shake my head. 'Half a century later Kōnosuke Tsuru had progressed to breakfast meetings with cabinet members. His interests span the Tokyo underworld and the Tokyo overlords, from drugs to construction – a handy portfolio in a country whose leaders' sole remedy for economic slumps is to pour concrete down mountainsides and build suspension bridges to uninhabited islands. But I digress. Kōnosuke's right-hand man was Jun Nagasaki. His left hand man was Ryūtarō Morino. Emperor

Tsuru, Admiral Nagasaki and General Morino. Are you with me so far?'

I give the patronizing slimer a slight nod.

'On his ninety-somethingth birthday Tsuru receives a massive heart attack and an ambulance ride to Shiba-koen hospital. This is February of this year. A delicate time – Morino and Nagasaki were played off against one another by Tsuru as a check on his underlings. Tradition would demand that Tsuru name a successor, but he is a tough old dog and vows to pull through. Nagasaki decides to usher in his manifest destiny seven days later by staging his Pearl Harbor – not against Morino's forces, which are on red alert, but on Tsuru's, which believed themselves to be sacrosanct. Over a hundred key Tsuru men are wiped out in a single night, all within ten minutes. No negotiation, no quarter, no mercy.' Daimon shoots me with his fingers. 'Tsuru himself managed to get himself lugged out of hospital – one rumour says he was battered to death with his own golf clubs, another rumour says he got as far as Singapore, where a relapse caught up with him. He's history. By dawn the throne was Nagasaki's. Any questions from the floor at this point?'

'How do you know all this?'

'Easy. My father is a bent cop in the pay of Nagasaki. Next.'

A blunt answer from a slippery liar. 'What are you doing here?'

'Let me go on. If this was a Yakuza movie, the Tsuru faction survivors would team up with Morino and stage a war of honour. Nagasaki broke the code and must be punished, right? Reality is less exciting. Morino dithers, losing valuable time. The Tsuru survivors work out which way the wind is blowing and surrender to Nagasaki's offer of amnesty. They are promptly killed, but never mind. By May Nagasaki not only has Tsuru's Tokyo operations under his thumb, but the Korean and Triad gangs too. By June he is helping to choose the godfather of the Tokyo governor's grandchild. When Morino sends an ambassador to Nagasaki proposing they divide the kingdom, Nagaski sends the ambassador back minus his arms and legs. By July Nagasaki has the lot, and Morino has sunk to scaring brothel owners for insurance money. Nagasaki is content to watch Morino go extinct, rather than dirty the sole of his boot by stamping on him.'

'Why does none of this make the newspapers?'

'You straight citizens of Japan are living in a movie set, Miyake. You are unpaid extras. The politicos are the actors. But the true directors, the Nagasakis and the Tsurus, you never see. A show is run from the wings, not centre-stage.'

'Are you going to tell me why you ended up here?'

'I fell in love with the girl Morino fell in love with.'

'Miriam.'

Daimon's mask slips and for the first time ever I see his real face. The door bangs open and Lizard appears. 'Are we comfortable, ladies?' He flicks open his knife, spins it, catches it and points it at Daimon. 'You first.' Daimon slides off the washbasin counter, still looking at me, puzzled. Lizard smacks his lips. 'The time has come to kiss yer oh-so-charming face goodbye, Daimon.' Daimon smiles in return. 'Is your dress sense a charity fund-raiser or do you actually believe you look cool?' Lizard smiles back. 'Cute.' As Daimon passes, Lizard whacks Daimon in the windpipe, grabs the back of his head and slams it into the metal door. 'I get such a hard-on from casual violence,' says Lizard. 'Say something cute again.' Daimon picks himself up, bloody-nosed, and stumbles into the corridor. The door is relocked.

Either I am losing my mind or the bathroom walls are bending inwards. Time bends too. My watch is dead so I have no idea how long I have been in here. Cockroach navigates the floor. I cup my hands and drink some water. I play a game I often play to console myself: searching for Anju in my reflection. I often catch sight of her around my eyes. I try this game: concentrate on my mother's face; subtract that face from my own; the remainder should be my father. Could my father be Ryūtarō Morino or Jun Nagasaki? Daimon implied Morino brought us here. But he also implied

Morino is washed up. Too washed up to own a fleet of Cadillacs. I suck a champagne bomb. My throat is sore. Mrs Sasaki will have decided Aoyama was right about me – I am an unreliable dropout. Cockroach reappears. I suck my last champagne bomb. Lizard watches me from the mirror – I jump. 'Here comes the moment you have been waiting for, Miyake. Father will see you now.'

Valhalla is one enormous leisure hotel. When it is completed it will be the plushest in Tokyo. Sugar chandeliers, milky carpets, cream walls, silver fittings. Air-cons are not installed, so the passageways are at the mercy of the sun, and under all this glass I am squeaking with sweat in thirty seconds. Thick smells of carpet underlay and fresh paint. On the far side of the building-site perimeter fence I see the vast dome of Xanadu, courtyards and even a fake river and fake caverns. The windows rob the world outside of all colour. Everything is in wartime newsreel tones. The air is as dry as a desert. Lizard knocks on room 333. 'Father, I got Miyake with me.'

I understand my stupendous mistake. 'Father' does not mean 'my father': 'father' means 'Yakuza father'. I would laugh if the afternoon were not now so dangerous. A voice rasps out a moment later. 'Enter!' The door is unlocked from inside. Eight people sit around a conference table in a spotless meeting room. At the head sits a man in his fifties. 'Sit the infant down.' His voice is as thirsty as sandpaper. Cavernous eye sockets, plump lips, mottled and flaky skin – the sort used on young actors playing old roles – and a wart in the corner of his eye bigger than a strayed nipple. My way-too-late fear was quite correct. If this troll is my father, I am Miffy the Bunny. I take the defendant's chair. I am being prosecuted by a group of dangerous strangers, and I don't even know what the charge is. 'So,' the man says. 'This is Eiji Miyake.'

'Yes. Who are you?'

Death gives me a choice. A point-blank bullet through the brain or a thirty-metre fall. Frankenstein and the stage manager of this black farce are placing bets as to which I will choose right now. Beyond hope is beyond panic. Here comes the Mongolian, strolling up the unfinished bridge. My right eye is so swollen the night swims. Yes, of course I am afraid, and frustrated that my stupid life is ending so soon. But mostly I feel the weight of the nightmare, stopping me waking. I am cattle in a cage, waiting for the bolt through my skull. Why gibber? Why beg? Why try to run when the only escape is a drop through blackness? If my head survived the fall, the rest of my body would not. The Mongolian spits, and folds a fresh strip of gum into his mouth. He pulls out his gun. After Anju I dreamed of drowning several times a week, right up until I got my guitar. In those dreams I handled fear by ceasing to struggle, and I do the same now. I have less than forty seconds. I unfold the photo of my father one last time. Dad is still uncreased. Yes, we do look alike. My daydream was right in that respect, at least. He is fatter than I thought, but hey. I touch his cheekbone and hope, somewhere, he knows. Down below on the reclaimed land Lizard whoops – 'A twitcher!' *Bang!* Picking off the wounded is more interesting to him than how I die. 'Yer got the wobblies too, huh?' *Bang!* 'Guns! The ultimate fucking video game!' *Bang!* One of the Cadillacs wheel-screeches into life. My father sits in the driving seat of the car in the photograph, smiling at whatever Akiko Katō is telling him as she gets in. A black-and-white day gone by. This is the closest we get. Stars.

'Who am I?' The Yakuza head repeats my question. His lips barely move and his voice is tone dead. 'My accountant calls me Mr Morino. My men call me Father. My subscribers call me God. My wife calls me Money. My lovers call me Incredible.' A ripple of humour. 'My enemies call me the stuff of nightmares. You call me Sir.' He retrieves a cigar from an ashtray and relights it. 'Sit down. Your trial is already behind schedule.' I do as I am told and look around at my jury. Frankenstein, chomping a Big

Mac. A weathered, leathered man, who appears to be meditating, rocking very slightly to and fro, to and fro. A woman is using a laptop computer, pianist fast. She reminds me of Queen of Spades' Mama-san until I realize she *is* Queen of Spades' Mama-san. She ignores me. To the left are three identikit men from the catalogue of Yakuza henchmen. A horn section on pause. Through an opening, visible out of the corner of my eye, a girl dressed in a loose yukata sucks a popsicle. When I try to meet her eye she retreats out of sight. Lizard takes the chair next to me. Ryūtarō Morino watches me, over the pile of junk-food Styrofoam boxes. The sound of breathing, the creaking of Leatherjacket's chair, the tappety-tap-tap of the computer keyboard. What are we waiting for? Morino clears his throat. 'Eiji Miyake, how do you plead?'

'What is the charge?'

Lizard's knife scores a deep cut along the table edge. It stops an inch from my thumb. 'What is the charge, *sir*?'

I swallow. 'What is the charge, *sir*?'

'If you are guilty you know the charge.'

'So I must be innocent, *sir*.'

I hear the ice-lolly girl in the next room titter.

'Not guilty.' Morino nods his head gravely. 'Then explain why you were at Queen of Spades on Saturday the ninth of September.'

'Is Yuzu Daimon here?'

Morino gives one nod, my face whacks the table-top, my arm is yanked above my head one degree away from snapping off. Lizard grunts in my ear. 'What d'yer suppose yer just did wrong?'

'Didn't – answer – the – question.' My arm is released.

'Bright boy.' Morino blinks. 'Explain why you were at Queen of Spades on Saturday the ninth of September.'

'Yuzu Daimon took me there.'

'Sir.'

'*Sir.*'

'Yet you told Mama-san here last Saturday that you didn't know Daimon.'

Mama-san glances at me. 'I warned you – I cannot tolerate whining juveniles. Can anyone tell me how to say "fifteen billion" in Russian?' Leatherjacket replies. Mama-san carries on typing. Morino waits for my answer.

'I didn't know Daimon. I still don't. I left my baseball hat in a games centre, went back, he had it, gave it me back, we started talking—'

'—and the rest, as they say, is history. But Queen of Spades is a choosy club. Yuzu Daimon signed you in as his stepbrother. Are you saying this is a lie?'

I wonder what the consequences will be.

'Did you hear my question, Eiji Miyake?'

'Yes, it was a lie. Sir.'

'I say that Jun Nagasaki sent you to spy.'

'Not true.'

'So you know the name Jun Nagasaki?'

'Since an hour ago, yes. Only the name.'

'You went to Queen of Spades with Yuzu Daimon to harass a hostess – you know her as Miriam.'

I shake my head. 'No, sir.'

'You went to Queen of Spades with Yuzu Daimon to persuade her to defect into Jun Nagasaki's circle of beagle-fucking traitors.'

I shake my head. 'No, sir.'

Violence stains Morino's motionless face. His voice is absolute zero. 'You are fucking Miriam. You are fucking my little girl.'

This is the crunch. I shake my head. 'No, sir.'

Frankenstein rattles fry splinters in a cup.

Morino opens a grey document wallet. 'So for your next trick, you will explain this photograph.' The horn section pass it down to me. An A4 black-and-white picture of a shabby apartment building. The zoom lens focuses on the third floor, where a kid my age is handing something through a door. A dog with its head in a lampshade pisses in a flower box. I recognize Miriam's apartment, and me. This is why I am here today. This is bad. No lie is going to get me out of here. But where will the truth get me? Morino clunks his knuckles out of their sockets. 'My breath is bated. As they say.' Morino clunks his knuckles into their sockets. My mouth is a sandpit. 'Now. Why did you show your zit-pus face at the home of my little girl?'

I tell him everything from Shinobazu pond in Ueno park to the conversation with Miriam. The only bit I leave out is Suga – I claim to do the library hacking myself. Morino nicks the tip off a new cigar. I finish, and judgment hangs in the air. Lizard swivels on his chair. 'Father?' Morino nods. 'It don't sound right to me. Computer dorks just don't lug suitcases around stations for a living.' Mama-san shuts her laptop. 'Father. I know Miriam matters to you very much, but we need to be in other places very urgently to keep the operation on track. This nondescript child from the beyond beyond who blundered on to private property is exactly what he appears to be. Nagasaki does not employ spies in diapers; his story fills the blanks in Daimon's; and he hasn't laid a paw on Miriam.'

Morino respects her. 'How do you know?'

'One – you had Miriam trailed by the best surveillance agent in Tokyo for the last two weeks. Two – I'm a woman.'

Morino narrows his eyes to read me. I lower my eyes. Frankenstein's mobile phone beeps. He goes into the adjoining room to answer. An airship floats into view behind Morino's head. Higher up, an airplane glints in high-altitude sunshine. Mama-san takes a disk from her computer and seals it shut in a case. 'Soon,' barks Frankenstein into his phone, 'soon.' He resumes his seat. Morino finishes reading me. 'Eiji Miyake. The court finds you guilty. Guilty of being a dumbfuck who sticks his nose through wrong doors. The mandatory sentence is having your testicles cut off, dipped in soy, and placed in your mouth, which will be gaffer-taped until said member is chewed and swallowed by the detainee.' I glance around at the jurors. Nobody is smiling. 'However, the court will suspend this sentence on condition you observe an exclusion order. You will never go near Queen of

Spades. You will never go near my little girl. Even if you see her in your dreams, I will discover your lapse, and the sentence will be executed. I make myself clear?'

I dare not taste the freedom I can smell. 'Completely, sir.'

'You will return to your pointless life. Without delay.'

'Yes, sir.'

Mama-san stands, but Morino doesn't dismiss me. 'When I was a boy half your age, Miyake, my friends and I would capture dune lizards on the Shimane coast. Dune lizards are cunning. You grab one, they detach their tails and skitter away. How do I know you are not leaving us with a tail?'

'Because you scare me.'

'Your father is also afraid of me, but that man has left me with a zooful of tails in his time.'

The horn players nod. I hear Popsicle giggle.

'Did you just say my father?'

Morino breathes smoke. 'Ye-es. You know I did.'

'My real father?'

'Ye-es.'

'As in . . .'

'As in the flesh-and-blood man who banged up your mother, Mariko Miyake, twenty years ago. Who else would I mean?'

'You *know* him?'

'Not intimately. We meet professionally, on occasion. You seem surprised.' Morino watches me flounder. 'So, my operative hit the nail on the head. Again. My, she *is* good. You really don't know who your father is, do you? To think, these things happen in real life. A semi-orphan comes to Tokyo in search of the father he has never met. So you thought the ATM messages I had my banking people send you were from your *real* father?' His lips bulge slightly in lieu of a laugh. Lizard snickers. Morino taps the document wallet. 'Everything about your father is in here.' He fans himself with it. 'You were buried deep, but my agent can dig up anything. I had you investigated – and your father crops up. We were surprised. Still. You can fuck off now.' He tosses the document wallet into a metal trashcan. Lizard stands and kicks my chair.

'Mr Morino?'

'Are you still here?'

'Please give me that document wallet.'

Morino narrows his eyes at Lizard and nods at the door.

'Sir, if you don't need that information any more—'

'I don't need it, no, but I enjoy causing you needless suffering. Son will escort you to the lobby. Your friend and mentor Yuzu Daimon is waiting for you. He is feeling drained. Now walk away from this room, or you will be beaten senseless and dumped in a skip.' I follow Lizard, glancing back one final time at the trashcan before door 333 closes on my father.

I resolved to walk past Yuzu Daimon, to show my contempt by just ignoring him. That was before I saw his body slumped on the sofa. I have known a few people who died, but I have never actually seen one – so pale, so utterly still. What do you do? My heart is this manic, mechanical punch-bag. The sofa creaks as his limbs shift. His eyes flicker open. His eyeballs wander, then find me. 'So – what did they – do to you?'

A sort of weird crunching of gears.

'What did they do to you, Miyake?'

I can finally speak. 'They let me go.'

'Two miracles in the same day. Untouched?'

'Scared shitless, but untouched. And not as scared shitless as I was a moment ago. I thought you were dead! What did they do to you?'

Daimon ignores this. 'Why – you went to . . . Miriam's – why?'

'She dropped a library book when we, uh, met by accident in Ueno park the day after your dawn exit. I took it back. That was all.'

A laugh tries to twitch the corners of his mouth.

'What did they do to you?'

'One litre of blood.'

I must have misheard. 'They took one litre of your blood? Isn't that . . .'

'Rather more . . . than a blood-bank tank, yes . . . I'll live. It was only my first . . . offence.'

'But what are they going to do with your blood?'

'Test it – sell it, I imagine.'

'Who to?'

'Miyake . . . please. I have no – energy – for an – exposé of illegal markets . . .'

'Can you move? I think you should get to a hospital.'

Speaking is costing Daimon a lot. 'Correct, Doctor, yes. I had a sixth of my blood removed as a payment in a Yakuza vendetta. Awful, isn't it? Yes, I know I'm lucky to be alive. Quite illegal, I agree. But please don't contact the police because my dad is on the take, too.'

'Okay, but hanging around in this building is a very bad idea.'

'One minute – two minutes – let me – get some breath.'

I explore the lobby. The exit will let us leave, but not re-enter. The passageway back to the interview room is blocked by a grille locked by Lizard. The glass walls of the lobby are covered by taped plastic sheeting. I peel back a corner – a building site, the perimeter fence and California beach lido, only a soccer-ball kick away. Sunbathers roast on the boardwalks. The Pacific is as glossy as a monster-movie sea. I sneeze. Not a cold, not now, please. I am afraid Daimon could slip into a coma if I don't haul him away. 'Try to stand up.'

'Leave me alone.'

'I want to call your parents.'

Daimon half sits. 'No, no, definitely, no. Believe me this once. Calling my parents is the very, very worst thing . . .'

'Why?'

Daimon shakes his head as if avoiding a fly. 'Politics. Politics.'

So now what? 'How much money have you got?'

'Every yen is yours if you leave me alone.'

'Don't tempt me. Near the entrance to Xanadu I saw a taxi rank.

You and me are going to walk over there. You can either give in now or make me shout at you for ten minutes and then give in. Up to you.'

Daimon sighs again. 'So masterful when you get roused.'

We get weird looks as we wade through the crowds, but everyone assumes Daimon is slouched on my shoulder because he is dead drunk. Atomic September sunshine drenches the day. My Japan Railway overalls are gluey with sweat. People flow into Xanadu and out again. The air is crammed with silvery helium balloons and tinsel music. Swarms of conversation pieces, smoke from a corn-on-the-cob stand. I see our reflection in a pair of mile-wide sunglasses. We look like shit. A giant black rabbit produces a midget magician from a top hat, and the world claps. Somewhere a piano and strings perform something beautiful. I feel Daimon heaving. 'Do you want to be sick?' I ask him. 'No. I was laughing at the funny side of today.' I wonder where the funny side is. 'Do you have any idea how embarrassing it is for me having my hide saved by you, Miyake?' Zax Omega leaps across our path, selling models of himself. 'Yeah,' I say. 'I imagine it must be pretty humiliating, considering.' Daimon says nothing more until we get to the taxi rank. His feet drag more heavily, and his breathing is rawer. The taxi door swings open all by itself – down south you still have to open them by hand. 'Do you know Kita Senju?' I ask the driver. He nods. 'Do you know the Tenmaya five minutes from the station?' The driver nods. 'This video store is right on the same street—' I scribble the Shooting Star's address. 'Please take my friend there.' The taxi driver looks dubious, balancing a very good fare against Daimon's grogginess. 'Only a bit of sunstroke. In ten minutes he'll be himself again.' The fare wins, and the taxi drives Daimon away. I turn back and face the way I came. I have an appointment back in Valhalla with a discarded document wallet in a metal trashcan.

The Mongolian is climbing nearer. A man-shaped hole in the dim dark. I can see his almost-smile. His cowboy boots count off my remaining moments. Lizard and the Cadillac headlights strobing the battleground may as well be events from another lifetime. Are Morino and Frankenstein still watching? If I take my eyes off the Mongolian, I am afraid my killer will halve the distance when I look back. My adrenalin is fighting my fever, but I have no way to use this energy loaned by fear. No amount of adrenalin will keep me alive when I hit the ground after that drop. No amount of adrenalin will let me disarm a real, live mercenary with a real, live gun. Fuck, no. I am dead. Who will miss me? Buntarō will find a new tenant by next Saturday. Mum will enter her cycle of guilt, blame and vodka. Again. Who knows what my father will feel? My stepmother will probably buy a new hat to celebrate. Akiko Katō will have a little paperwork to process. Cat will find a new pad. She was only ever in it for the milk. My uncles, their wives and my cousins back in Yakushima will be shocked and distraught at the news, of course, but they will all agree that Tokyo was trouble and Japan is not the fortress of safety it used to be. My grandmother will receive the news with a blank face and a long silence which will last half a day. Then she will say, 'His sister called him, so he went.' My list ends there. And this is assuming that my body turns up. Burying me in a pit under a future runway with the others down there would surely make a whole load more sense. Buntarō will report me in a week as a missing person, and everyone will shrug and say he trod in his mother's footsteps. Here he comes, checking his gun. What was it all for? Anju was overwhelmed by the ocean. I am just underwhelmed. I sneeze again. Sneezing, now! Why bother? The breeze is cool off the drained sea.

I decide to kill an hour before I re-enter Valhalla. First, I find a telephone. I call Mrs Sasaki at Ueno, but the moment I hear her voice I hang up in panic, or shame. Either I must tell her an outright lie – or I tell her the outright truth. I cannot do either. So I call Buntarō, who is easier – he jumps down the telephone line. 'Guess what, lad! Kōdai's eyes are actually open! Inside my wife! Open! Imagine that! And get this – he is sucking his thumb! Already! The doctor said this is unusual, so early on. Early developer, the doctor actually said that.'

'Buntarō, I—'

'I was watching this baby video earlier. Maternity is . . . beyond belief. Ever wondered if embryos get thirsty? They do! So they drink up the amniotic fluid, and then pee it out again! The same as being hooked up to a never-ending supply of Budweiser. Except amniotic fluid tastes better. Waiting to be born must be nine months of sheer bliss. Like a bar where you never have to pay the bill. Like the late sixties. And we never remember a thing.'

'Buntarō, a friend is—'

'Have you any idea how much pregnancy rearranges a woman's internals? By the third trimester, the uterus is touching the breastbone. Placental mammals really have it tough. That's why—' A woman in the background at Shooting Star screams her lungs out. 'Hang on, I'll turn down the volume. Watching *Rosemary's Baby*. Get a few pointers if Kōdai turns out to be the son of Satan. A midwife at the hospital was saying—'

'Buntarō!'

'Is anything the matter?'

'Really sorry, but I'm calling from a box and my card is about to die. A friend is coming to Shooting Star by taxi. He donated some blood, but they took too much and he needs a lie-down – please, when he gets there, would you show him up to my room? I'll explain later. Please.'

'And will his trousers needing pressing? Or how about a massage, or—'

The beeps go. Perfect. I hang up.

A platoon of boyfriends and girlfriends – not to mention the battalion of the bothered young families five years will transform the couples into – swill me down a shopping mall to a podium. Musicians perform something twiddly and ribboned. Mozart, maybe. By accident I find myself in the front row. A fat cellist, two thin violinists, a dumpy viola player and a girl playing a Yamaha grand piano. If dog owners grow to look like their pets, musicians turn into their instruments. Except pianists – how could a human resemble her piano? Complexity, maybe. Her hair covers her face – she bends over the keyboard, as if a god were whispering the tune. The pianist has one of those perfect necks – curves, smoothness, toughness, hollows, bumps, all just so. She is in a cream silk dress – sweat dapples mark her spine – and she plays barefoot. The music finishes and everyone claps. The string section bask in the applause – the pianist just turns around and gives a modest bow. Ai Imajō. It really is Ai Imajō. I look for a hiding place but I am walled in by handbags, pushchairs and melting ice creams. Ai Imajō looks right my way and a blush grenade goes off in my face. Then I realize she is looking but not seeing. She is still dazzled by the brightness of the music. Then she smiles at me – definitely – and mimes a head-butt. I manage a feeble wave before getting pushed back by penguins carrying tree-sized bouquets of flowers. A hippopotamus woman looped in beads makes the microphone scream with feedback. I wander off to find a shady corner of Xanadu where I can sit down. I don't want to embarrass Ai Imajō in front of her music student friends.

Valhalla blots out the sun. When my hour is up, I slip through a gap in the perimeter fence and into its unfinished shadow. I can see three security guards smoking in the mouth of the main entrance, but sneaking up between rows of blocks, piping, coils of cable and drainage channels is easy. If I am being watched from Valhalla itself I am in trouble; I hope seeing Ai Imajō has used up today's coincidence quota. I nearly trip over a coil of cable. It sidewinds into life and enters Valhalla through a ventilation duct. No place for a snake, Snake. Skirting the guards' field of vision, I get to the foot of the pyramid, and begin looking for a way in. The construction is vast – it takes about five minute per side. I pass the hotel lobby entrance, and curse myself for not leaving it wedged open with something – I could probably have forced the inner shutter somehow. Twenty minutes later I am back to the main entrance and its three guards. I consider trying to pass myself off as a boilerman or something – I am still in my work overalls – but when I creep close enough to overhear them discussing the best way to cripple a man, I change my mind. I backtrack to the basement ramp that Frankenstein drove down earlier in the afternoon. I spy on the guard lodge from behind a digger. Its window faces crossways, not up the ramp. I think if I stay against the wall I can reach it without being seen. Then, maybe, I can crawl past. The main danger is from any vehicles ascending the ramp as I am making my way down. Still, there were only three Cadillacs in the entire carpark. I think.

It works. I reach the lodge without being caught. On the guard's TV I hear 'And it's a clash of the Giants and the Dragons in front of sixty thousand on this sweltering afternoon in the Dome as homeboy Enoki limbers up, and I can well imagine what must be going through the mind of that young battler at this moment in time', and so on. I smell pork katsu and hear a microwave ping. I get down on my knees and scramble past – my foot slips in fine gravel, surely he must have heard, I carry on anyway, past his door, under the barrier arm and away into the dark, bracing myself for a shout and alarms. I dash behind a column, my heart percussion-capping. Nothing. He must be stone deaf. I am now an unauthorized intruder. Calm down. I am walking into a building to pick up a piece of unwanted refuse from a bin. The three Cadillacs are still parked in a row, which is not a good sign, but as long as my father is safe in the metal bin I can find a hiding place somewhere in the hotel and retrieve him when the coast is clear. Staying in the darkest wedges of shadow, I make my way to the portal door, and slip through. I sort of remember the way. The place is still deserted. Snake is wandering this maze of swinging doors, too. Grown to canoe length. I pass the toilet where Daimon and I were put on ice – abrupt laughter rings out. My nerves snap, I dart ahead, and clear the next corner just as the laughter spills into the corridor. It follows me for the next three turnings. Then it dies down. Then it changes direction and heads towards me – does it? I double back in panic – I thought I doubled back – and end up down a dead end with a drinks machine in the alcove. I listen. The voices of two men are getting nearer. Maybe I can squeeze down the side of this drinks machine – I can, but as I try to twist around behind it my foot gets caught in a loop of cable. At that moment the voices appear in front of the machine. I freeze. If I move they will hear me. If they look down the side of the machine they will see my leg. I feel a sneeze getting nearer. A transformer juts into the small of my back. It hornet-hums and is hot as an iron.

'My, my, my, what do we have here.'

'Imported Stella Artois. Nectar of the gods.'

'Time for a quick can?'

'Why not? And guess what? Kakizaki is AB rhesus negative.'

'My, my. I hope you bled him dry. AB neg is liquid ruby for the right billionaire.'

'Drier than dry, poor fucker. I see it as an act of mercy. You heard about the neck trusses on the lip of the pits? Fuck, this machine won't take five-thousands. Got anything smaller?'

I am going to sneeze right now.

Coins are fed in. 'Neck trusses? I thought Morino said to use gaffer tape.'

'We did, but Nabe wriggled too much. Morino ordered no sedatives. So there was nothing for it but neck trusses and nine-inch nails. Kakizaki's the lucky one. His meat's whiter than turkey; he'll hardly feel a thing.'

My sneeze vanishes. Beers clunk through the machine's guts. The men open their beers and walk away, still discussing carpentry. I sneeze and wallop my head on the side of the machine.

I find room 333 by accident while I am still looking for a hiding place. I press my ear against it. Apart from my pulse pounding my eardrums I hear nothing. I think. I test the handle. It is tightly sprung, but feels unlocked. Holding my breath, I open the door a sliver and peer in. I can see the metal bin with the document wallet. The window is slightly open, and a breeze combs the blinds. Remembering the adjoining room, I creep in. Nobody here. Relief washes through me, then triumph hoses me down. This insane risk has paid off. I open the document wallet and groan. A single photograph falls to the floor and lands blank side up. A message is ball-penned. *There is an Arabic proverb: "Take whatever you want," says God, "and pay for it." Pluto pachinko, Xanadu, now.* I turn the picture over. Two certainties. One: the woman is Akiko Katō. Two: from the angle of his jaw to the slope of his eyebrows, the man in the driving seat is my father. Without a doubt.

Pluto pachinko is so thick with sweat, smoke and sheer din you could swim up to the mirror-balls on the disco ceiling. I would swap a lung for a cigarette right now instead of waiting fifty years – but I am afraid if I delay for one moment I will miss Morino and Plan F, the best so far, will drive off with him. Never mind, just by breathing in here I can absorb enough nicotine to calm a rhino. Customers cram the aisles, waiting for a free seat. My eldest uncle – owner of the only pachinko parlour on Yakushima – told me that new places rig several of the machines to pay out more generously, so they can muscle in on the marketplace. The clatter and glitter of cascading silver balls hypnotize the ranks of drones and she-drones. I wonder how many babies are slowly cooking to death in the bowels of Xanadu's carpark. I start a second lap, searching for a staff-only door. Time is ticking. I find a girl in a Pluto uniform. 'Hey! Where's Dad's office!'

She is cowed. 'Whose office, sir?'

I scowl. 'The manager!'

'Oh – Mr Ozaki?'

I roll my eyeballs. 'Who else?'

She takes me behind the helpdesk, punches in a code on a combination door, and holds it open. 'Up these stairs, sir. I'd show you up myself, but I'm not supposed to leave the shop-floor.'

'I should hope not.' I close the door. A complex lock springs closed. Steep stairs leading to one door. Underwater quiet. I climb the stairs, and then nearly lose my footing when I notice Leatherjacket calmly watching me from the top step. 'Uh, hello,' I say. Leatherjacket looks at me and chews gum. He is cradling a gun. The first real gun I have ever seen. I point at the door. 'Can I go in?' Leatherjacket chews, and tilts his head a fraction. I knock twice and open the door.

I open the door and a man flies through the air, and through a mirror on the far side of the room. The mirror breaks into applause – the man drops out of view, to the drone-packed parlour below. The scene lurches. I gape – did I do that? Unabated pachinko din floods the office. Morino watches me from behind the desk with a finger on his lip and one ear cupped. I just have time to register the three horn players – they did the hurling – and Mama-san knitting before the chain reaction from below breaks out. Chaos, screaming, shouting. Morino rests his elbows on the desk. Contentment suffuses his face. A jag of mirror falls from the frame. From outside Leatherjacket closes the door behind me. The cyclone subsides as the stampede rushes out. Lizard and Frankenstein peer throught the frame to inspect the damage. Morino sort of smiles with his eyelids. 'Fine timing, Miyake. You witnessed my declaration of war. Sit down.'

I am trembling. 'The man . . .'

'What man?'

'The man they threw out through the window.'

Morino inspects a wooden box. 'Ozaki? What about him?'

'Won't he need' – I swallow – 'an ambulance?'

Morino unclips the box. Cigars. 'I expect so.'

'Aren't you going to call one?'

'Excellent! A Monte Cristo. Call an ambulance? If Ozaki wanted an ambulance called, he should have thought through the consequences of pissing on the shoes of Ryūtarō Morino.'

'The police will be here.'

Morino slides the cigar under his nose.

'Policemen?' Frankenstein watches the chaos flood out of Pluto pachinko. 'Policemen live in your world. We police our world ourselves.' He nods at Lizard and they leave. I am still sick to my core with the presence of violence. Mama-san's knitting needles click. The horn players are on pause.

Finally Morino unwraps the cigar. 'What do you know about cigars? Nothing. So listen. Learn. The Monte Cristo is to cigars what Tiffany's showroom is to diamond tiaras. Famous perfection. Pure Cuban – filler, wrapper, binder. For a rat's penis like Ozaki to even look at a Monte Cristo is blasphemy. I told you to sit down.' I obey, numb. 'You are here because you want information. Am I right?'

'Yes.'

'I know. This information cost me good money. How do you intend to pay?'

I try my best to ignore the fact that this man just had someone thrown through a window, and pull myself into focus. 'I would be grateful if . . .' My sentence dies.

Morino dabs the cigar with his tongue-tip. 'I am sure your gratitude is five-star gratitude. But I have metropolitan overheads. Your gratitude is worth fleashit to me. Try again.'

'How much?'

Morino takes a tool from the desk and circumcises the cigar. 'Why is it always money, money, money with kids nowadays? Little wonder Japan is becoming this moral and spiritual graveyard. No, Miyake. I do not want your money. Besides, we both know that most pigeons have more disposable income than you. No. I propose this. I propose you pay with your loyalty.'

'My loyalty?'

'Is there a fucking echo in here?'

'What would giving you my loyalty mean?'

'So like your old man. Living in small print. Your loyalty? Let me see. I thought we could spend the rest of the day together. Go bowling. An outing to a dog show. A bite to eat, and afterwards a get-together with some old friends. Midnight comes around, we give you a lift home.'

'And in return—'

'You receive—' He clicks his fingers and a horn player hands him another document wallet. Morino leafs through it. 'Your father. Name, address, occupation, résumé, personal history, pix – colour, black-and-white – itemized telephone bills, bank accounts, preferred shaving gel.' Morino closes it and smiles. 'You give me and my family a few hours of your time, and your historic search ends in crowning success. What do you say?' From the deserted pachinko floor below I hear glass crunching and electric shutters lowering. It occurs to me that saying 'No' may have consequences far worse than being denied a document wallet, bearing in mind what I witnessed.

'Yes.'

A wet dab, and a needle plunges into my left arm, just above the elbow. I yelp. Another horn player grips me tight. He shoves his face up to mine, and opens his mouth wide, as if he wants to bite off my nose. Pond-water breath. I have a close-up view of his mouth before I can turn away, then I turn back. His tongue is a clipped stump. A formless giggle. The horn players are all mutes. The syringe fills with my blood. I stare at Morino as a syringe in his arm fills up with blood. He seems surprised that I may be surprised. 'We need ink.'

'Ink?'

'For the contract. I believe in the written word.' The syringes are removed and my arm is released. Morino squirts both into a teacup, and mixes our blood with a teaspoon. My puncture is dabbed with disinfectant again. A horn player spreads a sheet of calligraphy paper in front of Morino, and hands him a writing brush. Morino dips the brush, breathes deeply, and in graceful strokes draws the characters for *Loyalty*, *Duty* and *Obedience*. *Mori*. *No*. He rotates the paper on the desk. 'Quickly,' he orders, and his mouth seems to be in his eyes, 'before the blood clots.' I pick up the brush, dip it and write *Mi* and *Yake*. Red already stiffening to dung. Morino watches with a critical eye. 'Penmanship. A dying art.'

'At my high school we practised with ink.'

Morino blows the paper dry, and rolls it into a scroll-case. Everything seems to have been prepared. Mama-san puts down her knitting needles and puts the scroll-case into her handbag. 'Perhaps now, Father,' she says, 'we can get down to the serious business?'

Morino puts down the cup of blood and wipes his mouth. 'Bowling.'

A basement shopping mall will connect Xanadu with Valhalla and Nirvana. It is still a gloomy underpass, lit by roadworker's lamps, and strewn with tarpaulins, tiles, wood planking, sheet glass and a prematurely delivered army of boutique dummies huddled naked in misty polythene. Morino is ahead, a megaphone in one hand. Mama-san walks behind me, and the horn players bring up the rear. Somewhere above my head in the sunlit real world, Ai Imajō is playing Mozart. Words from Morino could be the darkness speaking. 'Our ancestors built temples for their gods. We build department stores. In my youth I went to Italy with my father, on business. I still dream about the buildings. What we lack in Japan is megalomania.' Down here it is chilly and damp. I sneeze. My throat feels tight. Finally we climb to the surface on a dead escalator. *Welcome to Valhalla*, says Thor, a thunderbolt in one hand and a bowling ball in the other. Through a temporary door in a plywood wall we enter a vast darkness, sealed against the day. At first I cannot see a thing, not even the floor. I can only feel the emptiness. I follow the vapour trail and ember-light of Morino's cigar. A hangar? A glow clusters in the distance. This is a bowling alley. We walk past lane upon lane. I lose count. Minutes seem to pass, but this is impossible. 'Ever go bowling much on Yakushima, Miyake?' Sometimes his voice seems far away sometimes near. 'No,' I answer. 'Bowling keeps youngsters out of trouble. Safer than falling out of trees or drowning in undertows. Once, I went bowling with your father. A powerful bowler, your dad. An even better golf player, though.' I don't believe him, but I probe anyway. 'What golf course did you play at?' Morino waves his cigar at me – its tip is a firefly. 'Not a crumb until midnight. That is the deal. Then you stuff yourself with all the details you can stomach.' Suddenly we are here. Leatherjacket, Frankenstein, Lizard, Popsicle. Mama-san sits down and gets out her knitting. Morino smacks his lips. 'Our guests are accommodated?' Frankenstein jerks a thumb down the lit alley. Instead of tenpins are three wax human heads. The centre head moves. The left head tics. I should not be here. This is a nightmarish mistake. No. This is a sort of interrogation. Morino is not sick enough to hurl bowling balls at real people. He is at root a businessman. 'Father,' says Mama-san. 'I have to say. This is an unspeakable act.'

'War is war.'

'But what about their retinas?'

'I understand your concern, I really do. But my conscience rules out depriving a dead man a clear view of his destiny.'

'*Morino!*' shouts Centrehead, hoarsely. 'I know you're there!'

Morino raises his megaphone to his lips. His amplified voice is a dust-storm. 'Congratulations on a fine opening day, Mr Nabe.' Echoes slap away and back. 'There seemed to be a minor ruckus in the pachinko parlour, but I'm sure everything is ironed out now.'

'Release us! This instant! Jun Nagasaki owns this city!'

'Wrong, Nabe. Jun Nagasaki thinks he owns it. But I know I own it.'

'You are stark fucking *insane*!'

'And yer,' Lizard shouts back, 'are stark fucking *dead*!'

The megaphone crackles. 'You, Nabe, were always a walking lobotomy. Your death suits you perfectly. But you, Gunzo – I thought you had the sense to grab your pay-off and run for the tropics.'

Lefthead speaks. 'We're more useful to you alive, Morino.'

'But you are more pleasing dead.'

'I can show you how to strangle Nagasaki's supply lines.'

Morino hands the megaphone to Leatherjacket, who deposits his chewing gum in a tissue. 'Good afternoon, Gunzo.'

'*You?*'

'I favour customers who pay on time.' He has a dusky foreign accent.

'I don't fucking *believe* it!'

'Your inability to believe is the cause of your present dilemma.'

Centrehead shouts. 'Then you're dead too, you slimy Mongolian shit!'

The slimy Mongolian shit hands the megaphone back to Morino, smiles, and puts in a new stick of gum.

Lefthead cries, 'I can be your messenger to Nagasaki, Morino!'

'Yer ain't our messenger,' shouts back Lizard, 'yer our fucking message!'

'Most succinct, Son,' comments Morino approvingly. 'Most concise. You can throw first.' Lizard bows graciously and selects the heaviest bowling ball. I tell myself this is just a bluff. I should not be here. Lizard steps on to the concourse, and lines up a shot. 'Shoot us, Morino!' shouts Centrehead. 'Let us die honourably!' Frankenstein shouts back. 'What do you know about honour, Nabe? You sold your hole to Nagasaki faster than he could say "Bend over"!' Lizard steps one, two and – wham! A fast uncurving line, my gut knots, I try to wake myself up, look away for my own good, but when Centrehead screams I look, idiot that I am. Righthead – Kakizaki, I guess – is no longer recognizable. I want to vomit but nothing comes. I am glued. Kakizaki is a staved-in cavity of bone and blood. The horn players burst into wild applause. Lefthead is shut down with shock. Centrehead gasps, drowning, spattered with red specks. Lizard bows again and comes back to the console seat. 'Superb technique,' praises Frankenstein. 'Watch it on the replay, shall we?' I turn around and keel, putting my head between my knees. I jump up when the megaphone combusts 'Miyaaaaaakeeeeeeeee!' down in my ear. Lizard gestures at the bowling alley. 'Yer on.'

'No.'

The horn players mime confusion and surprise.

Morino stage-whispers: 'Yes. We signed a contract.'

'You said nothing about being an accessory to murder.'

'Your vow says you will do what the Father tells you to,' says Frankenstein.

'But—'

'A moral conundrum for a responsible young man,' considers Morino. 'To throw or not to throw. Throw, and you risk doing that double-dealing abomination down there some degree of damage. Not throw, and you cause a fire in Shooting Star and a twelve-week premature miscarriage in your landlord's wife. Which would weigh heavier on your conscience?' He wants to lock me into this violence, to ensure I will never talk. I can feel the locks, clicking shut. I get up and choose the lightest ball, hoping for an unseen plot twist to get me out of here. I pick up a ball, the lightest. It weighs a lot. No. I can't do this. I just can't. I hear laughter behind me. I look back. Lizard lies on his back with his legs apart and a balloon stuffed inside his jacket. Nipples, a navel and a triangle of public hair are scribbled on it with a black marker. Frankenstein kneels over him, lowering a long knife. 'No,' Lizard cries in falsetto, 'please don't yer hurt me, mister, I got a baby in my growbag.' 'Sorry, Mrs Buntarō,' sighs Frankenstein, 'but this is what you get for letting rooms to tenants who break vows with powerful men . . .' Lizard screams at the top of his lungs, 'Please! My baby, my baby! *Mercy!*' The knife tip presses down on Mrs Buntarō's rubbery belly, Frankenstein bunches his other fist into a sledgehammer and *Bang*! Popsicle lolls and rolls a tickled laugh. Mama-san knits, Morino claps. A huddle of faces hanging in blackness, glowing from the monitor and console lights. In a single motion they turn and stare at me. I cannot tell which floating face gives the final order. 'Bowl.' I must miss, but not obviously. I should not be here. I want to apologize to the heads, but how can I? I march on to the concourse, and try to breathe. One, I aim for the gutter, a metre down from Rightdeadhead. Two, my gut coils up and the ball flies away too early – my fingers made the holes sweaty. I crouch there, too sick to watch, too sick not to. The ball veers towards the gutter, and rolls along its edge for the middle third of the alley. But then spin swings the ball back – straight towards Centrehead. His face seems to refract, a wild howl grows from the rumble of the bowl, and the horn players behind me cheer in unison. And I close my eyes. Groans of disappointment from behind. 'You shaved his stubble,' consoles Morino. I'm trembling and I can't stop. 'Wanna watch the re-rerun?' leers Lizard. I ignore him, wobble back and collapse on the end seat. I close my eyes. The gleaming, clotting blood.

'Clear the decks!' Frankenstein halloos. 'My speciality, this – the windmill express!' I hear much grunting, his run-up and the thunder of a rocketing bowl. Three seconds later, rapturous applause. 'Eggshelled!' shouts Lizard. 'Bravo!' cheers Morino. Centrehead shrieks over and over, but Lefthead is ominously quiet. On the insides of my eyelids I can see the end of the alley. I scrunch my eyes up even more tightly, but I still have this Technicolor view. I probably will until I die. I should not be here in this twisted psychotic afternoon. My body refuses to stop trembling. I retch once, and twice, but nothing comes up. Noxious noodle fumes. When did I last eat? Weeks ago. If I could, I would walk away. Never mind the document wallet. But I know they won't let me. A hand slides into my crotch. 'Got any candy?' Popsicle. '*What?*' Champagne bombs? 'Got any candy?' Her breath is rotting yoghurt. Lizard grabs her hair and pulls her off. 'You cheap little fucking *slut*!' Slap, slap, lash. Morino picks up his megaphone. The survivor is still shrieking. 'Cut you a deal, Nabe?' The shrieks subside into strangled sobs. 'If you shut your racket up for the next bowl, you are a free man. Not a squeak, mind you!' Nabe breathes in hoarse throat-rips. Morino lowers the megaphone and looks at Mama-san. 'Will you?'

'My bowling days are behind me.' The knitting needles click.

'Father,' says Leatherjacket, 'I have grasped the fundamentals of this game.'

Morino nods. 'You are one of us. Please.'

'I'll tidy up Gunzo. I always disliked Gunzo.'

A steady roll, a clamped quaver of fear from Nabe, and a blat. Applause.

'Oh dear, Nabe,' bellows Frankenstein, 'I distinctly heard a squeak.'

'No!' comes the broken, bruised, buggered voice.

Morino gets to his feet. 'Try to see the funny side! Humour is the soul of the soul.' I should not be here. Morino takes his time. 'Yuk. This ball has been used already. Bits of Gunzo's scalp. Or Kakizaki.' Nabe is sobbing, softly, as if he lost a teddy bear and nobody cares. Morino paces – one, two – rumble, the bowl flies. One short saw-toothed howl. A chopstick snapping. Two heavy things thump into the pit.

Three Cadillacs glide down the fast lane. A nowhere land, not city, not country. Access roads, service stations, warehouses. Afternoon drains away the day into a hole of evening. I am branded with what I saw in the bowling alley. The burn will not hurt until the shock wears off and my nerves come back to life. I think about the places I could be if I never re-entered Valhalla. I could be chatting with Ai Imajō in a coffee shop. I could be feeding Cat and smoking with Buntarō. I could be bombing around the coastal road of Yakushima on Uncle Tarmac's motorbike. The moon rises over forest slopes. Where is this? The something peninsula. Frankenstein is driving, Leatherjacket is in the passenger seat. Morino and I sit in the middle seat. He blows wreaths of cigar smoke, and makes several phone calls about 'operations'. He makes a chain of telephone calls mostly no longer than 'Where the fuck is Miriam?' Popsicle is giving Lizard a blowjob in the back seat. We enter a tunnel. The roof lights barcode-scan across the windscreen. Mighty ventilators hang from the tunnel roof. I should not be in this nightmare. 'I wish you would stop saying that,' says Morino, apparently to me. 'It's getting on my nerves. We all get exactly the nightmare we deserve.' I am still trying to fathom this out when Frankenstein speaks. 'My nightmares always wind up in tunnels. I'm having this ordinary dream, nothing spooky or nothing, then I see the mouth of a tunnel and I think, "Oh yeah, here comes the nightmare." I drive into the tunnel and it starts. People hanged from the ceiling. Some guy I offed ten years ago come back and my shooter jams. The tunnel presses in closer and tighter till you can't breathe no more.' Popsicle slurps. Lizard groans slightly and speaks. 'Nightmares are yer law-of-the-jungle stuff. All yer modern gizmos stripped away. Yer just left there, alone, dinner for something bigger and badder and eviller. Watch yer teeth!' He slaps Popsicle, who whimpers. Morino taps ash into the tray. 'Interesting stuff, boys. My view is, a nightmare is comedy without a release valve. They tickle, but you can't laugh. And the pressure builds up and up. Like gas in lager. Got anything to add to our fascinating discourse, Miyake?' I look at this torturer, wondering if this is just another day for him. 'No.' Morino seems no longer to even need his lips to speak. 'Cheer up, Miyake. People die all the time. Those three killed themselves the moment they double-crossed me. You just helped deliver the sentence. You'll have forgotten all about them in a week. They say "Time is the greatest healer". Bollocks, that is. The greatest healer is forgetfulness.' Lizard comes with a contented smack of the lips. Popsicle sits up, wiping her mouth. 'Candy!' Lizard mutters and unzips something. 'Yer arm's a fucking pin-cushion. Show us yer thigh. I'll shoot you up there. Don't drool more than yer have to.' Leatherjacket speaks. 'In my homeland, it is said nightmares are our wilder ancestors returning to reclaim land. Land tamed and grazed, by our softer, fatter, modern, waking selves.' Frankenstein produces a steel comb and pulls it across his hair, keeping his other hand on the wheel. 'Sent by who?' Leatherjacket folds in a new stick of gum. 'Nightmares are sent by who, or what, we *really* are, underneath. "Don't forget where you come from," the nightmare tells. "Don't forget your true self."'

A neon poodle prances across its sign for all eternity. It wears a little doggie bow tie. Our Cadillac joins that of the horn players. Mama-san has taken the third away on business of her own. The men prime their guns and Frankenstein opens my door. 'Would you prefer to stay in the nice safe car with a scoobied-up sex nymphet tart?' Before I work out what to say Lizard swipes at my baseball cap. 'Pity. Yer can't.' We get out and walk towards the door of the poodle warehouse. An insect-o-cutor bristles every few seconds. From inside the warehouse I can hear a roaring, swelling and sinking. Two bouncers appear from the shadows of the entrance and approach the horn players. 'Evening, gentlemen. First, I gotta ask for any weapons. House rules – I lock 'em up safe. Second, we don't have your motors on the list. Who are you with?'

The horn players part and Morino walks through. 'Me.'

The bouncers blench.

Morino stares. 'I heard a rumour about a dog show tonight.'

The more colossal bouncer pulls himself together first. 'Mr Morino—'

'The old Mr Morino ended the day Mr Tsuru did. My name is Father now.'

'Yes, uh, Father.' The bouncer flips open his mobile phone. 'Just you give me a moment and I'll make sure the best, uh, ringside seat is cleared for you and your party—' Morino nods at Frankenstein, who knifes him about where his heart is. Right down to the hilt. A horn player jerks his head back and probably breaks his neck. It all happens too fast to register, and too fast for the victim to make a sound. The other two horn players fell the second bouncer. Lizard volleys the gun out of his hand and kisses the tumbled man. No he doesn't. He bites the bouncer's nose – and spits out specks of dark. At this point I look away. Thuds, grunts, blacken and bruise. 'Dump the fuckrats behind those crates,' orders Morino. The kicked-away mobile phone rings. Frankenstein crunches its shell with a single stomp. 'Taiwanese fucking tat. Nothing is made in Japan any more.' Lizard opens the warehouse door. Inside is mulchy and meaty. Row after dim row of pallets stacked with tins of dogfood. This place is enormous. Cheers and yells slosh from the distance. The horn players lead the way. I falter, and get a whack from Frankenstein in my coccyx. 'No stalling, Miyake. You're one of us until the clock strikes midnight.' I obey. I have to. All I can do to calm my survival instinct is to lower my baseball cap. Nobody in the shouting, hundred-plus crowd notices our approach. The horn players plough through the outer walls – Yakuza shirts and tattoos to a man. People whirl around angrily, catch sight of Morino, gape, and fall away. We reach the edge of a spotlit pit. A grey mastiff and a black Doberman are straining at their leashes, globs of saliva flying off their fangs. On the far side of the pit a man stands on a crate. He scribbles down the bets the crowd shout at him. Hairy fat diamonds bulge through his string vest. I am sandwiched between Frankenstein behind and Morino in front – as safe as it gets – so I have a decent view as Morino pulls a gun from his jacket and shoots the mastiff through the head.

Silence.

A stain eats up the pit floor around the dead dog's head. The Doberman whimpers behind its trainer. The horn players already have their weapons trained on the crowd. They fall back. I should not be here. The mastiff trainer regains his power of speech. 'You shot Mr Nagasaki's best dog!'

Morino acts confused. 'Whose best dog?'

'Jun Nagasaki, you, you, you—'

'Oh, him.'

The trainer is apoplectic. 'Jun Nagasaki! Jun Nagasaki!'

'I heard that name too much today. Don't mention it again.'

'Jun Nagasaki'll peel your skin off, you, you, you—'

Morino points his gun*Bang*! The trainer buckles over and lands on his mastiff. Their blood pools. Morino turns to Frankenstein. 'I warned him. Uncle? I warned him, yeah?' Frankenstein nods. 'Nobody can say you never gave a fair warning, Father.' The crowd is still anchored to the concrete floor. Morino hoicks, aims, and spits on the trainer. 'Guns, and fairy godmothers. They make your wildest wish come true. Every last pigfucking one of you will leave. Except Yamada here.' He levels the gun at the bookie on the crate. 'I want a word in your ear, Yamada. The rest of you – scram!

Go!' The horn players fire off a round each. The crowd drain away down the aisles and rows, ushered by the pistol-toting horn players – vampires before dawn don't melt away so fast. The bookie keeps his hands raised. Lizard jumps into the pit and tips the trainer's head over with his foot. Between his eyes is a bloodied joke-shop scab. 'Nice shot, Father.' From outside I hear cars screech away.

The bookie swallows hard. 'If you're going to kill me, Morino—'

'Poor Yamada-kun. You backed the wrong dog again. I am going to kill you, but not today. I need you to take a message to your new master. Tell Nagasaki I wish to discuss war reparations he owes me. Tell him I'll be waiting at midnight sharp. The terminal bridge for the new airport. Out beyond Xanadu on the reclaimed land. You think you can remember all that?'

The Mongolian halts ten paces away. His gun is cradled in his hand. The shots and lights from the reclaimed land seem far, far away. My heart shotguns inside my ribcage. My overalls are scratchy and stinking. My final memories of life are the stupidest things. An unclaimed Haruki Murakami novel I salvaged from lost property, half finished, in my locker at Ueno – what happened to the man stuck down his dry well with no rope? My mother laughing in Uncle Pachinko's yard garden, trying to play badminton, drunk but happy at least. Regret that I never did my Liverpool pilgrimage. Waking one morning to find a pencil-line of snow over me and Anju's futon, where it had blown in through a crack during an early fall. Is this junk the stuff of life? I hear my name, but I know it was only my imagination. I fight to keep control of my breathing, and sneeze. I never looked at Leatherjacket before, not properly. Yours is the last face I will ever see. Not how you imagine the face of death to look. Quite plain, mildly curious, taut with an immunity to emotion from the acts its master has made it witness. Do it. It would be too tacky to beg for my life. So what are my last words? 'I wish you wouldn't do this.' How profound. 'I suggest,' says Leatherjacket, 'that you crouch.'

'Crouch?' A crouch-style execution. Why?

'On the ground. A – how do you say? – foetus position.'

Why bother? Dead is dead.

'You should crouch for your own safety,' my killer insists.

I mangle a stillborn huff which Leatherjacket interprets as a no.

Leatherjacket primes his gun. 'Well, I warned you.'

So many stars. What are they for?

Tuna, abalone, yellowtail, salmon roe, bonito, egg tōfu, human earlobe. The sushi is piled high. The wasabi is mixed in with the soy to kill any impurities in the raw fish. It clots the soy, sticky blood. I must stop thinking about the bowling alley. I must. We have driven across the night since the dogs, it seems, but the clock here says only 22:14. Little over a hundred minutes to go, I tell myself, but I find it hard to believe in anything good. I am in the grip of a cold that will get much worse before it will get any better. I get some water down my throat; it bloats my stomach. Even breathing is hard. We have the restaurant to ourselves. A family was here, but they shuffled out the moment they saw us. The old waitress stays cool, but the chef stays out back, lying low. I would if I could. Frankenstein lobs a sausage at me. 'Why the starchfart face, cub scout? Anyone would think you lost your parents.' Lizard smears wasabi in the soy. 'Maybe he realized the mastiff I shot back at Goichi's was his long-lost papa.' Morino flicks his cigar-tip at me. 'Grin and bear it! Remember your heritage! You're a Japanese law-abiding straight! You grin and bear it until your Zimmer frame buckles and your drinking water is mercury oxide, and our whole country is one coast-to-coast parking lot. I'm not knocking Japan. I love it. In most places the muscle is at the beck and call of the masters. In Japan, we, the muscle, *are* the masters. Japan is *our* gig. So grin. Bear it.' I may have to bear it, but no way am I grinning about being dragged into a turf war between wolves with rabies. The only thing I can grin about is that until we leave this restaurant nothing can get worse. Lizard points to a corner of the room. 'Father!' Saliva-shiny sushi-cud. 'See what I spy with my little eye – they got a karaoke machine!'

'Joy of joys.' Morino looks at Frankenstein. 'Let loose the wings of song.' Frankenstein sings a song in English with a chorus that goes 'I can't liiiiiiiiive, if living is without yoo-ooo-ooo, I can't giiiiiiiiive, I can't take any mooooooore'. The horn players bay along with the vowels. The noise is so bad I watch for the sushi to sprout maggots. Leatherjacket sips a glass of milk in the corner. He doesn't seem to belong here either. Morino calls over the elderly waitress who has been nervously serving us. 'Sing.' Without arguing she performs an enka number called 'Cherry Blossoms of the Inland Sea', about a mah-jong gambler who dies to honour a gambling debt, but only after ninety-nine verses. Lizard sings a song called 'Electrode Incest' by a band of the same name. It contains no verses, choruses or chord changes. The horn players clap wildly as Lizard does a turkey dance on the table and wanks the microphone. Finally the song is over and Morino gestures me up.

'No,' I say flatly. 'I don't sing.'

A hail of sushi slaps my face. The horn players boo.

'I don't like music.'

'Bollocks,' says Morino. 'My pet investigator said you have twenty CDs, loads by that Beatle who got snuffed, a file of sheet music and a guitar.'

'How do you know that?'

'Nightmares do their homework.'

I swab rice off my face. 'You had my room broken into?'

Morino holds his glass for the waitress to fill. 'If I thought you had touched my baby girl, you virtual-orphan brat, I would have had *you* broken into. So be grateful.'

'I hate karaoke and I'm not going to sing.'

Lizard does a squitty imitation. '*I hate karaoke and I'm not going to sing.*' Then his fist fills my eye and the table becomes the ceiling.

I pick myself up. My eye sort of sings, throbbing up.

'I wanted to do that all day.' Lizard examines his knuckles. 'Father told you to sing.'

I should be afraid, but I shake my head. There is no blood.

Frankenstein places a chopstick over his index and ring fingers, belches, and snaps the chopstick with his middle finger. 'I say Miyake is in danger of a breach of contract, Father.'

Morino wags his finger. 'You have to make allowances. He was never the same after his sister drowned. They had their own little country. Fuck, they had their own language. What a pity he buggered off to Kagoshima the day she died, selfish fuck that he is. Hey!' He clicks his fingers at the waitress. 'More edamame beans!' Drugged with cold germs as I am, I can't guess whether Morino has a gift for inspired guesses or a skeleton key to the basements of minds. Either way, I want to spike his eye with my chopstick. I imagine myself doing it. Squirt. His wart throbs. I swear, the thing is watching me.

According to the Cadillac clock we enter the reclaimed land perimeter road at 23:04. Thirty minutes later we are still driving. Military band music pumps through the car and a fever pumps through me, or maybe the fever is in the car and the military music in me. Millimetres away from being a killer, I was. I am. Can a chance difference in spin and angle really make me not guilty? I threw. I had to. But I threw. One more hour and the document wallet will be mine. Plus a magnificent black eye. I was expecting the pretender to the Yakuza throne of Tokyo to be joined by fleets of armoured personnel, but no. Just these two Cadillacs. My nose streams uncontrollably, and my neck feels clamped in some sort of truss. Maybe some code of honour binds the two factions to non-violence. Or, please no, maybe this is a suicide mission. I tell myself if Morino was the kamikaze type he wouldn't have made it to his age, or even his body weight, but I no longer know what to think. Nobody says much. Morino calls Mama-san, at Queen of Spades, I guess. 'Is Miriam at work yet? I called her place. Tell her to call my mobile the moment she gets in.' Lizard and

Frankenstein smoke their Camels, Morino his cigar. I am too ill to want to smoke. Popsicle whimpers in her narcotic sleep. The sea is calm enough to walk on and the sky is stars, acre after acre. The full moon is a thirty watt bulb no more than several inches away. Morino makes another call, but nobody answers. 'Suicides tend to check themselves out when the moon is full, a nurse once told me. Suicides, and, for some reason, horses.' Finally we slow to a halt, parked at a strategic angle to the horn players' Cadillac, I guess. I get out. My cramped muscles hurt. Yet another building site. Tokyo suburbs are demolition dumps or building sites. The giant terminus building is still a giant foundation. Flat as a pool table, the reclaimed land extends all the way to the mountains. A bridge, with the central section missing, rises on either side of where we stand. I can hear the lazy sea a short distance over the embankment. 'Say, Miyake.' His lighter flame dances. 'You can monkey up that bridge.' I wonder what the catch is. 'Nagasaki is the opposition, and you don't fit the image. I don't want anyone thinking I'm recruiting from kindergarten.' Lizard snickers.

'Will you give me the document wallet?'

'You are boring me! Not until after fucking midnight! Go!'

I walk several paces, when Leatherjacket, standing on a mound of boulders, whistles. I thought it was to me but it wasn't. 'Our friends are coming. Nine vehicles.'

'Nine.' Frankenstein shrugs. 'I had hoped for more, but nine is not bad.'

I begin running up the slope. The bridge is the nearest thing to a safe haven. On the other hand, it is a perfect cell to keep me in. I get within a few metres of the top. I guess I am thirty metres up – high enough for vertigo to clamp my lungs and make my balls retract. I peer over the parapet and watch Nagasaki's cars draw up. They park semicircling Morino's two Cadillacs and flick their beams on full. They kill their engines. Four men in each vehicle file out, each with combat jackets, helmets and an automatic rifle, and take up firing positions. Not for the first time today, I feel I have strayed into an action movie. Morino and his men put on sunglasses. No guns, no night vision. Morino holds his megaphone in one hand and keeps the other in his pocket. Thirty-six heavily armed men to seven. A man in a white suit climbs out at leisure, flanked by two bodyguards. I wait for the order to fire. No document wallet. It was all for nothing. Morino's voice reverbs over the reclaimed land as if his megaphone is a pinhole for the night to talk through. 'Jun Nagasaki. Do you have any final requests?'

'I stand here frankly amazed, Morino. Have you really sunk so low so quickly? Rumours of your demise appear to be under-exaggerated. Five tired goons, one ex-arms dealer – I shall kill you myself, Suhbataar, so painfully that even you will be impressed – and an unarmed catamite hiding up a bridge.' So much for my safe haven. '*This* is your comeback squad? Do you have an aircraft carrier waiting offshore? Are you hoping to kill me by sheer anticlimax?'

'I summoned you here to deliver my verdict.'

'Are you a tertiary syphilitic? Are you Ultraman?'

'I'll allow you to apologize with honour. You may kill yourself.'

'This is beyond stupid, Morino, this is rude. Let me get this right. You *seriously* fuck up my opening day at Xanadu. Persuading the press that Ozaki fell by accident has been a logistical hernia. You hurl bowls at my three managers until their skulls are eggshell – original, I grant you, but annoying in the extreme – then you kill two innocent bouncers the old-fashioned way and shoot my finest dog. My dog, Morino, is what really hurts. You *amateur*. No operator of style ever, *ever* harms an animal.'

'Style? Importing uninspected shitferbeef burgers from the US and killing off Wakayama schoolchildren with O-157, and then getting your Ministry of Agricultural poodles to blame the radish farmers, is this "*style*"? Blackmailing bank executives over the figures you made them cook by refusing to pay back your bubble-economy loans: "*style*"? You call the "pay up, Mr Food Manufacturer, or pay for a razor blade in your baby products" scam "*style*"?'

'Your failure to grasp the fact that the world has progressed since 1970 is why I inherited and expanded Tsuru's interests and why you are still drawing your operational revenue on scaring loose change out of Shinjuku bar owners. How, oh *how*, do you suppose you will still be alive in five minutes?'

'You forgot my two secret weapons.'

'Did I! I am *ablaze* with curiosity.'

'The first weapon is your blazing curiosity, Nagasaki. Even in the old days, you spoke before you shot.'

'Is your second secret weapon as terrifying as your first?'

'I present to you, ladies' – it is hard for me to catch the next word – 'NimQ6.'

'"Nim – Q – 6"? A magic pissing goblin? A drain unblocker?'

'A plastic explosive developed by the Israeli secret service.'

'Never heard of it.'

'Of course you never heard of it. The Israelis do not advertise in *Time*. But microcells of NimQ6 are imbedded in the triggers of the guns your dumb fucking apes are holding. The casings of your swanky Kevlar helmets are peppered with the stuff. My colleague here, Mr Suhbataar, oversaw the customization of your equipment when he diverted them from his Russian military supplier.'

Some of Nagasaki's men turn to look at their boss.

Nagasaki folds his arms. 'In the sad history of sad dumb bluffing fucks with no real cards in their hands, Morino, you are the saddest, dumbest bluffing fuck of them all. Which weapons do you think I used to wipe out Tsuru, for fuck's sake? If there was a gram of truth in this booby-trap shit we would have found out by now.'

'You did not find out, because I needed you to bury the Tsuru faction. For this, I thank you—'

'Thank me when your lying guts are leaking through bullet holes. Now, I have a city to run. Stand away from the motors, you puppy dogs. I ordered those cars myself via our mutual Mongolian and I don't want to damage the paintwork.'

Morino stubs his cigar out on the paintwork. 'Shut up and learn. A gram of truth, you said. NimQ6 microcells weigh one twentieth of a gram. A dot on a page. It is a perfectly stable explosive, even under repeat-fire ricochet conditions, *until* – here is the beauty of the piece – it is oscillated by a specific VHF frequency. Then the microcell explodes with a force ample to blow away body parts. The single oscillator east of Syria is built into my mobile phone.' To me, shivering with cold heat thirty metres up, probably with a sniper aiming at my head, this does not sound overly convincing.

Nagasaki acts bored. 'Enough of this pseudo-science wank, Morino, I—'

'Humour me for ten more seconds. NimQ6 is the stuff of the future. I enter the code – I took the precaution of doing this prior to your arrival tonight – and simply press the dial button. Like this—'

Blossoms of explosions boom and flame and thunder.

I duck.

Shock waves scalp the air.

The reboom echoes off the mountains.

Finally I peer over the parapet. Nagasaki's men are scattered around where they were standing. The men who are out of the glare of the headlights are shadowy piles, but the ones who fell in the light – red as a slaughterhouse floor. Most of the torsos still have their legs attached, but the gun hands are blown away. And their heads – imploded by their combat helmets – are nowhere. I never learned the vocabulary I need to take this in. Only in war movies, horror movies: nightmares. The Cadillac door opens and Popsicle falls on to her knees. She gives a yelp of disgust, as if surprised by a spider in the bath. 'Yaaa!' Lizard bounders around. 'Yaaaaaaaaa! Fucking *yaaaaaaaaa*haaaaaaaaay!' Nagasaki is still alive – no helmet to remove his skull – and trying to get to his feet. Both arms are shredded stumps after the elbows. Morino struts over and puts the megaphone into his enemy's ear. 'Isn't science wonderful?' *Bang!*

The megaphone turns to me. 'Seasonal fireworks, Miyake. Now listen. Midnight has passed. So the document wallet in the Cadillac is all yours. Yes. Father keeps his word. Unfortunately, you won't be able to appreciate your hard-earned information because you'll be dead as a fucking dodo. I brought you along just in case Nagasaki wheeled your father out of retirement. I credited the cretin with too much cunning, so it seems we have one witness too many to the night's entertainment, instead of a possible bargaining chip. Mr Suhbataar has asked to put the bullet through your head, and as he is the chief architect of my master plan, how could I say no? Goodbye. If it makes you feel any better, you were a totally forgettable boy who would have lived a bored, stifled, colourless life. And yeah, your father is a meaningless jerk too. Sweet dreams.'

Why bother? Dead is dead.

'You should crouch for your own safety,' my killer insists.

My fear mangles my response to a stillborn huff.

'No?' Leatherjacket primes his gun. 'Well, I warned you.'

In his hand is not his gun but his mobile telephone. He enters a number, leans over the parapet, points down at the Cadillacs, and crouches.

The night rips open its guts, I am knocked over by a sheer wall of noise, the bridge shakes, a metallic, stony hail falls, I glimpse a flaming piece of car arcing overhead, and the document wallet containing my father is cinders. The night rezips. The echo sonic-booms off the mountains. Gravel presses into my cheekbone. I sort of stand – to my surprise, my body still works. Smoke pours upward from the craters where the Cadillacs were parked.

Leatherjacket enters another number into his mobile phone. I crouch, wondering what could be left to blow up – is he a walking bomb who explodes his own evidence? – but this time the mobile phone is only a mobile phone. 'Mr Tsuru? Suhbataar. Your wishes regarding Mr Nagasaki and Mr Morino have been realized. Indeed, Mr Tsuru. Just as they sowed, they reaped.' He puts his phone away and looks at me.

Burning and crackling.

My lip is bleeding where I bit it. 'Are you going to kill me?'

'I am thinking about it. Are you afraid?'

'I am very, very afraid.'

'Fear is not necessarily a weakness. I disdain weakness, but I disdain waste. To survive, you must persuade yourself that tonight was another man's nightmare into which you accidentally strayed. Find a place to hide by daybreak, and stay hidden for many days. If you assist the police in any way, you will be killed immediately. Do you understand?'

I nod, and sneeze. When I look up, smoke swallows up the night.

Five

ℌ

Study of Tales

MARGINS

Goatwriter peered out at the starless night. His breath misted up the windscreen. First frost floated a wafer of ice on eidelweiss wine. Goatwriter counted three noises. The candle spluttering on his writing bureau; Mrs Comb battling in her sleep, 'Don't care was made to care, Amaryllis Broomhead!'; and Pithecanthropus, snoring in his undercarriage hammock. The fourth noise, the whisperings which Goatwriter was waiting for, was still a way away, so Goatwriter rummaged for his respectable spectacles to leaf through a book of poems composed by Princess Nukada in the ninth century. Goatwriter unearthed this volume one thundery Thursday in Delhi. Since midsummer, every night went the same. The venerable coach parked, Goatwriter woke, and nothing would make him sleep again. One, two, three hours later the whisperings came. Goatwriter told nobody about his insomnia, not even Pithecanthropus, and certainly not Mrs Comb, who was sure to prescribe a ghastly 'curative' worse than the complaint. In the beginning, Goatwriter believed the whisperings were the local Aberdeen waterfalls, but this theory was scotched when the whisperings followed to other locations. Goatwriter's second theory was that he was insane. But with no other mental faculty affected, Goatwriter had come to believe that the whisperings had their origins in his fountain pen – the selfsame pen Lady Shōnagon wrote her pillow book with, over thirteen thousand crescent moons ago. Goatwriter heard a hush, a rustle, and his heart raced faster. He slid Princess Nukada back on the shelf and pressed his ear against the pen shaft. Yes, he thought, here they come. But tonight, the words were more distinct – listen! A 'queer' here, a 'pear' there, an 'ebony mare' everywhere. Goatwriter picked up the fountain pen and began to write, slowly at first, as the words spattered singly, but soon sentences flowed, filled and overspilled.

'Oh, sir, this is the giddy limit!' Mrs Comb opened the morning curtains. 'If you go gallivanting in the wee hours, wrap up proper! If your rheumatism plays up again, Muggins here'll have to do your lugging and carrying, mark my words.'

Goatwriter unpeeled his sticky eyes open. 'Unquiet slumbers, Mrs Comb – I dreamed of m-metal detecting for Norse nonagons in a delta where it was Wednesday m-morning for all eternity.'

Mrs Comb tied her apron strings tight. 'I told you ninety-nine times, sir – "*Creams and honey, dreams turn funny.*" But you insist on your Devonshire suppers. Now, up and about with you. Your breakfast is done. Earl Grey with Zanzibar kippers, grilled to your fancy.' Mrs Comb looked out at the landscape. 'A right dreary spot, and no mistake.'

Goatwriter found his pince-nez on a monocle chronicle and peered. The venerable coach had rolled to a cold shoulder of more still moored still moors. 'Inky landscape, paperpulp sky. I remain in little doubt, Mrs Comb, we are in the margins.' Hawthorn huddled in well-wallowed hollows.

'Drab name for a drab place,' Mrs Comb pronounced.

'The soil is too acidic for colour to take root. A m-marginal duke once tried to station a daffodil plantation, but the yellow bleached away. Even evergreens never greened. No bird is heard, no low crows fly by.'

'Aye, well, sir. Your kippers'll be growing cold.'

Goatwriter frowned. 'Strange to say, Mrs Comb, but of appetite I am bereft. Perhaps I might ask you to put the fish on a dish, and I shall eat them by and by. For now, a splash of tea would suffice—' Goatwriter lost the tail of his sentence. 'How vexatious! I wrote dozens of pages last night – but where are they now?' He looked beneath, between, behind his table – but the pages were gone. 'This is disastrous! I wrote fragments of a truly untold tale!'

Despite decades of service, Mrs Comb was cross about the kippers. 'You had another writing dream, I dare say, sir. Remember when you dreamed you wrote *Les Misérables*? It took your editor a week to persuade you not to take Victor Hugo to court for flagellism.' The door banged open and the wind sprang in. A fearsome prehistoric creature filled the frame with his hairy, mud-spattered torso. He grunted several times in the language of clay and blood. Mrs Comb glared fiercely. 'Don't you dare clomp your filthy mudluggers on my clean carpet!'

'A jolly good m-morning to you, too, Pithecanthropus.' Goatwriter forgot his missing pages. 'What are you holding there, my dear fellow?'

Pithecanthropus opened his cupped hands towards Mrs Comb. A delicate white flower drooped from its clod of earth. 'I say!' exclaimed Goatwriter. 'A Snowdonian snowdrop! In September! How exquisite! How rare!'

Mrs Comb was less impressed. 'I'll thank you for digging up your mucky weeds and carrying them elsewhere! Such a muckster I never beheld! And shut the door on your way out! Do you want me and Sir to catch our deaths?'

Pithecanthropus grunted dejectedly and closed the door.

'Nowt but a hairy savage, that one.' Mrs Comb scrubbed the kipper pan. 'A savage!' Goatwriter felt sorry for his friend, but he knew better than to come between Mrs Comb and her temper.

♌

So I wake up staring at another unfamiliar ceiling, and slip into my amnesia game. I am numb and I want to stay numb. I used to play this after Anju went, when I began my nine-year round of uncles' spare rooms and rice-cracker futons – 'Eiji is visiting this month' – and cousins who had the atomic warhead in any possible argument – 'If you don't like it here, go back to your grandmother's house!' Anyway, the object of the game is to hold on to this sensation of not knowing where I am for as long as possible. I count to ten but I am still clueless. I slept on a ballooning sofa in the middle of a living room, pale curtains covering a big bay window. I have a mouth ulcer the size of a hoofprint. *Bang!* goes the memory bomb. The heads in the bowling alley. I see Morino, cigar-lit. The Mongolian on the unfinished bridge. I flex my sore muscles. My nose and throat in the corked-up stage of a bad cold; my body sorts itself out despite its idiot brain. How long have I been asleep? Who fed Cat? A box of Lark cigarettes on the coffee table. Only three left, and I smoke one after another, lighting them with matches. My teeth feel clad in lagging. The room is warm. I slept in my clothes, my crotch and armpits are stewing. I should open the window, but I can't be bothered to move quite yet. While I lie here nothing new can begin, and more distance opens up between me and the deaths of thirty, forty men. I groan. I cannot unsee what I saw. It will be national news, if not international news. Yakuza Wars, from now until the new year. I groan. Forensics men will be crawling over the battleground with tweezers. The Serious Crime Squad will be interviewing Xanadu shoppers. A girl employed at the already infamous pachinko parlour will have told reporters about an impostor claiming to be the manager's son, moments before Mr Ozaki himself was thrown through the second-floor security window. Police artists will be making charcoal sketches. What do I do? What will the unseen Mr Tsuru want done to me? What has become of Mama-san and Queen of Spades? I have no plan. I have no cigarettes. I have no tissues to ungunge my nose. I listen hard, and I can hear . . . absolutely nothing.

How else would I shunt loose my morning dump if I gave up smoking? Bowel-shaking is one quality of cigarettes that never appears in the surf 'n' bronzed ads. I regret sleeping in my jeans, but I was afraid to undress in case I woke up to hear the door being jemmied and needed to bolt. I still am. This is worse than waiting for an earthquake. But what do I do if I think I hear an intruder? Hide? Where? I have no idea even how many floors this house has. I get up: first stop, toilet. Japanese-squat style, with a bowl of bitter herbs. A good clean birth – Western toilets increase the risk of complications. A Niagara Falls flush. The kitchen is terracotta and spotless – the owner loves cooking, judging from the flour-thumbed recipe books. Each cooking implement hangs on its own hook. Through the window I see an empty carport and a front garden. Roses, weeds and a bird table. A high privet hedge hides the house from the outside world. The cleaning cupboard is well stocked, but is too obvious to hide in. The living room is Japanese – tatami matting, a Buddhist altar with photographs of the recent and long dead, an alcove for flower arrangements, and a hanging scroll with kanji that would give me a headache if I tried to read them. There is no TV, no stereo and no telephone – just a receiver-less fax machine on the top of an ample bookshelf. The books are old, illustrated collections of tales. 'The Moon Princess', 'Urashima Tarō', 'Gon the Fox'. This house seems too orderly for kids. I open the curtains an inch. The back garden is somebody's pride and joy. The pond is bigger than my grandmother's – I can see carp lurking in the green. Late dragonflies skim over the duckweed. A stone lantern sits on an island. Pots of lavender, and a high bamboo grove, thick enough to hide in. Birds nest in an orange mailbox nailed to a silver birch. You could watch this garden for hours. It unfolds. No wonder there is no TV. I go upstairs. The carpet is snowy and lush under my bare feet. A lavish bathroom with seahorse taps. A master bedroom – the décor suggests a middle-aged couple. The smaller bedroom is only used for guests. Well. No hiding places here. You have to be nine years old to find good hiding places in the average house. Anju won by hiding in the washing machine one time. I assume my tour is complete, but notice a slatted cupboard door at the end of the landing. Its knob twizzles uselessly, but it swings open anyway. Its shelves are not shelves, but steep stairs. A knotted rope hangs down to help you haul yourself up. On the third step my head hits the ceiling, which shifts. I push, and a crack of daylight opens as the plyboard trapdoor swings up. I was way wrong. This is better than a hiding place. I emerge into a library/study with the highest book population density I have ever come across. Book walls, book towers, book avenues, book side streets. Book spillages, book rubble. Paperback books, hardback books, atlases, manuals, almanacs. Nine lifetimes of books. Enough books to build an igloo to hide in. The room is sentient with books. Mirrors double and cube the books. A Great Wall of China quantity of books. Enough books to make me wonder if I am a book too. Light comes in through a high triangular window. A sort of wickerwork light shade hangs down. Apart from the bookcases and sagging shelves, the only item of furniture is an old-fashioned writing bureau with square holes to lose papers and bills in. My grandmother had the same sort. Still does, I guess. On the writing bureau are two piles of paper – one white and blank as starched shirts, the other a manuscript laid in a special lacquer tray. I cannot help myself. I sit down and begin reading page one.

♌

Goatwriter worked all morning, trying to reconstruct the fragments of the truly untold tale which whispered before dawn, but it was as taxing as tracking tacks in a jonquil junkyard. Mrs Comb mangled wrangled sheets. Pithecanthropus returned the engine of the venerable coach. Goatwriter finally got up from his writing bureau to look up the correct spelling of *zwitterion* in his dictionary, but got sidetracked by *gustviter* and lured farther away by *durzi* and *theopneust*. Drowsiness ambushed. Goatwriter's last thought was that his dictionary was an impostor pillow, or possibly vice versa.

When Goatwriter awoke from his nap and returned to his writing bureau he thought he was still dreaming. The very pages he had written pre-snooze – they were gone! Impossible! Mrs Comb, he knew, never touched his writing bureau – there was only one explanation.

'Thief!' cried Goatwriter. 'Thief! Thief!'

Mrs Comb rushed in, dropping pegs. 'Sir! Whatever's to do?'

'Burglarized, Mrs Comb, while I lay sleeping!'

Pithecanthropus burst in clenching a French wrench.

'My reconstructed truly untold tale – spirited away!'

'But how could it be, sir? I was hanging out the washing but I seen nowt!'

'Perchance the thief is diminutive, and gained ingress and egress through the exhaust pipe!' This seemed rather far-fetched to Mrs Comb, but she followed Goatwriter and Pithecanthropus outside to the venerable coach's stern. Pithecanthropus knelt, sniffed the tyre-track mud. He grunted.

'An unwashed rodent?' verified Goatwriter. 'Slightly bigger than a mouse? Aha! Then we m-may conclude that the thief is a dirty little rat! Come, friends! We m-must apprehend this scallywag and teach him a thing or two about copyright law! My dear Pithecanthropus – lead the way!'

Pithecanthropus read the ground with his brow furrowed. An anvil cloud lugged past its sluggish mass. The tracks led off the beaten track, down the path not taken, through a sleepy hollow, over a tarn of brackish bilgewater. Mrs Comb caught sight of him first. 'Whatever next by 'eck!' A scarecrow, nailed to a 'T', staked into the lip of a dyke, in a sorry state. His eyes and ears were pecked away, and wispy hay bled from a wound in his side whenever the wind bothered to blow. Goatwriter approached him. 'Ahem. Good day, Scarecrow.'

Scarecrow raised his head, slower than moons over mown meadows.

'Frightfully sorry to trouble you,' began Goatwriter, 'but have you seen a dirty little rat scurry by carrying pages of a stolen manuscript?'

Scarecrow's mouth twitched more slowly than violence of violets. 'This day . . .'

'Splendid!' said Goatwriter. 'Can you tell me which way the thief went?'

'This day . . . we shall sit with my father in Paradise . . .'

At that very moment, two hellhounds hurdled the dyke, sank their slavering fangs into poor Scarecrow, ripped him off his T, and savaged him to windblown tatters. Goatwriter was knocked backward by a lashing paw. Pithecanthropus leaped and swept Mrs Comb into his arms. All that remained of the scarecrow were rags nailed to the wood. Goatwriter tried to recall what to do and what not to do with rabid dogs – play dead? Look them in the eye? Run like billy-oh?

'That'll learn 'im,' growled the top dog, 'to give the plot away!'

'Wot shall us do with these three, boss?' sniffed the underdog.

Goatwriter felt the heat of their breath. 'Good doggies.'

'Ee talks like a writer,' growled the underdog. 'Smells like one. Is one.'

'Ain't got the time,' the top dog barked. 'Our maker is getting away!'

'I want to practise on Beardy first!'

Pithecanthropus got ready to defend his friend, but the hellhounds bounded away over the rises and falls of the margins until they were blots on the wizened horizon. 'Well!' exclaimed Mrs Comb. Then she realized she was still nesting in the arms of Pithecanthropus. 'Put me down this very instant, you mucky lout!'

♌

A door bangs downstairs and the manuscript zooms out of focus. My heart goes seismic and I stop breathing. Somebody is here. Somebody is here for me. Buntarō would have called out by now. So soon? How did they find me? My survival instinct, so shredded by Morino, kicks in now. They are searching the living room, the kitchen, the garden, cranny by nook. My socks, which I left on the sofa. My empty cigarette box. I replaced the plyboard trapdoor and pulled up the rope, but did I close the slatted door? I can hand myself over and hope for mercy. Forget it. Yakuza just do not do mercy. Hide here, under books. But if I cause a book-slide I am done for. Is there anything up here that could serve as a weapon? I listen for footsteps on the shelves – nothing. The intruders are either working in silence, or I am only dealing with one. My default strategy is this: hold a three-ton three-volume set of *A Critical Review of the Japanese "I" Novel* above the trapdoor – when it opens wide enough, lob them through, and hopefully knock the guy backwards. Jump down, land on him – if he has a gun I'm in trouble – bust his ribs and run for it. I wait. And wait. Concentrate. I wait. Am I sure I heard the bang? I left the back window open an inch – suppose it was just the wind? Concentrate! I wait. Nobody. My arms are aching. I cannot stand this. 'Hello?'

The flurry of violence never comes.

Scared by a story I told myself. I am in a bad way.

Later in the afternoon, I go back down. In the spare bedroom closet I find some sheets and towels, and arrange them on the step-shelves behind the slatted door, so hopefully the intruder will think it is just a linen cupboard. I gather up any sign of me, and stuff it into a plastic bag under the sink. I must clean up any traces of myself, as I make them. I should be hungry – when did I last eat? – but my stomach seems to be missing. I need a cigarette, but no way am I venturing outside. Coffee would be fine, but I can only find green tea, so I make a pot. I blow my nose – my hearing comes back, but snots up again – open the bay window, and drink my tea on the step. In the pond carp appear and disappear. Whirligigs bend but never puncture the liquid sky. A ruby-throated bird listens for earthworms. I watch ants. Cicadas muzzzmezzzmezzzmezzzmezzzmuzzzzzzzz. Nowhere in the house is a single clock, or even a calendar. There is a sundial in the garden but the day is too hazy for a clear shadow. It feels three o'clock-ish. The breeze shuffles and flicks through the bamboo leaves. A column of midges hovers above the pond. I sip my tea. My tongue cannot taste a thing. Look at me. Four weeks ago I was on the morning ferry to Kagoshima, with a lunch box from Aunt Orange. I was sure I would find my father before the week was up. Look at who – what – I found instead. What a disaster, what an aftermath. The summer is lost, and other things too. The fax machine beeps. I jump and spill my tea. A message from Buntarō, telling me he'll be over around six, if the traffic lets up. When is six o'clock relative to now? Hours need other hours to make any sense at all. Hanging on the wall above the fax machine is a shell-framed photograph of an old man and woman, maybe in their fifties. I guess they own this house. They are sitting at a café table in the shade on a bright day. He is about to break into laughter at whatever she has just said. She is reading my reaction to see if I genuinely enjoyed her story, or if I am just being polite. Weird. Her face is familiar. Familiar, and impossible to lie to. 'True,' she says, 'we met before.' We look at each other for a while, then I go back to her garden for a bit where the dragonflies live out their whole lives.

♌

'Are you quite sure, m-my dear fellow,' prompted Goatwriter, 'that the tracks stop in this mound of mired mulch?' Pithecanthropus grunted a yes, waded in a yard and picked something up. 'Kipper bones!' squawked Mrs Comb. 'Then I must conclude,' said Goatwriter, 'we have hunted our quarry to its lair.'

'Nowt but an eyesore,' said Mrs Comb, 'and right whiffy to boot.' Upon closer inspection the dwelling proved carefully constructed – bricks of cans, pans and mottled bottles, and mortar of spud skins, burnt rice crusts and 'Vote for Me' leaflets. A bicycle mudguard ascended ramp-wise, to a hole as black as a Hackensack mac. Goatwriter squinted inside. 'So the burglar dwells in this hovel of stiltonic stench.'

'*Hovel?*' An irate rant shot back. 'Give me my *hovel* and stuff ya geriatric rust-bucket bus, *any* day of da month!'

'Aha! So you *are* in residence, thief! Unhand my manuscript forthwith!'

'Take a ☠✍ing hike, ya JoeSchmoe!'

'Soap and water!' gasped Mrs Comb.

Goatwriter lowered his horns. 'Fiend, there are ladies present!'

A tiny hand appeared in the whole and flashed the finger. 'If that scrawny bird is a "lady" I am Frank Sinatra's !☠✍! I'm warnin' ya, if ya ain't skedaddled by da time I count to five I'll slap harassment suits on ya so quick ya won't know your *X!X£*s from Tuesday!'

'Legality! Indeed. A most m-moot point! You broke into our venerable coach, and theived Zanzibar kippers and m-my truly untold tale! Furthermore, by Girton, we don't intend to go back empty-handed!'

'Oooh, a threat! I'm ✈/✹! ing in my didgereedungarees!'

Pithecanthropus grunted impatiently, waded up to the cone of rubbish and clefted the top quarter clean away. Inside was a shocked rat – who a moment later was a furious rat. 'Are ya *IXXX* ✹ing *deranged*? Ya nearly brained me, ya knucklescraping Neanderthal!'

Goatwriter peered through his pince-nez. 'Remarkable – the thief is an apparent relative of *mus musculus domesticus*.'

'I ain't no domestic nuffink, punk! I am da One, da Only, ScatRat! Yeah, yeah, so I *sampled* ya mouldy kippers – where's da big balooey, Huey? But I never lifted no stories. I got *Japanese Scientific Whalers' Weekly* 2 wipe my !● hole. And I swear, ya slander my good name once again my lawyer's gonna sue ya !✹✍s up ya *!#X$*s!'

'Scourers! Detergents!' Mrs Comb covered her ears.

ScatRat hollered all the louder. 'Act ya age, not ya egg size! Ya in da real world margins here!' ScatRat saluted with one finger. 'Rats, 4ever! In Union Are We Linked! ScatRat never never never, is extinct!' With that, the rodent vanished into the benthic bowels of his pyrrhic pile.

Pithecanthropus grunted a question.

'I agree, sir,' said Mrs Comb. 'Don't care should be made to care.'

Goatwriter shook his head sadly. His arthritis hurt. 'Certainly, friends, ScatRat is an exceedingly unpleasant character, but a lack of m-manners per se is no crime. I am afraid the m-mystery of my m-missing m-manuscript must go unsolved. Let us return to the venerable coach. I believe we will be leaving the m-margins tonight.'

Evening on the margins was an unrequited requiem. Mrs Comb was baking a burdock fairy cake to cheer Goatwriter up, and Pithecanthropus was repairing a hole in the roof. Goatwriter proof-read his last page, and laid it to rest in his manuscript tray. His rewrite lacked the magnificent glow that the original truly untold tale retained in his memory.

'Dinner-time, by and by,' called Mrs Comb. 'You must be starving, sir.'

'Peculiar to pronounce, I could not entertain a m-morsel.'

'But, sir! You haven't had a bite the livelong day!'

Pithecanthropus grunted in concern through the hole in the roof.

Goatwriter considered. 'So I haven't.'

'Still fretting about your missing stories, sir? We'll be leaving the margins and burglars and the like far behind.'

Pithecanthropus double-took and grunted frantically.

'By 'eck, you savage! Clap that trap! Sir is out of sorts enough as it is!'

Goatwriter frowned. 'M-my dear fellow, whatever is distressing you so?'

Mrs Comb dropped her cookery book. 'Sir! What are you eating?'

'Why, only a little paper cud—' Goatwriter's jaws froze. The truth dawned. Mrs Comb spelt it out. 'Sir! You were eating your own pages as you wrote them!'

Goatwriter's words stuck in his throat.

♌

When evening comes I turn off all the lights and wait for Buntarō in the kitchen, so nobody knows I am here, and so I can see Buntarō arriving and know it is him and not anyone else. I stare at a wall-tile whorl as minutes spin by and die. Here come the headlights of

Buntarō's car now, swinging into the car porch. It still seems weird to think of Buntarō existing anywhere except the counter at the Shooting Star. I hate needing. I spent the last nine years trying to avoid needing – generosity, charity, affection, sympathy, money. And here I am again. I unlock the front door. 'Hi.'

'Sorry I'm late. Heavy traffic. Has your fever gone?'

'It turned into this cold.'

'So that's why you sound like a parrot. Here, I bought you an emergency six-pack of Ebisu Export and a Hokka-Hokka take-out. Eat it before it gets cold and starts tasting like what it's made of.' He hands me the bag as he slips out of his sandals. 'And some cigarettes. Wasn't sure what you smoke, so I bought Peace.'

'Thanks . . . I'm sorry, but I lost my appetite.'

'No matter. I trust your nicotine craving rages unabated?'

'Peace is fine.'

'What are you doing all shut up in the dark?'

'No reason.' I switch the lights on as we go through to the living room.

'Whoah!' Buntarō looks at my black eye. 'A beaut!'

'Who's looking after Shooting Star?'

'My wife. Who do you think?'

'But she should be taking it easy. Being, uh, pregnant, I mean.'

'Worse than pregnant – bored and pregnant. In fact we had a mini-row this morning. She says she is tired of being treated like an invalid whale, and that if she sees another daytime TV programme about how to make pep bottles into traditional dolls she is going to buy a gun. Yes, if you are wondering, she knows what happened. But the good news is, it seems she is the only person in the whole wide world who does know.'

'What?'

'Nothing on the news. Nothing in the papers.'

'Impossible.'

Buntarō shrugs. 'Lad, it never happened.'

'It happened.'

'Not if it didn't happen on the news.'

'You do believe me?'

'Hey! I drove around all night, remember, you idiot.'

'So everything – the guns, the explosions?'

'Censored. Or probably cleaned up before the police even heard about it. Yakuza clean up their own shit, if only to hide how much they eat. Be grateful, lad. It gives us one less thing to worry about.'

'But what about the pachinko manager?'

'Who knows? Fell through a window while changing a light bulb.'

We go outside and smoke on the step. Dusk fades away. A carp plishes, now and then. I switch off the lights to keep the insects away. The frogs croak and crike. 'What's the difference between frogs and toads, country boy?' asks Buntarō.

'Toads live for ever. Frogs get run over.'

'My taxes went on your education.'

'Buntarō, one other thing. You remember I told you about a cat—'

'That animal? Yeah, her and my wife are already the best of friends. Her future is guaranteed. Time to feed the fish.' He goes inside and emerges with a box of mealy stuff that smells the same as the Hokka-Hokka take-out. We take it in turns to chuck a pinchful into the pond. Carp thresh and slurp.

'Buntarō, I really need to thank you.'

'Fish feed? Dirt cheap.'

'I'm not talking about the fish feed.'

'Oh, the cigarettes. Pay me back later.'

I give up.

♌

HUNGRY TOWN

Mrs Comb laid her final egg for the week. She nestled it in cotton wool, placed it with the others in her wicker basket, and covered them all with a tea towel. Then she ran through her shopping list a final time: size nine knitting needle, nit lotion, Indian indigo ink, Polish polish, Zanzibar marzipan, two cans Canadian toucan candles. A knock on her boudoir door was followed by Goatwriter's 'Ahem'.

'Yes, sir?'

The door creaked open and Goatwriter squinted over his glasses. 'I believe m-market day is with us again, Mrs Comb?'

'Aye, sir. I'm off to sell my eggs.'

'Splendid, splendid. I sense a shocking shortage of short stories hereabouts. I thought perhaps you could take one of my volumes to the m-market, and see if a storybroker comes along. You never know. Supply, demand, and all that . . .'

'Right you are, sir.' Mrs Comb was sceptical, but she didn't want to hurt Goatwriter's feelings, so she slipped the book into her apron pocket. The door banged open and the wind sprang in. Pithecanthropus stood on the threshold, and grunted a question to Mrs Comb. 'Aye,' she answered, 'I'm leaving now. And no, you can't come with me – I don't want you scaring away all the customers like that time in Marrakesh-under-marsh.' Pithecanthropus grunted a favour, and opened his cupped palms at Mrs Comb. She nearly dropped her basket. '*Worms!* In my boudoir! Respectable, well-fed folk live in these parts! Nobody eats *worms*! How dare you even think of putting those slimy creatures in with my lovely fresh eggs! Get away with you this instant! Lout!'

Bless my weathered feathers! thought Mrs Comb as she made her way across the blasted heath. Whatever became of this place? The landscape had once been beautiful, but now crops were dead or dying, trees stripped or ripped, and craters pocked the scorched, torched ground. Virile red-hot pokers thrusted from rusted, busted tanks through uranium shell-holes. Thistles whistled. A pipe dribbled sewage into a mire of wire. The stench made Mrs Comb cover her nose with her headscarf. 'By 'eck!'

Suddenly the sky screamed at the top of its lungs.

Mrs Comb barely had time to shelter her precious basket of eggs and cover her ears with her wings before the sonic boom hit, blowing her apron over her head and ballooning her knickerbockers. The shock waves ebbed away. Mrs Comb peered out and got to her feet. Looking up, she saw a peculiar sight – a hippie and his psychedelic surfboard, falling out of the sky, straight towards Mrs Comb! Acting on reflex, she scooped up her basket and fluttered behind a large barrel labelled 'Agent Orange'. The hippie hit the dirt at terminal velocity. Stones and collision noises showered from the impact crater. Mrs Comb watched the dust settle, too buffeted to say a word, even to herself. From the crater she heard a groan. 'Oh, *man*!' The hippie heaved himself over the edge. His dreadlocks were ginger, his sunglasses wraparound and his halo wonky. '*Man*.' Seeing Mrs Comb, he made the peace sign. 'Good day, ma'am.'

Mrs Comb found her tongue. 'That were a nasty tumble, and no mistake.'

'Darned Phantoms! *Totally* blew me away! Never even saw 'em coming. They must be bombing the town, if they can find anything left to bomb. Still, the munitions are there, so they gotta use 'em up.'

'Is owt broken?'

'Only my pride, ma'am, thanks for asking. I'm immortal, y'see.'

'I beg your pardon?'

'Immortal. My name's God. Mighty pleased to make your acquaintance.'

This unsettled Mrs Comb. Should she curtsy? 'Charmed, I'm sure. But if a town is about to be bombed, shouldn't you do something?'

God readjusted his halo. 'Would if I could, ma'am, but once the military decides to bomb the living bejesus out of a country . . . well.' He shrugged. 'Time was, we had a divine veto on wars, but our executive powers got whittled away, bit by bit, and now nobody even bothers consulting us.'

'Fancy . . . just what does it take to stop a war, may I ask?'

God made a 'search me' face. 'Tell you the truth, ma'am, I never wanted to be no God. My daddy insisted, it running in the family and all. I flunked the Ivy League divinity colleges, and wound up in California.' God grew nostalgic. 'Surf was high, the sand was gold, and the babes! The babes . . . Divine intervention was compulsory on the syllabus, but I skipped most of the lectures for the breakers on Big Sur! Stopping wars? One sticky spittoon of guacamole, ma'am. So, I graduated, third-class dishonours, and the only thing I learned was the water-to-wine scam. Daddy tried to pull strings, but heaven, ma'am' – God lowered his voice – 'is another word for nepotism. Golden City makes the freemasons look meritocratic. Ain't what you know – it's who you know and where you know 'em from. The cronies of the Almighty get given the stable democracies, and us nobodies get the war zones and peacekeeping missions. Ma'am, do you have the time?'

Mrs Comb checked her wristwatch. 'Five and twenty to eleven.'

'*Bonymaronie!* I gotta get my videos back to the shop or they'll fine me again!' God clicked his fingers and his surfboard levitated from the impact crater. God jumped aboard and waggled his sunglasses. 'Been mighty fine passing the time of day with you, ma'am. If you run into any trouble, just send me a wing and a prayer!' He crouched in a kung fu position and surfed away. Mrs Comb watched the dwindling divinity disappear. 'Aye. Well, I won't hold my breath.'

♌

In the parched fog and half-light I wake with a yell because an old woman in black leans over me. I sort of spasm, and fall off the sofa. 'Steady,' the old woman says, 'steady, child. You were dreaming. It's me, Mrs Sasaki, from Ueno station.' Mrs Sasaki. I unclench, breathe in, breathe out. Mrs Sasaki? Fog blows away. She smiles and shakes her head. 'Sorry I startled you so. Welcome back to the land of the living. Buntarō neglected to mention I would be visiting this morning, am I correct?'

I untense and breathe deeply. 'Morning . . .'

She puts down a sports bag. 'I brought you some items from your apartment. I thought they might make your stay here more comfortable. Though had I known about your black eye, I would have brought a T-bone steak.' I am embarrassed that Mrs Sasaki saw the mess I live in. 'I must admit, I thought you would be up by now. Why don't you sleep in the guest room, you foolish youth?'

My mouth is dust and glue. 'I feel safer down here, I guess. Mrs Sasaki – you, Buntarō – how did he know your number at Ueno? How do you know Shooting Star, and Buntarō?'

'I'm his mother.' Mrs Sasaki smiles at my astonishment. 'We all have a mother somewhere, you know. Even Buntarō.'

Pieces slot into place. 'How come neither of you said anything?'

'You never asked.'

'It never occurred to me to ask.'

'Then why should it occur to us to tell you?'

'My job?'

'Buntarō got you the interview, but you got the job yourself. None of this matters. We shall discuss your position at Ueno over breakfast. One thing at a time. First, you are to clean yourself up and shave. You look as if you spent the week camping out with the homeless in Ueno park. It is high time you stopped yourself going to seed. While you shower, I shall cook, and I expect you to eat more than me. What is the point in saving your hide if you go on hunger strike?'

I stay in the shower for ages, until my bone marrow is hot and my finger pads wrinkle. I body-shampoo myself three times from scalp to toes. When I come out, even my cold is better and I weigh less. Now I shave. I am lucky, I only need to shave once a week. The boys in my class at high school used to boast about how often they shaved, but there are a hundred other things I would rather do with my time than drag steel over my hair follicles. Still, a suggestion from Mrs Sasaki is more or less an order. Uncle Money gave me a shaver a couple of years ago, but Uncle Tarmac laughed when he saw it and said real men use blades. I am still on my first packet of Bic disposables. I splash on cold water, and rinse my blade under the cold tap – Uncle Tarmac says the cold makes the razor contract and sharpen. I think of him every time I shave. I smear on Ice Blue shaving gel, especially the groove between the upper lip and the nose – why is there no name for that? – and my chin cleft, and the lower jaw hinge where I usually cut myself. Wait until the gel stings. Then start on the flatlands near the ears where it hurts least. I sort of like this pain. Tugged, uprooted. Some pain is best conquered by diving into it. Around the nose. Ouch! Rinse away, stubbly goo, I chase it down the plug-hole. More cold water. I touch my black eye until it hurts. Clean boxers, T-shirt, shorts. I can smell cooking. I go downstairs and put my shaving stuff back in the sports bag. I catch the eye of the lady in the shell photograph. 'There, feeling better now? You worry too much. You are quite safe here. Tell me what happened. Give me your story. Speak. Give it to me.'

The Mongolian disappeared into thin air. The burning Cadillacs broke into fresh applause. My senses struggled back from wherever, and I knew I had to get away from that place as soon as possible. I started jogging down the bridge. Not running, I knew I had a long night in front of me. I did not look over the parapet again, and I did not look over my shoulder. I was not even tempted. The thick smoke spun with plutonium fumes. I willed myself to become a machine whose product was distance. I jogged a hundred paces, and walked a hundred, over and over, along the perimeter road, scanning the moonlit distance for cars. I could hide down the embankment if anything came – the slope was built of those shorefront prefabricated concrete blocks with big hollows. Horror, shock, guilt, relief: all the predictable things, I felt none of them. All I could feel was this urge to put distance between me and everything I had seen. Stars weakened. The fear that I would be caught and nailed to the crimes on the reclaimed land shook open emergency seams of stamina, and I kept my hundred-hundred regime up until the perimeter road curved through the roadblock and on to the main coastal road that led back to Xanadu. The dawn was scorching the horizon and the traffic on the main thoroughfare towards Tokyo was thickening. The aspirin moon was dissolving in the lukewarm morning. Drivers and passengers stared at me. Nobody walks out there, there was no pavement, just a sort of bulldozed-up ridge of ground – they assumed I had escaped from a mental hospital. I thought about hitch-hiking, but figured this could attract attention to me. How would I explain what I was doing there? I heard a fleet of police sirens approach. Luckily I was passing a family restaurant, so I could hide in the entrance and pretend to make a phone call. I was wrong – no police cars, only two ambulances. What should I do? My fever was taiko-drumming my brain. I had no plan of action beyond calling Buntarō and begging for help, but he wouldn't be at Shooting Star until eleven and I didn't have his home number, and I was afraid he would dump my stuff on the pavement when he found out what sort of company I kept. 'Are you okay, lovie?' asked a waitress behind the till. 'Do you need anything for that eye?' She looked at me so kindly that the only way I could stop myself blubbing was leaving rudely without answering. I envy her son. The route passed an industrial estate – at least I had a pavement to walk on. Every streetlight switched itself off simultaneously. The factory units went on for ever. They all made things for other factory units: stacking shelves, packing products, fork-lift gearboxes. The drumming was subsiding, but the fever was now steaming the contents of my skull. I had used everything up. I should try to get back to the family restaurant, I thought, and collapse in the lap of the angel of mercy. Collapse? Hospitals, doctors, questions? Twenty-year-olds don't collapse. The restaurant was too far behind me. There was a bench in front of a tiling sealant factory. I don't know why anyone put a bench there, but I sat down gratefully, in the shade of a giant Nike trainer. I hate this world. NIKE. THERE IS NO FINISHING LINE. Across a weed-strewn wasteland I could see Xanadu and

Valhalla. One great circle. A firing pistol went off somewhere, and the sun sprang up, running. A bird was singing – a long, human whistling note, then a starburst of bird code at the end. Over and over. Same bird lives on Yakushima, I swear. I willed myself to get up, and make it as far as Xanadu, where I could find some air-conditioning and a place to sleep until I could phone Shooting Star. I willed myself, but my body wouldn't move. A white car slowed down. Beep, beep. Beepy white car. Go away. The door opened from the inside, and the driver leaned over the passenger seat. 'Look, lad, I'm not Zizzi Hikaru but unless you know of a better offer coming along, I suggest you climb in.' An uncoupled moment as I realized the driver was actually Buntarō. A haggard, stressed Buntarō. I was too drained to even wonder how, who, when, why. I was asleep in thirty seconds.

♌

The market town was a razed maze of clubbed rubble and treeless scree. The mosque on the hill had taken a direct hit, its innards lobotomized and its windows blasted out. The building gazed blankly over the town. Trams lay toppled and stripped. Abandoned children lay by the roadside, skin shrink-wrapped around protruding bones. Flies drank from their tear ducts. Vultures circled near enough to hear the wind in their feathers, and hyenas skulked in the gutters. A white Jeep from a peacekeeping organization drove past, nearly running Mrs Comb over, taking lots of photographs and news footage. Mrs Comb came to an enormous statue reigning over the ruin. *The Beloved Commander*, read the plaque. In his shadow, a gaunt man sizzled worms over a fire for his family. The ballasted, bombastic, brassy, beetle-browed, bulging dictator on the plinth was the very opposite of the gaunt man beneath, whose skeleton seemed to have been twisted out of coat hangers. 'Excuse me,' said Mrs Comb, 'I'm looking for the marketplace.'

He glowered at her. 'You're standing in it.'

Mrs Comb realized he was quite serious. 'This wasteland?'

'There is a war on, lady, in case you haven't noticed!'

'But surely people still need to eat?'

'Eat what? We are under siege.'

'Siege?'

The gaunt man dangled a worm over the mouth of his son, who delicately took it from the chopsticks, and chewed without expression. 'Well, they call a "siege" "sanctions" these days. It is an easier word to swallow.'

'Fancy . . . who is the war between, exactly?'

'Sssh!' The man looked around. 'That's classified! You'll be arrested for asking questions like that!'

'Surely you know, when the soldiers fight each other?'

'The soldiers? They never fight each other! They might get hurt! They have a gentleman's agreement – never fire at a uniform. The purpose of war is to kill as many civilians as possible.'

'Shocking!' Then Mrs Comb said something rather unwise. 'Looks like I won't be able to sell my eggs, after all.'

A fertilizer bag flapped open and the gaunt man's wife crawled out. 'Eggs?' The gaunt man tried to shush her, but she shrieked, 'Eggs!' The still noon shook as the word spread like shockwaves. 'Eggs!' Orphans without forearms emerged from drains. 'Eggs!' Old women tapped their canes. 'Eggs!' Men appeared in doorless doorways, eye sockets hollow with hunger. 'Eggs!' A menacing mob encircled the statue. Mrs Comb tried to calm the situation. 'Now, now, no need to—' The mob surged – a hurricane huckus of hoohah, hubbub and hounding hands broke over Mrs Comb and swept her basket away. The mob roared. Mrs Comb squawked in terror as her eggs rolled away and were pounded to shell-spatted yolk and white underfoot. Mrs Comb flapped and rose above the crowds – she hadn't flown since she was a spring chicken, and couldn't stay airborne for more than a few seconds. The only nearby roosting place was the handlebar moustache of the beloved commander. The crowd watched her, awestruck. 'She flew! The lady flew!' Only a tiny fraction of the mob was near enough to fight for the gobs of crushed egg. The rest looked at Mrs Comb. A little kid said it first. 'She ain't no lady!'

'I most certainly am a lady!' retorted Mrs Comb. 'My father ruled the roost!'

'Ladies don't fly! She's a *hen*!'

'I am a *lady!*'

The word devoured the hungry town as wildfire devours thornbush thickets of Thales. Not 'lady', not 'hen' but: 'Chicken! Chicken! Chicken!'

♌

Mrs Sasaki ladles my miso soup from the pan into a lacquer bowl. Koiwashi fish and cubes of tōfu. Anju loved koiwashi – our grandmother used to serve it this way. The miso paste swirls at the bottom, deep-sea sludge. Yellow daikon pickles, salmon rice-balls wrapped in seaweed. Sheer comfort food. I exist on toast and yoghurt in my capsule, assuming I get up early enough: this is too much hassle to make. I know I should be ravenous, but my appetite is still in hiding. I eat to please Mrs Sasaki. When my grandmother's dog Caesar was dying, he ate just to please her. 'Mrs Sasaki, I have some questions.'

'I imagine you do.'

'Where am I?'

She passes me the bowl. 'You didn't ask Buntarō?'

'Yesterday was weird all day, I wasn't thinking straight. At all.'

'Well, you are staying in the house of my sister and brother-in-law.'

'Are they the couple in the seashell photo above the fax?'

'Yes. I took that photograph myself.'

'Where are they now?'

'In Germany. Her books sell very well there, so her publisher flew her over for a literary tour. Her husband is a scholar of European languages, so he burrows in university libraries while she does her writerly duties.'

I slurp my soup. 'This is good. A writer? Does your sister work in the attic?'

'She prefers "fabulist". I was wondering if you would find the study.'

'I hope it was okay to go up there. I, uh, even began reading some stories I found on the writing desk.'

'I don't think my sister would object. Unread stories aren't stories.'

'She must be a special person, your sister.'

'Finish those rice-balls. Why do you say that?'

'This house. In Tokyo, but it could be in a forest during the Kofun period. No telephones, no TV, no computer.'

Mrs Sasaki purses her lips when she smiles. 'I must tell her that. She'll love it. My sister doesn't need a telephone – she was born deaf, you see. And my brother-in-law says the world needs less communication, not more.' Mrs Sasaki slices an orange on the chopping board, and zest spray-leaks. She sits down. 'Miyake-kun, I don't think you should come back to Ueno. We have no proof those people or their associates want to find you, but nor do we have any proof that they don't. I vote that we shouldn't take any risks. They knew where to find you on Friday. As a precaution I ensured your Ueno records were misfiled. I think you should sit tight here, until the end of the week – if anybody comes asking for you at Shooting Star, Buntarō will tell them you skipped town. If not, the coast is clear enough.'

This makes sense. 'Okay.'

'Worry about the future from next week.' Mrs Sasaki pours the tea. 'In the meantime, rest. You don't so much solve problems as live through them.'

Green tea with barley grains. 'Why are you and Buntarō helping me?'

'"Who" matters more than "Why". Eat.'

'I don't understand.'

'No matter, Eiji.'

*

Later, the same day. The doorbell chimes and my heart coils up again. I put the manuscript down. Not Buntarō, not Mrs Sasaki, so who? I am up in the attic study, but I hear a key turned in the front door. I am learning the silences that fill this house, and I know what is in my head and what is not – there, the door swings open, feet in the entrance hall. The books are straining to hear, too. 'Miyake! Relax! This is Yuzu Daimon! Come out, come out, wherever you are! Your landlord gave me the key.' We meet on the stairs. 'You look better than when I last saw you,' I say. 'Most road-kills look better than me last Friday,' he replies. 'But you look worse. Sheesh! They did that to your eye?' His T-shirt reads *Whoever dies with the most stuff wins*. 'I came to bring you my apology. I thought I could chop off my little finger.'

'What would I do with your little finger?'

'Whatever. Pickle it, keep it in an enamelled casket: ideal for picking your nose in polite society. What a conversation piece: "It formerly belonged to the notorious Yuzu Daimon, you know."'

'I'd rather use my own finger, thanks. And' – I wave my hand, vaguely – 'going back was my decision, not yours.'

'Oh well, I bought you ten boxes of cigarettes to tide you over,' he says. I see he is still unsure whether or not I want to murder him. 'If I had to cut off a finger every time I needed to apologize, I'd be up to my shoulder blade by now. Marlboro. I remembered you smoked Marlboro in the pool hall on the fateful night. And your landlord thought you might like your guitar to keep you company, so I brought it over. I left it down in the entrance hall. How do you feel?' How do I feel? Weird, but not angry. 'Thanks,' I say. He shrugs. 'Well, considering . . .' I shrug. 'The garden is good for smoking.'

Once I begin – from the point where I loaded him into the taxi – I cannot stop until the end – the point where Buntarō loaded me into his car. I can't remember talking so long, ever. Daimon never interrupts, except to light our cigarettes and to get a beer from the fridge. I even tell him about my father and why I came to Tokyo in the first place. When I finally finish the sun has gone. 'What amazes me,' I say, 'is that none of what happened has been reported. How can forty people get killed – not quietly, either, but action-movie deaths – and it not be reported?'

Bees peruse swaying lavender. 'Yakuza wars make the police look crap and the politicos look bent. Which, as everybody knows, is true. But by admitting it, the voters of Tokyo may be prompted to wonder why they bother paying taxes. So it gets kept off TV.'

'But the newspapers?'

'Journalists are fed reports of battles already won and lost higher up the mountainside. Original, story-sniffing journalists get blacklisted from news conferences, so newspapers can't keep them on. Subtle, isn't it?

'Then why bother with the news at all?'

'People want their comic books and bedtime stories. Look! A dragonfly! The old poet-monks used to know what week of what month it was, just by the colour and the sheen of dragonflies' – whatd'yacall'em? – fuselages.' He plays with his lighter. 'Did you tell your landlord the uncensored version of what happened to you?'

'I toned down the violence. I also left out the death threats to his wife, since the man who made them is . . . dead. I still don't know what is right, and what will give him nightmares and paranoia.'

Daimon nods. 'Sometimes there isn't a right thing to do, and the best you can hope for is the least worst. Do you dream about it?'

'I don't sleep much.' I open a can of beer. 'What are your plans?'

'My dad thinks I should disappear for a while, and for once we agree. I'm going back to the States in the morning. With my wife.'

I splurt out beer. 'You're *married*? Since when?'

Daimon looks at his watch. 'Five hours ago.'

This is Daimon's sincere smile. I only see it once, and only for a moment.

'Miriam? Kang Hyo Yeoun?'

The smile is put away. 'Her real name is Min. Not many people know her real name, but we owe you. I gather she administered you her famous kick.'

'I sewed them back on. Min? Her name never stays the same.'

'It will from now on.'

We clink cans. 'Congratulations. Quick, uh, wedding.'

'That is the point of clandestine marriage and elopement.'

'I got the impression you hated each other.'

'Hate.' Diamon examines his hands. 'Love.'

'Do your parents know?'

'They've lived separately for ten years – always very respectably, of course. But they kind of forfeited their rights to advise me on . . .' Daimon plays with his lighter. '. . . relationship matters.'

'Shouldn't you be with, uh, Min-san?'

'Yes. I need to be leaving to pick up our air tickets. But before I go, will you show me the photograph of your father?' I unfold it from my wallet. He studies it closely, but shakes his head. 'Sorry, I never saw the guy. But listen, I'll ask my dad if he can't find out the contact details of the detective Morino was in the habit of using. Yakuza usually use the same one or two trusted people. I can't promise – the police department at City Hall is in pandemonium, nobody knows who's in bed with whom, and Tsuru is apparently back from Singapore, minus chunks of his memories and sanity, but maybe useful as a figurehead. But I can promise to try. After that you'll be on your own, but at least you may have a lead to a Plan B.'

'Plan G. Any lead is better than no lead.'

We go to the entrance hall. Daimon puts on his sandals. 'Well, then.'

'Well, then. Enjoy your honeymoon.'

'That is what I like about you, Miyake.'

'What is?'

He climbs into his Porsche, and gives me a quarter-wave.

♌

'Truss her!' howled one section of the mob. 'Baste her!' howled another. 'Roast her with spuds!' How Mrs Comb wished

Pithecanthropus would come running across the wrecked square and carry her away to safety. She wouldn't have complained, even if she found a flea in his hair. 'Chicken nuggets!' screamed a line of toddlers. 'Potato fries!' A ladder appeared, and with a fresh seizure of fear Mrs Comb realized they were going to climb up the statue of the beloved commander and cart her off to the ovens. How could Goatwriter possibly cope without her? He would starve. That was when Mrs Comb remembered the book he had given her. 'Hold your horses!' she squawked. 'And you'll dine on something tastier than stringy old chicken!'

The mob waited.

Mrs Comb waved the holy book. 'Stories!'

A hoochy-koochy hooker honked. 'Stories never filled *my* belly!'

The ladder moved nearer. Mrs Comb gulped. 'Maybe you never heard the right stories, then!'

'Prove it!' yelled a wolfman in ash and sackcloth. 'Tell us a story, and see if they fill us up!' Mrs Comb turned to page one, wishing Goatwriter's handwriting wasn't so spidery. '"Once upon a time a high-wire artist visited the waterfalls at Saturn to perform the greatest tightrope spectacle that was ever seen or, surely, ever will be seen. The long-awaited night arrived, and the artist set forth on his death-defying balancing act. Every ounce of concentration the artist possessed would be needed. Above his head spun many moons. Below his feet, the unending cataract of Saturn fell, fell, fell to the limitless ocean, too deep for sound. Halfway across this majestic silence, the high-wire artist was amazed to see a girl strolling across the wire towards him. Why describe this girl of his dreams? You already know what she looks like. 'Why are you here?' asked the artist. 'I came to ask if you believe in ghosts.' The artist frowned. 'Ghosts? Why, do you believe in ghosts?' The girl of his dreams smiled, and replied, 'But of course I do.' And she skipped off the wire. Horror-struck, the artist followed her slow fall, but long before she hit the water she had dissolved into the moonlight—"' A cobblestone missed Mrs Comb by an inch. 'I'm still hungry!' yelled the wolfman in ash and sackcloth. The ladder was propped up against the body of the beloved supreme commander. Tooth and nail, the mob fought to climb up. 'Wait, wait, you'll crack up laughing when you hear this one.' Mrs Comb flapped, lost her place, turned to page nine. '"Father! Father! Why hast thou forsaken me?"'

The noon sun browned, greyed, chilled and marooned.

The mob fell silent – then nervous – and then hysterical.

'Phantoms!' screamed the crowd as one. 'Run for the bomb shelters!' The men, women and children drained away into cracks, crannies and culverts, until Mrs Comb was left alone with the beloved commander and the body of a black marketeer whose skull had been staved in by the hurled cobblestone. 'Goodness gracious,' said Mrs Comb.

'*Great* balls of fire!' said God, hovering up on his surfboard. 'Ma'am.'

'God?'

'I believe you called?'

'I did?'

'This neighbourhood ain't what is used to be, ma'am. What say I give you a lift someplace else?'

Mrs Comb clucked with relief. 'Oh, God! You arrived in the nick of time! Nowt but cannibals in these parts, nowt but cannibals! If it isn't too much of an imposition, I'd thank you kindly to take me back to the venerable coach.'

'Climb aboard, ma'am.' God moved his surfboard alongside the handlebar moustache of the beloved commander. 'And hold on tight!' Mrs Comb tightened her headscarf, and watched the hungry town unroll below her. Why did humans despise what was beautiful and good? Why did they destroy the things they needed the most? Mrs Comb could not understand human beings. She really could not understand.

♌

Back on the balcony step I light another cigarette. The box of Marlboro is way too heavy. I look inside. Yuzu Daimon's platinum lighter. One side is inscribed in English, so I get a dictionary to work out what the words mean: *To General MacArthur on occasion of seventy-first birthday, January 1951, from Aichi Citizens Repatriation Committee – Earnest Beseech to Assist Countrymen Captured USSR*. So the lighter really was the real thing! It must be worth . . . what? A lot. Way too much. I go back to the entrance hall and peer through the front door, but Daimon is gone. The sound of a sports car – maybe Daimon's, maybe not – is swallowed by the afternoon neighbourhood. This is more than a little finger. Sort of sad, too. I wonder how many Aichi citizens ever made it home.

♌

QUEEN ERICHNID'S WEB

Pithecanthropus peered out of his undercarriage hammock. The venerable coach was on its juddery night journey. White lines and cat's-eyes sped from blurry darkness ahead like salmon in a river of hyperspace. Pithecanthropus loved the lullaby swing of the hammock as the coach banked, and the headwind combing his hair. A piebald rabbit, headlit, hypnotized and huddled, hurtled unharmed between the wheels – its nose nearly touched Pithecanthropus's. 'Hot diggetty!' thought the rabbit, finding itself alive after all. 'The angel of death is one ugly critter! Wait until I tell my relatives!' By and by, Pithecanthropus yawned, and slid back down his hammock, settling in the sediment of broken wishbones, flat batteries, oily rags, and Stilton rind. His final thought was that it wasn't the venerable coach which moved over the earth, it was the earth which spun beneath its ancient stationary wheels.

The vacuum cleaner of Mrs Comb in her boudoir directly above bumped Pithecanthropus out of his morning dreams, and he awoke a happy early man. The venerable coach had come to a standstill. Even in the undercarriage, Pithecanthropus could tell they were parked somewhere hotter than a Sahara saxophone sextet. After munching on dry-roasted locusts, he crawled out, and stood up in an arid ochre desert of pebbles, boulders and bleached behemoth bones. The naked eyeball of the sun stared unblinkingly from a sky pinkish with dry heat. A desert wind did nothing to cool the world it wandered through. The road ran as straight as a mathematical constant to the vanishing point. A quorum of quandom quokkas thumped off as Pithecanthropus flexed his powerful biceps, drummed his treble-barrelled chest and howled a mighty roar. The coach door opened and Mrs Comb shook the crumbs from the breakfast tablecloth. 'What an ungodly racket!' Goatwriter climbed down the steps and sniffed the desert air. 'Good morning.'

Pithecanthropus grunted a greeting and a question.

'I believe,' Goatwriter replied, 'we are in the Northern Territories, but of Australia or M-mars I cannot be sure. If one consults—'

Goatwriter never finished his sentence because a miraculous maelstrom of birds rose from nowhere and filled the air around the venerable coach – moogurning, phewlitting, macawbering, endizzying birds, many unseen since the days when mythology was common gossip. '*Archaeopteryx*!' exclaimed Goatwriter. 'Thewlicker's goose! *Quetzalcoatlus*! Greater Hopeless Auks! Nightjars at noon! Listen! Listen to the tune! Fragments! I hear fragments!' Goatwriter closed his eyes and a druggy smile graced his face. Pithecanthropus gazed too, remembering childhood days in fossilized forests. Mrs Comb had dived for cover beneath the venerable coach. The birds vanished thitherly as suddenly as hitherly. 'Extra*ordinary* avifauna!' declared Goatwriter. 'You can come out now, Mrs Comb! Do you know, I heard fragments of a truly untold tale! The birds were singing it! Excuse me, friends, I m-must return to m-my writing bureau this very instant!'

♌

Another two or three days of nothing weather go by. This is how I spend them. I get up late, smoke in the garden, and make some tea and toast. I watch my black eye dapple lighter. I clean up the living room and the kitchen, hide my rubbish, and go up to the attic to read. I feel safest up there. I am turning into a reading machine. I read detective stories by Kogorō Akechi. I read *Kitchen* by Banana Yoshimoto, and hate it, without being sure why. I read *The Makioka Sisters* by Junichirō Tanizaki, and love it. I read a weird novel by Philip Dick about a parallel universe where Japan and Germany won the Second World war, in which an author writes a weird novel about a parallel universe where America and England won. I read *No Longer Human* by Osamu Dazai, but the hero feels so sorry for himself that I want him to jump in the sea long before he does. Anju used to read, never me. Looking back, I was jealous of her books for the hours she gave them. And at high school we had those Japanese classes designed to maim the fun of reading, with all those questions like *Indicate the word most appropriately describing the emotion we experience when we read the following: "The mournful cries of the seagulls were borne over the waves as my father set sail for the final time." a] nostalgic. b] poignant. c] wistful. d] esoteric. e] heartful.* 'We.' Who is this 'We' jerk-off anyway? I never met him. This morning I am reading a French novel called *Le Grand Meaulnes*. I am fat on books. For snacks between meals I read the Goatwriter stories by Mrs Sasaki's sister. There are dozens of them. Mrs Sasaki says her sister wrote them for her nephew, Buntarō, when he was a little boy – Buntarō had a childhood? Weird. Now she writes them to warm up in the morning. Reading is hungry work. When I feel like lunch I go down to the kitchen and eat some food from the fridge, and an apple or banana. Afterwards I trawl the pond for fallen leaves with a big net and feed the fish. Then I go back up to the attic to read some more until it gets dark. I tape black-out paper to the triangular window, and play my guitar until Buntarō or Mrs Sasaki come. We eat together and chat – nobody has come looking for me at either Shooting Star or Ueno. So far. After supper, I lock, bolt and chain the door, do a load of push-ups and sit-ups, and take a shower. I still sleep downstairs on the sofa, where I stand a good chance of hearing an intruder before they get to me. I carry on reading until the early hours, and finally fall asleep. My dreams are shallow, floating dreams – zoom lenses, parked cars, people who smile knowingly at me . . .

I can smell again. I never noticed smells so much as now. I remap the house, this time in smells. The living room is polish, tatami, incense. The kitchen cooking oil, stainless steel, hard currants. The main bedroom is linen, jasmine, varnish. The garden is leaf juice, pond life and smoke tufts. This house is so quiet! The slightest noise is as impossible to ignore as the squawkiest mobile phone conversation on the metro trains. I hear things I never normally notice. Fluids mulching through my tubes, my joints clunking as I climb the shelves, the vibrations of cars. Crows and doors several streets away, a fly head-butting a windowpane, a futon being beaten.

The fax machine beeps. I put down *Le Grand Meaulnes*, go downstairs and find the fax lying on the floor. `MIYAKE. MORINO'S DETECTIVE WILL RECEIVE MAIL SENT TO ADDRESS BELOW. BE CAUTIOUS. DO NOT GIVE ADDRESS UNTIL SURE OK. WE BOARD FLIGHT 30MINS. HOPE YOU FIND THE MAN.` A post office box number in Edogawabashi follows. I write it down on a cigarette box flap, hide it in my wallet, and set the fax alight in an ashtray with General Douglas MacArthur's lighter. This is overdramatic, but I like flames. I glance up at the photo of Mrs Sasaki's sister. The wine in her glass is cool and scents the air. 'So,' she says, 'what happens in the next chapter?'

♌

Goatwriter sat down at his writing bureau. Luscious sentences swirled inches above his head, waiting for him to pin them on to paper. Goatwriter looked for his pen. Most odd, he thought, I recall quite clearly placing it here, on my blotter, when I heard Pithecanthropus perform his antemeridian grunt . . . He looked in all the places it should be, and then all the places it might be, and lastly all the places it couldn't possibly be. This left only one conclusion. 'Thief!' cried Goatwriter. 'Thief! Thief!' Pithecanthropus and Mrs Comb rushed in – she knew exactly what to do. 'Not again sir. Let me explain – your snack paper goes in here, and your writings and whatnot—' Goatwriter shook his head, numbly. 'No, Mrs Comb! My manuscript is not m-missing, but my fountain pen! The tongue of my imagination! The selfsame pen Lady Shōnagon wrote her pillow book with over thirteen thousand crescent moons ago! The birds nought but a didactic tactic, a decoy deployed while the thief struck!'

'Whatever's the world coming to?' said Mrs Comb. 'Rob thy neighbour!'

Pithecanthropus grunted a question.

'Who? A gloatload of connival rivals have the will to kill my quill!' Goatwriter groaned tearfully. 'Without my fountain pen, my career is over, moreover! The critics will de-re-un-in(con)struct me!'

'Over my dead body, sir! Never you fear! We found us a thief before and we'll find us one again! Won't we, you?' Pithecanthropus was so pleased to be addressed by Mrs Comb directly that he grunted happily, not wishing to point out yet that tracking in the muddy margin was easy, but tracking in a windy baking desert was a different prospect entirely

'As usual, Mrs Comb,' said Goatwriter, forcing himself to calm down, 'you are quite right. Let us apply logic to the dilemma. My pen is missing. Where does one find pens? At the end of sentences. Where does one find the ends of sentences? The ends of lines. Now, how many lines does one find in a desert?'

Mrs Comb looked through the window. 'Only one line out here, sir.'

'Which is that, m-my dear Mrs Comb?'

'Why, sir – the line running down the centre of the road!'

Goatwriter clapped his hoofs. 'Battle stations, friends! To war we go!'

*

Mrs Comb was tiring, perspiring beneath her parasol, wondering if the next egg she laid would come out hard-boiled. Pithecanthropus sweated profusely and the road cooked holes in his soles. Goatwriter saw mirages of verbs freeze and melt. The cruel sun shot dead hot lead at high noon. Time itself relapsed and collapsed. Goatwriter dabbed his brow with his drenched handkerchief and checked that what he thought he saw was truly true. 'Aha! Take heart, my friends! The white lines are veering off the road – my fountain pen cannot be far!' Mrs Comb insisted they drank a prickly-pear dessert before the desert. Without the white lines to guide them, even Pithecanthropus would have lost his way in the smoulderboulders, jags and crags, rocks and blocks. Reptiles stood still, on alternate legs. Pithecanthropus felt they were being watched, but said nothing for fear of distressing Mrs Comb. 'I say,' said Goatwriter, at the head of the expedition. 'We seem to be . . . here.' The three drew level at the lip of a porcelain crater, as steep as it was wide. A black hole emerged at the centre. 'Extra*ordinary*,' murmured Goatwriter. 'A primitive culture, evolving radiotelescope technology, unbeknown to the outside world . . .'

'You can call it a radiotellywhatsit, sir, but I know a kitchen sink when I see one. Must take a month o' Mondays to polish it, or—'

'Keeeeeeraaaaaaaaawk!' An evil-eyed, sawtooth-beaked pterodactyl appeared from the near rear to spear Goatwriter clear down the crater. 'Sir!' squawked Mrs Comb – Goatwriter's hoofs were unable to gain traction on the ceramic surface. 'Sir! I'm coming! I'll rescue you!' Mrs Comb swooped down on an intercept course, but Goatwriter vanished into the blackness. Mrs Comb, unable to pull out of her beak dive, promptly disappeared too. Pithecanthropus watched the pterodactyl circle around for another attack. 'Keeeraaawkeeeraaawkeeeraaaaaaaaaw!' Pithecanthropus wasn't afraid of dinosaurs – or anything else – but the thought of Mrs Comb facing danger alone made his cranium throb with worry. He tobaggoned down the crater. The bottomless blackness boomed.

♌

I sit at the writing bureau with a fresh sheet of paper, and for one moment my letter is perfect. The photograph of my father is open on the bureau too. How do you write a letter a real live private detective? *Dear sir, you don't know me, but* – rejected. *Dear sir, I am the late Mr Morino's personal assistant, and I am writing to ask for a replacement* – rejected. *Dear sir, my name is Eiji Miyake – you spied on me not so long ago for* – rejected. I decide to be uncunning and brief. *Sir: please send a copy of the ID file on Eiji Miyake to box 333* Tokyo Evening Mail. *Thank you.* If it works, it works; if it fails, nothing I could say would have persuaded him anyway. I go back down to the garden and burn the three drafts – if Buntarō or Mrs Sasaki found out, they would tell me I am insane – not to mention irresponsible – for seeking out anyone connected with Morino, and of course they are right. But surely if the man posed a threat we would know about it by now. He sifted through my capsule for Morino so he already knows my address. I put the note into an envelope, address and seal it. That was the easy part. Now I have to go out and post it.

I pull my baseball cap down low, take the key from the hook by the door and put my shoes on. I raise the latch on the main gate, and enter the real world. No brakes. No mysterious cars. Just a quiet, residential street, built down a sedate slope. All the houses are set back from the road behind high fences with automatic gates. Several have video cameras. Each building probably costs more than a whole village in Yakushima. I may rain, says the weather, but there again I may not. I wonder if Ai Imajō lives in this sort of street, with that sort of bedroom window, above that sort of privet hedge. I hear a girl laughing, and from out of an alley fly a junior high-school kid on a bike with his girl standing on the rear wheel spindles. 'What a *gross* story!' she repeats, over and over, laughing and flicking back her hair. '*Gross!*'

The slope leads to a busy main road, lined with shops. So weird, all this motion and noise. A mission in every vehicle. I feel as though

I am a ghost revisiting a place where I was never particularly happy. I pass a supermarket where mangoes and papayas lie exquisitely ribboned. Kids play tag in the aisles. In the supermarket carpark the men watch TV in their cars. A woman lifts a pooched-up doggy into her bicycle basket. A pregnant girl – my age – walks along, hands on her hump. Builders clamber along girders, a blowtorch hisses magnesium. I pass a kindergarten playground – children in colour-coded hats run along paths of Brownian motion. What is it for? What also weirds me out is that I am invisible. Nobody stops and points; no traffic crashes; no birds fall out of the sky; no 'Hey! Look! There's that kid who witnessed thirty or more men get blown away by gangsters three or four nights ago!' Do soldiers feel this, when they get back from a war? The utter weirdness of utter normality. The post office is full of babies bawling and pensioners staring into inner distance. I wait my turn, looking at the 'Have you seen this person?' posters of society's number-one enemies, with the plastic surgery faces they are fancied to have adopted. 'Do not attempt to apprehend these criminals. They may be armed and dangerous.' The person behind nudges me. The assistant asks for the third or fourth time. 'Yes, sir?'

'Uh, I'd like to post this, please.'

I pay, she gives me my stamps and change. It is true. What happened to me last Friday night is locked inside my head, and nothing shows on my face. I lick the stamps, stick them on, and balance the envelope on the lip of the box. Is this wise? I let the letter go; it falls with a papery slap. When did 'wise' ever come into it? Onwards, Plan G. I look up into the eye of a video camera. Outside, the air is heavier and gustier than it was, and swallows are diving low. Another video camera watches the supermarket carpark. Yet another is mounted on the bridge to meditate on passing traffic. I hurry back.

Evening ushers rain in slow motion. I am up in the attic. In the fading light the paper turned white to blue and now is nearly as grey as the ink. I watch the watercourses trickle down the windowpanes. I can almost hear the thirsty city make a frothing noise as its sponges up the rain. In Yakushima they boast about the rain. Uncle Pachinko says it rains thirty-five days per month. Here in Tokyo, when did it last rain? That summer storm, on the day of my stake-out. I was such a holy fool. Morino was a wake-up bomb. What if my father really has no interest in even meeting me? What if he is a Yakuza man too? Sometimes the watercourses follow the one before, other times they split off. Then my father owes it to me to tell me himself. His job – his way of life even – is not the point. In the street outside, the cars of ordinary husbands swish by on their way to ordinary homes. A car cuts its engine outside, and my sense of peace drains away. I peer through the triangular window: Buntarō's tired old Honda. Here comes my saviour, leaping over the flooding drain with a newspaper held over his head. His bald patch glistens in the rain.

I finish my noodles first so I broach the subject. 'Buntarō, I need to talk about money.' Buntarō fishes for tempura batter. 'What money?' Exactly. 'Rent for next month. I dunno how to tell you this, but . . . I don't have it. Not now the money from Ueno stopped. I know this is a hell of a lot to ask, but could you take it out of my deposit?' Buntarō frowns – at me or the elusive tempura? I go on. 'I am really ashamed, after everything you and Mrs Sasaki have done for me. But you should know now, so if, I dunno, if you wanted to give me my marching orders, I mean I would understand, really . . .'

'Got you!' Buntarō holds up the prawn between his chopsticks and delicately nibbles its head off. 'The wife had a better idea, lad. She wants a holiday before she gets too pregnant for the airlines to let her on. You know, we got to thinking how long it's been since we took a week off together. Guess how long? Never! Literally, never. Before I took over Shooting Star we were always too broke, and since then . . . well, a video shop can never sleep. When I work, she rests; when she works, I rest. Nine years have gone by like that. She phoned around a few hotels in Okinawa this morning

– off-season, loads of cheap deals. So, our proposal is this: you look after the shop next week, and that can take care of the rent for October.'

'*All* of October?'

'The hours are piggish – ten a.m. to midnight, seven days. Added up, it comes to a pretty measly rate. But it would give you a breathing space to land another job.'

'You would really leave me in charge of the shop?'

'No Al Pacino look-alike has come around asking for you. Hiding here was wise, but you can come out now.'

'No, I mean – would you trust me with your, uh, business?'

'My wife does, so I do. And I got a glowing reference from your previous employer.' Buntarō starts toothpicking. 'Running the shop is a doddle – I can teach you everything in thirty minutes. And my mom will drop by every evening to pick up the cash and do the accounts. What do you say? Do I tell the wife to book our hotel in paradise?'

'Of course. Sure. Thank you.'

'No need to, lad. This is business. Let's smoke a Marlboro on the step to seal a mutually beneficial package. But don't tell the wife. I'm supposed to be quitting in time for Kōdai's grand opening.' We go outside and get through most of a packet, listening to the frogs and the rain in the pond. The rain and smoke keep the mosquitoes away. 'By the way,' says Buntarō, 'does the name Ai Imajō happen to mean anything to you?'

I scratch the back of my head and nod.

'Friend or foe?'

'Friend, I hope. Why?'

'Apparently she appeared at Ueno lost property this morning to report a lost Eiji Miyake. My mother said you had left Tokyo unexpectedly for family reasons. The young lady made a "nice of him to let me know!" face, thanked my mother, and went away.' I stay poker-faced. 'Well' – Buntarō gets to his feet – I'll go and tell the wife our good news.' I walk through with him to the entrance hall. Buntarō pretends to check for dust. 'I must say, you keep this place neat as a palace. Neater than your luxury penthouse, anyway.' He taps his shirt pocket. 'Lad, I am a dolt! Clean forgot. This pictogram thing came for you today! I do beg your pardon. Pleasant dreams.' When Buntarō has gone I take the pictogram into the living room and inspect it by the lamplight. *Nagano, Mountain Paradise.* Something tells me Buntarō's memory lapse was no accident – this is from my mother, forwarded by Uncle Money. I sit down and balance it on my knee. It hardly weighs a thing, but it weighs so much. Skies grey with snow, mountainsides pink with cherry blossom, snow turquoise with sky, happy hikers, happy skiers. More intimate blame-shifting revelations. The creator of Goatwriter looks down at me from her shell-framed gloom. I cannot see her eyes but I can hear her voice. 'I don't think you're being very fair. Go on. Open it now and spare us all the agony.' Just like Mrs Sasaki, she is sympathetic and stern in equal measures. 'Ah,' she sighs, and the drowsy sea in the background sighs too, 'the young.'

♌

Pithecanthropus's long fall was broken by a semi-mesh of wires and cables. Far above, a pinhole let in a ray of light, to which the early man's nocturnal vision adjusted. He grunted. 'Yes,' replied Goatwriter, wobbling, 'm-my fall was providentially parried by a potpourri of porous packing. Mrs Comb, Mrs Comb – can you hear me?' The housekeeper clucked. 'It'll take more than that to knock *my* stuffing out, sir! An old bird I may be but I still have the use of my wings. But what is this cobwebby stuff everywhere? I can barely move!'

A wall of light opened up and a female voice blazed forth: 'Welcome!' A woman's face appeared. 'Welcome!' She wore a Technicolor crown and a shoulder-padded power suit. Her blond hair sunshone, her lips glistened, but she seemed two-dimensional because she was. The wall was a screen, lighting up a chamber strewn with electrical cables. The floor was soft with skin flakes and eyelashes. ‘Welcome, o Goatwriter! I am Queen Erichnid. This is my website.’

‘I am unfamiliar,’ Goatwriter began, ‘with your m-majesty’s genealogy.’

‘My genealogy is the media! My empire is the future!’

‘Right grand, doubtless,’ said Mrs Comb, ‘but we were looking for a stolen fountain pen and we have reason to suspect it might have ended up here.’

‘Indeed.’ Queen Erichnid deigned to look at Mrs Comb. ‘I had it stolen.’

‘Grand behaviour for a queen!’ cooed Mrs Comb. ‘Sneaking and snooping and off with decent folks’ possessions! We call your like *thieves* where I come from!’

‘Queen Erichnid never stole it herself, ya scraggy cutlet!’ rang a rodent retort. ‘*I* lifted ya poxy pen from under ya noncing noses, while her majesty digitalized da birdstorm!’

Pithecanthropus grunted in amazement. ‘ScatRat!’ gasped Goatwriter as he appeared on-screen with Queen Erichnid. He leered and harpstringed his whiskers. ‘Ya can refer 2 me as “Da Artist Formerly Known as ScatRat”.’ Mrs Comb huffed and clucked. ‘But how did you get here?’

‘Being marginalized was boring! I been trucking along in ya ■⌛ing rustbucket ever since ya caveman wrecked my scatpad. Dis morning, her divine majesty’ – a twenty-four-carat smile from the queen – ‘made me an offer no honest rat could refuse – I lure ya 2 her website, and she digitalizes me into da world’s #1 computer rat!’ Queen Erichnid tousled ScatRat’s ear and his tail quivered in ecstasy.

‘But why,’ – Goatwriter chewed his beard – ‘would you voluntarily renounce your solid state for the virtual?’

‘Why? *Why!* Da Internet is my rat-run, Goatee! I lightspeed down da cables I used 2 *!*😐☹-up my teeth chewing! Lemme cut 2 da quick. Queen Erichnid has granted ya dis audience to make ya da same offer, Goatee.’ Queen Erichnid close-upped until her kaleidoscope eyes filled the screen. ‘Indeed, o Goatwriter. I am offering to download you to the side of the screen where the future awaits! Link up with the cyberagents, the e-bookshops! The paper book is dying!' Her hair crackled static as her voice scaled operatic heights of passion. 'Compose your stories in a virtual paradise! I will act as your cyberagent, and—'

'Aye,' pecked Mrs Comb, 'the nub!'

'Silence, hen! Goatwriter, digitalization will perfect you! Iron out that troublesome speech d-d-defect! Sentences at the speed of light instead of the speed of amputee m-m-marathon day!'

Goatwriter glared proudly. 'My stammer distinguishes my true friends from the false, fawners, feigners and flatterers! I refuse!'

Queen Erichnid filed her nails. 'How very positive of you. Then I'll digitalize you anyway, ram-raid your virtual brain, synthesize every story you could ever make, and dump the leftover bytes along with your tedious companions Mr Id and Madame Ego.' Queen Erichnid clasped her bosom. 'O, the advances! The royalties! ScatRat! Bring the digitalizer on-line!' The evil queen's image receded to allow room for the awesome half-cannon/half-generator machine that ScatRat was lugging on-screen. 'Prepare 4 downloading, Goatee!'

Goatwriter struggled to move, but the web of cables held him fast. 'Where is the creative fulfilment in passing off another's stories as your own?'

Queen Erichnid looked puzzled. '"Fulfilment"! Writing is not about "fulfilment!" Writing is about adoration! Glamour! Awards! When I was a mere human I was deluded by "fulfilment". I learned the language of writers, o yes – I said "coda" and "conceit" instead of "ending" and "idea"; I said "tour de force" instead of "the good bit"; "cult classic!" instead of "this tosh'll never sell!" Did it bring me fulfilment? No! It brought me obscurity and overdrafts! But by capturing your brain, Goatwriter, the literary cosmos will be my cocktail bar! O ScatRat! Get ready to fire!'

'On ya word, Queen!'

Goatwriter lowered his horns. 'You forget one thing, Your Majesty!'

'Is that pose supposed to threaten me, o farmyard animal?'

'The riddle clause of the Evil Queen Law!' Goatwriter quoted. '"Any disagreements arising between evil queen and captive shall be settled by a riddle posed to the latter party by the former. Unless this riddle clause is properly executed it is illegal to store the captive in a retrieval system, transmit said captive in any form by any means, electronic, mechanical, photocopying, recording, without prior permission of captive and captive's publishers." Clear as a whistling thistle.'

Queen Erichnid's wintry eye filled the screen. 'ScatRat. Say it is not so.'

ScatRat twanged a whisker. 'Just an old formality, Majesty. Leave it 2 me. I'll zip 2 insoluableriddles@evilqueens.sup.org and get da number one brain /***er! Relax! Chinfluff's in da bag! He won't stand a *!☠Φ*s chance in a Bangkok *!Ψ*▦.' Queen Erichnid closed her eyes in cyberorgasmic delectation. 'Make it so! And then his stories' – gassy colours popped and fused – 'soul' – she tossed back her head – 'film rights and book deals in twenty-seven languages' – her laughing mouth consumed the screen and plunged the website into bronchial black – 'will be mine! Mine! Miiiiiiiine!'

Pithecanthropus, meanwhile, had slipped out of the wired jungle – he knew about jungles – and was exploring the edges of the cavernous website – he knew about caverns, too. He noticed that all the cables twisted into the same giant plug. Above this plug spun a ventilator fan to cool the circuits, and on the grille of this fan, hidden in a rack of Philips screwdrivers, was Goatwriter's beloved fountain pen. Through the grille Pithecanthropus could make out, using his night eyes, a ladder in a shaft beyond. He grunted thoughtfully, but slipped back to the screen when he heard ScatRat come on-screen again. The rat appeared in a glittering quizmaster jacket, clutching an envelope marked '$1 million riddles$'. 'Got it, Ya Majesty! Da riddle of da millennium!'

'Let us be quite clear,' said Queen Erichnid. 'When you fail to answer, your copyright reverts to me.'

'When Sir answers right' – Mrs Comb shook her tail feather – 'we go free – with Sir's fountain pen.'

'O, such a vivid imagination' – Queen Erichnid sneered – 'for a scratty-clawed home-help. ScatRat! Let the riddling commence!'

ScatRat slit the envelope open with his thorny fang. Drumrolling cued from hidden speakers: 'What is da most mathematical animal?'

'By heck.' Mrs Comb folded her wings. 'What kind of daft quiz is this?'

ScatRat flobbed nobby gob. It dribbled down the screen. 'Ya got 1 min, fetacheesepacker!' A sixty-second stopwatch appeared on-screen. 'From – now!' Countdown music began. Goatwriter chewed his beard. 'The most mathematical animal . . . Well, the case for humans is shattered by a minute of their television . . . Dolphins win the brain weight/body weight ratio discourse . . . However, no cleverer Euclidian geometrician exists than the bolas spider . . . yet the scallop's knowledge of Cartesian oval lenses is unsurpassed in the kingdom of fauna . . .' ScatRat chuckled. 'Ya got thirty seconds!' Queen Erichnid clapped with glee and danced a rampant rumba with her rodent rogue. 'I can taste those publishing lunches! Hear the rapture of *New Yorker* reviewers!' Worried, Mrs Comb searched her handbag for an inspirational snack, but all she found was an old chestnut. Pithecanthropus chose that moment to tap Mrs Comb's wing and slip Goatwriter's fountain pen into her handbag. In the glare of the screen Mrs Comb's sharp eyes spotted a creature from her direst nightmare jumping between Pithecanthropus's eyebrows. 'Fleas!' she shrieked. 'I knew it! All along! Fleas!'

'Yes, by jimminy, yes!' clopped Goatwriter. 'Of course! The most mathematical animal is the flea!'

Queen Erichnid's rumba halted. ScatRat's leer fell away. 'Ya gotta say why or it don't count!'

Goatwriter cleared his throat. '"Fleas subtract from happiness, divide attention, add to miseries and multiply alarmingly."'

ScatRat gazed up at his screen idol. 'Some ya win, Ya Majesty, and some ya—'

Queen Erichnid muted ScatRat with a double click. You failed me, you corrupted, bugged, *cybervermin*! Only one punishment fits this crime!' ScatRat's 'nooo-ooo-ooo . . .' dwindled to zero as the queen dragged him into the recycle bin. The queen's ire grew dire. 'As for *you*, o Bearded One, if you think some legal-eagle *babble* prevents me from seizing' – her eyes narrowed with wintry menace while megabytes crackled – 'the object of my desires, then even for a writer you are *cretinous* beyond *belief*! Stand by – for digitalization!' She primed the on-screen digitalizer. 'Five – four—'

'Sir!' Mrs Comb fluttered but was still meshed fast. 'Sir!'

Goatwriter strained against his cable harness. 'Deuced dastardly diabola!'

Queen Erichnid's teeth sparkled with silicon. 'Three – two—'

Pithecanthropus pulled out the plug.

The screen died, and the website vanished as if it had never existed, which in a sense it hadn't, for Goatwriter, Pithecanthropus and Mrs Comb found themselves sitting in the sun-blasted desert, too astonished to utter a syllable.

◆

17th September
A ski resort town in the Nagano Mountains

Eiji,

If you tried to contact me after I sprung myself from the clinic in Miyazaki, it was sweet of you, but I couldn't stay there any longer. Anywhere on Kyūshū is too close to Yakushima for comfort. (If you didn't, I don't blame you for a moment. I didn't really expect you to.) I may have problems but the patients there were so scary I figured I'd take my chances back in the big bad world. (At least they give you knives and forks out here.) Burn the last letter I wrote. Burn it, please. I won't ask you for a single thing but I'm asking you to do this. The only thing Dr Suzuki taught me is that there comes a point in your life, and when you pass this point you can't change. You are what you are, for better or worse, and that is that. I shouldn't have told you about the stairs incident. You must hate me. I would. Sometimes I honestly do. Hate myself, I mean. Be careful of counsellors, therapists, head doctors. They poke around, and take things to bits without thinking about how they'll put it all back together. Burn the letter. Letters like that shouldn't exist. (Especially on Yakushima.) Burn it.

So here I am in Nagano. What sunsets they make in these mountains! The hotel is at the foot of Mount Hakuba and the view from my room is swallowed up by the mountain. It needs a different word to describe it every day. You should visit Nagano, someday. In the Edo period all the missionaries from the capital used to 'summer' up here, to escape from the heat. I suppose we have the missionaries to thank for naming these mountains 'the Japan Alps'. Why do people always have to compare things with abroad? (Like Kagoshima, the Naples of Japan, that always sets my teeth on edge.) Nobody knows what the locals used to call the mountains before anyone knew the Alps, or even Europe, was out there. (Am I the only one who thinks this is depressing?) I'm staying as a non-paying guest in a small hotel opened by someone I knew from my days in Tokyo, years and years ago, after I left you in the care of your grandmother. He is a big-shot hotelier now, quite respectable, except for two very expensive divorces, which I'm sure he deserves. (He changed before he reached that critical point where your life is set in concrete.) He wanted me to help scout for a location for a new hotel he wants to build from scratch, but he doesn't know how much I drink yet, or he's persuading himself he can 'save' me. His favourite two words are 'project' and 'venture', which seem to mean the same thing. The snows are due in early November (only six weeks away. Another year on its last legs). If I have spent the good-old-days currency I have with my friend by winter, I may go in search of warmer climes. (Old Chinese proverb: guests are like fish – after three days they begin to stink.) I hear Monte Carlo is pleasant for 'wintering'. I hear Prince Charles of England may be available.

I had a dream about Anju last night. Anju, a Siberian tiger running past me in a subway (I knew it was Siberian because the yellow stripes were white), and a game where you had to hide a bone-egg in a library. Anju won't leave me alone. I paid a priest a fortune to perform pacifying rites but I should have spent the money on French wine for all the good it did. I never dream about you – in fact I never remember any of my dreams, except the Anju ones. Why is that? Dr Suzuki seemed to think . . . ah, who cares. Just burn the letter, please.

♌

STUDY OF TALES

Bats streamed beyond bracken-matted dusk. Goatwriter mulled at his writing bureau, watching the forest of moss until shadows danced. 'I declare, I could swear . . .' Goatwriter began. Mrs Comb was clog-polishing there on the stair. 'Not like that sewer-mouthed ScatRat, I hope, sir.' Goatwriter stroked the fountain pen of Sei Shōnagon. 'I could swear that in the arboreal soul of this forest . . . far and deep . . . I glean gleams of a truly untold tale . . .' Whether Goatwriter was thinking in words or talking in silence was unclear. 'The venerable coach penetrated this forest as far as the track permitted, and has not moved on for seven days . . . quite unprecedented . . . I do believe it is trying to tell me something . . .'

The evening cooled and Mrs Comb shivered. 'Foxtrot pudding for supper, sir. You give your eyes a rest and play a nice round of Blind Man's Scrabble.' She hoped the venerable coach would move on that night, but doubted it would.

The following morning, Pithecanthropus was digging through deep creaking coal seams in search of diamonds. Mrs Comb's birthday was coming up, and several nights ago the venerable coach had been overtaken by a convertible with a radio playing a song about how diamonds are a girl's best friend. Mrs Comb was no girl, it was true, but Pithecanthropus hoped that the friend part might rub off in his favour. Past tasty pockets of earthworms, truffles and larvae dug the early ancestor, past droll trolls, moles, addled adders and bothered badgers, down where Pithecanthropus could hear the earth furnace boom to a rhythm all its own. Hours cannot dig so far, and Pithecanthropus lost all track of time. 'You hulking great lout,' an impossibly distant voice found him, much later. 'Where are you the one time I need you?' Mrs Comb! Pithecanthropus swam upward with a mighty breaststroke, up through the loosened earth, and within a minute resurfaced. Mrs Comb was flapping in circles like a headless chicken, waving a note. 'Here you are last! Muck-grubbing around in a crisis!' Pithecanthropus grunted. 'Sir has upped and offed! I knew he wasn't himself last night, and this morning I find this note on his writing bureau!' She thrust it at Pithecanthropus, who groaned – all those squiggles skidding over their paper. Mrs Comb sighed. 'Three million years you've had to learn how to read! The letter says Sir has gone into this mucky forest! All on his own! He said he didn't want to drag us into nowt dangerous! Dangerous? What if he meets a mild cannibal much less a wild animal? What if the venerable coach drives off tonight? We'd never see Sir again! And he forgot his asthma inhaler!' Mrs Comb began sobbing into her apron, which wrung Pithecanthropus's giant heart. 'First his story, then his pen, and now he's lost himself!' Pithecanthropus grunted imploringly.

'Are . . . are you sure? You can track Sir in this thick-as-thieves forest?'

Pithecanthropus grunted reassuringly.

◆

I hear Buntarō let himself in downstairs. 'Hang on,' I yell, 'I'll be right down!' Two o'clock already – today is the last day of my exile. I feel tired again – it rained last night, and fat fingers kept prising me awake. I kept thinking somebody was trying to force a window somewhere. I arrange the pages of the manuscript how they were on the writing bureau, and pick my way between the books to the trapdoor. I shout down – 'Sorry, Buntarō! I lost track of time!' Goodbye, study of tales. I go down to the living room where a dark figure closes the door behind me. My heart rams itself up my throat. She is a middle-aged woman, unafraid, curious, reading me. Her hair is short, severe and as grey as a feared headmistress's. She is dressed in forgettable clothes, anonymous as a shot in a mail-order catalogue. You would pass her a hundred times and never notice her. Unless she suddenly appeared in your living room. How owlish and scarred she is. Her stare goes on and on, as if she has every right to be here, and is waiting for the intruder – me – to explain himself. 'Who, uh, are you?' I eventually manage. 'You invited me, Eiji Miyake.' Her voice you would not forget. Cracked as cane, dry as drought. 'So I came.'

A passing lunatic? 'But I never invited anyone.'

'But you did. Two days ago you sent an invitation to my letter-drop.'

Her? 'Morino's detective?'

She nods. 'My name is Yamaya.' She disarms me with a smile as friendly as a dagger thrust. 'Yes, I am a woman, not a man in drag. Invisibility is a major asset in my line of work. However, discussing my modus operandi is not why I am here, is it? Won't you offer me a chair?' All too weird. 'Sure. Please sit down.' Mrs Yamaya takes the sofa, so I take the floor by the window. She has the eye of a meticulous reader, which makes me the book. She looks behind me. 'Nice garden. Nice property. Nice neighbourhood. Nice hidey-hole.'

Over to me, it seems. I offer her a Marlboro from Daimon's

final box, but she shakes her head. I light mine. 'How did you, uh, trace me?'

'I obtained your address from the *Tokyo Evening Mail.*'

'They gave you my address?'

'No, I said I *obtained* it. Then I trailed Mr Ōgiso here yesterday evening.'

'With respect, Mrs Yamaya, I asked for a file, not a visit.'

'With respect, Mr Miyake, get real. I receive a note from a mysterious nobody asking for the selfsame file I compiled for the late Ryūtarō Morino three days before the night of the long knives. How coincidental. I earn a living by unpicking coincidences. Your note was a bleeding lamb tossed into a swimming pool of sharks. I had three theories – you were a potential client testing my professionality; someone with a potentially lucrative personal interest in Eiji Miyake; or the father of Eiji Miyake himself. All three were worth a follow-up. I do so, and I discover you are the son of the father.'

From the garden I hear a crow craw-crawing. I wonder what happened to Mrs Yamaya to make her so sad but so steel-willed. 'You know my father?'

'Only socially.'

Only socially. 'Mrs Yamaya, I would like to ask you more cleverly and indirectly, but, uh, will you please give me the file on my father?'

Mrs Yamaya forms a cage with her long, strong fingers. 'Now we have got to why I am here. To consider this very question.'

'How much?'

'Please, Mr Miyake. We are both perfectly aware of your financial non-position.'

'Then what are you here to consider? Whether or not I deserve it?'

The crow hops over to the balcony and peers in. It is as big as an eagle. Mrs Yamaya's murmur could hush a stadium. 'No, people in my line of walk must never allow "deserve" to enter the equation.'

'What does enter the equation?'

'The consequences.'

The doorbell rings and I twitch – hot ash falls on my legs. The doorbell rings again. What an invasion! A specially rigged light strobes on and off several times, for Mrs Sasaki's sister's deafness, I guess. I stub out my cigarette. It lies there, stubbed. The doorbell rings again – I hear a slight laugh. Mrs Yamaya doesn't move. 'Aren't you going to answer it?'

'Excuse me,' I say, and she nods.

Stupidly, I am too fazed to put the chain on the door, and the two young men seem so pleased to see me that for a moment I panic – this is a set-up organized with Mrs Yamaya, and I walked straight into it. 'Hi there!' they beam. Which one spoke? Immaculate white shirts, conservative ties, sheeny, computer-generated hair – hardly regular Yakuza garb. They irradiate health and positive vibes. 'Hey, feller! Is this a bad time? Because we have *great* news!' They are either going to produce guns or tell me about a spectacular discount kimono service.

'You, uh, do?' I glance behind me.

'You bet I do! You see, Lord Jesus Christ is waiting outside the door of *your heart* at this *very* moment – he wants to know if you have a few minutes to spare so he can tell you about the joy that will be yours – if you unlock your heart and let in His Love.' I breathe sheer relief – they take this as a 'yes' and turn up their zeal volume even higher. 'Your heart seems no stranger to trouble, my friend. We are here with the Church of the Latter Day Saints – perhaps you've heard of our missionary work?'

'No, no. I haven't actually.' Another stupid thing to say. When I finally close the door – these Mormons' smiles are ironed on – and get back to the living room nobody is there. I open the balcony doors, surprised. Did I imagine my grim visitor? 'Mrs Yamaya?' The crow is gone too. Nothing but the layered buzzes and summer creaks and hisses. A butterfly with gold-digger eyes mistakes me for a bush. I watch it, and moments telescope into minutes. When I go back in I notice what I missed at first – a brown envelope, lying on the sofa where Mrs Yamaya had sat. Any brief hope that she left me the document wallet on my father is snuffed out right away – the envelope is labelled 'Tokyo Evening Mail – Correspondence Box 333'. Inside is a letter, addressed to me in the spidery hand of a very old person. I sit down and slit it open.

♌

Where mossy drapes hung so thick that Goatwriter could no longer push onward, he sploshed in a babbling brook. The stream jaggered clattery underhoof not with rolling stones, but with dinner plates. The water was the colour of tea. Goatwriter sipped a mouthful – high-quality, cool tea. He drank his fill and his head cleared. 'A stream of consciousness!' he rejoyced. 'I must be in the Darjeeling foothills.' Goatwriter paddled upstream. Lantern orchids bloomed the noon gloom beneath spinster aspidistra. Opal-wingtipped hummingbirds probed syrup-bleeding figs. Far above the forest canopy was chalk-dusted with daylight. It seemed to Goatwriter that these random dabs of light formed words. 'All my life, I searched for the truly untold tale in the arcane, in the profound. Could my quixotic quest be a quite quotidian query? Does profundity hide in the obvious?'

Goatwriter paddled into a glade misty with sunlight. A girl with flaxen hair swing-swung, singing a melody with no beginning and no name. Goatwriter reached the foot of her tree. Her voice was that of the whisperings, heard by the old goat nightly since midsummer. 'You are in search of the truly untold tale.' She swung up, and Antarctica drifted unmeasured miles.

'Yes,' replied Goatwriter.

She swung down. Ursa Minor rose. 'Untold tales are in the highlands.'

'How m-might I find these highlands?'

'Go around the bend to the sacred pool, up the wall, and over the waterfall.'

'Over the waterfall . . .'

The girl with the flaxen hair swung up. 'Are you prepared to pay?'

'I've paid all my life.'

'Ah, but Goatwriter. You haven't paid everything yet.'

'What can be left to pay, pray?'

The swing fell to earth, quite empty.

When Goatwriter came to the sacred pool he removed his glasses to wipe away the waterfall spray, but to his surprise he found he could see better without them. So he left them on the marble rock and pondered the pool. Peculiar. Firstly, the waterfall was soundless. Secondly, the water did not fall from the precipice far above, but rose upward in a giddied, lurching, foaming – and silent – torrent. Goatwriter could see no path up the rock face. He spoke to himself, but no sound came out. 'I'm not a kid any more. I'm getting too old for symbolic quests.' He considered turning back, even at this eleventh hour. Mrs Comb would be distraught when he failed to return – but she had Pithecanthropus to care for, and to care for her. The writer within the animal sighed. And he thought of his truly untold tale, and he jumped from the marble rock. The pool was as cold and sudden as death itself.

Wednesday 20th September
Tokyo

Dear Eiji Miyake,

I hope you will forgive the sudden, unusual and possibly intrusive nature of this letter. Quite possibly, moreover, you and its intended recipient are not the same person, which would cause considerable embarrassment. Nonetheless, I feel it is a risk worth taking. Permit me to explain.

I am writing in response to an advertisement which appeared in the personal column of *Tokyo Evening Mail* on 14

September. The advertisement was brought to my attention only this morning by a visiting acquaintance. I should perhaps explain I am recovering from an operation to the valves in my heart. You appealed for any relatives of Eiji Miyake to respond. I believe I may be your paternal grandfather.

Two decades ago my son sired a pair of illegimate twins – a boy and a girl. He broke relations with their mother, a woman of lowly occupation, and, as far as I know, never saw his twins again. I do not know where the children were brought up, nor by whom – the mother's people, one presumes. The girl apparently drowned in her eleventh year, but the boy would now be twenty. I never knew their mother's name, nor did I see a picture of my illegimate grandchildren. Relations with my son have never been as cordial as one would wish, and since his marriage we have corresponded ever less. I did, however, discover the names of the twins he fathered: hence this letter. The girl's name was Anju, and the boy's name is Eiji, written not in the commonplace manner (the kanjis for 'intelligent' plus 'two' or 'govern'), but with highly unusual kanjis for 'incant' and 'world'. As in your case.

I would like to keep this letter short for the reason that the 'evidence' of the kanji remains inconclusive. A face-to-face meeting, I believe, will clarify this ambiguity: if we are related, I feel certain we will find points of physical resemblance. I shall be at Amadeus Tea Room, on the ninth floor of the Righa Royal Hotel (opposite Harajuku station), on Monday 25th of September, at a table reserved in my name. Please present yourself at 10 a.m., with any concrete evidence of your parentage which you may have in your possession.

I trust you appreciate the sensitive nature of this matter, and understand my reluctance to provide you with my contact details at this time. Should you be another Eiji Miyake with identical kanji, please accept my sincerest apologies for raising your hopes unnecessarily. Should you be the Eiji Miyake I hope you are, we have many matters to discuss.

Yours faithfully,
Takara Tsukiyama

For the first time since I came to Tokyo I feel clean, clear happiness. My grandfather wrote a letter to me. Imagine, meeting my grandfather as well as my father. 'We have many matters to discuss'! Here I was, despairing at the impossibility of it all, when contacting my father really was as straightforward as I always imagined. Monday – only two days away! My grandfather uses educated language – surely he holds more sway over family politics than my paranoid stepmother. I make myself a green tea and take it into the garden to smoke a Kent, Buntarō's brand of choice now all the Marlboros are gone. Tsukiyama – cool name – uses the kanji for 'moon' and 'mountain'. The garden hums with beauty, rightness and life. I wish Monday could start in fifteen minutes. What is the real time? I go back in and check the clock which Mrs Sasaki brought me mid-week. Still three hours until Buntarō gets here. My absentee host in her seashell frame catches my eye. 'Your luck has turned, at last. Call Ai. It was her idea to place the personal ad, remember? Go on. Shyness at the break of day is attractive in a way, but shyness buried in its shell will never serve you very well.'

'Was that supposed to rhyme?'

'Stop changing the subject! Go out, find a telephone and call her.'

Supermarket row is no different since my last visit, but I am. The world is an ordered flowchart of subplots, after all. Look at all these cars – driving past and never colliding. The order is difficult to see, but it is here, under the chaos. So, I lived through twelve hellish hours – so? People live through twelve hellish years and live to tell the tale. Life goes on. Luckily for us. I find a callbox under the emergency stairs in a Uniqlo. As mobile phones take over the world these things will become as rare as gaslights. I pick up the receiver and freeze. You coward! I decide to get a haircut first – you spineless worm, Miyake – and walk up the steps to Genji the Barber's. It has one of those red, white and blue stripy poles – Anju despaired of ever getting me to understand where the stripes unwound from and wound to. It was crystal clear to her. Genji's is a poky joint, wintry with air-con – I am the only customer – and was last painted when Japan surrendered. A silent TV shows horse-racing. The air is so thick with hairspray and tonic fumes that if you lit a match you would probably fire-bomb the whole building. Genji himself is an old man sprouting nasal hair, sweeping the floor with shaky hands. 'C'mon in, son, c'mon in.' He gestures towards the empty chair. I sit down and he flourishes a tablecloth over my shoulders. In the mirror my head seems amputated from the rest of me. I flinch as I remember Valhalla bowling alley. 'Why the long face, son?' asks Genji, dropping his scissors. 'Whatever's itching you, life can't be as bad as it was for my last customer. A businessman, doing pretty well for himself judging by his suit, but such a miserable old bugger I never saw!' Genji drops his comb. 'I said, "Forgive me if I'm speaking out of turn, sir, but is anything on your mind?" The customer sighs, and finally says: "Chintzywoo died last week." "Who was Chintzywoo – your poodle?" I ask.' Genji snips. '"No," the customer answers. "My wife."' Genji pauses to open a bottle of sake. He drinks half the bottle in one swig, and balances it on the shelf of the mirror. '"How tragic, sir," I say, "I hope you can find solace in hard work." "I was fired yesterday," the customer says. "How awful, sir," I say. "Were you fired in connection, y'know, with depression brought on by your bereavement?" "Not exactly," he sighs, "I was fired in connection with my espionage activities."' Genji pauses to finish his sake – he gropes for the bottle of hair tonic and drinks most of it without noticing. 'Well, this takes me aback, I can tell you! "Espionage? I never had a spy in my chair before. Who did you work for? China? Russia? North Korea?"

"No," he confesses, with some pride. "The most powerful country on the face of the globe. The Kingdom of Tonga."' Genji switches on the electric clippers – nothing happens, so he twirls the cord and whacks the head against the counter. They growl into life. 'So I say, "The Kingdom of Tonga? I never even knew they had a, y'know, secret service." "Nobody knows. Brilliant, isn't it?" "Well, sir, I guess you're a national hero over there. Why not emigrate? They'll welcome you with open arms."' Genji shaves around my ears. 'The customer frowns. "There was a palace coup three days ago. The militarists now in charge denounced me as a double agent, and I was sentenced to death by hanging yesterday." "Well, sir, at least you still have your health."' Genji hangs up the shaver and picks up his scissors. 'Well, at that moment the customer has this hacking coughing fit and I have to wipe blood off the mirror. "Mmm. Maybe you should go back to your old job, before you became a spy, y'know." He brightens up for the first time. "I used to be an airplane pilot," he says. "There you go, sir, why don't you apply for a position with an airline?" I suggest. He sneezes and, I swear, son, his right eyeball flies out! Rolls right across the room, it does! "Bugger!" he says, "that was my best one!" I'm getting pretty desperate by now, you can imagine. "How about writing your autobiography, sir? Your life could turn tragedy to Oscars." Genji snips, snips, snips. "The movie they made about me won three Oscars." "How wonderful, sir! I knew there was light at the end of the tunnel!" "It won three Oscars, eighteen months *after* the agent ran off with with my screenplay. A multimillion-dollar smash hit, and I never saw a yen. Worst of all, who do you think they got to play me? Johnny Depp I could have handled, but Bruce Willis?" Do you want me to cut it short, son?'

♌

Meanwhile, back in the forest of moss, Mrs Comb and Pithecanthropus found themselves caught between a rock, a hard place and sheaves of leaves. Pithecanthropus scratched his head and grunted. The truth was, Goatwriter's tracks had become confused with sacred cows and white elephants, but Pithecanthropus had said nothing for fear of disheartening Mrs Comb. Mrs Comb perched on a fungi-feathery tree-stump. 'It must be way past Sir's elevenses by now . . . if only he'd warned me he were off gallivanting, I could have rustled something up—'

A man crashed through the impenetrable vegetation and sprawled at their feet. Mrs Comb squawked up the hard place in surprise, and Pithecanthropus bounded to position himself between Mrs Comb and the man. He seemed no threat, climbing to his feet, brushing the leaf mould off his tweed jacket with leather elbow pads, and readjusting his sticking-plaster-fixed horn-rimmed glasses. Nor did he register any surprise at meeting a highly sentient hen and a long-extinct ancestor of *Homo sapiens* in this primeval forest. 'Have you seen them?'

Mrs Comb was mildly offended by his offhand manner. 'Seen who?'

'The word hounds.'

'Not those brutish, slavering, talking dogs we saw out in the margins?'

'That would be them.' Afraid, he pressed a finger to his lips and looked at Pithecanthropus. 'Hear anything?' Beams of silence you could bang your head on. Pithecanthropus grunted a 'No'. The writer slid out a long thorn from his crown. 'Many years ago I wrote a successful novel. I never thought anyone would actually want to publish it, you see, but they did, it was snatched from me, and the more I wished every extant copy would explode like a puffball, the more copies the lamentable thing sold. Its errors, its posturing, its arrogance! Oh, I would sell my soul to pyre the entire run. But alas, Mephistopheles never returned my fax, and the words I unloosed have dogged me ever since.'

Mrs Comb resumed the audience from her tree-stump. 'Why not retire?'

The writer rested against the rock. 'If only it were that simple. I hid in schools of thought, in mixed metaphors, in airport lounges of unrecognized states, but sooner or later I hear a distant braying, and I know my words are hunting me down—' His face changed from doleful weariness to suspicion. 'But what, exactly, brings *you* this deep into the forest of moss?'

'Our friend came gallivanting – have you seen him? Horns, a beard, hoofs?'

'If he isn't the Devil himself he must be a writer or a lunatic.'

'A writer. How do you know?'

'To be so deep in the forest he must be one of the three. Shhhhhhhhh!' The writer's eyes were wide with dread. 'A baying! Don't you hear that baying?' Pithecanthropus grunted softly and shook his head. 'Liars!' hissed the writer. 'Liars! You're in league with the hounds! I know your game! They're in the trees! They're coming!' And he tore off, crashing through the overgrowth. Mrs Comb and Pithecanthropus looked at one another. Pithecanthropus grunted. 'Bonkers,' agreed Mrs Comb, 'as a balmy balaclava!' Pithecanthropus examined the hole in the sheaves of leaves. He grunted. Beyond was a stream without sound.

'Hurry, slowcoach!' Mrs Comb fluttered from rock to rock, while Pithecanthropus waded against the tea-tinted current over the clattery dinner plates. So it was that Mrs Comb reached the sacred pool first. A second later she noticed Goatwriter's respectable spectacles lying on the marble rock. Third, she saw the body of her best and dearest floating in the water. 'Sir! Sir! Whatever's to do!' She flew forth across the pool without noticing the upwards waterfall or the glove of silence muffling. On her fifth flap she reached Goatwriter's head. Pithecanthropus's sixth sense told him that the sacred pool was death, and roared a warning – but no sound carried, and he could only watch in despair as his beloved slipped, dipped a tip of her wing and slapped lifeless into the water alongside Goatwriter. In seven bounds Pithecanthropus was atop the marble rock, where his body tore with eight howls of mute grief. He pounded the rock until his fists bled. And suddenly, our early ancestor was calm. He picked the sticky burrs from his hair, and climbed the rock face until the overhang browed.

He counted to nine, which was as high as Goatwriter could teach him, and dived for the spot between the bodies of his friends. A beautiful dive, a perfect ten. No thought bothered his head as Pithecanthropus entered the sacred pool. Serenity was never a word he knew, but serenity was what he felt.

♌

'Good afternoon. Jupiter Café. Nagamimi here.'

Donkey. I think. 'Uh, hello. Could I speak to Miss Imajō, please?'

'Sorry, but she isn't working today, see.'

'Oh. Could you tell me when her next shift is, then, please?'

'Sorry, but I can't do that.'

'Oh. For, uh, security reasons?'

Donkey hee-haws. 'No, not that. Miss Imajō's last shift was Sunday, see.'

'Oh . . .'

'She's a music student, and her college term is starting again, so she had to quit her part-time job here to concentrate on her studies, see.'

'I see. I was hoping to get in touch with her. I'm just a friend.'

'Yeah, I can understand that, if you're her friend and all . . .'

'So, might you have her telephone number? On a form or a record?'

'We don't keep forms or records here. And Miss Imajō was only here for a month, see.' Donkey hums as she thinks. 'We don't keep files and stuff like that here, see, 'cos of space. Even our cloakroom, it's got less room than one of those boxes what magicians put swords through. It isn't fair. At the Yoyogi branch, see, they have this cloakroom big enough to—'

'Thanks anyway, Miss Nagamimi, but . . .'

'Wait! Wait! Miss Imajō *did* leave me her number, but only if someone called Eiji Miyake phoned.'

Kill me now. 'Yes. My name is Eiji Miyake.'

'Really?' Donkey hee-haws.

'Really.'

'Well, really! Isn't that a funny coincidence?'

'Isn't it just.'

'Miss Imajō said only if somebody called Eiji Miyake calls. And you call, and your name is Eiji Miyake! Like I always say, see. "Truth is stranger than reality." I saw you hit that nasty man with your head. It must have hurt!'

'Miss Nagamimi, please could you give me Miss Imajō's number?'

'Right, hang on a moment, where did I put it, I wonder.'

Ai Imajō's number is ten digits long. I get to the ninth, and feel the paralysis of fear creeping down my arm. What if my call embarrasses her? What if she thinks I'm some slimeball who won't leave her alone? What if her boyfriend answers? Her father? What if Ai Imajō answers? What do I say? I look around Uniqlo. Shoppers, sweaters, space. My index finger presses the final digit. The number connects. A telephone in a distant apartment begins to ring. Somebody is getting up, maybe pausing the video, maybe putting down their chopsticks, cursing this interruption—

'Hello?' Her.

'Uh . . .' I try to speak but a sort of dry spastic noise comes out.

'Hello?'

I should have planned this better.

'Hello? Do I get to know who you are?'

My voice comes back all on its own. 'Hello, is this Ai Imajō?' Stupid question. I know this is Ai Imajō. 'I, uh, my, uh . . .'

She sounds sort of pleased. 'My knight in shining armour.'

'How do you know?'

'I recognized your voice. How did you get my number?'

'Miss Nagamimi at Jupiter Café told me. Eventually. If this isn't a convenient time to call, I can, uh . . .'

'Nope, this is perfectly convenient. I tried to track you down at Ueno lost property office, where you said you worked, but they told me you suddenly left town.'

'Yeah, uh, Mrs Sasaki told me.'

'Was it to do with your relative?'

'Sort of. I mean, no. In a way, yes.'

'Well, that's that sorted out, anyway. Where did you disappear to at Xanadu the other weekend?'

'I figured lots of, uh, organizer people and music people would want to come and talk with you.'

'Exactly! I needed you to head-butt some for me. How is your head, by the way? No lasting brain damage?'

'No, my brain is normal, thanks. Sort of normal.'

Ai Imajō finds this funny.

We both begin talking at the same moment.

'After you,' I say.

'No, after you,' she says.

'I, uh' – the electric chair must be more pleasant than this – 'am wondering if, I mean, it's perfectly all right if not, you know' – never commit your army without a clear path of retreat – 'but if, uh, it's okay for me to, uh, call you.'

A pause.

'So, Miyake, you are calling me to ask me if it is okay to call me, right?'

I really should have planned this better.

♌

Walking was pleasant since Goatwriter sloughed off his arthritic body in the sacred pool. The bamboo swayed sideways to let him pass, and whippoorwills wavered quarter quavers. Up ahead, he saw a house. It was a strange building to encounter in the Lapsang Souchang plateau. It would not have seemed out of place in a sleepy suburb, with its pond of duckweed and dragonflies. A stone lantern glowed on an island. A piebald rabbit disappeared amid a rhomboid rhubarb riot. Beneath the gable was an open triangular window. Whisperings filled the air. Goatwriter took the path to the front door. Its lockless knob twizzled uselessly, the door swung open, and Goatwriter climbed the lightening stairs to the attic. 'Good afternoon,' said the writing bureau. 'Greetings,' said the pen of Sei Shōnagon.

'But I left you in the venerable coach!' exclaimed Goatwriter.

'We travel anywhere you go,' explained the bureau.

'And since when did you learn to speak?'

'Since *you* learned to unblock your ears,' answered Sei Shōnagon's pen, who had sharpened her nib on the whetstone of her original mistress's wit. 'Shall we make a start?' suggested the writing bureau. 'Mrs Comb and Pithecanthropus will be along, in a little while.' Goatwriter took out a fresh sheet of paper. Outside, over the highlands, lowlands, rainforests, slums, estates, islands, plains, the nine corners of the compass, peace dropped slowly from the mist-melded sky. Reality is the page. Life is the word.

Six

回天

Kai Ten

Amadeus Tea Room is a wedding-cake world. Icing-pastelled, fluted and twirly. Aunt Money would award it her highest decoration: 'Rapturous'. Me, I want to spray-paint its creamy carpets, milky walls and buttery upholstery. I found the Righa Royal Hotel immediately, which left over an hour to kill walking around Harajuku. Dreamy shop-girls cleaned boutique windows in the morning cool, and florists hosed down pavements. I poke the ice in my water. My grandfather is due here in fifteen minutes. 'Grandfather', as a word, will acquire a new meaning. Weird, how words slip meanings on and off. Until last week, 'grandfather' meant the man in the grainy photo on my grandmother's family altar. 'The sea took him off,' was all she ever told us about her long-dead husband. Yakushima folklore remembers him as a thief and a boozer who disappeared off the end of the harbour quay one windy night.

Amadeus Tea Room is posh enough to support a butler. He stands behind a sort of pedestal at the pearly gates, examines the reservations book, orders the waitresses, and pedals his fingers. Do butlers go to butler school? How much are they paid? I practise pedalling my fingers, and at that very moment the butler looks straight at me. I drop my hands and look out of the window, acutely embarrassed. On neighbouring tables wealthy wives discuss the secrets of their trade. Businessmen peruse spreadsheets and tap sparrow-sized laptop keyboards. Wolfgang Amadeus Mozart looks down from his ceiling fresco, surrounded by margarine cherubs blasting trumpets. He looks puffy and pasty – little wonder he died young. I badly want to smoke one of my Clarks. Mozart certainly has a great view through the panoramic window.

Tokyo Tower, PanOpticon, Yoyogi park – where the dirty old men hang out with telephoto lenses. On a soaring chrome block a giant crane builds a scale model of itself. Water tanks, aerials, rooftops. The weather is stained khaki today. A silver teaspoon is struck rhythmically against a bone-china teacup – no, it is the carriage clock on the mantelpiece announcing the arrival of ten o'clock. Butler bows, and guides an elderly man this way.

Him!

My grandfather looks at me – I stand up, flustered, suddenly under-rehearsed – and he gives me that 'Yes, it *is* me' look you put on when you turn up for an appointment with a stranger. I cannot say he looks like me, but I cannot say he doesn't. My grandfather walks with an cane, wears a navy cotton suit and a bootlace tie with a clasp. Butler zips ahead and prepares a chair. My grandfather purses his lips. His skin is sickly grey and mottled, and he fails to hide how much effort walking costs him. 'Eiji Miyake, one presumes?' I give an eight-eighths bow, searching for the right thing to say. My grandfather gives an amused one-eighth. 'Mr Miyake, I must inform you at the outset that I am not your grandfather.'

I unbow. 'Oh.'

Butler withdraws, and the stranger sits down, leaving me marooned on my feet. 'But I am here at your grandfather's behest to discuss matters pertinent to the Tsukiyama family. Be seated, boy.' He watches my every motion – his eyebrows are sunken, but the eyes inside are laser sharp. 'The name is Raizo. Your grandfather and I go back many decades. I know about you, Miyake. In fact, it was I who brought your personal column advertisement to my friend's attention. Now. As you are aware, your grandfather has been convalescent, in the wake of major heart surgery. His doctor's original forecasts were overly optimistic, and he is obliged to remain in hospital for another three days. Hence I am here, in his stead. Questions.'

'Can I visit him?'

Mr Raizo shakes his head. 'Your stepmother is helping to nurse him in the ward, and . . . how can I express this?'

'She thinks I am a leech who wants to suck money from the Tsukiyamas.'

'Precisely. Just for the record: is that your intention?'

'No, Mr Raizo. All I want is to meet my father.' How many times must I say this?

'Your grandfather believes that secrecy is the wisest strategy to belay your stepmother's misgivings, at this point. Young lady!' Mr Raizo crooks his finger at a passing waitress. 'One of my gigantic cognacs, if you please. Your poison, Miyake?'

'Uh, green tea, please.'

The waitress gives me a well-trained smile. 'We have eighteen varieties—'

'Oh, just bring the boy a pot of tea, dammit!'

The waitress bows, her smile undented. 'Yes, Admiral.'

Admiral? How many of those are there? '*Admiral* Raizo?'

'That was all many years ago. "Mr" is fine.'

'Mr Raizo. Do you actually know my father?'

'Blunt questions earn blunt answers. I make no secret of the fact I despise the man. I have avoided his company for years. Since the day I learned he sold the Tsukiyama sword. It had been in his – your – family for five centuries, Miyake. Five Hundred Years! The snub that your father dealt five centuries of Tsukiyamas – not to mention the Tsukiyamas yet to be born – is immeasurable. Immeasurable! Your grandfather, Takara Tsukiyama, is a man who believes in blood-lines. Your father is a man who believes in joint stock ventures in Formosa. Do you know where the Tsukiyama sword presently resides?' The admiral rasps. 'It resides in the boardroom of a pesticide factory in Nebraska! What do you think of that, Miyake?'

'It seems a shame, Mr Raizo, but—'

'It is a crime, Miyake! Your father is a man devoid of honour! When he separated from your mother he would happily have cut her adrift without a thought for her future! It was your grandfather who ensured her financial survival.' This is news to me. 'There are codes of honour, even when dealing with concubines. Flesh and blood matter, Miyake! Blood-lines are the stuff of life. Of identity! Knowing who you are from is a requisite of self knowledge.' The waitress arrives with a silver tray, and places our drinks on lace place mats.

'I agree that blood-lines are important, Mr Raizo. This is why I am here.'

The admiral sniffs his brandy moodily. I sip my soapy tea. 'Y'know, Miyake, my doctors told me to lay off this stuff. But I meet more geriatric sailors than I do geriatric doctors.' He drinks half the glass in one gulp, tips his head back, and savours every molecule. 'Your stepsisters are dead losses. A pair of screeching vulgarities, at some half-wit college. They rise at eleven o'clock in the morning. They wear white lipstick, astronaut boots, cowboy hats, Ukrainian peasant scarfs. They dye their hair the colour of effluence. It is your grandfather's hope that his grandson – you – have principles loftier than those espoused in the latest pop hit.'

'Mr Raizo, forgive me if . . . I mean, I hope my grandfather doesn't see me as any kind of, uh, future heir. When I say I have no intention of muscling my way into the Tsukiyama family tree, I mean it.'

Mr Raizo makes rumbles impatiently. 'Who – meant – what – where – when – why – whose . . . Look, your grandfather wants you to read this.' He places a package on the table, wrapped in black cloth. 'A loan, not a gift. This journal is his most treasured possession. Guard it with your life, and bring it when you rendezvous with your grandfather seven days from now. Here. Same time – ten hundred hours – same table. Questions?'

'We never met – is it wise to trust me with something so—'

'Brazen folly, I say. Make a copy, I told the stubborn fool. Don't entrust some boy with the original. But he insisted. A copy would dilute its soul, its uniqueness. His words, not mine.'

'I, uh . . .' I look at the black package. 'I am honoured.'

'Indeed you are. Your father has never read these pages. He

would probably auction them to highest bidder, on his "Inter Net".'

'Mr Raizo: could you tell me what my grandfather wants?'

'Another blunt question.' The admiral downs the rest of his cognac. The jewel in his tie-clasp glimmers ocean-trench blue. 'I will tell you this. Growing old is an unwinnable campaign. During this war we witness ugly scenes. Truths mutate to whims. Faith becomes cynical transactions between liars. Sacrifices turn out to be needless excesses. Heroes become old farts, and young farts become heroes. Ethics become logos on sports clothing. You ask what your grandfather wants? I shall tell you. He wants what you want. No more, no less.'

A coven of wives blowhole wild laughter.

'Uh, which is?'

Admiral Raizo stands. Butler is already here with his cane. 'Meaning.'

♎

1st August, 1944

Morning, cloudy. Afternoon, light rain. I am on the train from Nagasaki. My journey to Tokuyama in Yamaguchi prefecture will take several more hours, and I will not reach Ōtsushima island, my destination, until tomorrow morning. Over the last weekend, Takara, I was torn between two promises. One promise was to you: to tell you every detail about my training in the Imperial Navy. My second promise was to my country and the emperor: to keep every detail regarding my special attack forces training an absolute secret. The purpose of this journal is to resolve my dilemma. These words are for you. My silence is for the emperor.

By the time you read these words, Mother will have already received a telegram informing you of my death and posthumous promotion. Perhaps you, Mother and Yaeko are in mourning. Perhaps you wonder what my death means. Perhaps you regret you have no ash, no bones, to place in our family tomb. This journal is my solace, my meaning, and my body. The sea is a fine tomb. Do not mourn immoderately.

Let me begin. The war situation is deteriorating rapidly. Our emperor's forces have suffered severe losses in the Solomon Islands. The Americans are invading the Philippines with the clear aim of possessing the Ryūkū chain. To prevent the destruction of the home islands extraordinary measures are called for. This is why the Imperial Navy has authorized the kaiten programme.

A kaiten is a modified mark 93 torpedo: the finest torpedo in the world, with a cockpit for a pilot. A kaiten can be steered, aligned and rammed into an enemy vessel below the waterline. Destruction of the target is a theoretical certainty. I know you are fond of technical data, Takara, so here goes. A kaiten measures 14.75 metres in length. It is propelled by a 550hp engine, and fuelled by liquid oxygen which leaves no wake of air bubbles on the surface, thereby allowing an invisible strike. A kaiten can cruise at 56 kph for 25 minutes, thus outpacing capital target vessels. A kaiten is tipped with a 1.55-ton TNT warhead which detonates on impact. Four kaitens will be mounted on I-class submarines. The submarines will sortie to within strike range of enemy anchorages, where the kaitens will be released. This new, deadly manned torpedo will reverse the recent losses in the Great East Asian Co-Prosperity Sphere, will dismay and ultimately decimate the American Navy. The Pacific Ocean will become a Japanese lake.

From the naval airbases at Nara and Tsuchiura, 1375 volunteers offered their lives for the kaiten programme. Only 160 passed the stringent selection procedures. You can see, my brother, how the Tsukiyama name shall be honoured and remembered.

2nd August

Hazy morning; a hot, cloudless afternoon. I awoke with other kaiten trainees in cells at the military police barracks in Tokuyama – regular billets were destroyed in bombing raids last month. A bomb struck the fuel depot, and in the ensuing destruction the port and large districts of the town were razed to the ground. From this wreckage a launch took us to Ōtsushima. The short voyage takes only 30 minutes, but the contrast could not be more complete. Ōtsushima is a body and head of peaceful wooded hills, terraced with rice-fields. The kaiten base and torpedo works lies on the low-lying 'neck' of the island.

Sub-Lt Hiroshi Kuroki and Ens Sekio Nishina, the two co-inventors of the kaiten, paid us the inestimable honour of meeting our launch. These men are living legends, Takara. Initially, Naval High Command was reluctant to sanction the use of special attack forces, and rejected the kaiten proposals submitted by Sub-Lt Kuroki and Ens Nishina. To convince High Command of their utmost sincerity, they resubmitted their proposals, written in the ink of their own blood. For all this, they are cheerful, unassuming fellows. They showed us to our quarters, joking about the 'Ōtsushima Hotel'. They led the technical debriefings that took up the rest of the day, and postponed the tour of the base until tomorrow.

3rd August

Windy conditions. Sea choppy. The perimeter fence of the kaiten base encloses an area of approximately six baseball grounds, and accommodates between 500 and 600 men. Security is tight – even the islanders are unaware of the true purpose of the base. The base includes a barracks, refectory, three torpedo factories, a machine-shop to convert the mark 93 torpedoes to kaitens, an exercise yard, a ceremony square, administrative buildings, and the harbour. From the machine-shop, a narrow-gauge railway enters a tunnel blasted through 400 metres of rock to the kaiten launch pier, where training began tonight. I jankenned with Takashi Higuchi, a classmate from Nara, for the privilege of the first kaiten run co-piloted with Sub-Lt Kuroki. His stone beat my scissors! Never mind, my turn will come tomorrow.

4th August

Sultry, humid, hot weather. Tragedy has struck so soon. Last night, Sub-Lt Kuroki and Lt Higuchi failed to return from their run around the northern body of Ōtsushima. Frogmen spent the night searching for their kaiten. It was finally found shortly after dawn, a mere 300 metres from the launch pier, embedded in the sea-floor silt, 16 hours after launching. Although kaitens have two escape hatches, these may only be opened above water. Underwater, the water pressure clamps them closed. A kaiten contains enough air for about 10 hours – with two pilots, this time was halved. They ensured their sacrifices were not in vain by writing 2000 kana of technical data and observations, pertaining to the fatal malfunction. When their paper was used up, they scratched words on the cockpit wall with a screwdriver. We just returned from their cremation ceremony. Ens Nishina has sworn to carry the ashes of Kuroki aboard his kaiten when he meets his glory. The atmosphere on the base is one of mourning, obviously, but tempered with a determination that the lives of our brothers shall not be lost in vain. My own heart was burdened with guilt. I begged a private audience with Commandant Ujina and told him about how I felt a special responsibility to Higuchi's soul. Cmdt Ujina promised to consider my request that I be included in the first sortie of kaiten attacks.

9th August

Weather extremely hot. Forgive the long silence, Takara. Training has swung into full gear, and finding even ten minutes to sit down with my journal during the day has been impossible. At night, I am asleep as my head touches my pillow. I have wonderful news. During the morning roll-call, the names for the first wave of kaiten attacks were announced and 'Tsukiyama' was among them! Kikusui is our unit emblem. This is the floating chrysanthemum crest of Masashige Kusunoki, champion of Emperor Godaigo. Kusunoki's 700 warriors withstood an onslaught of 35,000 Ashikaga traitors at the Battle of Minatogawa, and only after sustaining 11 terrible wounds did he commit seppuku with his brother, Masasue. The symbolism is obvious. We are the 700. Our devotion to our beloved emperor is ultimate.

Four fleet subs will each transport 4 kaitens. *I-47*, captained by *the* Lt-Cdr Zenji Orita, will carry Ens Nishina, Sato, Watanabe, and Lt Fukuda. *I-36* will carry Lt Yoshimoto and Ens Toyozumi, Imanishi and Kudo. Aboard *I-37* will be Lt Kamibeppu and Murakami, and Ens Utsunomiya and Kondō. *I-333*, captained by Cpt Yokota, will transport Lts Abe and Gotō, and Ens Kusakabe and Tsukiyama Subaru. After the announcement we were reallocated dorms, so members of the same sortie can sleep in the same room. *I-333* is on the second floor, at the end, overlooking the rice terraces. At night the croaking of frogs drowns out the foundries. I remember our room in Nagasaki.

12th August

Weather cool and calm. Sea as smooth as Nakajima river where we sailed our model yachts. Today I will write about our training. After breakfast we divide into Chrysanthemums and Drys. Because there are only 6 kaitens available for training, we are given priority practice privileges. At 0830 we proceed through the tunnel to the kaiten pier. After boarding, a crane lowers us into the sea. Usually we sail two to a cockpit. Of course, we have no room, but this doubling up helps to save fuel, and 'a drop of petrol is as precious as a drop of blood'. Our instructor knocks on the hull, and we knock back to show we are ready to embark. First we run through a series of descents. Then we solve a navigation problem, using a stopwatch and gyrocompass. We locate a target ship, and simulate a hit by passing under the bow. One must be careful not to clip the upper hatch on the keel – two kaiten pilots died in Base P this way. We also dread being stuck in silt, like Sub-Lt Kuroki and Lt Higuchi. If this misfortune occurs, one is supposed to blast compressed air into the warhead (filled with seawater rather than TNT) which should, in principle, buoy the kaiten to the surface. None of us are eager to be the first to test this flotation theory. What we dread most, however, is surviving the loss of a training kaiten. This occurred to a hapless trainee from Yokohama five days ago. He was dismissed, and his name is never mentioned. After returning to the pier or the base harbour, depending on our course, we attend debriefing sessions to share our observations with the Drys. After the worst of the afternoon heat is over, we practise sumō wrestling, kendō fencing, athletics, rugby. Kaiten pilots must be in prime physical condition. Remember our father's words, Takara: the body is the outermost layer of the mind.

14th August

Weather fine at first, clouding over by midday. As my training session was cancelled today owing to engine failure, I have a spare hour to write to you about my *I-333* brothers. Yutaka Abe is our leader, aged 24, of old Tokyo stock and a graduate of Peers. His father was aboard *Shimantogawa* at the glorious Battle of Tsushima back in 1905. Abe is a superhuman who excels in every field. Rowing, navigation, composing haiku. He let it slip that he has won every chess match he has played for the last 9 years. The motto on his kaiten is to be 'Unerring Arrow of the Emperor'. Shigenobu Gotō, aged 22, is from a merchant family in Osaka and has a wit that can kill at twenty paces. He gets love letters nearly every day from different girls, and complains about the lack of women on the base. Abe responds with a single word: Purity. Gotō can impersonate anybody and anything. He even takes requests: Chinaman attacked by snake in privy; Tōhoku fishwife being blown through tuba. He uses his voices to distract Abe when they play chess. Abe wins anyway. The message on Gotō's kaiten is to read: 'Medicine for Yankees'. Our third member is Issa Kusakabe. Kusakabe is a year older than me, quiet, and reads anything he can get his hands on. Technical manuals, novels, poetry, old magazines from before the war. Anything. Mrs Oshige (our 'mother' on Ōtsushima, who believes we are testing a new type of submarine) arranged for a boy to bring Kusakabe books from the school library every week. He even has a volume of Shakespeare. Abe questioned whether the works of an effete Westerner were appropriate for a Japanese warrior. Kusakabe explained that Shakespeare is English kabuki. Abe said Shakespeare contained corrupting influences. Kusakabe asked which plays Abe was thinking of. Abe let it drop. After all, Kusakabe would not have volunteered to be a kaiten pilot if his ethics were in any way questionable. He is inscribing not a slogan, but a line of verse on his kaiten. 'The foe may raise ten thousand shouts – we conquer without a single word.' I must not neglect Slick, our unit chief engineer. His nickname is derived from his hands, which are always oily and black. Slick is one of the oldest men on the base. He is vague about his age, but he is old enough to be our father. Gotō jokes that he probably is our father. Slick's real children are his kaitens. By the way, I have elected to leave my kaiten without a motto. My sacrifice shall be its motto and its meaning.

I put the journal under the counter of Shooting Star to give my eyes a rest – the pages are laminated, but the pencil marks are fading away to ghost lines. Plus, many of the kanji are obscure, so I have to keep referring to a dictionary. I open a can of Diet Pepsi and survey my new empire: video racks, stacks, shelves. Mucus aliens, shiny gladiators, squeaky idols. Soft rock pumps away. In my week away the old shoe repairer next to Fujifilm has been turned into a Kentucky Fried Chicken outlet. A spooky life-sized statute of Colonel Sanders stands outside, under a limp 'Opening Fayre' banner. He is as fat and grinny as a statue of Ebisu in a temple. Does KFC make you that fat?

Buntarō and Machiko will be on their JAL airplane now, somewhere over the Pacific. Buntarō was in a near-frenzy when I got back from my meeting with Mr Raizo, even though he had ninety minutes before the taxi came. What would happen if the computer crashed? If the monitor broke down? If it rains tap-dancing conger-eels? Machiko hauled him into the taxi. I

I can watch anything on the monitor, but there are too many films to choose, so I leave the same Tom Hanks movie running all day. Nobody will notice. Between two and five, business is pretty quiet; once offices and schools start winding up I get much busier. The regulars gape when they see me – they immediately assume that Machiko has suffered a miscarriage. When I tell them the Ōgisos are on holiday, they act as if I said Buntarō and his wife turned into teapots and flew to Tibet. The question of who I am is a trifle delicate – my scuzzy landlord sublets my capsule without troubling the tax office. Schoolkids cluster around horror, office ladies hire Hollywood movies with blond stars, salarymen hire titles like *Pam the Clam from Amsterdam* and *Hot Dog Academy*. Several customers bring videos back late – you always have to check the dates. Mrs Sasaki arrives at 7.30 – I dash upstairs to feed Cat, and then across to KFC to feed myself. Colonel Sanders' chicken is made of sawdust. Mrs Sasaki tells me about my replacement at Ueno, which makes me sort of nostalgic for my old job. She leaves me the *Tokyo Star* – Monday has the jobs pages. If I want a career in kitchen portering, telesales, shelf-stacking or mailbox-stuffing then Tokyo is heaven on earth. Cat appears on the stairs – during my week in hiding she learned how to open my capsule door. I tell her to go back but she ignores me, and after replacing a stack of returned videos I find her settled on the counter chair, so I have to make do with a wobbly stool. Fujifilm says 10:26. Business drops off.

♎

2nd September

Hot weather, but cooler in the evenings now. I received your letter today, Takara, and the parcel from Mother and Yaeko containing the thousand-stitch belt. Given the special attack nature of my mission, the five-sen coins sewn into the belt will not avert death, but I shall wrap it around my middle every time I climb aboard my kaiten. Abe, Gotō, Kusakabe and I read aloud our letters from home, and I was proud as Tengu when I told them my younger brother is already a junior squadron leader at the bullet factory. Your games resemble authentic military training – charging at Roosevelts and Churchills with bamboo bayonets. My thoughts are also with Yaeko at the parachute factory. Her stitches may save the lives of my former classmates at Nara Naval Air Academy. It must pain Mother to trade Tsukiyama family treasures for rice, but I know Father and our ancestors understand. War changes rules. It is wise of you to tape Xs over the windows, to guard against bomb blasts. Nagasaki was ever a most fortunate city, and if raids come the enemy will target the shipyards rather than our side of town. All the same, every precaution should be taken.

I will write a reply to your letter very soon. By now, you will understand why my reply fails to provide answers to all the questions you asked.

9th September

Weather: warm, mild, balmy. I am 20 years old today. To celebrate my birthday in a time of national emergency is inappropriate, so after a warhead study session I sneaked away before supper. I gratefully accepted the sunset as my birthday present. Inland Sea sunsets are special. Tonight's was the colour of Yaeko's plum preserve. Do you remember the story of Urashima Tarō? About how he saved the giant turtle, and stayed in the undersea palace for three days, but upon his return three generations had come and gone? I wondered about how this place will look in ninety years, when the Greater East Asian War is but a distant memory. Bring your children to Ōtsushima when the war is won. The local sea bream is delicious, as are the Inland Sea oysters. I was about to return to the refectory, when Abe, Gotō and Kusakabe appeared. Somehow Abe had found out about my birthday and told Mrs Oshige, who managed to prepare chicken skewers on a stick. Kusakabe built a fire and we had supper on the seashore and some home-brew sake which Gotō appropriated from a canteen assistant. The drink was rough enough to paralyse our faces, but no meal ever tasted better, with the exception of Mother's.

13th September

A warm morning, a muggy afternoon. An attack of flu has been around the base. I myself have been in the sickbay for 24 hours with a temperature of 39 degrees. I am recovering now. I suffered from strange dreams. In one, I was in my kaiten cruising around the Solomon Islands in search of an enemy aircraft carrier. Everything was so blue. I felt indestructible, like a shark. Suddenly Mrs Shiomi's son, the boy who threw himself under a Russian tank with a bomb at Nomonhan, was in my kaiten. 'Did nobody tell you?' he said. 'The war is over.' I asked who won, and I saw that Shiomi's eyes were missing. 'The emperor entertains the Americans with duck shoots in the palace grounds. In this fashion he seeks to save his skin.' I decided I should sail into Tokyo harbour and sink at least one enemy vessel, and pointed my kaiten north. The acceleration forced my body back, and when I woke I felt I was remembering being born, or perhaps dying, the last time or the next time. Kusakabe and Gotō visited me later, to share notes they had taken in our navigation class, but I said nothing about my dream.

2nd October

Drizzle all day. The Kikusui target sites were announced at a secret meeting this afternoon. *I-47* and *I-36* will head for Ulithi, a vast lagoon in the Philippines captured by the Americans only 10 days ago. *I-37* and *I-333* will simultaneously attack Kossol Passage anchorage in the Palau Islands. The purpose of a dual-site attack is to ensure maximum damage to enemy morale. Find the Palau Islands in Father's atlas, Takara. You can see how vividly blue the seas are. When you wonder where I am, remember: your brother is the blue of the sea.

Disharmony grows between Abe and Kusakabe. Our unit leader challenged Kusakabe to a game of chess, and he declined. Abe teased him: 'Are you afraid of losing?' Kusakabe made a strange reply: 'No, I am afraid of winning.' Abe retained his smile, but his irritation was plain. Brothers who shall die together should not quarrel in this way.

10th October

Weather clear. Dew on the grass this morning. Slick, his ground crew and I were hauling our kaiten through the tunnel to the launch pier this afternoon when the air-raid siren sounded. No drill had been scheduled. The tunnel filled up with men from the launch pier while the commandant shouted orders over the loudspeakers. TNT was secured in the deep bunker, the submarines manoeuvred out of the bay, and we waited anxiously for the sound of B29s. If a bomb scores a direct hit on the machine-shops, the project could be delayed crucial weeks. Slick wondered aloud if an attack on the mainland means the Americans are attacking Okinawa already. We hear so many rumours but reliable news is scant. After a nervous forty minutes the all-clear siren sounded. Maybe a jumpy lookout post mistook our own Zeros for enemy planes.

13th October

Pleasant afternoon sun. Clouds by evening. Rereading this journal, I notice that I have failed to describe the atmosphere of the base. It is unique, in my experience. Engineers, instructors, pilots and trainees all work together towards the same end. I have never felt so alive as in these weeks. My life has a meaning – to defend the Motherland. Discipline is not lax. We undergo the same drills and inspections as any military bace. But the excesses of ordinary camps, where green recruits are hazed and where soldiers are hung upside down and beaten, are unknown on Ōtsushima. We receive regular rations of cigarettes and candy, and real white rice. My one regret is that I cannot share my meals with you, Mother and Yaeko. I am stockpiling my candy for you, however, and refuse to gamble with it like Gotō and most of my co-trainees.

18th October

Steady rain all day. The *Zuikaku* is still afloat and Father is therefore almost certainly alive! Abe arranged for me to use military channels to dispatch a telegram to Mother immediately. I received the news from Cpt Tsuyoshi Yokota of *I-333*, which docked in Ōtsushima today. Cpt Yokota had himself spoken to Admiral Kurita aboard the *Atago* only seven days previously while on patrol in the Leyte Gulf. The news that Father is still well and thinking of us heartens me beyond words. One day he may hold this very journal in his hands! Cpt Yokota says that *Zuikaku* is regarded as a charmed ship since Pearl Harbor. Remember that civilian mail to the South Seas is a very low priority, so do not be discouraged if you hear nothing. This evening, a 4-day leave was announced for the Kikusui Group men, before we depart for the target zone.

20th October

Clear day, refreshing breezes. Good fortune begets good fortune. During dinner, Cmdnt Ujina broadcast the evening news over the camp speakers, and we heard of the extraordinary kamikaze successes in the Philippines yesterday. Five American aircraft carriers and six destroyers sunk! In a single wave! Surely even the American savages will realize the hopelessness of invading the home islands. Lt Kamibeppu stood on his bench and proposed a toast to the souls of the brave aviators who had given their lives to our beloved Emperor Hirohito. Rarely have I heard such a moving speech. 'Pure spirit, or metal? Which is the stronger? Spirit will buckle metal, and blast it with holes! Metal can no more damage pure spirit than scissors can cut a rope of smoke!' I confess, I imagined the day when similar toasts shall be drunk to our souls.

28th October

Light rain today. The new *I-333* kaitens became operational today. They handle more smoothly than the training kaitens. After a longer-than-expected test session, I ran back through the rain across the exercise ground and nearly collided with Kusakabe, who was leaning against the supply shed, staring intently at the ground. I asked him what had caught his attention so. Kusakabe pointed at a puddle, and spoke softly. 'Circles are born, while circles born a second ago live. Circles live, while circles living a second ago die. Circles die, while new circles are born.' A very Kusakabe comment. I told him he should have been born a wandering poet-priest. He said maybe he was, once. We watched the puddles for a while.

2nd November
The dying heat of 1944. I just returned from Nagasaki for the final time. Those memories are yours too, so I have no need to describe them here. I can still taste Mother's yōkan and Yaeko's pumpkin tempura. The train journey took a long time because the engine constantly broke down. The military carriage was commandeered by a high-ranking party of officers, so I travelled with a carriage full of refugees from Manchūkuo. Their stories of the Soviets' cruelty and their Chinese servants' treachery were terrible. How grateful I am that Father never joined the colonists over the past two decades. One girl younger than you was travelling alone to find an aunt in Tokyo. This was her first time in Japan. Around her neck was an urn. It contained the ashes of her father, who died in Mukden, her mother, who died in Karafuto, and her sister, who died in Sasebo. She was afraid she would fall asleep and miss Tokyo, which she imagined was a small place like her frontier town. She believed she could find her aunt by asking people. At Tokuyama I gave her half my money, wrapped in a handkerchief, and left before she could refuse. I fear for her. I fear for all of them.

'Golems,' I explain, lying showered and naked in after-midnight capsule darkness with Ai on the other end of the phone, 'are totally different to zombies. Sure, they are both undead, but you mould golems from graveyard mud in the image of the dead man buried below, and then you inscribe his rune on the torso. You can only kill golems by erasing the rune. Zombies you can easily decapitate, or set alight with a flamethrower. You make them from body parts, usually stolen from a morgue, or else you simply reanimate semi-rotten corpses.'

'Is necrophilia a compulsory subject in Kyūshū high schools?'

'I work in a video shop now. I have to know these things.'

'Change the subject.'

'Okay. What to?'

'I asked you first.'

'Well, I always wanted to know what the meaning of life is.'

'Eating macadamia-nut ice cream and listening to Debussy.'

'Answer seriously.'

Ai hums as she changes position. 'Your question is seriously wrong.'

I imagine her lying here. 'What should my question be, then?'

'It should be "What is *your* meaning of life?" Take Bach's *Well-Temper'd Clavier*. To me, it means molecular harmony. To my father, it means a broken sewing machine. To Bach, it means money to pay the candlestickmaker. Who is right? Individually, we all are. Generally, none of us is. Are you still thinking about your great-uncle and his kaiten?'

'I guess. His meaning of life seemed rock-solid valid.'

'To him, yes. Sacrificing your life for the vainglory of a military clique isn't my idea of "valid", but to your great-uncle learning how to play the piano as well as my united brain, nerves and muscles will allow wouldn't have seemed very worthwhile.' Cat walks in at this point. 'Maybe the meaning of life lies in the act of looking for it.' Cat laps water in the thirsty moonlight.

◆

'So much space!' Buntarō yells into a telephone on a windy morning. 'What do you do with all this space? Why did I never come here years ago? The plane took less time than my dentist. Do you know when I last took a holiday outside Tokyo?'

'Nope.' I stifle a yawn.

'Me neither, lad. I arrived in Tokyo when I was twenty-two. My company made transformers, and they sent me up for training. I get off the train at Tokyo station, and twenty minutes later I find the exit. Would I ever *hate* to spend my life living in this hell-hole! I think. Twenty years on, look at what I did. Beware of holidays in paradise, lad. You think too much about what you never did.'

'Does everyone in paradise get up so early?'

'The wife was up before me. Strolling on the beach, under the palm trees. Why is the ocean so . . . y'know . . . blue? You can hear the waves crash from our balcony. My wife found a starfish washed up. A real, live starfish.'

'That's the sea for you. Is there, uh, anything specific you wanted to talk to me about?'

'Oh, yeah. I thought I'd run through your problems.'

'Which ones, uh, did you have in mind?'

'Your problems with the shop.'

'Shooting Star? There are no problems.

'None?'

'Not one.'

'Oh.'

'Get back to paradise, Buntarō.'

I try to get back to sleep – I was talking with Ai until after three a.m. – but my mind is moving up its gears. Fujifilm says 07:45. Cat laps water and leaves for work. The morning plugs itself in. I doodle blues chords for some time, smoke my last three Lucky Strikes, eat yoghurt – after spooning out a mould colony – and listen to *Milk and Honey*. A kite of sunlight settles on Anju.

For two days she was classed as missing, but nobody was cruel enough to tell me not to give up hope. True, tourists go missing on Yakushima all the time, and often turn up – or get rescued – a day or two later. But locals are never so stupid, not even local eleven-year-olds – we all knew Anju had drowned. No goodbye, just gone. My grandmother had aged ten years by the following morning, and looked at me as if she scarcely knew me. There was no big scene when I left that day. I remember her at the kitchen table, telling me that if I hadn't gone to Kagoshima, her granddaughter would still be alive. Which I thought – and think – is only too true. Being surrounded by Anju's clothes and toys and books was unbearable, so I walked to Uncle Orange's farmhouse and my aunt cleared a corner for me to sleep in. Officer Kuma called round the evening after to tell me that the search for Anju's body had been called off. My Orange cousins are all older girls, and they decided I needed nursing through my grief – they kept saying it was okay to cry, that they understood how I felt, that Anju dying wasn't my fault, that I had always been a good brother. Sympathy was also unbearable. I had swapped my sister for one never to be repeated goal. So I ran away. Running away on Yakushima is simple – you leave before the old women stir and the fog goes home seawards, tread quietly through the weatherboarded alleyways, cross the coast road, skirt the tea-fields and orange orchards, set a farm dog barking, enter the forest and start climbing.

After the head of the thunder god vanishes into the ocean, I skirt the ridge above my grandmother's house. No light is on. An autumn morning, when rain is always ten minutes away. I climb. Waterfalls without names, waxy leaves, berries in jade pools. I climb. Boughs sag, ferns fan, roots trip. I climb. I eat peanuts and oranges, to make sure I can disappear high and deep enough. Leech on my leg, creeping silence, day clots into grey afternoon, no sense of time. I climb. A graveyard of trees, a womb of trees, a war of trees. Sweat cools. I climb. Way up here, everything is covered in moss. Moss vivid as grief, muffling as snow, furry as tarantula legs. Sleep here, and moss covers you too. My legs stiffen and wobble so I sit down, and here comes the foggy moon through a forest skylight. I am cold, and huddle in my blanket, niched in an ancient shipwreck of a cedar. I am not afraid. You have to value yourself to be afraid. Yet for the first time in three days, I want something. I want the forest lord to turn me into a cedar. The very oldest islanders say that if you are in the interior mountains on the night when the forest lord counts his trees, he includes you in the number and turns you into a tree. Animals call, darkness swarms, cold nips my toes. I remember Anju. Despite the cold, I fall asleep. Despite my tiredness, I wake up. A white fox picks its way along a fallen trunk. It stops, turns its head, and recognizes me with more-than-human eyes. Mist hangs in the spaces between my boughs, and birds nest in what was my ear. I want to thank the forest lord, but I have no mouth now. Never mind. Never mind anything, ever again. When I wake, stiff, not a tree but a snot-dribbling boy again, throat tight with a cold, I sob and sob and sob and sob and sob and sob.

Milk and Honey over, my Discman hums to a stop. The kite of sunlight has slid to my junk shelf, where Cockroach watches me, fiddling its feelers. I leap up, grab the bug-killer, but Cockroach does a runner down the gap between the floor and the wall – I zap in about a third of the can. And here I stand, in mammoth-hunter pose, empty of everything. I ran away into the interior to understand why Anju had grown with me, cell by cell, day by day, if she was going to die before her twelfth birthday. I never did discover the answer. I made the descent without mishap the following day – the Orange house was having collective hysterics about me – but, looking back, did I ever really leave the interior? Is what Eiji Miyake means still rooted on Yakushima, magicked into a cedar on a mist-forgotten mountain flank, and my search for my father just a vague . . . passing . . . nothing? Fujifilm says I have to get Shooting Star ready for business. Another day too busy to worry about what it all means. Luckily for me.

7th November

Mild weather, fish-scale clouds. I am in our dorm after our pre-departure banquet. I am fat with fish, white rice, dried seaweed, victory chestnuts, canned fruit, and sake, which was presented by the emperor himself. Because the weather was fine today, the Kikusui graduation ceremony was held outside, in the exercise yard. Everyone on the base was in attendance, from Commandant Ujina down to the lowliest kitchen boy. The rising-sun flags on base and on the ships and submarines, were all raised in unison. A brass band performed the kimigayo. We wore uniforms especially tailored for the kaiten division: black, cobalt trimmings, with green chrysanthemums embroidered on the left breast. Vice-admiral Miwa of the 6th Fleet gave us the honour of a personal address. He is a fine orator as well as an unequalled naval tactician, and his words inscribed themselves on our hearts. 'You are avengers, at last face to face with those who would murder your fathers and violate your mothers. Peace will never be yours if you fail! Death is lighter than a feather, but duty is heavier than a mountain! 'Kai' and 'Ten' signify 'Turn' and 'Heaven' – therefore, I exhort you, turn the heavens so light shines anew on the land of the gods!' One by one, we ascended the podium, and the vice-admiral presented each of us with a hachimaki to tie around our heads like the samurai of old, and a seppuku sword, to remind us that our lives are His Imperial Majesty's possessions, and to avert the indignity of surrender should disaster prevent us from striking our targets. During the closing kimigayo we bowed before the portrait of the emperor. A priest then led us to a shinto shrine to pray for glory.

Abe, Gotō and Kusakabe are writing letters to their families, so I will do the same, and clip off some hair and nails for cremation. I shall write my final orders to you in this letter, but I shall reiterate them here: Takara, you are the acting head of the Tsukiyama family until Father returns. Whatever trials lie ahead, preserve the sword. Impress upon your sons, and their sons, the integrity and purity of the Tsukiyama blood-line. After deification my soul will reside at Yasukuni shrine, with my myriad brothers who also gave their lives to the emperor. Come to pray, bring our sword, and let the light dance on the blade. I shall be waiting.

8th November

Weather: fair, hazy. The maple leaves are flaming scarlet. *I-333* departed from Ōtsushima. The departure ceremony was held on the dock at 0900. A camera crew was present to make a newsreel of our departure. I waved at the camera as I passed, Takara, in case you and your friends see me at the cinema in Nagasaki. Lt Kamibeppu gave a speech on behalf of the Kikusui unit, thanking our trainers, apologizing for our blunders, and promising that every kaiten pilot will do his utmost to make our country proud of us. After this, we thanked Mrs Oshige individually. She was choked with emotion and unable to speak, but words may sully the message of the heart. The officers toasted us with omiki libation, and boarded the submarines to cries of 'Banzai'. We stood atop our kaitens, and waved back at our classmates on shore, until we rounded the western head of Ōtsushima. A small flotilla of fishing boats and training canoes saw us into the open sea. Gotō looked at the fishermen's daughters through Kusakabe's binoculars. Abe has just announced that our maintenance check has been brought forward an hour, so I'll wait until tomorrow to tell you about *I-333*.

9th November

Weather: rain in the morning; a clear afternoon with swelling waves. Gotō, who has a way with words, describes life in a submarine as being 'corked into a tin flask and thrown into a flood'. Into this tin flask is fitted the forward torpedo room, officers' qtrs, forward battery, pump room, conning tower, control room, mess, crew qtrs for 60 men, fore/aft engine rooms, after-torpedoes. Slick likens *I-333* to an iron whale. I marvel at the crew: they have been on active duty since the war began with only 10 days' shore leave! After one day, I am already aching to run, or throw a baseball. I miss our futons on Ōtsushima – on *I-333* we sleep on narrow shelves, with sides to stop us falling out. The air is stale and the light is sepia. I must emulate the endurance of the crew. Even walking requires contortion, especially at the beginning of a voyage when the gangways are used for food storage. There are only two places one can be alone. One is the kaitens, which can be accessed from the inside of the submarine via specially adapted tubes between the submarine deck and the kaiten lower hatch. The other is the toilet. (However, submarine toilets are not conducive to lingering.) Additionally, we have Cpt Yokota's permission to use the bridge when conditions permit. Of course, I must inform the duty officer when I go above-decks, so I can be accounted for if we have to make an emergency dive. After our evening calisthenics session I joined the ensign on lookout duty, starboard of the conning tower. At night the control room is 'rigged for dark' – only red lights are permitted, so Cpt or observers may switch above-and below-decks without loss of night vision. I watched the white spray on the bow and the foam wake to the rear. On moonlit nights these are telltale signs for bombers. The ensign told me the coastline to the west was Cape Sata-misaki, in Kagoshima prefecture. The end of Japan was lost in scarlet clouds.

'EjjjMyake!' Masanobu Suga bumper-cars into Shooting Star from the neon night, trips over and wallops the floor. He noses the ground, and grins at me – he is so drunk that his brain cannot understand how much his body hurts. Suga wobbles up to a one-legged kneel, as if he is about to ask for my hand in marriage. I dive around the counter to pick up his glasses before he grinds them to splinters. Suga thinks I am trying to help him up, and elbows me away with a 'grfffme!' He stands up, as stable as a newborn giraffe, and falls backwards into a rack of war movies. The rack topples and a hundred video boxes cascade. A customer – only one, luckily – stares death rays at us through her half-moon glasses. Suga glares at the fallen video rack. 'Poltygeists liv'nn heeer, Miyake. Needter leanov'r theeer a mo, mo-mo, justamo . . .' He tightrope-walks to the counter, lifting his head towards the monitor. '*Cassyblanca*.' The movie is actually *Bladerunner*. I right the rack and collect the videos boxes. Suga dangles his head, broken-puppet-style. 'Myaki.'

'Suga. Nice to, uh . . .'

Suga loses spittle control. I intercept the saliva stalactite with the *Tokyo Post*. 'Notdrunk, nvergetdrunk, notme. Happy, happy, he-he-hep-py, yes, mebbe, butnotnever out-of-cont. Roll.' He sinks to his knees, his knuckles gripping the edge of the cliff. Even Uncle Pachinko on a whisky bender is not this hopeless. 'Wentaseeya, Mishish Shashashaki sedyja quit. ByebyeUenobyebye, badvibes, bad, badbadbadvibes in Ueno, where allverlostnf'gottn orphans ended after the war, did did y'knowthat? Died like flies, poorlittlpootlittl . . .' Tears blossom in Suga's eyes and one runs down his pocked cheeks. Death-Ray Specs has a rape-alarm-in-a-library shrill: 'Too much! The way you youngsters behave today makes me vomit out my own lungs!' She leaves before I can begin an apology. For a moment I wish Suga would pass out – I could pretend not to know him and maybe an ambulance would take him away. 'Suga! You need to get home! You drank too much!'

Suga sniffs and focuses on me with puffy dogfish eyes. 'I'm curshed.'

'Have you got enough money for a taxi?'

'Curshed.'

'Can you tell me your address, Suga?'

He clenches his eyes and deliberately whacks his head back on the front of the counter as hard as he can, which luckily is not too hard as his neck control functions are off-line, but even so his face is bright with pain. I hold his head and he pushes me away. 'I'm curshed, Miyake! Dontchoogettitt? Curshed! One donut! For one fcknmeashly *donut*! Littlkid, kindygartn littlkid, waiting jushinside th'bakery doordoor, hewuzcryin'seyes out . . .' The tears begin again and Suga trembles. A scared dog sort of shiver.

'Suga, my room is upstairs, I'm going to—'

'*One*' – whack! – '*meashly*' – whack! – '*donut*. I opnd the door, littlkid runs out, fastazafastaza.' Sugas eyes screw up in pain. 'Batman'n'Robn on his T-shirt, littlkid, straight intr the middlvthe . . . road . . .' Suga blubs and his breathing is chopped and sliced. 'Wtchythink Idid, Miyake? Swoooooopd t'th'rescue, d'ythink? Nope, Miyake, nope nope nope rootd, rootd, I's rootd. T'th'spot, Miyake. Saw. Heard. Audiovshl. Car. Brakes. Littlkid. Wham, wham, wham. Flew, littlkid, flew like a baggashopping, *ber-lattt*, bowlingball, bloodontheroad, markerpen . . .' Suga's fingers claw for a ripcord on his face to pull – I grip his hands in my fists. Suga is losing his will to resist. 'Mum, she . . . pushpass-pusspashme, wailing right . . . *AaarrrAaarrrAaaaaarrrrrr* . . . I ran. Ran ran ran . . . Ran, Miyake, nverstppd never, run, Suga run, you *MUR-DER-RER* . . . Suga the mudderer.' Suga swallows a stone of grief. 'Betchawishdyr poisoned th'pineapple now, doncha? Howdjathink I got this pizza cheezgraterskin? Curshed. Icrossaroad, Isee Littlkid. Iseeanuvva Littlkid, Isee Littlkid. Curshed. Curshed.' His eyes ease themselves shut.

I see.

I take the key from the till, and manhandle the sack of Suga upstairs. 'Toilet. If you piss my futon I'll blowtorch your computers, okay? Suga? You hear me?' Suga nods, bleared and mumbly beyond grammar. 'I'll be downstairs.' Down at the till a girl in a cow-print T-shirt stands holding every Brad Pitt video in the shop. She studies her watch and emits a sigh of pain. 'Sorry to keep you waiting,' I say. She ignores me. I hear Suga barf. Barf one, Cowgirl looks puzzled. Barf two, Cowgirl breaks her vow of non-interaction and stares at me questioningly. Barf three, Cowgirl says, 'Can you hear anything?' I look at her as if she is an utter lunatic. 'Nothing. Why?' She leaves and I rearrange the fallen video cases on the rack. My toilet flushes, which is sort of encouraging. A flurry of custom follows. I have lost track of who is human and who is a replicant on *Bladerunner*. I wonder how many years Suga has been carrying his cursh around with him. I forget that other people in the world have broken parts too. Eleven o'clock swings around, and the night shows no sign of cooling. I hear a thump or two upstairs: at least I don't have a dead body on the premises to explain to Buntarō. I hear the drumming of water, and for a moment think the heat has turned to rain – then I realize that no, to answer the last question he asked me three weeks ago, Suga cannot piss straight when he wazzes. Another treat in store tomorrow morning. I crank up the air-con a notch, and retrieve my grandfather's journal and kanji dictionary from under the counter. The warmth between Subaru and Takara his younger brother is in stark contrast to the cold between my father and Takara my grandfather. Admiral Raizo's mention of a 'feud' makes me uneasy. The Yakushima aunts happily used me as ammo in their endless polite battles, and I cannot shake the feeling that I am on the edge of another war zone.

10th November

Conditions too poor to permit access to bridge. Abe reminds us we are irreplaceable components of our kaitens. Moreover, *I-333* rolls about too much to allow maintenance checks on our kaitens. We have sensed a certain reserve between ourselves and *I-333*'s crew. A certain distance is perhaps natural, but at times their conduct borders on coldness. For example, I discovered that Radioman First Class Hosokawa in communications grew up in Nagasaki, and when we passed in the corridor after dinner I addressed him in our local dialect. He looked startled, and replied using rigid formal speech. When Abe suggested that the kaiten pilots contribute to the cleaning docket, Cpt Yokota replied with terseness that our offer was generous but unthinkable. Abe believes the men regard us as incumbent gods, and are merely suffering from excess veneration. Gotō pointed out that 3½ years of dodging depth-charges would put a strain on anyone's mental state. Kusakabe speculated that the men may consider us insane. This angered Abe. Kusakabe calmly observed that submariners spend their lives slipping away from the jaws of death, while we seek to meet it head-on. Abe pulled rank and ordered Kusakabe – and Gotō – never to voice such thoughts again, because he was demeaning the dedication and patriotism of our hosts. I said nothing for the sake of harmony but inwardly I sympathized with Gotō. Even the youngest crew members have the eyes of old men.

11th November

Fine conditions prevail. The mercury in the thermometer climbs as the sea warms. It is impossible to remount the kaitens on the submarine deck once released, so we are unable to make test runs in our vessels. We must, however, spend time in our kaitens checking that the engines and other systems are in perfect working order. Watching the sea rush by through the kaiten periscopes is most enjoyable, especially when *I-333* is submerged. As we proceed south, I notice changes in the animal kingdom. For example, today I saw a manatee. It swam how a cow might swim. We passed through a school of tropical fish coloured marigold, snow and lilac. Two dolphins appeared this afternoon, swimming alongside us. The creatures appeared to be laughing at such a peculiar fish. May fortune similarly smile on our mission. Gotō made a joke. 'If a Chinese bandit, an American imperialist and a British general jumped off a building at the same time, who would hit the ground first?' Nobody knew, so Gotō gave us the punch line. 'Who cares?'

12th November

Weather thundery, but no rain, yet. Cpt Yokota is outspoken in his criticism of the Tokyo government, to say the least. If a civilian spoke in such a disrespectful manner he would be surely be arrested by the secret service. At dinner tonight, the captain opened a bottle of rum. I never experienced the drink outside pirate tales of my boyhood. It certainly loosens the tongue. Abe drank least, being a weak drinker, but Cpt Yokota can knock it back like cool tea on a hot day. Cpt Yokota first savaged the Admiralty for failing to learn from the Midway fiasco instead of suppressing news of the defeat and turning the very word into a taboo. 'The sole strategy of our navy,' according to Cpt Yokota, 'is to lure the enemy into a "Decisive Naval Engagement" like the Battle of Tsushima against the Russians. But it isn't going to happen in this war. The Americans are not so stupid.' Prime Minister Tōjō is 'an army idiot of the highest magnitude' for ordering the invasion of uninhabited Alaskan islands: 'For what? To liberate seabirds from Anglo-Saxon tyranny?' Prince Higashikuni is 'so stupid he couldn't pour piss out of a boot if the instructions were written on the heel'. Gotō laughed, Kusakabe smiled, and Abe turned a polite pink. I was unsure of the appropriate response. Cpt Yokota maintains the East Indies oilfields would still be Japanese territory if the wings of the military had fought together and not against each other, and if radar technology had been seriously developed. Now we must resort to begging the Germans for radar sets. He accuses the Imperial Army of operating subs undeclared to High Command as 'wheelbarrows', to support troops stranded on Rabaul and islands the enemy have bypassed. Most worrying of all is the Cpt's firm conviction that our secret codes have been cracked. Abe, perhaps rashly, observed that the codes were invented by a Tokyo Imperial University cryptologist to be undecipherable to the occidental brain. Cpt Yokota retorted that no Tokyo Imperial University cryptologist was ever ambushed on the high seas by a pack of destroyers that knew his vessel's exact whereabouts.

'But what if' – I unpick loops in my phone cord – 'you are right, and meaning is just something the mind "does", how come different people have different meanings of life? How come some people have no meaning? Or forget the meaning they started with?'

'Experiences, influences, diseases, divorces. What *is* that noise?'

'Suga snoring.'

'What cat snores that loud?'

'Suga is human. Sort of.'

'Oh. And is Suga a he, or a she?'

I hunt in vain for traces of jealousy. 'He. A drunk friend crash-landed far from home. I let him kip on my floor but he took my futon. You were saying.'

'I forget . . . I remember. Want to hear something private, about myself?'

I sit up. 'Sure I do.'

'I am a full-blown diabetic. Every evening, for the last thirteen years, I have injected insulin into my arm. I conform to a meal plan. If I neglect this, I may go into a hypo. If my hypo is severe enough, I may die. The meaning of my life is to balance death and sugar. People without time bombs built into their genes are not likely to have the same meaning. Maybe the truest difference between people is exactly this: how they see why they are here.'

Suga growls in his sleep. My cigarette glows. 'Mmm.'

'What's up with you tonight, Miyake?'

I tap my cigarette into a beer-can ashtray. 'Meeting my father has been my meaning. Now I am about to – what do I do after I meet him?'

'Why worry about it now?'

'I dunno. I worry about things and I can never stop.'

'Eiji Miyake, I want to sleep with you right now.'

I choke on a lungful of smoke. '*What?*'

'Only a joke. I wanted to prove that you can stop worrying if you want to. Anyway, Debussy never worried about his meaning of life.'

'Debussy? What band was he in?'

'Claude Debussy. Tell me you are joking.'

'Claude Debussy . . . played drums for Jimi Hendrix, right?'

'Do not blaspheme the sacred, even in jest, or eagles will peck out your liver. I'm playing him for my tone piece in tomorrow's audition. Want to hear?'

'Sure.' This is a first.

I hear her clunk and shuffle about. 'Lie back and gaze at the stars.'

'Above Kita Senju the night sky is all neon murk.'

'Then I'll play you *Et la lune descend sur le temple qui fut.*'

'Help.'

'"And the moon sets o'er the temple that was."'

'You speak French as well as everything else?'

'I've been planning to run away to France since I was six, remember.'

'France. What an elegant meaning of life.'

'Shush, or you won't hear the stars.'

The oil in the frying pan spits. I botch the second egg, feel shell fragments between my fingers, and the spermy mess drops in. I love the way the clear part skins over white. I rescue the toast, nearly in time, and scrape the charcoal into the sink. The pile on my futon stirs – 'Uuuoooeeeaaaiii.' Suga – this unclodded lungfish – winches his head and surveys my capsule. I stub out my Philip Morris in an eggshell, draw the curtains and the unwashed morning streams in over three days of washing-up and a major spillage of socks and papers. Suga is not pretty. He neck is boiled-octopus pink and a volcanic island chain of mosquito bites trails over his face. He blinks. 'Miyake? What are you doing here?'

'I live here.'

'Oh. What am I doing here?'

'This is where you died last night.'

'I gotta do a dinosaur piss. Which is the pisser?' I point with a nod. Suga gets up and goes. And goes, and goes. He comes out sighing, zipping up his flies. 'Your toilet smells as bad as Ueno. Smells like a serious upchuck.'

'How about a nice fried egg for breakfast, swimming in tasty oil?'

'Did *I* puke last night?'

'You kindly got most of it down the toilet. Come any time.'

'I need to drink a swimming pool.'

I fill a beer mug with tap water. Suga downs it in a marathon gulp. 'Thanks. Any chance of a coffee?' I give Suga mine and start another pan of water boiling. Suga bunches the futon into a log, sits at the table, drinks his coffee, goes 'aaaaaah', and rolls down his shirtsleeves to hide his eczema. 'I never knew you played the guitar. Is that kid on the swing your little sister?' Near enough. 'Yes.' I tip the eggs on to the toast, clear junk and sit down to eat. 'Then the man in the funny sunglasses is your father?' My yolk bleeds yellow. 'Not quite. John Lennon.' Suga plies his temples with his thumbs. 'I heard of him. In the Beach Boys, right? So where am I exactly?'

'Above a video shop in Kita Senju.'

'When did I get here?'

'About eleven last night.'

'You live above your workplace? The commuting must be a bitch.'

'Be grateful I had somewhere near by to drag your carcass, otherwise a dog would be pissing on you in the gutter right now. How did you get here last night? Did you get a taxi from the station? You were in no condition to walk far.'

Suga shakes his head blankly. 'I really can't remember.'

The eggs are good. 'And why did you come to visit me?'

Suga shrugs. 'Miyake, when I was blotto last night . . . I don't suppose I blabbed any stupid stories or anything? I spout utter drivel when I drink. If I said anything, there wasn't, y'know, a word of truth in it. Pure bull. Everything I said. Or may have said.'

'Fair enough.'

'But I didn't actually say any, y'know, crazy stuff, did I?'

'No, Suga. Nothing.'

Suga nods confidently. 'Yeah, I thought as much. Me and alcohol. Pfff.' In strolls Cat and immediately recognizes Suga as a soft touch. 'Hello, beautiful!' Suga pets Cat while Cat susses out the food situation. 'What are you doing shacking up with this dubious character, then?'

'Your gratitude overwhelms me.'

'Why did you leave Ueno only two weeks after a life sentence?'

'Family stuff. So, do you have, uh, seminars today?'

Suga shrugs. 'What day are we on?'

'Thursday.'

'I don't know where I'll go today.'

'Not questing for Holy Grail?'

'Pointless.' Suga takes off his glasses and pinches the bridge of his nose. The gesture makes him look sixty-something. 'Deep time-waste. I quit hacking.'

'Am I hearing this right?'

'I back-doored the Pentagon two weeks ago. Guess what?'

'No Holy Grail?'

Suga combs his hair with his fingers. 'Nine billion Holy Grails. I looked inside one. I found another nine billion Holy Grails. And in each of them?'

'Nine billion Holy Grails?' I have to get ready for work.

Suga sighs. 'The whole thing was just some government nerd practical joke. Every hour I spent hacking – and it adds up to months – I could have spent more profitably with my finger up my fat one. Even looking at a computer makes me ill.'

'So what do you do at university?'

'I don't. I walk. Sleep.'

'Why not just find another site to hack?' I fetch a clean T-shirt from my curtain rail. It is dry but crumpled, so I plug in my iron.

'For hackers,' Suga sighs, 'well, for the best ones, Holy Grail is the ultimate *meaning* of hacking, right. Non-hackers couldn't understand this. Imagine if you suddenly discovered, say, that your father isn't who you thought he was. I don't even have the heart to post the news. They would never believe me, anyway. They'd think I'd gone over to the other side.'

I add my plate to my sink collection and try to find two socks that match, sort of. 'Nine billion Holy Grails filled with nine billion Holy Grails.' I flick out the legs of my ironing board and set it upright. 'What a great hiding place for a Holy Grail.' It was an off-the-cuff comment, and Suga opens his mouth to answer, but changes his mind. He strokes Cat, who cruises at ninety purrs per minute. My iron breathes steam. Suga opens his mouth. 'No,' he says. 'I checked hundreds of sample Grail files, from all over the document field. Holy Grail is just an exercise in infinity. In meaninglessness.'

♎

13th November

Weather unknown at present. We are silent-running. Ten minutes ago the lookout sounded the alarm – a squadron of Lightnings heading straight this way. Rehearsed pandemonium ensued as the crew prepared the *I-333* for diving before we were spotted. 'Lookouts below! Dive! Dive!' Abe, Gotō, Kusakabe and I returned to our bunks. 'Hatches secured!' Seawater filled the ballast tank. A high-pitched wail as air was forced out through the topside vents. *I-333* tipped at 10 degrees. Light bulbs exploded. Dull pain rings in my ears. Our lives are in the hands of the crew now. We are down to a maximum of 80 metres. The hull of *I-333* groans like nothing I ever heard. Nobody dares make a sound. Cpt Yokota has told us of rumours about buoys dropped by the enemy that emit sonar, and allow acoustic-guided missiles to locate and destroy submarines. Maybe Cpt Yokota is right: courage is the highest quality for a soldier, but technology is a fine substitute. I keep thinking about all the water above us. What I detest most about *I-333* is the smell: it assaults my senses whenever I return from the bridge. Sweat, excrement, rotting food, and men. Men, men, men. Ashore, surprises are often welcome. They break dull routine and bring excitement. Aboard a sub, surprises can prove lethal. I am writing these words to distract my mind. Abe is meditating. Gotō is praying. Kusakabe is reading. A kaiten pilot is the most dangerous agent of destruction in maritime history, but how vulnerable I feel now.

14th November

Weather deteriorating. *I-333* is about halfway to our destination. Relations between Abe and Kusakabe have worsened. Yesterday evening Abe challenged him to chess, and when Kusakabe declined said, 'Seems strange for a kaiten pilot to be afraid of losing a game.' The accusation was dressed up as a joke, but jokes are usually other things in disguise. I think Abe is jealous of the territory Kusakabe refuses to share. Without a word Kusakabe put his book down and set up the chessboard. He destroyed Abe like you would destroy a six-year-old. He took about ten seconds per move. Abe took longer to move, his face grew grimmer, but he could not bring himself to resign. Kusakabe promoted a pawn to a queen three times while Abe's king waited in a corner for the inevitable. When Abe knocked his king over, he joked: 'I only hope your final mission is as great a success as your chess-playing.' Kusakabe replied, 'The Americans are formidable opponents, Lieutenant.' Gotō and I were afraid these insults could only lead to violence, but Abe calmly put the chessmen away. 'The Americans are an effete race of cowards. Without his gun, the Yankee is nothing.' Kusakabe folded the board. 'We have lost this war by swallowing our own propaganda. It poisons our faculties.' Abe lost control, grabbed the chessboard, and flung it across our cabin. 'Then exactly why are you here, kaiten pilot?' Kusakabe stares back defiantly at our superior officer. 'The meaning of my sacrifice is to help Tokyo negotiate a less humiliating surrender.' Abe hissed with rage. 'Surrender? That word is an anathema to the Yamato-damashii spirit! We liberated Malaya in ten weeks! We bombed Darwin! We blasted the British from the Bay of Bengal! Our crusade created a co-prosperity sphere unrivalled in the East since Genghis Khan! Eight corners united under one roof!' Kusakabe was neither angry nor bowed. 'A great pity the Yamato-damashii spirit never figured out how to stop the roof collapsing in on us.' Abe shouted hoarsely. 'Your words disgrace the insignia on your uniform! They insult your squadron! If we were on Ōtsushima I would report you for seditious thought! We are talking about good and evil! The divine will made manifest!' Kusakabe glared back. 'We are talking about bomb tonnage. I wish to sink an enemy carrier, but not for you, lieutenant, not for the regiment, not for the blue-bloods or the clowns in Tokyo, but because the fewer planes the Americans have raining bombs on Japan, the greater the chance my sisters will survive this stupid bloody war.' Abe struck Kusakabe's face with his right hand, twice, hard, then hooked him under the chin with the left. Kusakabe staggered, and said 'An excellent line of reasoning, lieutenant.' Gotō got between them. I was too shocked to move. Abe spat at Kusakabe and stormed out, but there are not many places to storm to on a submarine. I got a damp cloth to bathe the bruise, but Kusakabe picked up his book as if nothing had happened. So calm, I almost suspect him of provoking Abe in order to be left in peace.

15th November

Weather: rain and wind, tail of a typhoon. I am suffering mildly from diarrhoea, but sickbay dispensed some effective medicine. We have lost contact with *I-37*, our sister submarine on this mission. An all-systems kaiten service took up most of the day. Following yesterday's incident, Abe avoided speaking unless he had to. Kusakabe addressed him with rigid politeness. His left eye is half closed by a bruise. Gotō told the crew that Kusakabe fell out of his bunk. I asked Kusakabe if his offer to lend me his book of English kabuki was still open, and Kusakabe said sure, and recommended a play about the greatest soldier in Rome. Listen: 'Let me have war, say I; it exceeds peace as far as day does night; it's spritely, waking, audible, and full of vent. Peace is very apoplexy, lethargy; mulled, deaf, sleepy, insensible; a getter of more bastard children than war's a destroyer of men.' Even when Abe came into our cabin I carried on reading it. Western military values are perplexing, however. The soldier, Coriolanus, talks about honour, but when he feels betrayed by the Romans, instead of registering his disapproval by hara-kiri, he deserts and fights for the enemy! Where is the honour in that? This afternoon an unescorted American freighter was sighted, but Cpt Yokota is under strictest orders not to fire a conventional torpedo until the kaiten mission is completed. Gotō swore he for one would never breathe a word to Admiralty HQ if Cpt Yokota ignored this directive. *I-47* sent a communiqué warning of two enemy destroyers SSE 20 kms, so we let the freighter escape. Later, Gotō and I fabricated a model warship from card, and practised kaiten approach angles with a mock periscope. Then, as casually as a comment on the weather, Gotō said, 'Tsukiyama, I want to introduce you to my wife.' For once, he was quite serious. He wedded her on our final weekend leave. 'If she wants to remarry after my death,' he said, more to himself than to me, 'she has my blessing. She may have more than one husband, but I will only ever have one wife.' Gotō then asked me why I volunteered for special attack forces. It may strike you as odd that we never discussed this topic at Ōtsushima or even Nara, but our minds were too intricated in the 'how' to see the 'why'. My answer was, and is, that I believe the kaiten project is the reason I was born.

Suga lumbers downstairs. 'Hey.'

'Hey.' I close the journal. 'How are you feeling?'

'A ten-megaton headache.'

'My boss keeps a first-aid box somewhere—'

'I have a unique immunity to painkillers. I cleaned your toilet. I never cleaned one before. I hope I used the right cloths and stuff.'

'Thank you.'

Suga sniffs and watches the screen for a while. It is an American movie – not many aren't – I chose at random called *An Officer and a Gentleman*. From the box I thought it might be about the Pacific war and the navy my great-uncle fought, but I was way wrong. The star – he has a pained-rodent face – is stuck in boot camp in the 1980s. 'Well,' says Suga, 'I see why you jacked in Ueno. Is this all you do? Sit on your butt and watch movies all day?'

'Same as sitting on your butt and watching computer screens.'

Suga inspects the new-releases rack. 'Living on borrowed time, these video shops. Pretty soon people will download all their videos via the Net, right. DCDI format. The technology is already here, just waiting for marketing to catch up. I meant to ask: what happened with that Korean babe you were chasing?'

'Uh, mistaken identity.'

A kryptonite-green Jeep, throbbing with time-travel music, mounts the pavement. Lolita in the passenger seat spits cherry pips out of the window, while Dalai Lama darts in, nursing a fluffy white ferret – it sports a pink-and-lime bow tie – in one arm and three videos in the other. '*Jason and the Argonauts* thrilled us, *Sinbad* chilled us, *Titanic* killed us. Myths are no longer what they used to be. I should know – I wrote them.' I check the return-by dates and thank him. Dalai Lama moonwalks out and waves the ferret's paw at us. The ferret yawns. The Jeep jets off, red-shifting music into a squashed blur. Suga watches through the door. 'I wish I had a friend like that. I could phone him up every time I felt like a misfit, right, just to remind myself how normal I actually am.' Suga yawns, cleans his glasses on his T-shirt, and steps outside to consult the sky. 'So, a new day.'

'Audition hall waiting rooms are nurseries for lunatics,' says Ai, the noise of the wind a hazy crackle of static, 'or psychological warfare students. Musicians are worse than those world-class chess players who kick each other under the table. One boy from Tōhō music school is eating garlic yoghurt and reading French slang from a phrase book. Aloud. Another is chanting Buddhist scriptures with his mother. Two girls are discussing best-loved music academy suicides who couldn't take the pressure.'

'If your music sounds half as good to the judges as it did to me last night, you should walk it.'

'I think you may be biased, Miyake. They don't give points for necks. Anyway, nobody walks it to a Paris Conservatoire scholarship. You drag yourself there by your fingernails, over the corpses of slaughtered co-hopefuls. Like the Roman gladiators, except when you lose you have to simper politely and congratulate your nemesis. Playing over the phone to you is not the same as performing for a panel of dug-up A-class war criminal look-alikes who control my future, my dream, and my meaning as a human being. If I blow this audition, it will be private lessons to cutey-cutey Hello Kitty daughters until the day I die.'

'There will be other auditions in the future,' I point out.

'Wrong thing to say.'

'When are the results announced?'

'Five o'clock today, after the final candidate has performed – the judges fly back to France tomorrow. Hang on – someone's coming—' I get an earful of static swish and covered mumble. 'That was my on-in-two-minutes call.'

Say something powerful, encouraging and clever. 'Uh, good luck.'

Her breathing changes as she walks. 'I was thinking earlier . . .'

'About?'

'The meaning of life, of course. I changed my mind again.'

'Yeah?'

'You find your own meaning by passing or failing a series of tests.'

'Who passes or fails you in these tests?'

Her footsteps echo and static breezes. 'You do.'

Customers come, customers go. A steady stream of movies about the end of the world get rented – must be something in the air. I wonder how Ai is doing in her audition. I thought my guitar-playing was okay, but compared to her I am a no-fingered amateur. A hassled mother comes in and asks me to recommend a video that will shut her kids up for an hour. I resist the temptation to slip her *Pam the Clam from Amsterdam* – 'Well, madam, it *did* shut them up, didn't it?' – and suggest *Sky Castle Laputa*. I go to the door – the sky is one of those opal marmalade sunsets. A Harley Davidson growls by, a strolling lion. Its chromework is cometary, and its driver is a kid with leather trousers, a designer-gashed T-shirt saying DAMN I'M GOOD and an army outrider helmet with a cartoon duck stencilled on. The girlfriend, her perfect arms disappearing into the T-shirt, blond hair catching amber sunlight, is none other than Coffee. Love hotel Coffee! Same pout, same time-zone-straddling legs. I hide behind a Ken Takakura poster, and watch the motorbike weave through the clogged traffic. Definitely Coffee – or her clone. Now I am not so certain. Coffee has millions of clones in Tokyo. I sit down and open my grandfather's journal. What would Subaru Tsukiyama say about Japan today? Was it worth dying for? Maybe he would reply that *this* Japan is not the Japan he did die for. The Japan he died for never came into being. It was a possible future, auditioned by the present but rejected with other dreams. Maybe it is a mercy he cannot see the Japan that was chosen. I wonder what angle to take when I meet my grandfather next Monday. I wish I could do angles like Daimon. I wish Admiral Raizo had given me a pointer. Should I applaud the samurai spirit stuff? Does it matter? All I want is for my grandfather to introduce me to my father. Nothing more. I wonder how I would have fared in the war. Could I have calmly stayed in an iron whale cruising towards my death? I am the same age as my great-uncle was when he died. I guess I would not have been 'I'. I would have been another 'I'. A weird thought, that – I am not made by me, or my parents, but by the Japan that did come into being. Subaru Tsukiyama was made by a Japan that died with surrender. It must be tough being a product of both, like Takara Tsukiyama.

♎

18th November

Weather: tropical heat, blinding sunshine. This morning I spent thirty minutes on the lookout platform fore of the periscopes. The lookout lent me his binoculars. Our position is 60 kilometres west of Ulithi atoll. A high-altitude reconnaissance plane from Truk reported 200 enemy vessels including 4 carriers. Enemy radio transmissions grow ever busier. Cpt Yokota made the decision not to wait for *I-37*, as 5 days have elapsed since last contact. Hailing her on VLF radio would be hazardous so close to an enemy stronghold. I hope she has only been delayed. Being sunk so close to the target area would be a cruel irony for the kaiten pilots. We wished *I-36* and *I-47* good hunting and turned east towards the Palau Islands. *I-333* approached Peleliu around 1800. The archipelago is as beautiful as places from old stories, but as outlandish as the landscapes I used to doodle on my copybook. I saw coral islets, twisted outcrops, gorges, peaks, swamps, and sandbars. Recent battle damage was much in evidence. The 14th Division of the Kwantung Army will have made the enemy pay dearly for the invasion of these islands. The bases and airfields were among the most battle-ready in the war, because the Palaus were Japanese territory since the League of Nations mandate of 1919. But the enemy cannot guess the true price of anchoring in the Kossol Passage. The lookout spotted an enemy scout plane and we dived. As tonight's meal will, in all probability, be our final one, Captain Yokota produced his wind-up gramophone and two records. I instantly recognized a tune which father used to play, before jazz was banned because of its corrupting influence. The musician's name is Jyu Keringuton. How strange to be listening to American jazz before setting out to kill Americans.

19th November

Weather: fine, calm conditions prevailing. A quiet last night. *I-333* conducting submerged periscope watch. Slick has promised to visit Nagasaki and hand this journal to you personally, Takara. My co-Kikusui pilots are composing their final letters. Kusakabe asked Abe's advice regarding an obscure kanji for a haiku he was composing. Abe answered without rancour. I have little talent for poetry. Slick is presently servicing our kaitens for the final time, and the kaiten release mechanisms are being tested. Captain Yokota is approaching the mouth of Kossol Passage in a slow curve. We prayed at the special shrine and left incense as gifts to the god of the shrine. Gotō burned his card aircraft carrier and offered the ashes. We studied a cartographical chart of the target zone, with depth soundings. At our final supper we thanked the crew for bringing us here safely. We drank banzai toasts to the success of our mission and to the emperor. I went up to the bridge one final time to see the moon and stars, and shared a cigarette with the ensign on duty. The moon was full and bright. It reminded me of the mirror Yaeko and Mother use to apply cosmetics. This moon will allow me to choose my target in under three hours from now. Three hours. This is all my lifeline has to run, if all goes well. My thoughts are now occupied with how I can best utilize my training to be sure of making a lethal hit. I will now entrust this journal to Slick.

Live my life for me, Takara, and I will die your death for you.

Live long, little brother.

I never heard Ai sound miserable. I never thought it was in her repertoire. I stroke Cat. 'Your father knows how much the Conservatoire means to you?'

'That Man knows exactly how much it means.'

'And he knows how few scholarships get awarded?'

'Yes.'

'Why has he forbidden you to go? Why isn't he brimming over with pride?'

'Niigata was good enough for him, so Niigata will be good enough for me. He refuses to use the word music. He says "tinkling" instead.'

'What does your mother think?'

'My mother? "Think"? Not since her honeymoon. What she says is "Obey your father!" Over and over. She let him finish her sentences for her for so long that now he starts them too. She actually apologizes to my father for making him yell at her. My sister married the owner of the biggest concrete works on the Japan Sea coast because our father told her to, and now she is turning into my mother. It's creepy. She heard they have big ozone holes over Austria so—'

'Austria? Doesn't she mean Australia?'

'Their knowledge of the world outside Japan only extends as far as they can swim offshore. Sorry if I sound bitter. Then my brother was drafted. He runs That Man's branch office, so you can imagine how sympathetic he was. I am wrecking the family harmony, he said. French food will play havoc with my diabetes – as if *he* ever cared about my diabetes – and the sheer worry will cause my mother's blood pressure to rise, and she may actually explode. Then I will be guilty of blowing up Mother as well as disobeying That Man. What's making that noise? Not Suga again?'

'Cat, this time. She feels sorry for you, but doesn't know what to say that wouldn't sound feeble. She hopes it will all work out okay.'

'Thank her. At times like this I wish I smoked.'

'Hold your mouth to the receiver – I'll blow smoke down the line.'

'Teenagers often fantasize that their parents are not their real parents. After this evening I can see the appeal. Truth is, That Man hates the idea of me not needing him. He wants to hire and fire the world as he sees fit. He is afraid of his employees finding out he can't control his daughter. What a family of sand fleas I come from! I swear, sometimes I think I would be better off as an orphan. Oh. Oh . . . sorry, Miyake . . .'

'Hey, don't worry.'

'Today has blown my tact chip. I should switch myself off and leave you in peace. I've done nothing but whinge for thirty minutes.'

'You can whinge all night. Isn't that right, Cat?'

Cat, bless her, miaows right on cue.

'See? So whinge.'

'You look five years younger,' I tell Buntarō when he gets back from Okinawa on Sunday evening, and he really does. 'So if I go on four holidays do I get to look like a twenty-year-old?' He presents me with a key-ring of Zizzi Hikaru – like most idols, Zizzi is Okinawan – who sheds her clothes when you breathe on the plastic casing. 'Hey, thanks,' I say, 'this will be a family heirloom. Good to be back?'

'Ye-es.' Buntarō looks around Shooting Star. 'No. Yes.'

'Right. Did Machiko-san enjoy herself?'

'Way too much. She wants to move there. Tomorrow.'

Buntarō scratches his head. 'Kōdai being born soon . . . it changes the way you see things. Would you want to be brought up in Tokyo?'

I remember my mother's first letter, the balcony one. 'Maybe not.'

Buntarō nods and checks his watch. 'You must have a thousand things you want to do, lad.' I don't, but I can see he wants to catch up on paperwork, so I climb up to my capsule and round up dirty laundry. I try calling Ai, but nobody answers. Netherworld noises vibrate down the apartment building tonight. Husband bawling, baby screaming, washing machine spinning. Tomorrow is Monday – grandfather day. I lie on my futon and begin decoding the final three pages of the journal. These are written on different paper, in cramped letters that get harder and harder to read. Across the top of the paper is stamped in red ink, in English: 'SCAP' – which is not in my dictionary – and 'Military Censor'. These half obscure a pencil inscription in Japanese: ' . . . these words . . . moral property . . . . . . Takara Tsukiyama . . .' An address in Nagasaki is illegible to me.

♎

20th November

Weather – unknown. Dead but still alive. Alone in kaiten. Last 6 hours. At 0245 Cpt Yokota came to cabin – announced the kaiten attack commence 15 mins. Stood in a circle and tied hachimaki of brother before us. Gotō: 'Just another training run, boys.' Abe to Kusakabe: 'You are a demon chess player, Ensign.' Kusakabe: 'Your left hook is the demon, Lieutenant.' Toured *I-333* – thanked crew for bringing us here safely. Saluted, man by man. Shook hands before entered kaitens via chutes. Slick sealed the hatches on us. His face last I saw. *I-333* dived for final approach. Radioman First Class Hosokawa maintained telephone link until release, providing last-minute orientation. Abe released 0315. Heard clamps fall loose. Gotō released 0320. Kusakabe floated free 0335. Next 5 minutes I thought many things, focus difficult. Hosokawa in Nagasaki dialect: 'I'll be thinking of you. May glory be yours.' Final human words. Foreclasps released. Started engine. Rears released. Floated free. Thrust sharp left avoid conning tower/periscope shears. Proceeded ESE heading, holding depth 5 metres. Surfaced 0342 confirm position with visual fix. Enemy fleet clearly silhouetted harbour lights. Troop carriers, transport ships, fuel tankers, at least 3 battleships, 3 destroyers, 2 heavy cruisers. No carriers, many fat targets. Eating, asleep, shitting, smoking, drinking, talking Americans. I, their executioner. Strange sensation. At strategy meeting on *I-333* agreed first kaitens should target distant vessels – guesswork required. Used kids choosing-chant: Do – re – ni – shi – ma – sho – ka? Ka – mi – sa – ma – no – iu – to – explosion. Shock waves rocked kaiten. Steadied periscope, saw fuel tanker, plum-blossom fire, smoke already obscuring stars. Secondary explosion. Orange. Beautiful, terrible, could not tear eyes away. Flares climbed, lit Passage brighter than day. Hunted, I dived. Waking dream. Being, not doing. Chose nearest large naval ship and manouevred to appropriate angle. Klaxons, engines, chaos. Another major explosion – kaiten, nearby depth-charge, no knowing. Patrol boat? Vibrations nearer, nearer, nearer – dived to 8 metres – passed over. Sizable explosion to starboard. Loneliness – afraid brothers leave me here among hostile strangers not my race. Slowed to 2 kph, surfaced for position check. Fires/smoke/after-explosions 2 locations. Chose large outline due west – light cruiser? 150 metres. Eyes dazzled by searchlight, but cloaked by chaos on-shore. Dived to 6–7 metres. Throttled to 18 kph. Flying, strange air. Cut to dead halt. Surfaced, final check. Cruiser filled the night. 80 metres. Saw figures streaming. Ants. Fireflies. Dived 5 metres. Primed warhead. One thought: 'This is my final thought.' Opened throttle lever to maximum velocity. Acceleration shoved me back, hard . . . 70 metres closing, 60, 50, 40, 30, 20, impact next moment, impact now

Clang like temple bell. Wild spinning – up = down, down = up, drilling, flung left right up down, loose objects flying, me too. Lungs empty. So this death, I think, then I think, Can dead think? Pain rings from head erased further thought. Lurching crunch > hung downwards > judder halt. Engines howling, rudder control dead and free in hand, scream noise from engines, heat climbing, burning oil smell – same moment I realize not dead and must cut engines, engines die. Failure. Warhead did not detonate. Kaiten glanced off hull = bamboo spear off metal helmet. Periscope sights slashed face, broke nose. Sat, listened to noises from surface. Tried to ignite TNT manually, strike casing with wrench. Tore off fingernail in attempt. Impact broke chronometer. Minutes or hours, cannot tell. Periscope blackness> blueness now. Flask of whisky. Will drink, put these pages into flask. Takara. Message in bottle in dead shark. Learn this song, Takara?

Corpses adrift and corpses swollen,
Corpses abed in the swollen sea,
Corpses adream in the mountain grasslands,
We shall die, we shall die, we shall die for the emperor,
and we shall never look back.

Abed in the swollen sea. Air thinner. Or imagine air thinner. Now? Divers may discover me – typhoon shakes me loose, beaches me – remain here end of time. Kaiten was not way to glorious death. Kaiten is urn. Sea is tomb. Do not blame us who die so long before noon.

◆

'No hope,' answers the woman who is not Ai. It is after midnight but she sounds more amused than angry. She has a brick-thick Osaka accent. 'Sorry.'

'Oh. Can I ask when, uh, Miss Imajō is expected back?'

'Feel free to ask, but whether I answer is another Q.'

'When is Miss Imajō due back? Please?'

'And tonight's top news story: Ai Imajō is summoned to the ancestral seat in Niigata in a last-ditch attempt to break the diplomatic deadlock. When reporters asked the defiant Miss Imajō how long the summit would last, we were told: "As long as it takes." Stay tuned!'

'Days, then?'

'My turn. Are you the karate kid?'

'No. The head-butt kid.'

'Same kid. Nice to meet your disembodied voice at last, karate kid. Ai calls you head-butt kid, but I think karate kid sounds wittier.'

'Uh, for sure. When Ai gets back could you—'

'I inherited my granny's psychic powers. I knew it was you calling. Don't you want to know who I am?'

'Are you Ai's shy, retiring flatmate, by any chance?'

'Hole in one! So. Is Ai dating a human being, or are you another psycho gremlin?'

'Not exactly dating . . .' I take the bait. '"Psycho gremlin"?'

'Fact. Eighty per cent of Ai's admirers go on to successful careers in the horror movie industry. The last one was the Creature from the Black Lagoon. Webby, floppy, water-resistant, caught bluebottles with his tongue. Phoned at midnight and croaked until dawn. Drove a Volvo, wore blazers, gave out CDs of himself singing madrigals, and confided unsolicited fantasies when Ai begged me to say she was out. He and Ai would marry at Tokyo Disneyland, tour Athens, Montreal and Paris with their three sons, Delius, Sibelius and Yoyo. One time his mother called – she wanted

Ai's parents' number in Niigata so she start marriage negotiations directly with the manufacturer. Me and Ai had to concoct an ex-boxer boyfriend in prison who half strangled Ai's last admirer.'

'I can promise, my mother will never call. But—'

'Ever worked in a pizza kitchen, karate kid?'

'A pizza kitchen? Why?'

'Ai says you need a job as from tomorrow.'

'True, but I never worked in a kitchen before.'

'No worries. Chimpanzees could do the job. In fact, we have hired lots of furry, tree-dwelling higher primates in the past. The hours are lousy – midnight to eight a.m. – the kitchen is hotter than the core of the sun but on the graveyard shift the money is good. Central location – the Nero's opposite Jupiter Café, site of legendary head-butt. Plus, you get to work with me. Has Ai mentioned my name?'

'Uh . . .'

'Obviously I am the last thing on her mind. Sachiko Sera. As in "*Che Sarà, Sarà,* whatever li-lah, li-lah." Well, almost. Can you start tomorrow evening? Monday?'

'I don't want to talk you out of giving me a job I need so badly, Ms Sera, but, uh, don't you want to meet me first?'

Sachiko Sera does a beyond-the-tomb voice. 'Eiji Miyake, native son of Yakushima . . . I know *everything* about you . . .'

'Mr Miyake?' At Amadeus Tea Room, Butler stops pedalling his fingers. Arched eyebrows: butlership is all in the eyebrows. 'Please follow me. The Tsukiyamas are waiting for you.' Tsukiyama*s*? Could my grandfather have persuaded my father to come too? The place is busier than last week – a funeral party is meeting here, many of the customers are in black – and I have trouble trying to locate an elderly man and a middle-aged one who looks like me. So when Butler pulls a chair out at a table where a woman and a girl my age are seated, I assume he has made made a mistake. His eyebrows tell me there is no mistake, so I gawp, while they assess me. 'Will you require an additional cup, madam?' asks Butler. The woman dismisses him with a 'most certainly not.' The girl stares at me – a 'will the turd round the U-bend?' sort of stare – while my memory grapples with a similarity . . . Anju! A chubby, crinkle-cut, scowly Anju. We have the same feather eyebrows. 'Eiji Miyake,' she says, and I nod as if it were a question, 'you are one sorry, shameless creep.' All at once, I understand. My half-sister. My stepmother fingers the bronze torc around her neck – thick enough to halt an axe-swing – and sighs. 'Let us try to keep this meeting as brief and painless as possible. Sit down, Mr Miyake.'

I sit down. Amadeus Tea Room continues in the background, as if on a video screen. 'Mrs Tsukiyama' – I grope around for pleasantries – 'thank you for your letter last month.'

Fake surprise. '"Thank you"? Irony is your opening move, Mr Miyake?'

I look around. 'Uh . . . actually I was expecting my grandfather . . .'

'Yes, we know all about that. Your little rendezvous was recorded in his diary. Regrettably, my father-in-law is unable to attend.'

'Oh . . . I see.' Have you locked him in a cupboard?

Half-sister has a slappy voice. 'Grandpapa passed away three days ago.'

Slap.

A waitress passes with a tray of raspberry cheesecake slices.

Stepmother openly fakes a smile. 'I am frankly astonished that you failed to see how sick he was last Monday. Running around at your beck and call, plotting conspiracies. I only hope you are proud of yourself.'

This makes no sense. 'I never met him last Monday.'

'Liar!' slaps Half-sister. 'Liar! Mother already told you – we have his appointment diary! Guess whose name we found for a meeting here one week ago!' I want to wrap this girl's mouth in carpet tape.

'But my grandfather was still in hospital last Monday.'

Stepmother does a head-resting-on-hands pose. 'Your lies really are rather embarrassing, Mr Miyake. We know my father-in-law left his hospice last Monday to meet you! He didn't ask for permission from the duty nurse, because he wouldn't have received it. He was far too sick.'

'I am not lying! My grandfather was too sick to come, so he sent his friend.'

'What friend?'

'Admiral Raizo.'

Stepmother and Half-sister look at each other. Half-sister snickers a jerky laugh and Stepmother smiles so that her mouth shrinks to a lipsticked tip. Those lips kiss my father. 'Then you did meet Grandpapa,' slaps Half-sister, 'but you were too dumb to recognize him!' My temper takes the strain. I look at Stepmother for an explanation. 'My father-in-law's last practical joke.'

'Why would my grandfather pretend to be this Admiral Raizo?'

Half-sister thumps the table. 'He is *not* your "grandfather"!' I ignore her. Stepmother's eyes glint with war. 'Did he give you any documents to sign?'

'Why,' I repeat, 'would my grandfather pretend to be somebody else?'

'Did you sign anything?'

This is going nowhere. I put my hands behind my head, lean back, and study the ceiling while I calm down. 'Yes, my friend,' observes Mozart, 'you have a problem here. But it is your problem. Not mine.' I badly want to smoke. 'Mrs Tsukiyama, is this bad blood necessary?'

'"Bad blood",' mutters Half-sister. 'Nice expression.'

'What do I have to do to prove to you that all I want is to meet my father?'

Stepmother tilts her head. 'Do calm down, Mr Miyake—'

This makes me boil over. 'No, Mrs Tsukiyama, I am tired of calming down! I do not—'

'Mr Miyake, you are making a—'

'Shut up and listen to me! I do not want your money! I do not want favours! And *blackmail*! How did you come up with the theory I wanted to *blackmail* you? I am so, so, so *tired* of scrubbing around this city trying to find my own father! You want to despise me, fine, I can live with that. Just let me meet him – just once – and if he tells me himself that he never wants to see me again, okay, I will vanish from your lives and start my own, properly. That is it. That is all. Is this too much to comprehend? Is this too much to ask?'

I am so drained.

Half-sister is unsure of herself.

Stepmother has finally put away her unbearable sneer.

I think I got them to listen. And half the customers in the Amadeus Tea Room.

'Actually, yes.' Stepmother pours herself and her pouty, piggy daughter weak tea from a fluted teapot. 'It is too much to ask. Let us concede that I accept you mean my family no malice, Mr Miyake. Let us even concede that I feel some sympathy for your position. The basic situation still stands unchanged.'

'The basic situation.'

'There is no nice way to say it. My husband does not wish to meet you. You seem to believe in a dark conspiracy keeping you away from him – this is simply not true. We are not here to confuse your trail. We are at the behest of my husband to ask you, *please*, to leave him in peace. He has paid for your upkeep not to maintain hopes of a future reunion, but to buy his right to privacy. Is this too much to comprehend? Is this too much to ask?'

I want to cry. 'Why won't he just tell me this himself?'

'In a word' – Stepmother sips her tea – 'shame. He is ashamed of you.'

'How can he be ashamed of a son he refuses to meet?'

'My husband isn't ashamed of who you are, he is ashamed of what you are.'

At the far side a customer abruptly stands up, sliding his chair behind him.

'You are causing pain for him, for us, for yourself. Please stop.'

The waitress walks into the chair. Teacups and raspberry cheesecakes slide off her tray, and fine bone china chimes to pieces in a ripple of 'Ooooooooo's. Stepmother and Half-sister watch with me. Butler paraglides over to supervise the clean-up operation. Apologies, counter-apologies, assurances, orders, carpet sponges, dustpans. Sixty seconds later no evidence remains of the great cheesecake crisis. 'Okay,' I say.

'Okay?' Half-sister returns.

I address the woman my father chose to marry. 'Okay, you win.' She did not expect this. Neither did I. She searches my face for a catch. There is none. 'My father – just by never getting in touch himself – made his, uh, position clear a long time ago. I . . . I . . . dunno, I never wanted to believe it. But tell him' – an apricot carnation sits in a glass tear vase – 'hi. Hi and goodbye.'

Stepmother keeps her gaze steady.

I stand up to go.

'Did you get that from Grandpapa?' slaps Half-sister. She nods at the kaiten journal, wrapped in its black cloth. 'Because if so, it belongs to the Tsukiyamas.'

I look at this anti-Anju. If she had asked nicely, I would have agreed and handed it over. 'This is my lunch box. I have to go to work.' I walk out of Amadeus Tea Room without looking back taking the journal with me. Butler summons an escalator and bows as the doors close. I have the box to myself – the muzak is 'On Top of the World' by the Carpenters, a tune which makes my teeth throb, but I am too drained to hate anything now. I am stunned at the decision I just took. I watch the floor numbers descend. Do I mean it? My father never wants to meet me . . . So my search for him is . . . not valid? Finished? My meaning is cancelled? I guess, yes, I do mean it. 'Ground floor,' says the elevator. The doors open and a crowd of very busy people surge in. I have to fight my way out before the doors close and I get taken back to where I came from.

Seven

Cards

Sachiko Sera, my third boss in four weeks, was not exaggerating: the Nero kitchen is hot as hell and a monkey could do my pizza-by-numbers job. The kitchen is a rat-run – it measures five paces by one, with a sort of cage at one end with lockers and chairs where the delivery bikers wait. Sachiko and Tomomi take the orders by telephone or from walk-in customers and pass the slips through the hatch from the front counter. I dress the crusts in the correct toppings by matching the pizza name to the giant chart that takes up an entire wall, coded with coloured icons for monkeys who never learned to read. So, for example, in the big circle marked 'Chicago Gunfight' are little pictures of tomato puree, minceballs, sausage, chilli, red and yellow peppers, cheese; Hawaii Honeymoon is tomato, pineapple, tuna, coconut; Neromaniac is pepperoni, sour cream, capers, olives and chariot prawns. Then you have the crust types: thick, crusty, herb, mozzarella-filled. The toppings live in a cave-sized fridge – each container lid has a picture of the contents. When dressed, you slide the pizzas into a two-lane gas-fired inferno. Rollers convey the pizzas through its molten innards at about ten centimetres per minute, although if the orders are piling up you can reach in with a pair of forceps and give the pizza a premature birth. 'Timing is the trick,' says Sachiko, tying back her hair. 'Ideally, the pizza lands in its box – tape the order slip to the lid thusly – the same moment the biker lands from his last delivery.' After half an hour, Sachiko leaves me to it. It is sort of fun, and the orders never stop, not even at 1 or 2 a.m, so unlike Ueno lost property or Shooting Star I never have much time to think. Our customers include students, card sharks, businessmen working through the night – Shinjuku is a nocturnal jungle. I drink litres of water, sweat litres of water, and never need to piss once. There is an extractor fan as loud as a ferry and a tinny radio that only picks up one local station trapped in the 1980s. There is a gunk-smattered world map to taunt the slaves of the inferno with thoughts of all the countries in the world – and their diversely tinted women – where we are not free to go. A clock lurches forward. Sachiko is how I imagined her on the telephone – loopy, organized, neurotic, stable. Tomomi is an evil hag who has been at Nero's since Admiral Perry sailed into Old Edo Bay and has no intention of upsetting her cosy life by ever getting promoted. She chats with her friends on the phone, flirts with privileged bikers, selects arts courses she will never get around to applying for, and drops heavy hints about the affair she had with the owner of Nero's x years ago and the damage she could inflict on his marriage if her pleasant equilibrium were ever threatened. Her voice could slice sheet steel, and her laugh is a loud glittery fake. The bikers come and go week by week, but tonight they are Onizuka and Doi. Onizuka has a lip spike, custard-yellow hair and wears a death's-head biker's jacket instead of the Nero Pizza uniform. When Sachiko introduces us, he says this: 'Last guy before you, he fucked up the orders. Customers gave me shit. Don't you fuck up the orders.' He comes from Tōhoku and still has a northern accent as thick as crude oil – this worries me, in case I mistake a mortal threat for a weather remark. Doi is ancient, over forty, walks with a limp and has a Jesus-being-crucified expression. Suffering, spaced-out screensaver eyes, not much hair on his head but loads on his chin. 'Don't let Onizuka get you down, man,' he tells me. 'The man is mellow. Saw to my motor for free, man. Smoke dope?' When I say no, he shakes his head sadly. 'Youth of today, man, you misspend the prime of your life, you'll repent at your leisure, man. Got friends who know how to party? Premium quality, discreet service.' Tomomi enters the cage – she is a gifted eavesdropper. 'Discreet? As discreet as a mile-wide UFO playing the *Mission Impossible* music over the Imperial Palace.' At 3 a.m. Sachiko brings me a mug of the thickest coffee known to chemistry – thick enough to stand pencils in – which makes my body forget how tired it is. Onizuka waits in the staff cube at the end of my rat-run, but never says another word to me. Twice I smoke a JPS outside the shopfront. I have a prime view of PanOpticon. Anti-aircraft lights blink on and off from dusk till dawn. Very Gotham City. Both times the inferno summons me back before I can finish the cigarette. While I am waiting for a Health Club to emerge from the inferno – asparagus, sour cream, olives, potato wedges, garlic – Doi leans over the hatch. 'You know how hungry I am, Miyake?'

'How hungry are you, Doi?'

'I am hungry enough to cut off my thumb and chew it.'

'Really hungry, then.'

'Pass me that knife, will you?'

I make a 'do I have to?' face.

'Pass me the knife, man, this is a hunger crisis.'

'Be careful with that knife. Razor sharp.'

'Why else would I want it, man?' Doi places his left thumb on my chopping board, places the blade over it, and thumps the handle with his right fist. The blade slices clean through the knuckle. Blood spills over the counter – Doi reins in his breath. 'There, that wasn't so bad! He picks up his thumb with his right hand and dangles it in his mouth. Plop. I gargle dry air. Doi munches slowly, deciding if he likes the taste. 'Gristly, man, but not bad!' Doi spits out his thumb bone, sucked shiny and white. I drop whatever it was I was holding. Sachiko appears in the hatch – I point, and glug. 'Doi!' scolds Sachiko. 'You prima donna! You just can't resist a captive audience, can you? Sorry, Miyake, I should have warned you about Doi's little hobby: magic school.' Doi mimes a kung-fu retaliatory shuffle. 'The Sacred Academy of Illusionists ain't no hobby, chieftainess. One day there'll be queues outside the Budōkan to see me perform.' He waggles his two attached thumbs at me. 'You can tell from his eyes that Shiyake is one cat in sore need of the magic arts.' 'Miyake,' corrects Sachiko. 'Him too,' says Doi. I don't know how to respond to all of this – I am just relieved that the blood was only tomato juice. Five o'clock. Morning comes in for landing. Sachiko asks me to prepare some mini-salads, so I wash some lettuce and cherry tomatoes. The pizza orders thicken again – who eats pizzas for breakfast? – and before I know it Sachiko is back, doing a high-court voice. 'Eiji Miyake, by the powers vested in me by Emperor Nero, and in view of your satisfactory behaviour, I declare your life sentence suspended for the period of sixteen hours. You will, however, present yourself at this correctional institution at midnight, for a further eight hours hard labour.' I frown. 'Huh?' Sachiko points at the clock – 'Eight o'clock. Surely you have a home to go to?' The shop door slides open. Sachiko glances around, and looks back at me with an 'aha!' look. 'The prisoner has a visitor waiting outside the gates.'

Ai says anywhere except Jupiter Café, so we walk towards Shinjuku to find a breakfast place. Talking is a bit awkward – we have not actually met since the day in Jupiter Café, even though we must have spent over twenty-four hours on the telephone last week. 'If it was any more humid than this,' I venture, 'it would be raining.' Ai tilts her face skyward. 'Y'know, it is raining.' She caught a coach back from Niigata yesterday evening, and looks travel-worn. I am as sweaty and dishevelled as a whorehouse bed. I imagine. 'So how did it go with your father?' Ai hums. 'Pointless. I knew it would be . . .' she begins. I make the right noises at the right time, but as usual when people discuss parental problems, I feel as if I am being told about a medical condition in an organ I lack. Still, I am booming with pleasure that Ai came to meet me for breakfast. We pass a tiny shrine – Ai breaks off to look at the trees, torī gate, straw ropes and twists of paper. A jizō statue sits behind an orange, a bottle of Suntory whisky and a vase of chrysanthemums. An old man is having a good long pray.

'Are musicians superstitious?' I ask.

'Depends on the instrument. String players, technically including pianists, have the luxury of being able to practise until we get it right, and any mistakes we do make usually get swallowed up by the orchestra. Woodwind, and especially brass, have it tougher. However good you are, one unlucky blast and Bruckner's celestial ninth gets blasted open with a – well, my last conductor's metaphor – a shotgun fart. Most trumpet players I know have beta-blockers instead of cookies with their morning coffee. Are Yakushima pizza chefs superstitious?'

'The last time I went to a shrine it was to, uh, decapitate its god.'

'With a lightning bolt?'

'I only had a junior carpenter set hacksaw.'

She sees I am serious. 'Didn't the god give you what you wanted?'

'The god gave me exactly what I wanted.'

'Which is why you sawed his head off?'

'Yep.'

'My, I must be careful about giving you what you want.'

'Ai Imajō – I, Eiji Miyake, swear I will never saw your head off.'

'That's okay, then. But isn't destroying religious artifacts a borstal-sized offence?'

'I never told anyone until this morning.'

Ai gives me a look with ninety-nine possible meanings. McDonald's has an electronic signboard above the door which reports how many seats are vacant – it flits in and out of single figures. Detectors are built into the seat, I guess. Ai tells me to go upstairs and find a table while she queues, and I am too exhausted to argue. McDonald's stinks of McDonald's but at least it will disguise the stink of Miyake the unshowered kitchen slave. Upstairs a flock of student nurses smoke, bitch and shriek into their mobiles. I add up the money I just earned and feel a little less tired. It is Europe Week in McDonald's – a video screen hangs on the wall, and scenes of Rome glide by while soporific music sucks you in. Ai appears at the top of the steps holding the tray, looking around for me. I could wave, but I enjoy looking at her. Black leggings, a sky-blue T-shirt under a berry-juice silk shirt, and amber magma earrings. If Ai were a nurse I would break a major bone to get a bed in her ward. 'They were out of chocolate shake,' she says, 'so I chose banana. I see you have a kinky fetish for nurse uniforms.'

'They must have, uh, followed me in.'

Ai sticks the straw through my lid. 'In your dreams – anyway, you reek of cheese. Sachiko says a lot of your customers are nurses – they train across the road. That squat grey building is Sensō-ji Hospital.'

'I thought it was a prison. Are you only having green tea?'

'Green tea is all that my meal plan allows until lunch.'

'Oh – I forget again. Sorry.'

'No need to be. Diabetes is a medical condition, not a sin.'

'I didn't mean—'

'Relax, relax; I know. Eat.'

A mighty river of drones flows below the window – civil servants rushing to get to their desks before their section chief is at his. 'Once upon a time,' says Ai, 'people use to build Tokyo. But that changed somewhere down the line, and now Tokyo builds people.'

I let a squirt of shake dissolve on my tongue. 'Back to your father: he said if you ignore him and go to Paris, you are never welcome in Niigata.'

'So I said he can have it his way.'

'So you won't go to Paris?'

'I am going to Paris. But I am never going back to Niigata.'

'Does your father mean what he said?'

'That was a thermonuclear threat aimed at my mother, not me. "If *you* want to be looked after by your own daughter in your old age, *you* make her stay." In fact, he left shortly after to go and play pachinko. My mother broke down in gales of tears, just as he knew she would. I am thinking: what century is this? You know, there are mountain villages in Niigata that import Filipina wives wholesale in groups of twenty, because as soon as the local girls come of age they are on board the fastest shinkansen out of there. The men wonder why.'

'So you won. You can go to Paris.'

'In disgrace, but I am going.'

I light a JPS. 'You are so tough, Ai.' She shakes her head. 'The gap between how other people see you and how you see yourself is . . . a mystery, for me. I think *you* are tough. I think *I* am as tough as your shake – which is nine parts pig lard, incidentally. I desperately want my parents to be proud of me. Real strength is not needing the approval of other people all the time.' On a Roman balcony one slanting evening a girl puts sunflowers in a terracotta jar. She sees the cameraman, scowls, pouts, flicks her hair and vanishes. Ai dangles her teabag in and out of the hot water. 'I honestly think they would have been happier if I had done a two year course in applying cosmetics at a women's college, married the family dentist and spawned a hive of babies. Music. You eat it, but it eats you too.' I swallow hashbrown-and-fries cud. 'Still. Compared to the Miyakes, your family are the Von Tripps in *The Sound of Music*.' Ai spins her teabag. 'Von Trapps.'

A five-year-old comes up to our table from nowhere and looks at Ai. 'Where do babies come from before they get into their mummies' tummies?'

'Storks bring them,' says Ai.

The kid looks dubious. 'Where do the storks get them, then?'

'Paris,' I tell her and get a smile out of Ai. The girl's father appears at the top of the stairs carrying a tray of bright food and she runs off. He looks like a good dad.

Ai looks at me. I see her face as a very old woman, and also as a very little girl. I never looked into anyone's eyes this long since my who-will-blink-first games with Anju. If this were a movie and not McDonald's we would now kiss. Maybe this is more intimate. Loyalty, grief, good news, bad days. 'Okay,' I finally say, and Ai does not say 'okay what?' She rubs her thumbnail over a McTeriakiburger scratchcard. 'Look. I won a baby robot turkey lunch box. Must be a good omen. Will you let me buy you a new baseball cap?'

'This one was a present from Anju,' I reply before I change my mind.

Ai frowns. 'Who?'

'My twin sister.'

Ai frowns more deeply. 'You said you were an only child.'

No going back now. 'I told you a lie. Only the one. I want to untell it. I have a whole load of other stuff to tell you too: my grandfather contacted me – thanks to the personal ad you suggested – and my stepmother and half-sister met me. More of an ambush than a meeting, actually. I also figured that trying to find someone who obviously doesn't want to meet me, even if he is my father, will only make me miserable, so I quit . . . What is it?' Ai is frying with exasperation. 'That is so *you* of you, Miyake!' I try to understand. 'What is?' Ai knocks on her forehead with her knuckles. 'Okay, okay. Start with your twin sister. Then do the stepmother. Go.'

I float back to Shooting Star around noon as buoyant as a light wave. Ai has classes for the rest of today, but she is coming round to my capsule tomorrow . . . Wednesday' – I have to stop to remember which day I am on. I am thinking about Ai about ninety times an hour. It was funny when we said goodbye at Shinjuku – we got hopelessly lost because I was following her while she was following me. The walk from Kita Senju station is pleasant today. Shrubs, autumn trees, kids in pushchairs slurping lollies – today they defeat the bog ugliness of Tokyo. 'Good morning, Eiji-kun,' says Machiko pleasantly, 'you reek of cheese.' She is watching a Beat Takeshi movie set in Okinawa. 'Good director, but only truly cool actors dare act uncool roles.' Machiko shows me her holiday photos and gives me a picture I like of an orange orchard vanishing up a rain-hazed hillside. We talk about Nero's for a while. Machiko has this gift of making me feel I am interesting – and I nearly tell her about Ai but I am afraid I would sound slushy, and besides, there still is not much to tell, so I climb up to my capsule.

'Eiji-kun! I forgot to give you this. It was delivered this morning.' I turn around, and go back down for the package – one of those padded envelopes, the smallest size they come in. The addressee is

Mr Fujin Yoda – who? – living in Hakodate up in Hokkaido. An INCORRECTLY ADDRESSED message has been stamped on the front. On the back is my name and address, printed under SENDER on a stick-on label. 'Anything wrong?' asks Machiko.

I keep my wits about me and say, 'Nothing.' Something is wrong, however – I never posted it. Up in my capsule a shredded tea towel puts the mysterious package out of my mind – Cat, purely out of spite, because she slept alone last night. I hope she stops shredding before she starts on my shirts. I shower, tidy up the scraps of clawed cloth and thrash out a Howlin' Wolf version of 'All You Need Is Love' on my guitar. I should be dropping with tiredness, but I am immune to sleep. Then I remember the package. I slit it open. Inside is a computer disk wrapped in a letter. I twist some ice from the ice-tray into a glass and fill it with water. I love the sound the cubes make as fissures shoot through.

Tokyo, 1st October

My name is Kozue Yamaya. However unlikely or brutal this account of the last nine years of my life appears, I ask you to read it until the end. In your hands is my final testament. I shall ask you to be my legal executor.

Endings are simple, but every beginning is made by the beginning before. The one I shall choose is a night in the rainy season nine years ago. In those days my name was Makino Matani. She was a housewife with a two-year-old son, and married to the owner of a financial services company. She was a recent graduate in Business Studies from a respectable women's college in Kobe. Every New Year she exchanged greetings cards with her ex-classmates who were married to dentists, judges and civil servants. An ordinary life. The rainy season came. I remember those last moments perfectly – my son was playing with a plastic train set, and I was cleaning the rainy-season mould in the shower cubicle. I could hear the television reporting flash floods and landslides in western Japan.

The doorbell rang. I answered it, and three men barged the door and snapped the chain my husband had trained me to use. They demanded to know where my husband was hiding. I demanded to know who they were. One slapped me hard enough to dislodge a tooth. 'Your husband's case officers,' he snarled, 'and *we* ask the questions.' He and another searched the house while the third watched me try to reassure my screaming son. He threatened to maim my son if I didn't tell him where my husband was. I called my husband at work and discovered he had phoned in sick that morning. I called my husband's mobile and discovered the number had been disconnected. I called his pager – dead. I was nearly hysterical by now – the thug poured me a shot of my husband's whisky, but I couldn't swallow it. My son watched with big scared eyes. The two other thugs returned with a box of my husband's personal effects and all of my jewellery. Then the bad news really began. I learned then my husband had run up debts of over fifty million yen with a Yakuza-backed credit organization. Our life assurance policy had been doctored to name this organization as sole beneficiary in the event of his suicide. The house and contents were their property if my husband defaulted on repayments. 'And that,' said the most violent of the three, 'includes you.' My son was taken into the next room. I was told I was now responsible for my husband's debts. I was then beaten and raped. Photographs were taken 'to guarantee my obedience'. I had to endure this torment in silence, for the sake of my son. If I failed to obey their orders, the photographs would be sent to every name in my address book.

A month later I was living in a single windowless room in a Buraku area of Osaka. I was indentured to a brothel, and I was not allowed to leave the building or have any contact with the outside world, beyond sex with my customers. You may doubt that sexual enslavement is practised in twenty-first century Japan. Your ignorance is enviable, but your disbelief is precisely why such enslavement can prosper unchecked. I myself would have doubted that 'respectable' women could be turned into prostitutes, but the owners are masters of control. I was dispossessed of every item from my old life which could have reminded me who I was – except my son. I was allowed to keep my son – this prevented me from escaping by suicide. My customers not only knew about my imprisonment, they derived pleasure from it, and would have been implicated in the crime had it become public. The final wall between me and the real world was perhaps the strongest: a phenomenon psychologists label 'hostage syndrome' – the conviction that my fate was deserved and that no 'crime' was being perpetrated. After all, I was a 'whore' now – what right did I have to bring shame to my old friends or even to my mother by appealing for assistance? Better that they carry on believing I had disappeared overseas with my bankrupt husband. Six other women, three with babies younger than my son, shared my floor. The man who raped me was our pimp – it was to him we had to beg for food, medicine, even nappies for our children. He also supplied narcotics, in careful quantities. He administered them personally to ensure we couldn't overdose. We created fake names for ourselves, and in time our old lives became detached from what we had become. All of us dreamed of killing the owner at some vague point in the future after our escape, but all of us knew we would never dare return to Osaka. We were required to take care of each other's children while their mothers were working. The pimp told us that after we had worked off the amounts the defaulting members of our families had embezzled we would be free to go, so the harder we worked to please our customers, the quicker we would be out of there. In autumn, a girl who had been working in the brothel for two years was released. So we thought.

My 'release' came sooner, because over the following new year my resilience exhausted itself and I suffered a nervous breakdown. The customers complained to the pimp that I was no longer trying. The pimp talked to me for a while. He could be gentle when he chose. It was one of his weapons. He said he had talked to my creditors and that I would be transferred with my son to another branch that night. We drank gin and tonic to celebrate.

I awoke wrapped in a blanket in a black airless place. My head was groggy and drugged. My son was not with me. I was still in my brothel nightshirt. For a terrible moment I thought I had been buried alive, but groping around, I realized I was in the boot of a stationary car. I found a jack, and finally forced an exit. I was in a lock-up garage. I saw the pimp's reflection in the wing mirror and froze. He was asleep. Then I saw that his nose was missing. Someone had put a gun to his nostrils and pulled the trigger. There was no sign of my son. I ran – but before I had got out of the garage my senses began to return. I was lost, penniless, believed to have vanished by anyone who remembered me. My former owners would jump to the conclusion that I had been taken or killed by the same gang who killed my pimp. I hesitated – but I ran back, groped inside the pimp's jacket for his wallet. I found a travel bag strapped around his groin. The bag contained a wad of ten-thousand-yen notes inches thick. I had never seen so much money. When I found my way out of the lock-up I found myself in the precincts of the vast Osaka central hospital, the only place in the city where a woman with a sick-as-death complexion in nightclothes could blend into the background.

*

I do not have time to tell you much about the years that followed. I lived for a year in women's refuges, cheap hotels. My bank accounts were in false names. The meaning of my life had become the search for my son. My ex-husband was now a ghost I never thought of. I hired a private investigator to investigate the Yakuza branch that had incarcerated me. The investigator returned my advance one week later – he was warned away. Out of sympathy and guilt, he ended up hiring me as a secretary/accountant. This was a smart business decision, because three-quarters of his customers were women wanting their husbands trailed to fatten divorce settlements. They preferred discussing the sordid details with another woman. As with gynaecology, so for marital infidelity. They recommended our agency to their friends, and business thrived. I began accompanying my boss on fieldwork. Women are virtually invisible, even to the most paranoid of men. (Furthermore, I discovered that the brothel organization had deleted every computer reference to me and my son. I enjoy the privileges of being a non-existent woman.) My life in the brothel had hardened me as deeply as it had scarred me. After three years my boss offered me a partnership, and when his cancer finally killed him I took over the business. All this time, I was researching the organization that had killed Makino Matani and her son, and created Kozue Yamaya. It is gargantuan, nameless, and many-headed. It has no name. Its membership is in excess of six thousand. I swung introductions to its leaders, even invitations to the weddings of their children. I entered its employ as a freelance researcher. My status as a semi-insider gave me greater access to its secrets, and deflected suspicion.

My son was murdered in order to sell his organs to extremely rich, desperate parents of the élite in Japan. The home market is most lucrative, because the parents will pay for pure, home-grown stock, but the export market to eastern

Asia, North America and Russia is also significant. This fate is shared by the children and eventually the women enslaved in the brothels. The disk I have enclosed in this package contains the names, digital images and personal histories of the men who head this organization; the law enforcers who protect them; the surgeons who carry out the work; the politicians who blanket the operation; the businessmen who launder the money; the men and customs officers who freeze and transport the organs.

Tomorrow is October 2nd. It is the day I plan to go public. I shall hand my data over to my contacts in the police and the media. One of two things will happen: the media will scream, and Japanese public and political life will be hit by a vice scandal which will send shock waves from hospitals in Kyūshū to the parliament building; or I shall be killed by those I seek to expose. If the latter comes to pass copies of this disk and letter are to be sent on to an audience I have selected for widely differing reasons.

Understand this: you are holding a letter from a dead woman. My revenge on the men who abduct women and children to harvest their organs failed. My hope and life's work are now in your hands. Act with your eyes open, as your conscience dictates. I cannot advise you – my best attempt has already failed. The Yakuza is a ninety-thousand-strong state within our state. If you attempt to use ordinary police channels, you will achieve only the issue of your own death warrant. You are holding a high card for a very dangerous game into which you never asked to be dealt. But for the repose of the soul of my son Eiji Matani, who was killed by these people, and for countless others, past, present and future, I implore you to act.

Please.

Kozue Yamaya

Why me? Her son and I share a name with the exact same kanji – *ei* for incantation, *ji* for earth. I never encountered this combination before, but this alone cannot account for Kozue Yamaya putting me on her trustee list. I sift my memory of the time we met for clues, but find none.

No way to find out, either.

I call downstairs. 'Machiko? Any big stories in the paper today?'

'What?' says Machiko, 'Don't tell me you haven't heard?'

'What?'

Machiko reads from the front page: '"Top Politican in Honesty Shocker – 'I'm Not on the Take!' Integrity Revelation by Minister Stuns Colleagues!"'

I manage a smile, and close the door. So Kozue Yamaya is dead too. I feel hollow with pity for that scarred person who visited me during my week at the study of tales. But I would be a fool to get involved in this. Keeping this disk is suicidally dangerous. I stow it in the most unused corner of my apartment – my condom box under my socks – until I figure out what to do. If no foolproof idea comes today or tomorrow, I should drop it in the river and hope another addressee is in a wiser, stronger position. Uneasily, I imagine us lined up in a row on the bridge, all dropping our disks in, acting on the same cowardly impulse. I change the water for Cat, switch on my fan, unroll my futon and try to sleep. Despite not having slept for twenty hours, I keep thinking of Mrs Yamaya. I sense a weird week ahead, one with sharp teeth. My pulse thuds. An unbreakable spear striking an impenetrable shield.

I arrive at work as Tuesday gasps its last. By the time I have changed into my chef apron and white bandana Wednesday is born. A big group of off-duty taxi-drivers stops by to order an office-party quantity of pizzas, and I am kept busy for ninety minutes. The FM radio keeps changing frequency at whim, swinging between

Chinese-, Spanish- and Other-speaking stations. 'Tagalog, man,' reckons Doi. 'The stratospheric ether is hyper-pure tonight, man, I can feel it in my sinuses.' He waits for the inferno to deliver his pizza, smoking a cigarette of his own creation in the cage. He rubs his eye. 'Miyake, I got something stuck in the corner here – pass me a toothpick, man?' I ignore my misgivings and pass him a toothpick. 'Thanks.' Doi uses it to pluck his eyelid down. 'No good. Would you mind looking? I think a tiny fly flew in.' I walk over, and peer close. Doi suddenly sneezes, his head jerks down and the toothpick punctures his eyeball. A jet of white fluid spatters my face. 'Shit!' screams Doi. 'Oh shit! I *hate* it when that happens!' I just stand there, unable to believe that reality is this grotesque. Sachiko appears in the hatch. I gibber – she shakes her head – I stop gibbering. 'Falling for him once is cute, Miyake, but two strikes and you're Mr Gullible. Doi, if you waste many more of those coffee whiteners you're going to force me to be Ms Assistant Manager and dock your salary. I mean it.' Doi snickers and I realize I have been had again. 'Hear and *ooo*bey, chieftainess.' Sachiko addresses a supernatural agency above the inferno. 'Is it my karmic destiny to oversee lunatic asylums, lifetime after lifetime, over and over, until I get it right? Miyake – one double Titanic, thick base, extra shark meat.' I box up Doi's pizza. He leaves in total victory. I keep thinking about the package from Mrs Yamaya. Tomomi slinks into the cage for one of her perpetual coffee breaks. She tells me how frantically busy her life is – 'busy' is definitely her favourite word – and asks how I know Ai doesn't fakes her orgasms when we have sex, because while she was having her affair with Mr Nero she felt obliged to *busy* things up on a number of occasions, because men are so insecure about performance. Tomomi has a tarantula-in-underpants effect on me. She sharpens her fingernails and keeps prodding for an answer. I am sort of saved by a toy-helicopter-sized wasp that flies in – Tomomi shrieks 'Kill it! Kill it!', and runs back through to the front. The hatch doors slam shut. The wasp buzzsaws around for a minute, warily sussing me out through its multi-lens eyes, and lands on Laos. Hard to concentrate on the pizzas, but I prefer its company to Tomomi. I stand on the counter and clap a plastic tub over south-east Asia. The wasp strikes up a death-by-flugelhorn noise and tries to knock a hole through the side – I get unbearably itchy and, instead of making a portable wasp release-box, semi-panic and shove the tub over the extractor fan, which is flush to the wall. The flugelhorn stops with a nearly inaudible crackle. 'Last of the action heroes,' says Onizuka, fingering the spike in his lower lip. He always arrives in the cage quiet as a ghost, and he speaks so softly I have to semi-lip-read. He nods at the inferno, where a pizza is waiting to be boxed. 'That my Eskimo Quinn for the KDD building? Customers give me shit if their pizzas get cold.' The hatch opens a crack. 'Is it dead?' ask Tomomi. 'The wasp is fine,' says Onizuka, 'but Miyake got mushed trying to leave through the extractor.' Tomomi performs an overture laugh to see if she can rile me. Onizuka departs with his pizza without another word. Doi arrives back a minute later – I could swear his *left* leg was limping yesterday, but today it is his right – and Tomomi tells him about the wasp. The drug pusher and the queen of all evil discuss whether I am guilty of the murder of a life form. 'It was only a wasp,' I say, 'there are plenty more where they came from.' This is not good enough for Tomomi: 'There are plenty more humans where we come from, so does that make homicide okay?' This is too stupid to argue about – especially as Tomomi was shrieking 'Kill it! Kill it!' – so I watch pizzas inching through the inferno. When I tune in again Doi and Tomomi are talking about crows. 'Say what you want,' Tomomi says, 'crows are cute.' Doi shakes his head. 'Crows are winged Nazis, man. The porter in our building, he chased one away with a broom. The next day, the same crow dive-bombed him and pecked his head hard enough to draw blood, man. A crow? Attacking a uniformed porter? Freaky, man. Kinda short-circuits nature.' Tomomi sharpens her eyeliner pencil and snaps open her hand mirror. 'The weak are meat, the strong eat.'

◆

Ueno to Kita Senju is easy, even during rush hour, because outbound submarines are empty except for night-shift workers and eccentric billionaires. The subs heading the other way into Ueno are human freight wagons. Tokyo is a model of that serial big-bang theory of the universe. It explodes at five p.m. and people-matter is hurled to the suburbs, but by five a.m. the people-matter gravity reasserts itself, and everything surges back towards the centre in time for the next day's explosion. My commute is against the natural law of Tokyo. I feel dead-beat. Giving up on my father is taking some getting used to. Ai is coming over to my capsule after her rehearsal, at about five in the afternoon. Her dinner is my breakfast. To my relief she asked if she could do the cooking – she prefers to choose what she eats because of her diabetes. To call my culinary repertoire 'limited' would be boastful. As I walk back from Kita Senju to Shooting Star, a weird cloud slides over half the sky. Cyclists, women with pushchairs, taxi-drivers stop to stare up at it. Half the sky is clear October blue – the other half is a dark funnelling churn of storm-cloud. Plastic bags get caught in vortexes and fly out of sight. Buntarō is in the shop early to bring the accounts up to date after his week away. He looks up at me and sniffs. 'I know,' I say, 'I know. I stink of cheese.' Buntarō shrugs, all innocence, and goes back to his calculator. I crawl upstairs. Cat bids me good morning and slips away to her own dimension. I wash her bowl, change her water, shower, and decide to have a quick nap before cleaning up for Ai.

My face is melted out of position. My tongue is a pumice stone. Saliva, collected in my tongue-root gully, drools out on to my pillow. At my table, Ai chops carrots and apples. For a moment I think – I married Ai, and she is making dinner for our nine children – but then I smell the apple. Nutmeg too. Cat is licking her paws and watches me. Buntarō lets Ai up, she knocks, I am too deeply asleep to wake up, Buntarō confirms I am definitely up here, Ai peers in, sees me, goes out and buys food for a salad. Life is sheer bliss when it wants to be. Ai must trust me, to be alone with me in my capsule while I am dressed – or not dressed – how I am. Being trusted makes me trustworthy. Carrot and apple go together great. She is chopping walnuts – I never much cared for walnuts until this moment – and raisins, and sprinkles them over lettuce. She is wearing old jeans and a faded yellow T-shirt lighter than her skin, and her hair is up. Here is that mythical neck. She scrapes peelings into the garbage bag. She wears thick black-framed glasses that suit her in a quirky sort of way. Ai never, ever tries to impress, and that impresses me *so* much. She has a pirate silver earring. 'Hey, Kyūshū Cannibal,' she says – I realize all this time she knew I was watching her – and chords inside me change from A flat to loose-string D minor. 'Why do you keep letters in your freezebox?'

'Watch out,' says Ai, 'I think there may be fish in these bones.'

'It tastes great.'

'Do you live entirely on pot noodles?'

'I vary my diet with pizza, courtesy of Nero. Mind if I finish the salad?'

'Do, before you die of scurvy. You never told me about your view.'

'That is no view. Yakushima has views.'

'It beats the view me and Sachiko have now. We used to overlook a low-security prison exercise yard. That was quite nice. I used to leave the windows open and play Chopin waltzes back to back. But then I returned from class one day to find a vertical rotary carpark had sprung up since breakfast. Now we have a view of concrete six inches away. We want to move, but paying a deposit would wipe us out. Even honest estate agents, if that isn't an oxymoron, skin you alive. Plus, it's nice to know that if a fire broke out we could climb out of the window and abseil to safety by breathing in and out slowly.'

The telephone riiiiiiiings. I answer: 'Hello?'

'Miyake!'

'Suga? Where are you?'

'Downstairs. Mr Ōgiso tells me you have company – but would you mind if I come up?'

I do, to be honest. 'Sure'.

When Suga enters my capsule I gape. He has had a body transplant. His eczema has vanished. He has a contoured haircut that must have cost ten thousand yen. He is wearing the suit of a Milanese diamond robber, and has the hip rectangular glasses of an electric-folk-singer. 'Are you going for an interview?' I ask. Suga ignores me and bows shyly at Ai. 'Hi, I'm Masanobu Suga. Are you Miyake's Korean girlfriend?'

Ai bites the head off a celery stick and looks at me quizzically.

'No,' I garble 'Suga, this is Miss Imajō.'

Ai munches. 'Suga the Snorer?'

Now Suga looks confused. 'I – er – Miyake?'

'Uh . . . Some other time.'

'There won't be another time for a long time – I came to say goodbye.'

'Leaving Tokyo?' I chuck a cushion down for him. 'Near or far?'

Suga slips out of his sandals and sits down. 'Saratoga.'

'Which prefecture is that in?'

Ai has heard of it. 'Saratoga, western Texas?'

'Heart of the desert.'

'Beautiful,' Ai munches, 'but wild.'

I find a sort of clean cup. 'Why are you going to a desert?'

'I'm not allowed to tell anyone exactly why.'

I pour his tea. 'Why not?'

'I'm not allowed to tell anyone that, either.'

'Is any of this to do with your Holy Grail?'

'After I left here last week, I went to my office and I got my brain back in gear. So offensively obvious. Write a search program, smuggle it into the file field, and get it to scan through the nine billion files to see if a real Holy Grail site had been hidden anywhere, right. My first attempt backfired. In megabyte terms it was like trying to squeeze China through the Sumida tunnel. The Pentagon immune system recognizes the program as an alien body, zaps it and launches a tracer program. I only just get out in time.' '*The* Pentagon?' Ai asks. Suga twiddles his thumbs, modest and boastful. 'So I sleep on the problem for a couple of days, then deep genius busts the door down. Dawn raid of inspiration. I break into the Pentagon immune system, softjack its own OS, muzzle it, and get *it* to search the very files its job is to protect! Like retraining your enemy's sniffer dogs to show you his hidey-hole. I make it sound easy, I know, but first I had to boot my flight path through six different zombies across six different cellphone networks. Second—'

'You did it?'

Suga lets the details slide. 'I did it. But the number of Holy Grails it had to check was, right, deeply cosmic. Think about it. Nine billion files, at the apex of nine billion pyramids, each one built of nine billion files – as far as I had dared to look. After turning loose my search program, I drowse off. Deep Sleep City. It is eleven in the morning by now, right – I worked at my computer since seven the evening before. What next? I wake up to find three men searching my office. Mid-afternoon, deep shock. One guy – a hacker, I can tell – is downloading all my personal files on to a hand-held drive I never even saw before. Second guy, an older headmaster type, is making an inventory of my hardware. The third is this fat sunburned foreigner in a cowboy hat leafing through my Zax Omega mangas and drinking my beer. I was too amazed to be scared. The headmaster guy flashes some ID at me – Data Protection Agency, ever heard of that? – and tells me I have violated the Japan/United States Bilateral Defence Treaty and that I have the right to remain silent but that if I don't want to be tried for espionage under US jurisprudence at the nearest military base, I had better get down on my knees and blab for dear life.'

'Is all this true?' Ai asks me.

'Is all this true?' I ask Suga.

'I was wishing to hell that it wasn't. The buggery scene in

Shawshank Redemption keeps flashing before me. The headmaster gets out a matchbox-sized recorder and starts firing questions. I'm expecting him to strap electrodes to my balls. How had I got into the Pentagon in the first place? How had I softjacked their anti-viral OS? Was I working alone? Who had I spoken to since? Had I heard of any of the following organizations – I hadn't, I can't even remember them now. They know what schools I went to, where I live, everything. Then the hacker guy talks technical data – I can see he is impressed with my zombie ring. Even so, it gets dark, and I don't know what they plan to do to me. Finally, the foreigner, who has been flicking through my photo albums and *MasterHacker*, speaks to the headmaster, in English. I realize he is the one in charge here. I ask if I can take a leak. The younger hacker accompanies me – I ask him for some more lowdown but he shakes his head. We get back to my office and headmaster offers me a job or prosecution under some very scary-sounding law. He describes the job, and the money – serious wooow! Artificial intelligence, missile shield systems—' Suga bites his lip. 'Oops. That's the only downer. I can't go around telling anyone about it.'

'What about IBM and your university?'

'Yeah, that was my next question. Headmaster nods at the foreigner – the foreigner barks an order into his mobile. "Already taken care of, Mr Suga," the headmaster tells me. "And we can arrange a PhD if your parents are worried about qualifications. Would MIT be acceptable? Other details can be worked out later." In fact, I fly out the day after tomorrow, so I have a million things to do. I brought you a present, Miyake. I considered tropical fruit, but this is a bit more personal. Here.' He produces a square case, flips it open and unclips a black flat thing. 'This is my finest home-cultivated computer virus.' For the second time in two days I am being given a computer disk. 'Uh . . . thanks. Nobody ever gave me a virus before.' Ai mutters something, and then speaks up: 'If those things get into hospital systems they put lives at risk. Do you ever think about that?' Suga nods and slurps his tea. 'Ethical cyberexplorers are responsible, right. Ghosts in the machine, not nerdish vandals. We are a growing breed. Over sixty-five per cent of top-flight systems explorers are ethical.' Ai gives Suga a black look. 'And over eighty-five per cent of all statistics are made up on the spot.' Suga soldiers on. 'Take this virus – "Mailman", I call it – it delivers your message to every addressee in the address book of whoever you send it too. Then it duplicates itself and delivers itself to all the addresses in those address books – and so on, for ninety-nine generations. Neat or what? And totally harmless.' Ai looks unconvinced. 'Spreading junk mail to tens of thousands of people doesn't strike me as especially ethical.' Suga has a proud-father beam. 'Not junk mail! Miyake can spread whatever message of joy and peace he wants to hundreds of thousands of users. It isn't the sort of thing I can take to Texas, being as how Saratoga is a top-secret research installation, right, and it would be a shame to let it go to waste.'

Suga leaves, I finish the salad and slice a melon for dessert. I take some down to Buntarō, who nods at the ceiling, and waggles his little finger questioningly. I pretend not to understand. No way am I going to make a pass at Ai. There is a sort of not-yetness between us. I tell myself. She is clearing a space on the table. 'Time for my insulin. Want to watch, or are you squeamish about needles puncturing human skin?'

'I want to watch,' I lie.

She gets a medical box from her bag, prepares the syringe, disinfects her forearm, and calmly slips the needle in. I flinch. She is watching me watching her as the insulin shoots into her bloodstream. I suddenly feel humble. Making a pass at Ai would be as uncouth as yelling at a flower to hurry up. Plus, if she rejected me I would have to microwave myself out of existence. 'So, Miyake,' says Ai as the needle slides out. 'What's your next move?'

I swallow dryly. 'Uh . . . what?'

She dabs a droplet of blood with sterilized cotton wool – 'Are you going to stay in Tokyo now you've changed your mind about tracking down your father?' I get up and wipe my frying pan. 'I . . . dunno. I need money before I can do anything else, so I'll probably stay at Nero's until something better comes along . . . I want to show you a couple of letters my mother wrote to me.'

Ai shrugs. 'Okay.'

I brush the ice granules off the plastic – she reads them while I finish the dishes and take a shower.

'Long shower.'

'Uh . . . when I take a shower I feel I'm back on Yakushima. Warm rain.' I nod at the letters. 'What do you think?'

Ai folds them neatly into their envelopes. 'I'm thinking about what I think about them.' Fujifilm says ten o'clock. We have to leave – Ai wants to be home before the stalkers leave their bars, and I have to get to work before midnight. Downstairs, Buntarō munches Pringles and watches a movie full of cyborgs, motorbikes and welders. 'Have a nice salad?' he asks so innocently I could kill him. I nod at the screen.

'What are you watching?'

'I am testing the two laws of cinematography.'

'Which are?'

'The first law states "Any movie with a title ending in '-ator' is pure drivel".'

'The second?'

'"The quality of any movie is in inverse proportion to the number of helicopters it features."'

'In a way,' Ai says as we arrive at Kita Senju station, 'I wish you hadn't shown me those letters.'

'Why not?'

Ai jangles loose change. 'I don't think you'll like hearing what I really think.' The last moths of autumn swirl around a stuttering light.

'Hearing what you really think was the point of showing you.'

Ai buys her ticket – I show my pass – and we walk down to the platform. 'Your mother wants you in her life, and your life could be a whole load richer with her in it. Your standoffishness isn't helping you or her. Those letters are a peace treaty.'

I feel sort of jabbed by that. 'If she wanted me to contact her, why didn't she give me her Nagano address?'

'Did it occur to you she might be afraid of giving you the power to reject her?' Ai hunts out my eyes. 'Anyway, she did tell you where she is – "Mount Hakuba".'

I shake my gaze free. '"Mount Hakuba" is no address.'

Ai stops walking. 'Miyake, for someone so bright' – bzzzzzzzzz! goes my sarcasm detector – 'you are one virtuoso self-delusionist. There can be no more than ten hotels at the foot of Mount Hakuba. Compared to finding a nameless man in Tokyo, finding your mother is a breeze. You could find her by tomorrow evening if you actually wanted to.'

Now the girl is trespassing. I know I should leave it but I can't. 'And why exactly do you think I don't want to?'

'I'm not your shrink.' Ai shrugs curtly. 'You tell me. Anger? Blame?'

'No.' Ai is clueless about all this. 'She had seven years to unabandon us, and another nine years to unabandon me.'

Ai frowns. 'Okay, but if you don't want to know what I really think about your issues, then talk about the weather instead of showing me personal letters. And hell, Miyake—' I look at her. 'What?' Ai semi-snarls. 'Do you *have* to smoke?' I put away my MacArthur lighter and slide my Parliaments back into my shirt pocket. 'I had no idea it bothered you so much.' Once the words are out I know they are way too snide. Ai snarls, full on. 'How could it not bother me? Since I was nine my arm has been a pin-cushion, just so my pancreas doesn't kill me. I endure a hypo twice a year while you line your lungs with cancer – and the lungs of everyone downwind – just so you can look like the Marlboro Man. Yes, Miyake, your smoking *really* bothers me.'

I cannot think of a single thing to say.

The evening is in pieces.

The train arrives. We sit next to each other back to Ueno, but we may as well be sitting in different cities. I wish we were. The jolly citizens of advertland mock me with their minty smiles. Ai says nothing. We get off at Ueno, which is as quiet as Ueno ever gets.

'Mind if I walk with you to your platform?' I ask, as a peace offering.

Ai shrugs. We walk down a corridor as vast as the suspended animation chamber in a space-ark. A rhythmic fierce whacking noise starts up from ahead – a man in orange is pounding something with a sort of rubber mallet. Whatever – whoever – is being minced is hidden behind a column. We both alter our course to give the man a wide berth – we have to walk past him to get to Ai's platform. I seriously think he is beating somebody to death. But it is only a paving tile the man is trying to coerce into a hole too small for it. *Whack! Whack! Whack!* 'That,' says Ai, probably to herself, 'is life.' From the tunnel an approaching train wolf-howls and Ai's hair swims in its wind. I feel miserable. 'Uh . . . Ai . . .' I begin, but Ai interrupts me with an irritated shake of her head. 'I'll call you.' Does that mean "It's okay, don't worry", or "Don't you dare call until I decide to forgive you"? Perfect ambiguity from the Paris Conservatoire scholarship student. The train comes, she gets on, sits down, folds her arms and crosses her legs. Without thinking about it I wave goodbye with one hand, and with my other hand pull my Parliaments from my shirt pocket and lob them down the gap between the train and the platform. But Ai has already closed her eyes. The train pulls away. She never even saw.

Shit. *That*, I think to myself, *that* is life.

My Nero rat-run shrinks every evening. The inferno gets hotter. Sachiko says nothing about Ai. Wednesday night is the busiest so far. One o'clock, two o'clock spin around. Emotions are so tiring.

I guess this is why I avoid them. The moment anything becomes good, it is doomed. Doi sucks ice cubes, scratches inside his nostril with his finger and shuffles his playing cards. 'Take a card,' he says, 'any card.' I shake my head – I am not in the mood. 'Go on! This is ancient Sumerian enchantment with third-millennial twists, man. Take a card.' Doi thrusts the fanned cards at me and looks away. So I take a card. 'Memorize it, but don't say what it is.' Nine of diamonds. 'Okay? Replace and shuffle! Anyway, anyhow, anywhere, bury the mortal remains of your card . . .' I do so – no way could Doi have seen. Tomomi drapes herself in the hatch. 'Miyake! Three Fat Mermaids, extra seaweed and squid. Doi – nose-picking doesn't suit a hippie of your years.' Doi scratches outside his nose: 'Muzzle the grizzly, man . . . ain't you had an intra-nasal zit before?' Tomomi stares at him. 'I have an intra-nasal zit right now. Its name is Doi. That delivery to the spine doctor's wing-ding is due seven days ago – if they phone to complain I'm shoving the headset inside your ear and you can deal with their negative energy. Man.' Doi does a whoah! gesture. 'Lady, I am mid-trick here.' Tomomi whistles inwards. 'Do you *want* me to tell Mr Nero about the aromatic substances in your scooter hotbox?' Doi returns his cards to their box and whispers to me as he leaves: 'Fear not, man, this trick is to be continued . . .' The minutes jog up the down escalator. Onizuka takes a break after a long-distance delivery. He broods in the cage, ripping a grapefruit to bits. I box up the Chicken Tikka and mini-salad for his next delivery. To hurry the night along I practice clock-management: before checking the time I kid myself it is twenty minutes earlier than the time I truly believe it is, so I can pleasantly surprise myself. But tonight, even my doctored guesses are way too optimistic. Doi reappears in the cage, listening to a song on the radio in ecstasy – 'Riders in the Storm, man . . .' He could be a songbird fancier in a deep wood. 'Me on my pizza scooter.' He drinks butter-vomit Tibetan tea from a flask and practises making cards appear from his ears. He has forgotten about the unfinished trick, and I don't remind him. 'The human condition is a card game, man. Our hand is dealt in the womb. During infancy we lay a few cards down, pick up a few more. Puberty, man – more cards – jobs, flings, busts, marriage . . . cards come, cards go. Some days, you got a strong hand. Other days, your winning streaks end in bad gongs. You bet, call, bluff.' Sachiko enters the cage for her break. 'And how do you win this game?' Doi peacock-tails the cards and fans himself. 'When you win, the rules change, and you find you lost.' Sachiko rests her feet on a box of Nero ketchup sachets. 'Doi's metaphors always make my head spin more than the abstract idea they're supposed to simplify.' Tomomi feeds through an order for a Satanica, crisp crust, treble capers. I lay out the base and imagine Ai, asleep, dreaming of Paris. Suga is dreaming of America. Cat is dreaming of cats. Pizzas come, pizzas leave. The wodge of completed orders climbs up the spike. Another hot dawn glows in the real world outside. I peel cucumbers until eight o'clock brings the new chef, a slap on the back and a ninety-decibel 'Miyake Go Home!' Going back to Kita Senju on the Chiyoda line, I plug myself into my Discman. No music. Weird I changed the batteries yesterday evening. I press 'Eject' – there is no CD inside, only a playing card. Nine of diamonds.

A message is waiting on my capsule answerphone. It is not from Ai. 'Uh . . . well, hello, Eiji. This is your father.' Laughter. I freeze – the first time I feel cold since March. 'Hey, I said it. This is your father, Eiji.' A deep breath. He is smoking. 'Not so difficult. Well. What a mess. Where do I start?' A 'phew' noise. 'First – believe me – I did *not* know you had come to Tokyo to search for me. That sadist Akiko Katō dealt with my wife, not me. I was in Canada for conferences and business since August – I only got back to town last week.' Deep sigh. 'I always hoped this day would come, Eiji, but I never dared make the first move. I never thought I had the right. If that makes sense. Second – about my wife. This is so embarrassing, Eiji – can I call you Eiji? Anything else seems wrong. My wife never breathed a word about the letter she wrote to warn you away, nor about meeting you last week . . . I only found out when my daughter let it slip out an hour ago.' Ruffle-shuffle. 'Well, I went ballistic and I only just calmed down enough to call you. How petty. How suspicious. What right did she have to keep you away from me? And on the heels of the death of my father, too . . . I shudder to think what kind of family you must think we are. There again, you might be right. My wife and I – our marriage, it is not exactly . . . Never mind.' Pause. 'Third. What is third? I'm losing track. This is the past. The future, Eiji. I want very badly to meet you, in case you were wondering. Right now, if possible. Today. We have so much to say, where do I start? Where do I stop?' Bemused laugh. 'Come to my clinic today – I'm a cosmetic surgeon, incidentally, if your mother never told you. We won't be disturbed by my wife or any hostile parties – or we could go to a restaurant if you haven't eaten by the time you get this . . . Look, I cleared my afternoon surgery. Can you make one o'clock? This is my surgery number.' I scribble it down. 'Get to Edogawabashi metro station, call, and Ms Sarashina – my assistant, completely trustworthy – will come and meet you. Only a minute away. So. Until one o'clock this afternoon . . .' An amazed sort of coo noise. 'I've been praying this day would come for years, and years, and years . . . Every time I went to the shrine, I asked . . . I can hardly—' He laughs. 'Enough of this, Eiji! One o'clock! Edogawabashi metro station!'

Life is sweet, rich and fair.

I forget Ai Imajō, I forget Kozue Yamaya, I lie back, and I replay the message over until I have every word, every mannerism, by heart. I get out the picture of my father and animate his face so he speaks the words. An educated, warm, dry voice that inspires respect. Not so nasal as mine. I want to tell Buntarō and Machiko – no, I want to wait. Later today, I will walk calmly into Shooting Star with a mysterious gentleman behind me and let drop a 'By the way, Buntarō, may I introduce you to my father?' Cat watches me warily from the closet – 'Today is the day, Cat!' I iron my good shirt, shower, and then try to doze for an hour. No hope. I listen to John Lennon's *Live in New York City*, and it is lucky I set my alarm clock, because the next thing I know it is eleven-thirty and the clock is ringinginginginginging inside my ears. I dress, fuss Cat, and put out her dinner six hours early in case I have to go straight to work after my father. Luckily Buntarō is on the phone to the distributor so he cannot pry under my halo of joy.

Edogawabashi station. I scan the midday crowds so intently that I miss her. 'Excuse me? I'm guessing you're Eiji Miyake, from your baseball cap.' I nod at the smartly dressed woman, not exactly young, not exactly old. She smiles with blackcurrant lips. 'I'm Mari Sarashina, your father's assistant – we spoke on the phone just now. What a thrill it is to have you visit.'

I bow. 'Thank you for coming out to meet me, Ms Sarashina.'

'No trouble at all. The clinic is a stroll away – Well, this is a very special day for your father. Cancelling an afternoon of appointments—' she shakes her head. 'Unprecedented in six years! I thought to myself, "Is the emperor visiting?" Then he said his son was visiting! – his words, not mine – and I thought, Aha! All is explained! He meant to fetch you from Edogawabashi himself, you know, but lost his nerve at the last minute – between you and me, he's afraid of emotional displays, et cetera. Enough gossip. Follow me.' Ms Sarashina walks and talks unswervingly. A cat-sized dog crosses our path. Oncoming pedestrians and cyclists make way for her. She navigates side streets of labelless boutiques and art galleries. 'Your father's clinic is a state-of-the-art establishment in the beautician sphere. We have a loyal word-of-mouth clientèle, so we avoid ostentatious advertising, unlike the downmarket clip-and-tuck shops.' A mouse-sized cat crosses our path. 'Here we are – see, you could pass by none the wiser.' A tall, anonymous building, sandwiched by flashier neighbours. The ground floor is a jewellery business, viewing by appointment. Set down a short corridor is a steel door. Mari Sarashina points to a brass plaque. 'This is us – *Juno*. Zeus turned her into a swan.' Her fingers dance over a security keypad. 'Or was it a bull?' A video camera watches us. 'Rather draconian security, I know, but our client list includes television stars, et cetera. You would not believe' – Mari Sarashina glares at heaven – 'what the grubbier paparazzi will do for a quick peek. Your father reviewed security after a reporter, disguised as a health ministry inspector, tried to bluff his way into our client files. Jackals, those people. Leeches. He had fake ID, name-card, the works. Ms Katō, your father's lawyer, bled them dry in court, naturally – although I gather she's not exactly flavour of the month, vis-à-vis yourself.' An elevator arrives. Mari Sarashina presses '9'. 'A room with a view.' She smiles reassuringly. 'Apprehensive?'

I nod, hollow with nervous excitement. 'A little.'

She brushes fluff off her cuff. 'Quite natural.' She stage-whispers. 'Your father is three times jumpier. But – relax.' The doors open on to a gleaming white reception area decked with lilies. Perfumed antiseptic. Pin-striped sofas, slab-of-glass tables, a tapestry of swans on a lost river. The walls curve into the ceiling – whorled and delicate, bones inside an ear. Celtic harp music accompanies the aircon hush. Ms Sarashina jabs the intercom on her desk – 'Dr Tsukiyama? Congratulations, it's a boy!' She shows me her perfect teeth. 'Shall I send him in?' I hear his voice crackle. Mari Sarashina laughs. 'Fine, Doctor. Coming up.' She sits down in front of her computer and gestures towards the steel door. 'Go on, Eiji. Your father is waiting.' I move, but real time is on 'Pause'. 'Thanks,' I tell her. She makes a 'don't mention it' face. One door away now – go! I turn the handle – the room beyond is airtight. The steel door opens with a kissing sound.

My arms are swung behind my back, my body is rammed against the wall, my feet are kicked away, and the cold floor slams into my ribs. One set of hands frisk me while another set holds my arms way past the angle they were designed to bend – the pain is record-breaking. Yakuza again. If I did have a concealed knife I would stick it into myself for being so stupid. Again. I consider volunteering to give up the Kozue Yamaya disk until a foot in the small of my back knocks the thought from my head. I am flipped over, and hauled to my feet. At first, I think I am standing on the set of a medical drama. A trolley of surgical equipment, a drugs cabinet, an operating table. The edges are shadowy, with ten or eleven men whose faces I cannot make out. I smell sausages. A man is filming me with a handycam, and on a large overhead screen I see myself. Two men with the bodies of Olympic shotputters are holding an arm each. The handycam zooms in, and captures my face from various angles. 'Light!' comes an old man's voice, and whiteness fills my eyeballs. I am dragged forward a few paces, and sat down. When I can see again I find myself at a card table. Here is Mama-san and three men. Near enough to touch is a smoked glass screen taking up most of the wall. An intercom clicks on, and the voice of god fills the room. 'This lamentable specimen is him?'

Mama-san looks at the smoked glass. 'This is him.'

'I had no idea,' says God, 'Morino had fallen on such hard times.'

Now I really know I am in trouble. 'The man on the telephone?' I ask her.

'An actor. To save us the trouble of sending someone to get you.'

I try to rub life back into my arms, and glance at the three men also sat at the card table. From their postures and faces, I can tell that they are also here against their will. A sweat-shiny fat-as-a-donut asthmatic, a man who keeps twitching as if his face is under attack, and an older guy who was once handsome but who has had scars gouged upwards from the corner of his mouth which fix his face in a mockery of a smile. Mr Donut, Twitcher and Smiley all fix their eyes on the table.

'We are gathered here today,' says God, 'for you to pay your debts to me.'

I cannot address a disembodied voice so I address Mama-san. 'What debts?'

God replies first. 'Major damage to Pluto Pachinko. Compensation for loss of trading time on the opening day. Two cadillacs.

Lost insurance premiums, cleaning bills and general indemnities. Fifty-four million yen.'

'But Morino caused that damage.'

'And you,' says Mama-san, 'are the last living disciple of his faction.'

I want to be sick. 'You know I was no disciple.'

God rattles his speakers. 'We have your contract! Signed in your mixed blood! What more binding an ink is there?'

I look at the smoked glass. 'How about her?' I point at Mama-san. 'She was Morino's accountant.'

Mama-san is nearly smiling. 'Child, I was a spy. Now shut up and listen or one of these bad, evil men will take a scalpel and slice your tongue in two.'

I shut up and listen.

'Mr Tsuru has selected you, his most hopeless debtors, to play a card game. A simple card game, with three winners and one loser. The winners will leave this chamber free men, owing not a penny. The loser will donate organs to needy patients. A lung,' she stares at me, 'a retina, and a kidney.'

Everyone in the room behaves as if this is quite normal.

'I am supposed to say,' I have to start again because no voice came out the first time, 'I am supposed to say "Sure, fine, let's gamble with my body parts"?'

'You are free to decline.'

'But?'

'But you will then be declared the loser.'

'Decline, kid,' jeers Twitcher, opposite me. 'Stick to your principles.'

I smell mustard and ketchup. I have no logic to combat any of this. 'A game?'

Mama-san produces a pack of cards. 'You shall cut to decide shuffling order. Aces high, highest shuffles first, the other players follow clockwise from the starter. Then we begin the game proper. In the same order, you shall turn over the top card until the queen of spades appears.'

'Whoever she chooses,' says God, 'loses.'

I feel how I felt back in the bowling alley.

'Is that voice him?' I ask Mama-san. My vocal chords are dry as sand. 'Is that Mr Tsuru?'

Twitcher claps sarcastically.

So, Tsuru is God. God is Tsuru. I try to buy time. 'Even you,' I say to Mama-san, 'must think this is insane.'

Mama-san's mouth becomes a tight slit. 'I take my orders from the company president. You take yours from me. Cut.'

My hand feels as heavy as a brick. The jack of spades.

Mr Donut draws the ten of diamonds.

Twitcher cuts the two of clubs.

Smiley turns over the nine of spades.

'The boy is the first to shuffle,' says Tsuru from behind his smoked glass.

The players look at me.

I clumsily flicker-shuffle the pack. Up on the screen, hands many times the size of my own do the same. Nine times, for luck.

Mr Donut wipes his hands on his shirt. The cards fly from hand to hand in gymnastic formation.

Twitcher makes a magical gesture with three fingers and cuts once.

Smiley shuffles in precise, circular motions.

Mama-san slides the pack to the centre of the table. It sits there innocently. I look at it as I would a bomb, which is exactly what it is. I wait for an explosion, an earthquake, a gunshot, an 'It's the cops!'

I hear sausages spitting on a grill.

The slow breathing of men.

'Take the top card now,' prompts Tsuru's voice gently, 'or a guard will remove your eyelids, and you will never be able to close your eyes again, not even to blink.'

I turn over the nine of diamonds.

Mr Donut's breathing grates as his asthma worsens. He cuts the ace of clubs.

Twitcher intones *Namu amida butsu* three times – he had a Buddhist education – before his hand darts out and snatches the ace of spades. 'Thank you,' he says.

Smiley is the coolest of us all. He calmly turns over the seven of spades.

My turn again. I feel as if Miyake is operating Miyake by remote-control. I look at myself on the screen. Myself stares back, I never knew I looked like that. My hand extends—

A narrow door in the smoked glass swings open and a waggy labrador skitters out, chomping on a sausage and slipping on the polished marble. 'Bring her back!' cries Tsuru, his real voice emerging from the entrance, only half picked up by the microphone and speakers. 'She mustn't run on a full stomach! Her digestion is delicate!' Two of the guards eventually shepherd the dog back to its master.

'We,' murmurs Smiley, 'are just TV dinner for the mad old fuck.'

All eyes in the room on me again.

Something alien is under my tongue.

I turn over the six of hearts.

I lick my forearm, taste salt, and see a tiny black insect.

Mr Donut's arm leaves a sweat patch on the felt. The three of diamonds.

Twitcher prays to Buddha and flips over the joker. 'Thank you.'

Smiley sighs and turns over the five of clubs.

Twelve cards gone out of fifty-two, fifty-four including two jokers.

I look at the backing of the top card for a clue, and two trapezoid eyes stare straight back at me. I know those eyes.

What is life like without half your organs?

No, Tsuru would never let the loser walk away to tell the tale, with a torso of scars and holes to prove it. The silence of the lucky winners can be relied upon, but the loser would end up the same way as Kozue Yamaya's son.

How did I get here?

I look at the screen Miyake. He has no answers either.

Mama-san opens her mouth to threaten me—

I turn over the card, and the black queen looks into my eyes.

The room slants from side to side.

'Fuck,' says Twitcher, 'I thought the kid found the bitch, not her sister.'

'So,' says Smiley, 'does the kid.'

What are they talking about? Smiley nods at my death notice on the table. 'Look closer.'

It is the queen of clubs, not spades. Clubs.

Mr Donut says, 'I need my inhaler'. Mama-san nods, and he fishes it out of his jacket pocket. He holds his head back, breathes in a blast, holds it, and breathes out. Then he turns over the queen of spades.

Nobody says anything.

The screen Mr Donut is sweating worse than a man dying of plague.

Me, I am trembling and wracked with relief and guilt and pity.

Mama-san clears her throat. 'Your queen has appeared, Mr Tsuru.'

The speakers stay silent.

'Mr Tsuru?' Mama-san frowns at the smoked glass. 'Your queen has spoken.'

No response.

Mama-san leans over and knocks on the glass. 'Mr Tsuru?'

A guard wrinkles his nose. 'What's he cooking now?'

Another guard frowns. 'Well it aint sausages . . .'

The guard nearest the door in the glass pushes it open and peers in. 'Mr Tsuru?' He breathes sharply, as if blocking a karate kick with his stomach. 'Mr Tsuru!' He stays where he is, and turns around to face us, blankly.

'Well?' demands Mama-san.

His jaw moves but nothing comes out.

'What?'

He swallows. 'Mr Tsuru has grilled his face to the hotplate.'

A riot of improvised theatre breaks out. All I can do is close my eyes.

'Mr Tsuru Mr Tsuru Mr Tsuru! Can you hear me?'

'Scrape his head off!'

'Turn the gas off!'

'His lip has fused to the metal!'

'Ambulance ambulance ambulance someone call a—'

'Fuck! His eyeball just popped!'

'Wipe it off on your own shirt!'

'Get that fucking dog out of here!'

Someone vomits noisily.

The dog barks joyfully.

Mama-san scrapes a metallic object down the smoked glass. The screech is unbearable, and the chamber falls silent. Her composure is perfect, as though she scripted this moment many years ago and has rehearsed it ever since. 'Mr Tsuru's entertainment has been overtaken by a *deus ex machina*. It appears the excitement was too much, triggered a second stroke, and since our dear leader chose his barbecue to fall on, it no longer matters particularly when that ambulance gets here.' She now addresses the two or three older men. 'I am appointing myself the acting head of this organization. You shall obey me, or oppose me. Make your intentions known. Now.'

The moment is dense with calculations.

The men look at us. 'What will we do with them, mama-san?'

'Card games are no longer company policy. Show them the door.'

I dare not trust this new development, not until I am outside and running. Mama-san addresses us. 'If any of you go to the police and somehow convince a recently-graduated detective that you are not a lunatic, three things will occur, in this order. One: you will be taken into protective custody. Two: a bullet will be put through your head within six hours. Three: your debts will be transferred to your next-of-kin and I will personally ensure that their lives are destroyed. This is not a threat, this is standard procedure. You will now indicate that you understand.'

We nod.

'We have been in business for thirty years. Draw your own conclusions about our ability to protect our interests. Now get out of here.'

The cinema is full. Couples, students, drones. The only free seats are in the front, where the screen looms over your head. Everything in Tokyo is nearly full, full, or too full. There was no trace of Mari Sarashina in the reception outside the chamber. 'If I was you guys,' said the guard as the elevator doors closed, 'I'd buy a fucking lottery ticket.' In the seat next to me is a girl – her boyfriend's hand has been edging over the back of her seat. The elevator began its long, slow descent. Mr Donut dropped his cigarettes. We watched them lying there where they fell. Mr Donut began shaking, but with laughter or fear or what, none of us knew. Smiley closed his eyes and tilted his head back. I kept my eye on the descending floor numbers. Twitcher picked up a cigarette and lit it. This movie is brutal and cheap and fake. If people who dream up violent scripts ever came into contact with real violence, they would be too sickened to write such scenes. When the elevator doors opened we plunged into the afternoon crowds without a word. The sunny weather was a sick prank. I came to a place where street performers twisted balloons into crocodiles and giraffes, and had to dig my fingernails into my arm to stop myself crying. The movie finishes and the audience files out. I stay and watch the credits. The key grips, the animal trainers, the caterers. A new audience files in. I re-watch the movie until my brain starts to melt. After the balloon man, I wandered wherever the crowds looked thickest. I cursed myself for not leaving Tokyo after Morino. I should have known. In the cinema foyer I call Ai and quickly hang up when she answers. I get on a Yamanote circle line submarine, and sit with the drones. I wish I was a common drone. The stations roll by, and by, and by, and repeat themselves. I am too full of fear-pollution to ever sleep again.

A conductor gently shakes me awake. 'You gone around six times, kid, I thought I should wake you up.' His eyes are kind and I envy his son.

'Is it night or are we underground?'

'Quarter to eleven, Thursday the fifth. Know what year we are in?'

'Yeah, I know that.'

'You should get home while the trains are still running.'

I wish. 'I have to get to work.'

'What are you, a grave-robber?'

'Nothing so exotic . . . Thanks for waking me up.'

'Any time.'

The conductor moves down the compartment. Above the seats opposite, behind the swaying hand-rings, is an ad for an Internet advertising company. An apple tree grows from a computer chip, and from its computer chips fruit grow more apple trees, and from these apple trees grow more computer chips. The forest grows out of the frame and invades the advertising spaces either side. I was unaware that any part of my brain was thinking about the Kozue Yamaya disk, but an enormous idea occurs to me. I am wide, wide awake.

My mind is not here, but I never need my mind in Nero's. When I arrive on the last stroke of Thursday, I get a weird look from Sachiko – she knows about my argument with Ai – but it is hard to care. I think about the twenty-four-hours-ago Eiji Miyake, chicken-cooping up and down these same three-by-one square metres of Tokyo giving birth to his pizzas. Lucky, blind, cursed idiot. I wish I could warn him. I knock back a genki drink to ward off sleeplessness and start work on the backed-up orders. 'You got a nine of diamonds for me, man?' asks Doi when he returns. I forgot it. 'No. Tomorrow.' Doi congratulates himself. 'Magic is the manipulation of coincidence, man. In this life, coincidences are the only thing you can count on.' I wash my hands and face. Every time the door buzzes, I am afraid it could be a Tsuru thug. Every time the telephone rings, I am afraid Sachiko or Tomomi will appear in the hatch and hand the receiver through, saying: 'A call for you, Miyake. No name.' Doi is super-talkative tonight – he tells me how he got dismissed from his last job. He was a night-watchman in a multistorey cemetery where the ashes of the dead are stored in hives of tiny locker-shrines. He was fired for substituting his own music for the tapes of Buddhist funerary mantras. 'I figured, man, if *I* were stuck in a box for all eternity, which would I prefer? Priests making opening-seriously-larger-than-expected-phone-bill moans, or the golden age of rock'n'roll? No contest! I could *feel* the vibes in the place change, man, whenever I put on my Grateful Dead tapes.' Doi slashes his throat with his forefinger. I hear Doi without really listening to him. His pizza comes through for delivery. I box it and off he goes. The radio plays 'I Heard It on the Grapevine' – a sweaty, scheming song. Sachiko opens the hatch – 'You have a mystery caller on line three!'

'Ai?'

'Nooo . . .'

'Who?'

'She said it was a personal call.' Sachiko leans through to the kitchen wall phone, presses a button and hands me the receiver.

'Hello?'

The caller does not respond.

Fear makes my voice sharp. 'I don't owe you anything now!'

'Is two a.m. good morning or good night, Eiji? I'm not very sure.' A middle-aged woman, not Mama-san. She is as nervous as I am, I think.

'Look, would you just tell me who you are?'

'Me, Eiji, your mother.'

I lean against the counter.

Tomomi is studying me through the crack in the hatch. I close it.

'This is, uh, a surprise.'

'Did you get my letters? My brother said he forwarded them on to you. He said you're living in Tokyo now.'

'Yeah.'

Yeah, I got your letters. But therapy that closes wounds in you just opens wounds in me.

'So . . .' we both begin.

'You first,' she says.

'No, you first.'

She takes a deep breath. 'A man has asked me to marry him.'

What do I care? 'Oh.' Tomomi inches open the doors. I bang them shut savagely. Hope I broke the bitch's nose. 'Congratulations.'

'Yes. The hotelier in Nagano I told you about in my last letter.'

A hotelier, huh? Nice catch. Especially with your history.

Why are you telling me this now?

You never bothered telling us about your life before.

You never cared what we thought. Not remotely.

You want me to be happy for you? To say 'Sure, Mum, great news!'?

I very nearly put us both out of our misery and hang up.

'Where are you calling from?' I end up saying.

'I'm back at the clinic in Miyazaki. The . . . drink, you know. I was poorly for a very long time. That's why . . . But now, he – the hotelier, his name is Ōta by the way – he says after we marry my problems are his problems too, and so . . . I want to get better. So I came back here.'

'I see. Good. Good luck.'

'Mrs Ōta.' Ordinary, married, respectable. RESET. A new patron, a new set of bank cards, a new wardrobe. Nice. But answer my question: Why are you telling me this now?

I see.

Mr Ōta doesn't know about us. You never told him. You want to make sure I'll agree to keep your nasty little secrets to myself. Am I right?

'He'd love to meet you, Eiji.'

How nice of Mr Ōta. Why would I want to meet this owner of fat hotels?

Twenty years is a little late to start playing the dutiful mother, Mother.

Fact is, you only ever make me unhappy. You are making me unhappy now.

So fine. Get over your drink problem, get married, live happily ever after and leave me alone. You neurotic, grasping, betraying witch.

The hatch opens – a pen with a white flag waves – Sachiko's untouchable Doraemon mug appears on the shelf, emitting coffee particles. The hatch closes.

'Eiji?'

The DJ cuts 'I Heard It on the Grapevine' short.

Why I say what I say now, I could never explain, not even to myself.

'Mum, how about I, uh . . . come and see you in Miyazaki tomorrow?'

When I finish explaining, Sachiko nods. 'Not the sort of humanitarian mission I could stand in the way of, is it? But my last order as your superior officer in the great army of Nero is this: phone my flatmate before you leave Tokyo.'

'Did she, uh, say anything?'

'I can tell her mood by her piano-playing. While you were calling her last week Ai played Chopin and nice stuff. Yesterday evening, I had to get ready for work to those blocky-cocky Erik Satie pieces he wrote to evict his neighbours.'

'I, uh, sort of messed up, Sachiko.'

'Ai is no Miss Twenty-four Hour Sunshine. Life is short, Miyake. Call her.'

'I dunno . . .'

'No. "Dunno" is not acceptable. Say: "I hear and obey, Miss Sera."'

'I really—'

'Shut up and say it or you'll never make pizza in this town again.'

'I hear and obey, Miss Sera.'

'Tomomi tells me you had a heavy session, man . . .' Doi appears in the cage with a mini food blender. 'Know what I do to subdue all those spike-vibes, man?'

I turn away. 'Doi, this is my last night. Have mercy.'

'No tricks, man! Just a magic anti-stress cocktail . . .' Would he put me through this if he knew I had come within one card and a burst artery of having my organs removed this afternoon? Probably, yes. 'First, strawberries!' Doi empties a punnetful into the blender. He pulls a black velvet hood over the blender and liquidizes them. He removes hood and lid. 'Then, tomatoes!' He drops three overripe tomatoes in. 'Red food massages away stress waves. Green aggravates. That's why rabbits and veggies are so uptight . . . What next? Raspberry juice . . . raw tuna . . . azuki beans . . . all the major food groups.' Doi replaces the lid, the hood, and blends. 'And last of all, the crowning glory—' With a flourish he produces a pink budgerigar from a handkerchief. It flaps, blinks and tweets. 'In you go, little guy!' He gently lowers it into the bright red liquid mush, and replaces the lid and hood. I know it is a stupid trick, so I refuse to look shocked. He lowers the blender behind the ledge between the cage and my rat-run – where he switches blenders, perhaps? – and then shakes the blender jug, cocktail-barman-style, to the Hawaiian slide guitar music on the radio.

'Doi!' Sachiko comes into the cage with her clipboard.

Doi jumps and puts down what he is holding guiltily.

'I hate to inconvenience you with this annoying "work" business, but . . .'

'Still on my break, chieftainess! Three more minutes! I'm showing Miyake my peace potion . . .' He picks up the blender jug, still in its black hood, and liquidizes the contents for thirty seconds.

Sachiko, defeated, sits down. Doi removes the hood, the lid, and drinks the soupy liquid straight back. 'Deeelicious.'

'Wow . . .' Sachiko stands up, putting blender B – I knew it – on the ledge, minus velvet hood. 'Did you make this imitation budgie? It's so realistic. What's it made of?' She is genuinely impressed.

'Ladyboss! You gave my trick away!'

'Then don't leave your props lying around the kitchen!'

'Don't call my Tutu a prop! Budgies have feelings too, diggit?'

'Tutu doesn't look very animated for a live budgie.' Sachiko extracts the bird from the red gunge. Its head comes off in a shower of white powder.

'Doi,' I say, 'please tell me this is a part of the trick.'

'Doi's eyes bulge in pure panic. 'Oh, man . . .'

After the ambulance takes Doi to hospital for a stomach pump and rabies injections, I offer to do the scooter deliveries. Sachiko says she should because she knows the area better. Tomomi mans the phones alone. I prepare and box up three El Gringo – thick base, gorgonzola, spicy salami, tomato and basil crust – by the time Onizuka gets back. Tomomi tells him what happened to Doi – for a moment I think Onizuka may abandon his principles and smile, but the danger passes and he reverts to his miserable self. Business slackens a little. By 07.30 I have already memorized the breakfast news round-up. Trade talks, summits, visiting dignitaries. This is how to control entire populations – don't suppress news, but make it so dumb and dull that nobody has any interest in it. The weather on Friday, 6th October will start cloudy, with a 60 per cent chance of rain by mid-afternoon, and a 90 per cent chance of rain by evening. I scour down the counters, hoping that no more orders come in during the next thirty minutes. I need to work out the cheapest way to get to Miyazaki. I peer into the inferno – six pizzas inching onwards, glowing karma-like. The radio plays a song called 'I Feel the Earth Move under My Feet'. Radios and cats both go about their business whether anyone is there or not. Unlike guitars, which sort of stop being guitars when you close their cases. Sachiko lays an envelope on the counter of my rat-run. 'I fiddled petty cash, but this is what Nero owes you.'

'Sorry to leave you in the lurch.'

'Well, the Nippon index will plummet once the news breaks, but somehow we'll pull through. I may even don the chef's apron myself, if head office can't send anyone. It has been known. Call me, when you come back to Tokyo – I can't promise to keep your job open in this branch, but I can get you in anywhere there's a vacancy.'

'I appreciate it.'

'Any idea how long you'll be away?'

'Depends on . . . lots of things. If I can help my mother get well.' I fold the envelope into my starved wallet.

'Phone Ai. I don't want to be the one to tell her that you've skipped town.'

'I, uh, don't think I'm friend of the month at the moment.'

'Ai has no friends of the month, you idiot. *Phone* her.'

Tomomi slouches in the hatch. 'If you can spare the energy to prepare one final pizza before your happy families reunion, the Osugi Bosugi man has ordered his weekly kamikaze.' She slaps the order slip on the ledge and disappears. I frown at Sachiko, feeling as if my feet are sliding away. 'Osugi and Bosugi? PanOpticon?'

'A regular order since time began. "Kamikaze" is a pizza not on the wallchart – we should get around to putting it up, only nobody else in Tokyo could stomach it. Mozzarella crust, banana, quail eggs, scallops, octopus ink.'

'Unchopped chillis.'

'One of the other chefs mentioned it?'

This is a mystery to me. 'I guess . . .'

'It is an unforgettable creation. Speaking of which, I have to go and write Doi's accident report.' So she doesn't see my face when I look at the order slip. Tomomi's handwriting is an clear as malice. *Tsukiyama, Osugi & Bosugi, PanOpticon.*

First I laugh in disbelief.

Then I think: another trap.

Then I think: no trap. Apart from the fact that nobody knows I know my father's name, since Tsuru died nobody wants to trap me. Mama-san let me go once already. This is no trap, but a card trick that Tokyo has performed. How is it done? Look at it stage by stage. I know 'Kamikaze' because . . . here it is. I remember. Weeks ago, that night when Cat came back from the dead, a man misdialled, called my capsule thinking I was a pizza restaurant, and ordered this same pizza. Only he never misdialled. That man was my father.

The rest is simple. My father is not Akiko Katō's client – he is her colleague.

Akiko Katō is why I watched PanOpticon from Jupiter Café.

Jupiter Café is why I met Ai Imajō.

Ai is why I met Sachiko Sera.

Sachiko Sera is why I am standing in Nero's, preparing a pizza for my father.

No more misdirections, jumped conclusions, lies. To my father, I was a sixty-second amusement. Then I was a zero. Now I am an embarrassment. I feel so, so . . . stupid. I dress his pizza. It looks as disgusting as it sounds. I feed it into the inferno, watch the black gunge glow orange. Why 'stupid'? How about 'angry'? Since I wrote to Akiko Katō my father has known how to contact me. Morino, Tsuru, everything . . . if only he had just told me to go away two months ago. I would have been disappointed, sure, but I would have obeyed. This time, I decide what happens. I don't know what I will do when I confront him, but now that Tokyo has unearthed the man, I am going to see him. I open the hatch. No sign of Tomomi. Sachiko gnaws a Biro. 'If I say that a wild budgie flew into the blender of its own accord, d'you think head office will believe me?'

'Only if they want to.'

'Lot of use you are.'

'But I could deliver this Kamikaze for you.'

Sachiko checks her watch. 'Your shift ends in two minutes.'

'PanOpticon is on my way to Shinjuku.'

'You are a biped blessing sent from heaven, Miyake.'

The door to PanOpticon revolves in perpetual motion. Palm trees sit in bronze urns. Gaudy, people-eating orchids watch me pass. Nine identical leather armchairs wait for occupiers. A one-legged man crutches across the polished floor. Rubber squeaks, metal clinks. Behind the desk is the chubby security guard who threw me out when I tried to see Akiko Katō two months ago. A smear of shaving foam is under one ear. He yawns as I approach. 'Yeah, son?'

'I have a pizza for Mr Tsukiyama in Osugi and Bosugi.'

'Do you?'

I hold my box up.

'"Never fear-O, it's a Nero." No explosives in there now, are there? You international terrorists always smuggle weapons into buildings using pizza boxes.' He thinks this is very amusing indeed.

'Put it through a scanner, if you want.'

He waves a baton thing at the elevators. 'East elevator, ninth floor.'

The Osugi and Bosugi reception appears deserted. A console, piled with files, plants dying of sun starvation, a monitor on screensaver mode – a computer face drifts from anger to surprise to jealousy to joy to grief and back to anger. A single corridor runs to a pane of morning. A photocopier intones. Where do I go? A human head rises up from a swamp of sleep. 'Yes?'

'Morning. Pizza for Mr Tsukiyama.'

She drags herself to a higher plane of consciousness, clips a headphone over her ear, and presses a button on her console. She lights a cigarette while waiting. 'Mr Tsukiyama, Momoe here. Pizza boy with breakfast. Shall I send him along or are you still projecting positions with your client?' She suctions in her cheeks while my father replies. 'Received and understood, Mr

Tsukiyama.' She jerks a thumb up the corridor and removes her headphone. 'All the way, turn right at the end. Mr Tsukiyama is dead ahead. And knock first!'

The carpet is worn, the air-con is old, the walls need repainting. A door ahead opens and – bang on cue – Akiko Katō appears carrying a wire basket of shuttlecocks. Her silver sea-urchin earrings dangle. She catches me sneaking a glance at her as I catch her sneaking a glance at me. I keep walking, reminding myself that I am doing nothing illegal. I reach the end of the corridor, and nearly collide with a woman adjusting her shoe. She is my age, with sexier legs than Zizzi Hikaru. I smell perfume and wine. She regains her balance and walks the way I came. Ahead is a single door, ajar – *Daisuke Tsukiyama, Partner*. Inside, a man – my father, I guess – is on the telephone. I eavesdrop. 'Darling, *I know*! You're overreacting – you – just – darling – *listen to me!* Are you listening? Thank you. I *had* to spend the night here because if I give this one to the underlings they'll fuck it up and then I'll have to spend even more nights here sorting out the mess and my client will be fucked off too and take his account somewhere swankier, so my bonus gets slashed and then how am I supposed to pay for the fucking pony in the first fucking place? Stop – stop it, darling – yeah, I know her friends all have ponies, but all her friends' daddies are judges with more money than fucking Switzerland . . . You think I *like* doing this overtime-slave shit? You think I *like* – what? *What*? Oh, oh, oh, *this* is what we're really talking about, is it? Paranoia strikes back! Ever occurred to you, *darling* . . . *What*? You didn't! No. Tell me you didn't. You did. Well, this is your morning bombshell. A private investigator. You stupid little woman. Of *course*, private investigators feed you bullshit! Why? Because they want repeat business! I am too outraged' – a filing cabinet bangs – 'to continue this conversation. I have a company to run. And if you have cash to throw away on those games, why all the hurry to sell off the shares the old man left? Yeah, you have a nice day too. *Darling*.' He hangs up. 'And throw yourself off the balcony, *darling*.'

I take a deep breath—

He may recognize me—

He may not recognize me, and I may tell him—

He may not recognize me, and I may not tell him—

I knock. A pause. Then a cheerful 'Come!' I recognize my father from the photograph I got from Morino. He lies on a vast sofa, wearing a dressing gown. 'Pizza boy! You overhear my telephone call?'

'I did my best not to.'

'Let it be a lesson to you.'

'I'm sorry, I—'

'Remember: it costs more to keep a pony in straw than a whore in fur.'

'I can't imagine ever needing to remember that.'

My father grins – a grin that is used to getting what it wants – and beckons me over. There is a great view of skyscrapers in the background, but I drink in every detail. The too-black hair. The racks of shoes in his closet. The photo of Half-sister on his desk as a ballerina swan. The shape of his hands. The way he swivels upright. His body seems to be in better shape than his company – I guess he works out at a gym. 'You're not Onizuka, and you're not Doi.'

No, I am your son by your first mistress. 'No.'

'So?' My father waits. 'You are?'

'The chef.'

'Oho! So *you* make my delectable Kamikazes.'

'Only this week. I'm temporary.'

He nods at the pizza box. 'Then I betcha never came across anything quite like my kamikaze, am I right?'

I place the box on the coffee table. 'It's an unusual combination.'

'Unusual? Unique!'

I smell perfume and wine.

My father smiles and frowns at the same time. 'Are you all right?'

I tell you now, or I go away for ever.

He grins. 'You look like your night was almost as long and hard as mine.'

How you love yourself. 'Goodbye.'

Mock-offended surprise. 'You don't want me to sign anywhere?'

'Oh. Yeah. Here, please—'

My father scribbles on the receipt.

I want to smash your skull with your golfing trophy.

I want to shout and I think I want to cry.

I want you to know. Your consequences, your damage, your dead. I want to drag you down to the seabed between foot rock and the whalestone.

'Hell-o-oo-ooo!' My father waves his hand. 'I said, is Doi back next week?'

I swallow and nod and leave this man who I will never meet again. I look back once – his eyes close as his jaws sink into black stodge.

Outside PanOpticon, I buy a pack of Hope, sit on a bollard and watch the traffic stop and start. Twenty years translated to two minutes. I smoke one, two, three. The cloud atlas turns its pages over. Crows dissect a pile of trash. Tokyo is a dirty eraser. Summer left town without leaving a forwarding address. Drones in Jupiter Café tuck into their breakfasts. I want to stop a passer-by, and tell the story of the last six weeks, from PanOpticon stake-out up until this moment. How do I feel? Oh, I cannot begin. But hey, Anju, I kept my promise. I wish Ai were working at the Jupiter Café today. I would ride in on my Harley Davidson like Richard Gere in *An Officer and a Gentleman*, and she would climb on, and we would vanish down the narrow road to the deep north. I watch the pedestrians crossing *en masse* when the green man says so. I join them. I cross Kita Street – I feel disappointment that our father turned out exactly how all the evidence said he would. I wait for the man to turn green. I cross over Ōmekaidō Avenue –

I feel shame that his blood is in my veins – and I wait for the man to turn green. Then I cross back over Kita Street – I feel sad that I found what I searched for, but no longer want what I found. I wait, and cross back over Ōmekaidō Avenue. I feel release. I complete one, two, three circuits. I can go now. I hear my name. Onizuka has pulled up on his Nero scooter. I am immune to surprise, now and maybe for ever. I don't know what he wants, but I rule out walking away from Onizuka in case he knifes me in the kidneys. 'C'm here.' He hoicks and spits. 'Been looking for you.'

'You found me.'

'Been watching you walking in circles.'

'Squares. Not circles.'

He toys with his lip-stud. 'Want to ask you something.'

I go up to him.

He thumbs towards Nero's. 'Tomomi the Mouth says you're going to Miyazaki.'

'Tomomi the Mouth is right.'

'Your mum's ill?'

'She is, yeah.'

'Short of dosh?'

Where is this going? 'I'm not exactly the Bank of Japan, no.'

'My stepdad runs a haulage business. Said one of his drivers'll get you to Osaka, then sort out a rig for Fukuoka.' Onizuka never jokes, and he hasn't started now. He hands me a slip of paper. 'Map, address, phone number. Be there by noon.'

I'm too surprised – too grateful – to say anything.

Onizuka drives off even before I properly thank him.

'You want to visit your mother in Miyazaki, but you can't be sure when you'll be back,' Buntarō announces as I step into Shooting Star. My landlord folds his *Okinawa Property Weekly*. 'As if I could say "No!", lad! My own mother would murder me. Yes, my wife will take care of the cat. Like old times. Your rent is covered until the end of October, and your deposit can take care of November, unless you need me to return it, in which case I'll pay it into your bank account, box your stuff and put it into storage. Call me from Miyazaki when you know what your plans are. Shooting Star isn't going anywhere. My wife has made you a lunch box.' He rubs his gold tooth, and I realize that it is Buntarō's lucky amulet. 'Go on then,' he says. 'Pack!' My capsule is exactly as I left it twenty hours ago. Socks, yoghurt cartons, scrunched pillows. Weird. Cat is out, but Cockroach waits on the window ledge. I get the death spray, creep up on it, and – Cockroach is motionless. Daydreaming? I hassle him with the corner of a cookie wrapper. Cockroach is a dead husk.

Onizuka TransJapan Ltd is near Takashimadaira station out on the Tōei Mita line. Through the gates is a walled yard with a loading bay and three medium-sized trucks. It is only eleven. I walk back towards the station, where the giant electronics store is opening. Inside is cold as pre-dawn February. Two identical receptionists at the helpdesk chime 'Good morning' in such angelic harmony that I am unsure which to speak to. 'Uh, which floor are the computers, please?'

'Basement, third level,' answers Miss Left.

'Mind if I leave my backpack with you?'

'No problem at all,' answers Miss Right.

I float on the down escalator. Souls of shoppers float with me. Everywhere is draped with tinselly maple leaves to announce the coming of autumn. Miniature TVs, spherical stereos, intelligent microwaves, digital cameras, mobile phones, ionizing freezers, dehumidifying heaters, hot-rugs, massage chairs, heated dish-racks, 256-colour printers. The escalator announcement warns me not to stand on the yellow lines, to assist children and old people at all times, and orders me to enjoy quality shopping. Goods sit on their shelves, watching us browse. Not a single window. In the computer section I am greeted by a tame Suga in a clip-on tie. His skin has a clingfilm gleam. I wonder if they have Vitamin B-emitting strip lights down here to compensate for the total absence of natural light. 'You look like a man with his mind made up, sir!'

'Yes, I'm thinking of upgrading one of my PCs.'

'Well, I promise we can spoil you for choice. What's your budget?'

'Uh . . . I've got a research grant to burn through. My modem's from the twenty-fifth century – now all I need is the hardware to match it.'

'No problem. What's your modem?'

I overdid it. 'Uh . . . a very fast one indeed.'

'Yes, sir, but which make?'

'Uh, a Suga Modem. Saratoga Instruments.'

He bluffs. 'Verrrrrrrrry nice machines. Which uni are you at?'

'Uh, Waseda.'

I have used a magic word. He produces his card and bows low enough to lick my shoes. 'Fujimoto – at your service. We do operate an academic discount scheme. Well. I'll let you play – you just call me if I can assist.'

'I will.'

I pretend to read the specifications on a few machines, gather a sheaf of brochures, and choose a machine to sit at. I click on to the Internet, and find the e-mail address of the Tokyo Metropolitan Police home page. I write it on my hand. I glance around, hoping no hidden video cameras are watching. I load Suga's disk. `A hearty welcome to the mailman virus!` Suga made his virus more user-friendly than he ever made himself. `Do you want to enter your message to the masses via keyboard or load it from disk?` I press D. `Okay. Load your disk and hit ENTER.` I eject the Suga disk, insert the Kozue Yamaya one, and press Enter. The virus program takes over. The drive buzzes and blinks. `Okay. Now enter address of lucky recipient.` I type in the police home page address off my hand. `Hit ENTER to lick stamp!` The cursor pulses, my finger hovers – the consequences of pressing this key swarm – click. Too late to change my mind now. `Mailman is delivering your letter to primary addressee . . . Flash. Mailman is forwarding your letter to second generation addressees . . .` Short pause. Third generation addressees . . . Long pause. Fourth generation, [yawn]. The screen clears. Mailman will continue to generation99. The message scrolls off-screen. Log off now/leave the crime scene/run like hell. Beep. Bye-bye. Bye-bye, Suga. I eject the Yamaya disk and put it into my shirt pocket. I am a plague-spreader. Only this plague might cure something. 'Excuse me.' An older salesman strides over. 'What did you just download into our system, exactly?' I grope for a plausible lie, but find nothing. 'Uh, well. I was morally obliged to release information about a Yakuza network which steals people, cuts them up and, uh, sells the body parts. Using your computer seemed the safest way to go about exposing them. I hope that was okay?' The salesman nods gravely, trying to figure out where I am on the harmless to knife-slashing spectrum of lunacy. 'Glad we could help, sir.' We thank each other, bow, and I let the escalator whisk me away. I retrieve my backpack from the helpdesk, unhassled, and walk out into the warm traffic fumes. I drop the two disks down the nearest storm drain. From a phone booth near Onizuka TransJapan I try calling Ai at home, then on her mobile, but nothing doing. Quarter to noon. I had better find Onizuka's stepfather and introduce myself. I am so tired nothing seems real.

Eight

The Language of Mountains is Rain

I dribble my soccer ball along a busy shopping mall in downtown Tokyo. No flashy retailing hot spot, this – the shops are all in decline, selling pan-scrubbers in bulk, blouses of thirty summers ago, flimsy exercise aids. Light clots with jellyfish from ancient seas. How or when I won possession of the soccer ball, I cannot say, but here it is – a curse, not a blessing, because the enemy goalposts could be hidden anywhere in Japan. If I pick up the ball, the referee will cut off my hands with rusty shears. If I lose the ball to the enemy, I will be spat at by schoolchildren and bitten by dogs until the day I die. But players are chosen, they do not choose. I must find the enemy goalposts and blast the ball home. Familiar faces eddy by in the stream of shoppers – a Kagoshima music shopkeeper, my father's secretary, Genji the barber, snipping with finger-scissors – but I know that one lapse in concentration is all an enemy player needs to rob the ball. The mall descends into a swampy fog and the air cools. Jellyfish fall from the air and die. I wade through their clear bodies, kneeing the ball along in draining slurps. I know the enemy are tracking me on radar units obtained from Nazi Germany, so why do they let me penetrate so deep into their territory? Here comes Claude Debussy, walking on the swamp-surface in snowshoes. 'In possession, Monsieur Miyake? *Fantastique!*' He stage-whispers: 'I bring a classified message from your great-uncle. One of our team has turned traitor! Trust nobody, not even me!'

'Buntarō?'

'Machiko-san?'

Shooting Star was abandoned years ago. Tatty posters hang by single pins. I bolt the door behind me – a wise precaution, I see, as enemy players unmask themselves and gather on the pavement. The derelict state of the shop is why the enemy chose to hide their goalposts in my capsule. I push the ball behind the counter, and face the problem of the stairway, which is nine times higher than I imagined it. I boot the ball up, but it rebounds back. Meanwhile the enemy batter-ram the window with a wooden statue of the god of laughter – the glass bends, but does not yet break. I grip the ball between my feet, and amphibian-wriggle my way up, step by step. I am nearly at the top when I hear glass smashing. If I wriggle any faster the ball will slip and bounce down to the enemy. The enemy roar – traffic news – the top step – the enemy boom upward – I jam the doorlatch with pool cues.

My capsule is a gloomy warehouse, empty except for building rubble.

Ahead is my glory – the enemy goal.

Mr Ikeda screams in my ear: 'What have you done?'

I turn to face my father. 'I came to score the goal.'

'This is our goal, not the enemy goal! Traitor! You showed them the way!'

The pool cues snap and splinter.

An ogre shakes my knee with one hand and grips the steering wheel with the other. 'You were dreaming, son. Mumbling, you were.' He is a sad ogre. I gaze at my surroundings, clueless. Amulets from temples and shrines festoon the cab of a truck. Ogre's pool-ball eyes aim in different directions. 'Who knows what you were mumbling? Not me. You made no sense at all.' All at once Eiji Miyake and the last seven weeks come back to me. 'No sense in any language ever recorded, that is,' continues Ogre, whose name is Honda, I think, but it is too late to check now. I feel a weird lightness. I met my father this morning. I feel loss, I feel victory, but most of all I feel free. And now, in a perfect reversal of the way I imagined things, I am headed to Miyazaki to see my mother for the first time in six years. At less than 5 kph. Four lanes of traffic, crawling at slug-speed. The dashboard clock blinks 16.47. I have been asleep for over three hours, but still have a hefty overdraft at the bank of sleep. If Suga's mailman virus works the way he boasted, Kozue Yamaya's file has already spread to every e-mail contact on every address book of every e-mail contact on every address book, etc., for ninety-nine generations. That adds up to . . . more computers than there are in Japan, I guess. Way, way beyond the ability of anyone to cover it up. It is out of my hands now, anyway. 'Going nowhere fast past Hadano, we are,' says Ogre. 'Traffic news says a milk-rig overturned ten clicks downstream.' Urban Tokyo has unfolded into zones and charted rice-fields. 'On a fine day,' says Ogre, 'you can see Mount Fuji over to the right.' Drizzle fills the known world. Rain stars go nova on the windscreen, wipered away every ninth beat. Radio burbles. Tyres hiss on the wet Tomei expressway. A minibus of kids from a school for disabled children overtakes on the inside. They wave. Ogre flashes his headlights and the kids go wild. Ogre chuckles. 'Who knows what makes kids tick? Not me. Alien species, kids.' Line after line of hothouses troop by. I feel I should stoke the conversation to pay for my fare, but when I start a sentence a yawn splits my face in two. 'Do you have any kids?'

'No kids, not me. Me and marriage, never in the stars. Many truckers have girls in every port. Say they do, anyway. But me?' Ogre has a story, but it would be rude to probe. 'Cigarette?' Ogre offers me a box of Cabin, and I am about to light up when I remember. 'Sorry, I promised a friend I'd give up.' So I light Ogre's and try to smoke my craving. Traffic nudges. Ogre inhales, leans over the giant steering wheel, and taps ash. 'Was your age, once, believe it or not. Got a job at Showa-Shell driving ginormous tankers. How ginormous? Ginormous. Freight division had its own on-site training programme – those babies are not your regular engine boxes, you get me? Dormitories were ex-barracks, outside Yamagata. Bleak spot, it was, sleet and frost even in March. Fourteen guys, all sharing one long corridor, small partitions for privacy, get the picture?' I rub my eyes. We overtake the kids in their minibus. They press their faces against the glass and do zoo faces. I think of drowning men in submarines. 'Now, I never sleepwalked in my life. Ever. Until my first night in Yamagata. Not just walking – doing things. So, say I dream of walking around my home town: I sleepwalk down the corridor saying, "Afternoon. Nice weather. Afternoon." If I dream of being a famous artist, then we wake up to find toothpaste smeared on the mirrors. Harmless, it was. I always cleaned up my mess. A laugh, us trainees thought. They never woke me up – everyone knows the rule, "Never wake a sleepwalker", although nobody really knows why.' The radio whips and spikes. Ogre tries to retune it. 'I learned why – the worst sixty seconds of my life. One moment, I am strolling around a shady market on a hot day in China. The next moment, two guys are sitting on me, shouting – two others are grabbing a hand each – two others grappling my fingers loose. What was I holding? A cleaver. Taken it from the canteen, I had. Lethal, fuck-off cleaver, the sort you chop up frozen carcasses with. Walked from partition to partition, waking up my co-trainees by tapping them on the side of their heads.' On the road ahead, ambulance lights pulse in the slow dusk. A silver container truck lies on its side. Its cabin is crushed and shredded. A car is being winched on to a pick-up. Traffic controllers wave three lanes into one. They have glowing batons and fluorescent flak jackets. Others hose the road. Ogre strokes an amulet. 'Rock solid, you believe the world is. Then everything jolts and shocks, and it all melts away.' Traffic crawls through a coned bottleneck, and Ogre gropes for his box of Cabin. 'Got a lighter?' I light one for him, wondering if the story is over. 'My dream. Baking hot day in China, it was. I was parched. I came across a watermelon market. Sweet snow watermelons. Would have sold my soul for one, I would. My mother whispered in my ear: "Be careful, son! They'll try to sell you rotten fruit!" Something half buried in the dust catches my eye – a dagger, the sort archaeologists dig up. Walked from stall to stall, tapping watermelons with its blade. From the sound quality, I judged if the flesh was rotten or firm.

I knew: the first good fruit I came to, I would whack in half, and eat it, there and then.' We clear the bottleneck and Ogre begins to climb through the gears. 'Medication stops the sleepwalking. Out cold, I am. But it goes on my licence, so union jobs and hazardous cargo are out. And a wife? And kids? Too afraid of what I might do to them one night, if it starts up again. So you see . . .' Ogre inhales all life from his cigarette. 'Be very careful what you dream.'

'Scientists call it the Ai Imajō Effect.' Her voice is so clear she could be in the next room. 'The brightest minds in psychology have given this mystery their best shot, but results are still inconclusive. Why, oh why, whenever I fix a meal for a man, does he jump on the next truck out of Tokyo?'

I was not expecting a joke. 'I tried calling this morning.'

'It would be handy to blame my mood swings on my old friend diabetes, but really I have to blame my old friend me.'

'No way, Ai, I was—'

'Shut up. No. It was my fault.'

'But—'

'Accept my apology or the friendship is off. Me – of all people – lecturing you on how to behave towards your mother.'

'You were right. My mother called me from Miyazaki. Last night.'

'Sachiko said. Good, but being right is no excuse for being preachy. Anyway. I'm on my piano stool, varnishing my toenails. So where are you, absconder?'

'Being eaten alive by mosquitoes outside a trucker's café called Okachan's.'

'There are ten thousand trucker's cafés called Okachan's.'

'This one is between, uh, nowhere and . . . nowhere.'

'Must be Gifu.'

'I think it is, actually. One truck driver dropped me off here, after calling his mate – called Monkfish – to pick me up when he passes by on his way to Fukuoka. Before me, he has a fist-fight with a crooked gas station attendant who made improper suggestions about his wife.'

'Pray he wins unconcussed. Poor Miyake – stuck in a Nikkatsu trucker film.'

'This is not the fastest way to Kyūshū, but it is the cheapest. I have news.'

'What?'

'Put your nail varnish down. I don't want you to stain your piano stool.'

'What is it?'

'For the last nine years I grew up in the quietest village on the quietest island in the quietest prefecture in Japan. Nothing happened. Kids say that everywhere, but on Yakushima it really is true. Since I saw you last, everything that never happened, happened. It was the weirdest day I ever lived through. And when I tell you who I met this morning—'

'It sounds as if I should call you back. Give me the number.'

'Eiji!' She perches on the high windowsill, hugging her knees. Bamboo shadows sway and shoo on the tatami and faded fusuma. 'Eiji! Come quickly!' I get up and walk to the window. Dental-floss cobwebs. From the window of my grandmother's house I see Ueno park, but everyone has gone home. But there is Anju, kneeling before an ancient shipwreck of a cedar. I climb out. Anju's kite of sunlight is tangled in the highest branches. It shines dark gold. Anju is in despair. 'Look! My kite is caught!' I kneel down with her – seeing her in tears is unbearable – and try to cheer her up. 'Why don't you set it free? You're fantastic at climbing trees!' Anju airs her recently acquired sigh. 'Diabetes, genius, remember?' She points down – her legs are a pin-cushion of syringes, drips and torture instruments. 'Set it free for me, Eiji.' So I begin climbing – my fingers claw at the reptile bark. Sheep bray in a far valley. I find a pair of my discarded socks, dirty beyond redemption. After a lifetime dark rises, winds swirl, crows come looking for soft places. I am afraid the sunlit kite will rip and shred before I can get to it. Where in this storm of leaves can it be? Minutes later I find him on the top branch. A man still without a face. 'Why are you climbing my tree?' he asks. 'I was looking for my sister's kite,' I explain. He frowns. 'Chasing kites is more important than taking care of your own sister?' Suddenly I realize I have left Anju alone – for how many days? – in our grandmother's house without thinking about food or water. Who will open her canned dinner? My concern is heightened when I see how tumbledown the place is now – shrubs grow out of the eaves, and one harsh winter would topple the house. Has it really been nine years? The lockless knob twizzles uselessly – when I knock the entire door frame falls inward. Cat shadows slide behind rafters. In my capsule is my guitar case. And in the guitar case is Anju. She cannot open the escape hatches from the inside, and she is running out of air – I hear her knocking helplessly, I scramble, scrabble, but the locks are so rusty—

'And I woke up and it was all a dream!' Monkfish glows in the dashboard lights, all skin and string vest. Croaked laughter, one two three. He has the rubberiest lips any human being had, ever. I am in another truck crossing rainy hyperspace. A road sign flies by at light speed – Meishin expressway *Ōtsu exit 9 km.* The dashboard clock glows 21.09. 'Funny things, dreams,' says Monkfish. 'Did Honda tell you his sleepwalking story? Load of crap. Fact is, ladies find him repulsive. Plain and simple. Dreams. I read up on 'em. Nobody really knows what dreams are. Your scientists, they disagree. One camp says your hippocampus shuffles through memories in your brain's left side. Then your brain's right side cobbles together tall stories to link the images.' Monkfish does not expect me to say anything back – he would be having this conversation with the Zizzi Hikaru doll if I were not here. *Kyoto exit 18 km.* 'More like scriptwriting than dreaming. Whatever.' A hairy fly strolls across the windscreen. 'Ever tell you my dream story? We all have one. I was your age. I was in love. Or maybe mentally ill. Same difference. Whatever. She – Kirara, her name was – was one of those pampered daughters-in-a-box. We went to the same swimming club. I had quite a body in my day. Daddy was the fascist mastermind of some evil organization. What was it? Oh yeah, the Ministry of Education. Which put Kirara way above my class. Made no difference. I was obsessed. I copied out a love poem from a book at school. I got a kiss! I still have this goaty appeal to the fairer sex, and Kirara succumbed. We started going out in my cousin's car for sessions at the reservoir. Counted the stars. Counted her birthmarks. Never knew bliss like that, never will again. But then her father got wind of our dalliance. I was not prince material for her princess. Whatever. One word from Daddy and she dropped me like a scabby corpse. Even changed swimming club. For Kirara, I was just an entrée to be nibbled, but to me, she was the entire menu at the restaurant of love. Well, I was distraught. Insane. I sent her more poems. Kirara ignored them. I stopped sleeping, eating, thinking. I decided to prove my devotion by killing myself. I planned to hike out to the Sea of Trees at the foot of Mount Fuji and overdose on sleeping pills. Hardly original, I know, but I was eighteen and my uncle had a forest cabin out there. The morning I left, I posted a letter to Kirara saying that as I couldn't live without her love I had no choice but to die, and describing where I would perform the deed – not much point dying for love if nobody notices, is there? Took the first train out, got off at a quiet country station and started hiking. The weather grew uncertain, but me, never. I was never so sure about a decision in my life. I found my uncle's cabin, and walked past it until I came to a glade. This was the place, I decided. And guess what I see, up in the air.'

'Uh . . . a bird?'

'Kirara! My beloved with a noose around her neck! Feet doing the clockwise-anti-clockwise biz. What a sight! Bloated, shitted, crows and maggots already at work.'

'That is . . .'

'So ghastly that I woke up, still on the early train to Mount

Fuji. Talk about a revelation! I got off at the next station, caught the next train back home. I found my suicide note, unread and unopened, on my doormat, *Return to Sender* scrawled across the front in blood-red pen. Kirara – or her father – returned it without even reading it. Did I feel stupid? Then she went off to university, and . . .' Monkfish slows to let a truck pass. The driver waves. 'Saw Kirara again, years later. At Kansai airport, from a distance. Flash husband, gold jangly things, brat in a pushchair. Guess what flashed through my head?'

'Jealousy?'

'Nothing. I felt not – one – thing. I was ready to hang myself for her, but I never even loved her. Not really. Only thought I did.' We enter a tunnel of echoes and air. 'Stories like that need morals. This is my moral. Trust what you dream. Not what you think.'

More tunnels, valley bridges, service stations. The truck judders down Chūgoku expressway to dawn. A twenty-first-century thirty minutes covers distances of days for noblemen and priests in earlier centuries. Half-rain, half-mist, half-speed windscreen wipers. Shapes get their names back, and names their shapes. Islands in estuaries. Herons fishing. Lavender concrete mixers sealing riverbanks. Bricked-up hillside tunnels. A beer crate depot, unending and uniform as Utopia. I imagine my mother lying awake, hundreds of kilometres ahead, thinking about me. I am still shocked at how I invited myself to Miyazaki. Is she as surprised? Is she as nervous as I am now? *Okayama exit.* Smoke unravelling from factory stacks. Monkfish hums a tune over and over again. Vehicles rule the highways, not their drivers – trucks change drivers as easily as oil. The visits our mother made to Yakushima were torture. Between the time she dumped us and the day Anju drowned she turned up about once a year. *Fukuyama exit.* Flame licking the corner of a mist-field. Land cleared of trees in a week, levelled in a month, asphalted in an afternoon – forgotten ever since. Cracked, greened, smothered and uprooted.

Lines and wires, sagging and tautening from pole to pole, fingers of speed jamming on a loose-strung guitar. My grandmother refused to see her, so we always stayed at Uncle Pachinko's in Kamiyaku – the main port – the night before. We always wore our school uniform. Aunt Pachinko took us to the barber's especially. Everybody knew, of course. She took a taxi from the ferryside, even though Uncle Pachinko's house is less than ten minutes on foot. She would be shown into the best room, returning our aunt's small talk with a savage attention to pointless detail. *Hiroshima exit.* Monkfish turns off the wipers. Hoardings advertise a bank that crashed many months back. Mountains, marching back years to the Sea of Japan coast. Non-coloured suburbs of rerun cities. Uncle Tarmac told me years later – after a six-pack of beer – that Uncle Pachinko made our mother visit, as a condition of the allowance he sent her. He meant well, I guess, but it was wrong to force us together. We answered the questions she asked. Always the same questions, ducking the hazardous topics: What subjects did we like best at school? What subjects did we like least at school? What did we do after school? We spoke in the manner of inspector and inspected. No glimmer of fondness. *Tokuyama exit.* This is where Subaru Tsukiyama, my great-uncle, spent his final weeks in Japan. He would not recognize Yamaguchi prefecture today. A golf-range hacked out of a hill, shrouded in green netting. Micro-figures swing. I re-remember the mailman virus, and wonder if it is still spreading Kozue Yamaya's ugly news. It feels nothing to do with me, now. Visible consequences are iceberg tips: most results of most actions are invisible to the doer. A dirty rag of bleached sky – the morning forgets it was raining, as suddenly as a child forgetting a sulk she planned to last years. Anju would have been more chatty with our mother, I think, but she sensed my distrust and she clammed up too. Our mother chain-smoked. Every image I have of her is dim with cigarette smoke. Aunt Pachinko never asked her questions about herself, at least not in front of us, so all we knew was what we overheard behind partitions. Then she took the late afternoon jetfoil back to Kagoshima, and everyone breathed a sigh of relief. Once, she stayed two days – that must have been when Anju saw our mother tempura her ring – but the extended visit was never repeated. *Yamaguchi exit.* A tree moves by itself on a windless hillside. The mountains level out. She was away for Anju's funeral. Gossip, the island blood sport, reported that she flew to Guam for 'work' the day before Anju died, without leaving an emergency telephone number. Other stories did the rounds, too, less sympathetic ones. I armoured myself in three-inch thick indifference towards her. The last time we met – and the only time without Anju – I was fourteen. It was in Kagoshima, at Uncle Money's old place. Her hair was short and her jewellery was garish. She wore dark glasses. I was there under orders. I guess she was, too. 'You've grown, Eiji,' she said when I shambled into the room and sat down. I was determined to be disagreeable. 'You haven't.' Aunt Money hurriedly said, 'Eiji's rocketed up over the last months. And his music teacher says he's a natural guitar player. Such a pity you didn't bring your guitar, Eiji. Your mother would have loved to have heard you.'

I spoke to the bridge of her glasses. 'A mother? I don't have one of those, Aunt. She died before Anju drowned. I have a father somewhere, but no mother. You know that.'

My mother hid herself with cigarette smoke.

Aunt Money poured tea. 'Your mother has come a long way to see you, and I think you should apologize.' I was ready to stand up and walk out, but my mother beat me to it. She collected her handbag and turned to Aunt Money. 'There really is no need. He said nothing I disagree with. What I disagree with is forcing us to endure these family discussions when there is quite clearly no family and nothing to discuss. I know you act out of niceness, but niceness can leave nastiness for dead when you count the damage. Give my regards to my brother. There is an overnight train for Tokyo in fifty minutes and I intend to be on it.' Maybe the passing years have altered the script a little, but this is the gist of what was said. Maybe I added her dark glasses, too, but I have no memory of my mother's eyes.

Monkfish opens a can of coffee and switches on the radio. The sun switches on, too, as we cross Shimonoseki bridge. I am back on Kyūshū. I smile for no reason. A soul returning to a body it gave up for dead, amazed to find that everything still works – this is how I feel. Broken fences, wildflower riots, unplotted space. Kyūshū is the run-wild underworld of Japan. All myths slithered, galloped or swam from Kyūshū. Monkfish remembers I am here. 'As my dear old mum said, every single morning, "Rise early – the first hour is a gift from paradise." Whatever. Twenty minutes to Kitakyūshū . . .'

♦

'Mr Aoyama! Please accept my sincerest condolences on, uh, your death.'

Mr Aoyama lowers his binoculars and fiddles with the focusing. He is wearing his JR uniform, but looks much more distinguished than he ever did at Ueno. 'Death is not so bad, Miyake, not when it actually happens. It is like being paid. And I must apologize for accusing you of espionage.'

'Forget it. You were under loads of stress. Obviously.'

Mr Aoyama strokes his upper lip – 'I shaved off my moustache.'

'Good move, Station-master. It never suited you, to be honest.'

'One should commemorate major life shifts, I believe.'

'And you don't get much more major than death.'

'Indeed, Miyake.'

'May I ask how I died?'

'You are very much alive! Your body is on the Kitakyūshū-Miyazaki coach. This is only a dream.'

'I never had such an . . . undreamlike dream before.'

'Dreams of the living can be calibrated by their Dead. Look closely—'

We are flying. Mr Aoyama is flying Superman-freestyle. I have a Zax Omega jetpack strapped to my pack. Below us are pink meringue clouds. Reams of Earth unroll away. 'Another privilege we dead are afforded – unlimited freedom to marvel at the majesty of creation.'

'Are you my Dead?'

'I hired you and you hired me.'

'Why has Anju never visited?'

'Quite.' Mr Aoyama checks his watch. 'The matter in hand.'

'Do the dead really, uh, mingle with the living?'

'No big deal.'

'You can really see . . . everything?' I think of my Zizzi Hikaru sessions.

'If we so choose. But would you bother watching a billion-channel TV? So little warrants attention. Wrongdoers imagine their sordid crimes to be so unique, but if only they knew. No. My purpose in your dream this morning is redemption.'

'Uh . . . yours or mine?'

'Ours. I treated you poorly at Ueno. Even if you did spit in my teapot.'

'I feel bad about that.'

Mr Aoyama looks through his binoculars. 'Newspapers of two days hence will be bad beyond belief. Look. Redemption approaches.' Mr Aoyama points downward. The clouds part, as in ancient scrolls – and I see the secret beach, foot rock and the whalestone. Sitting on the whalestone is a girl, hunched up, miserably alone. Anju, of course. 'Unfinished business, Miyake.'

'I don't understand.'

'You will.'

My jetpack misfires and dies. My mother – a face on the jacket of a horror video – but already she and the ninth-floor balcony hurtle away into the Tokyo sky. I spin, see a playground flying this way at terminal velocity, and remember that if I don't wake up before I hit the ground I—

♠

I awake with a 'Gaaaghhh!' on the back seat of a coach – its doors hiss shut as it lurches forward. I sit up, blinking. Yes, the coach.

Monkfish offered to ask around some Kitakyūshū truckers for a ride south to Miyazaki, but my mother is expecting me early this afternoon. I don't want to risk being late. An old lady has joined me on the back seat since I fell asleep. She knits, has a face as round and chipped as the moon, and does aromatherapy, I guess, because I can smell . . . a herb with a name I can't remember. She is sunburned shiny orange. Between us is a basket of persimmons. Not watery Tokyo persimmons – these are persimmons from tales. Persimmons worth risking the wrath of enchanters to steal. I drool – I have eaten nothing but crap for a day and a half. 'I propose a barter,' says Mrs Persimmon. 'One persimmon for your dream.'

Embarrassing. 'Was I mumbling?'

She keeps her eyes on her stitches. 'I collect dreams.'

So I tell her my dream, leaving out the fact that Anju is my sister. Her knitting needles make the sound of swords clashing on a distant hill. 'I will not be short-changed, young man. What did you omit?' So I admit that Anju is my twin sister. Mrs Persimmon considers. 'When did she leave, this unfortunate?'

'Leave where?'

'This side, of course.'

'This side of . . .'

'Life.' No, her knitting needles make the sound of a blind man's stick.

'Nine years ago. How did you know?'

'I shall be eighty-one on Thursday week.' Her mind is wandering, or mine is plodding. She yawns. Tiny, white teeth. I think of Cat. She unpicks a stitch. 'Dreams are shores where the ocean of spirit meets the land of matter. Beaches where the yet-to-be, the once-were, the will-never-be may walk amid the still-are. You believe I am an old woman hoary with superstition, and possibly deranged to boot.' I could not have put it that well. 'Of course I am deranged. How else could I know what I know?'

I am afraid of offending her, so I ask what she thinks my dream means.

She smiles toothily. She knows I am patronizing her. 'You are wanted.'

'Wanted? By . . . ?'

'I do not give free consultations. Take your persimmon, boy.'

Miyazaki is toytown after Tokyo. At the bus station I go to the tourist information office to ask about the clinic where my mother is staying. Nobody has heard of it, but when I show the address I am told I will need to get on a local bus headed for Kirishima. The next one is not for over an hour, so I go to the station bathroom, clean my teeth, and sit down in the waiting room drinking a can of sweet cold coffee, watching the buses and passengers come and go. Miyazaki people amble. The clouds are in no hurry and a fountain makes rainbows under palm trees. A retired dog with cloudy eyes comes to sniff hello. A very pregnant mother tries to control a clutch of floppy, spring-heeled children. I remember my persimmon – my grandmother says pregnant women must never eat persimmons – and peel it with my penknife. I get sticky fingers, but the fruit is pearly and perfect. I spit out shiny stones. One of the boys has just learned to whistle but he can only do one tune. The mother watches the kids leap along the plastic seats. I wonder where their father is. Only when they start playing with a fire extinguisher does she say anything: 'If you touch that, the bus men will be angry!' I go for a walk. In a gift shop still with its unsold 1950s stock I find a bowl of faded plastic fruit with smiley faces. I buy it for Buntarō to get him back for my Zizzi key-holder. At a Lawsons I buy a tube of champagne bombs and read magazines until the bus arrives. I should be nervous, I guess, but I lack the energy. I don't know what day it is, even.

I expect a smartish institution with carparks and wheelchair ramps on the outskirts of town – instead, the bus follows a lane deep into the countryside. Over a thousand yen later a farmer on the bus points me down a country road and tells me to walk until the road becomes a track and the track runs out. 'Can't miss it,' he insists, which usually spells disaster. A hillside of pines sheers up on one side; on the other, early rice is being harvested and hung out to dry. I find a big, flat, round stone on the track. Crickets trill and ratchet in Morse. I put the stone in my backpack. The cosmos is flowering mauve, magenta and white. All this space. All this air. I walk, and walk. I begin to worry – after twenty minutes I can see the end of the lane, but there is still no clinic in sight. Comic-horror scarecrows leer. Big heads, bony necks. The road runs out of tarmac, and I can see that the track dies altogether at a group of old farm buildings at the foot of an early autumn mountain. Sweat pools in the small of my back – I must smell none too fresh. Did the bus driver let me off at the wrong stop? I decide to ask at the farmhouse. A skylark stops singing and the silence is loud. Vegetable plots, sunflowers, blue sheets hanging in the sun. A traditional thatched teahouse stands on a small rise in a rockery taken over by couch grass. I am already past the gate when I see the hand-painted sign: Miyazaki Mountain Clinic. Despite the signs of life, nobody is around. I see no bell or buzzer near the front door, so I just open the door and enter a cool reception room where a woman – a cleaner? – in a white uniform is organizing mountains of files into hills. It is a losing battle. She sees me. 'Hi.'

'Hello. Could I, uh, speak to the nurse in charge, please?'

'You can speak with me, if you like. Suzuki. Doctor. You are?'

'Uh, Eiji Miyake. I'm here to meet my mother – a patient. Mariko Miyake.'

Dr Suzuki makes an ahaaaaaaaa noise. 'And a very welcome guest you are too, Eiji Miyake. Yes, our prodigal sister has been on tenterhooks all morning. We prefer the word 'members' to 'patients', if that doesn't sound too cultish. We were expecting you to call from Miyazaki: did you have any trouble finding us? I'm afraid we are rather a long way out. I believe solitude can be therapeutic in our hemmed-in lives. Have you eaten? Everyone is having lunch in the refectory.'

'I had a rice-ball on the bus . . .'

Doctor Suzuki sees I am nervous about meeting my mother with an audience looking on. 'Why don't you wait in the teahouse, then? We are rather proud of it – one of our members was a tea-master, and will be again, if I have any say in the matter. He modelled it on Senno-Soyeki's teahouse. I'll go tell your mother her visitor is here.'

'Doctor—'

Dr Suzuki swivels around on one foot. 'Yes?'

'Nothing.'

I think she smiles. 'Just be who you are.'

I take off my shoes and sit in the cool, four-and-a-half-mat hut. I watch the humming garden. Bees, runner beans, lavender. I drink some barley tea – warm now, and frothed up – from the bottle I bought in Miyazaki. Kneeling on the ceiling, a papyrus butterfly folds its wings. I lie back and close my eyes, just for a moment.

New York billows snow and grey crows. I know the driver of my big yellow taxi, but her name escapes while I look for it. I wade through journalists and their bug-eyed lenses into the recording studio, where John Lennon is swigging his barley tea. 'Eiji! Your guitar had given up all hope.' Since I was twelve, I have wanted to meet this demi-god. My dream has come true, and my English is a hundred times better than I dared hope, but all I can think of to say is 'Sorry I'm late, Mr Lennon'. The great man shrugs exactly like Yuzu Daimon. 'After nine years of learning my songs you can call me John. Call me anything. Except Paul.' We all laugh at this. 'Let me introduce you to the rest of the band. Yoko you already met at Karuizawa one summer, on our bicycles—' Yoko Ono is dressed like the Queen of Spades. 'It's all right, Sean,' she tells me, 'Mummy's only looking for her hand in the snow.' This strikes us as very funny indeed. John Lennon then points to the piano. 'And on keyboards, ladies and genitals, may I introduce Mr Claude Debussy.' The composer sneezes and a tooth flies out, which causes a new round of laughter – yet more teeth fall out, causing yet more laughter. 'My pianist friend, Ai Imajō,' I tell Debussy, 'worships your work. She won a scholarship for the Paris Conservatoire, only her father has forbidden her to go.' My French is perfect, too! 'Then her father is a beshatted boar with pox,' says Debussy, on his knees to gather up his teeth. 'And your Ms Imajō is a woman of distinction. Tell her to go! I always had a penchant for Asian ladies.'

I am in Ueno park, among the bushes and tents where the homeless people live. I feel this is a slightly inappropriate place for an interview, but it was John's idea. 'John – what is "Tomorrow Never Knows" actually about?'

John pulls a philosopher pose. 'I never knew.'

We giggle helplessly. 'But you wrote it!'

'No, Eiji, I never . . .' He dabs his tears away. 'It wrote me!'

At that moment Doi lifts the tent flap and delivers a pizza. When we open the box, it contains cannabis compost. Picture Lady – it seems we are her guests – produces a cake knife with a polished stoat skull. We are each served a thin slice – it tastes of green tea. 'Which is your favourite song by John, Eiji-kun?' I realize that Picture Lady is in fact Kozue Yamaya working undercover – we all laugh at this.

'"#9dream",' I answer. 'It should be considered a masterpiece.'

John is delighted with this answer, and mimes an Indian deity, singing, '*Ah, bowakama pousse pousse.*' Even the perspex whale outside the science museum giggles. My lungs fill up with laughter and I am having serious trouble breathing. 'Truth is,' John continues, '"#9dream" is a descendant of "Norwegian Wood". Both are ghost stories. "She" in "Norwegian Wood" curses you with loneliness. The "Two spirits dancing so strange" in "#9dream" bless you with harmony. But people prefer loneliness to harmony.'

'What does the title mean?'

'The ninth dream begins after every ending.'

A guru is furious. 'Why are you quitting your search for enlightenment?'

'If you're so bloody cosmic,' scoffs John, 'you'll know why!'

I am laughing so hard that I—

♦

'I woke up. And there was my mother, standing in the tea house entrance.'

Ai turns her music off. 'You giggled yourself awake? What must she have thought?'

'Later, she admitted she thought I was having a seizure. Even later, she said that Anju used to laugh in her sleep when she was a toddler.'

'You talked for quite a long time?'

'Three hours. Right through the midday heat. I just got back to Miyazaki.'

'Neither of you were exactly lost for words, then?'

'I dunno . . . A sort of unspoken agreement happened. She dropped any "Mother" role, and I dropped any sort of "Son" role.'

'From what you told me, you never played those roles.'

'True. What I mean is, I agreed to not judge her against a "Mother" standard, and she agreed not to compare me to a "Son" standard.'

'So . . . where does that leave you now?'

'I guess we'll start as, uh, sort of . . .'

'Friends?'

'I don't want to pretend this was a summer of love and peace festival. There was a minefield of stuff we both skirted around, that we will have to face, one day. But . . . I sort of liked her. She is real person. A real woman.'

'Even I could have told you that.'

'I know, but I always thought of her as a magazine cut-out who did *this* and did *this* but who never actually felt anything. Today, I saw her as a woman in her forties who has not had as easy a life as the rumour machine on Yakushima reckons. When she talks, she is in her words. Not like her letters. She told me about alcoholism, about what it does to you. Not blaming it or anything, just like a scientist analysing a disease. And guess what – my guitar? It turns out to be hers! All these years, my guitar was her guitar, and I never even knew she could play.'

'Was the hotelier from Nagano there?'

'He visits every two weekends: not today. But I promised to go back next Saturday.'

'Good. Ensure his intentions are honourable. And your real father?'

'That was one of the minefield issues. Another time, maybe. She asked how I liked Tokyo, and if I had any friends. I boasted about my one friend, the genius pianist.'

'What an élite club. Where are you staying tonight?'

'Dr Suzuki offered to find a futon in a corner somewhere, but I'm catching a train down to Kagoshima to stay with my uncle—'

'Uncle Money, right? And tomorrow morning you board the Yakushima ferry and visit your sister's gravestone.'

'How did you know?'

Urgent clouds stream across a cinema sky.

'I do listen when you tell me about Anju, you know. And your dreams. I have perfect pitch.'

The bored horizon yawns. These tidal flats touch the Hyuga Nada Sea, south of Bungo Straits, where my great-uncle sailed on his final voyage aboard the *I-333*. If binoculars were powerful enough to bring the 1940s into focus, we could wave at one another. Maybe I will dream him, too. Time may be what prevents everything from happening at the same time in waking reality, but the rules are different in dreams. I smell autumn fruit. 'My, what a small world,' says Mrs Persimmon. 'Hello again. May I sit here?'

'Sure.' I dump my backpack on the overhead rack.

She sits as if afraid of bruises. 'And did you enjoy my persimmon?'

'Uh, it was delicious. Thank you. How was my dream?'

'Had better.' The weird old lady pulls her knitting out.

'May I ask, what do you do with the dreams you, uh, gather?'

'What do you do with persimmons?'

'I eat persimmons.'

'Old ladies also require nourishment.'

I wait for an explanation, but Mrs Persimmon gives none. A nuclear power station slides by, a frigate at anchor, a lonesome windsurfer. I feel I should make polite conversation. 'Are you going to Kagoshima?'

'Between here and there.'

'Are you seeing relatives?'

'I attend conferences.'

I wait for her to tell me what sort of conference eighty-year-olds attend – fruit farming? Stitchwork? – but she concentrates on her knitting. I think of atoms decaying. 'Are you some sort of dream interpreter?'

Her irisless eyes are not safe to look into for very long. 'My younger sister, who handles the business side of things, describes our profession as that of "channellers".'

I assume I mishear. 'You collect Chanel accessories?'

'Do I appear to be such a person?'

Try again. 'Channeller? Is that, uh, a sort of engineer?'

Mrs Persimmon shakes her head in mild exasperation. 'I told my sister. This word-meddling confuses people. We are witches, I told her, so "witches" is what we should call ourselves. I have to begin this row again. This is a scarf for my grandmother. She moans if it isn't perfect.'

'Excuse me – did you say you are a witch?'

'Semi-retired, since I turned five hundred. I believe in making room for the young ones.'

She is winding me up very wittily, or she is beyond mad. 'I would never have guessed.'

She frowns at her knitting. 'Of course not. Your world is lit by television, threaded by satellites, cemented by science. The idea of women fuelling their lifespans by energy released in dreams is as you say, beyond mad.'

I hunt for an appropriate answer.

'No matter. Disbelief is good for business. When the Age of Reason reached these shores, it was us who breathed the deepest sigh of relief.'

'How can you, uh, eat dreams?'

'You are too modern to understand. A dream is a fusion of spirit and matter. Fusion releases energy – hence sleep, with dreams, refreshes. In fact, without dreams, you cannot hold on to your mind for more than a week. Old ladies of my longevity feed on the dreams of healthy youngsters such as yourself.'

'Is it wise to go around telling people all this?'

'Whyever not? Anyone insisting it were true would be locked up.'

I vaguely regret eating that persimmon. 'I, uh, need to use the bathroom.' Walking to the toilets it seems that the train is standing still but the landscape and I are flying by the same swaying speed. My travelling companion is beginning to scare me – not so much what she says, but how she says it. I wonder how I should handle her. But when I return to my seat I find she has gone.

♦

Red plague eradicated all human life from the globe. The last crow has picked the last flesh from the last bone. Ai and I alone survive, thanks to our natural immunity. We live in Amadeus Tea Room. Satellites' orbits spin lower and lower, and now the electronic rafts float by our balcony, near enough to touch. Ai and I entertain ourselves by going on long walks through Tokyo. I choose diamonds for Ai, and Ai picks the finest guitars for me. Ai performs Debussy's *Arabesque* live at the Budōkan, then I run through my Lennon repertoire. We take it in turns to be the audience. Ai still makes delicious salads, and serves them in TV dishes. We have lived this way, as brother and sister, for a long time.

One day we hear a meeeeeeeeep noise on the balcony. Meeeeeeeeep. We peer out, through the ajar window, and see a hideous bird strolling towards us. Pig-big, turkey-scrotumed, condor-shaggy. Its beak is a hacksaw blade. Its alcoholic eyes are weeping sores. Every few steps it vomits up an eyeball egg, and then sits on it, wriggling to push it up its butt-hole. 'Quick!' says Ai. 'Close the window! It wants to get in!' She is right, but I hesitate – that beak could sever my wrist in one snap. Too late! The bird leaps in, flumphing off a chair, rolling on to the carpet. Ai and I take a step back, afraid, but curious. Great evil might follow, but so might great good. The bird struts and peers at the decor with the critical eye of a potential buyer. It finally roosts on a wedding cake, and says – its voice is Doi's – 'The cat in the wig on the ceiling will have to go, man, and that is just for starters. Dig?'

'You again, Miyake!' says Ai, but she sounds pleased. 'I saw on the news, Kagoshima has a typhoon warning. Are you there already?'

'Not yet. I have to change trains at' – I read the sign – 'Miyakonojō.'

'Never heard of it.'

'Only train drivers know it. Am I interrupting anything?'

'I was smooching with a very sexy Italian called Domenico Scarlatti.'

'Just to make me and Claude jealous.'

'Scarlatti is even more dead than Debussy. But wow, his sonatas . . .'

'I had this dream: you were in it, with this scabby turkey—'

'Eiji Miyake and his killer charm. This is why you called me?'

'No, actually I called you to tell you that, uh, when I woke up I realized I am probably in love with you, and that I thought it was the sort of thing you ought to know about.'

'You are *probably* in love with me? That must be the most romantic thing any man ever said to me'

'I said "probably" because I was afraid of seeming too forward. But if you insist, uh, yes, I am definitely in love with you.'

'Why tell me this now, when you are a thousand kilometres

away? Why didn't you make a pass at me when I visited your capsule?'

'Did you want me to?'

'You thought I trekked out to Kita Senju for your pre-dinner conversation?'

An egg cracks on my head and yolky happiness dribbles. 'Why didn't you say anything?'

'You are the man. *You* have to take *your* dignity and self-respect to the pawnbrokers.'

'That is so unfair, Miss Imajō.'

'Unfair? Try being a woman some time.'

'This has crept up on me. I didn't know about it when you visited. I mean, I certainly wouldn't have thrown you out if, uh . . . but then I went and showed you the letters, and . . .'

'It took a dream of a putrid turkey.'

'Scabby, not putrid. And it was sort of cute, too. Do you mind?'

'I have Scarlatti's permission to play you K.8 in G minor. Allegro.'

Ai performs until my phonecard dies. I think she likes me.

The train pulls into Kagoshima JR under an end-of-the-world evening sky. Ghosts of K.8 in G minor tango, waltz and chicken-dance inside my head. Every time I think of the girl my heart sort of squid-propels itself. The conductor announces that owing to typhoon eighteen, all train services are cancelled until further notice – tomorrow morning, at the earliest. Half the passengers groan in unison. The conductor adds that bus and streetcar services have also been suspended. The other half groan in unison. I have an immediate problem that love will not fix. Uncle Money lives over the ridge of hills to the north of Kagoshima – it takes two hours on foot. I call him, hoping to blag a lift, but the line is engaged. I guess I should walk to the port and doss down in the ferry terminal. Powerful gusts of wind kick-box across the bus square. Palm trees take the strain, banners flap, cardboard boxes run for their lives. Nobody is about, and businesses are closing early. Turning the corner into Port Boulevard, I nearly get picked up and free-kicked to Nagasaki by a juggernaut wind. I lean into it to walk. Sakurajima the volcano island is there but not quite real tonight. The dark sea is crazed with waves. A hundred metres later I see I am in serious trouble – the electronic signboard says the entire terminal complex is closed. I could get a taxi to Uncle Money's – too embarrassing, as he would have to pay. I could stay in a hotel – and then not be able to pay in the morning. Being poor sucks sometimes. I could beg for mercy in a police box – no. I could shelter in an arcade doorway – maybe not. I decide to walk to Uncle Money's after all – I'll be there by about nine o'clock. I take a short cut across the school pitch where I scored the only goal of my short career, nine years ago. Grit swarms and claws at my eyes. I walk past the station and push on along the coastal road, but walking is wading and progress is slow. No cars. I try to get through to Uncle Money from a callbox, but it sounds as if the lines are down now. Unaerodynamic objects sail by – car shrouds, beer crates, tricycles. Sea booms, wind wails, salt water banzais the sea defences and spray slaps me. I walk past a roofed bus shelter without a roof. I consider stopping at one of these houses and asking if I can sleep in the entrance hall. I walk past a tree with a bus-shelter roof embedded in its trunk. Then I hear a whoooooosh. I crouch on reflex, and a black animal bounds by – a tractor tyre! I am now afraid of winding up as road mush. I draw level with Iso-teien garden. I was brought here on school outings and I remember brick buildings with alcoves which I can probably shelter in. I scale the wall – the wind flicks me over the top, and I land in thrashing bougainvillea. The peaceful summer garden is now a demonic possession movie. A madwoman is banging a door, over and over. Over there – I scramble, pummel, swim – flying twigs sting my face. Up a steep slope, and I trip into the hut. Compost smell, tarpaulin, twine – I am in a potting shed. The latch is smashed, but I drag over a sack of soil and succeed in wedging fast the door. The whole structure judders, but any inside is better than outside. My eyes adjust to the darkness. A whole arsenal of spades, trowels, gardening forks, rakes. There is a narrow partition down one wall but it is too dark to see behind. First, I gather up the pots and repair the damage caused by the wind's break-in as best I can. Second, I arrange a makeshift bed. Third, I finish a bottle of green tea that I bought at Miyakowherever. Fourth, I lie down, listen to the typhoon rhino-whipping the old structure, and worry. Fifth, I give up worrying and try to identify single voices in this lunatic roaring choir.

♠

My bladder is outside my body – a golden embryo-shaped sac. It sags painfully off my groin. I am in Liverpool – I know this because of the mini cars and bee-hive haircuts – and I am looking for a toilet. Gravity is stronger in England – hauling myself up the steps of this cathedral exhausts me. The door is a manhole. I shuffle through on my back to keep my bladder-baby safe on my stomach. 'One moment, Captain!' says Lao Tzu from behind a wire grille. 'You need an entrance ticket.'

'I already paid at the airport.'

'You didn't pay enough. Cough up another ten thousand yen.'

This is an exorbitant price, but I either pay or piss my pants. With difficulty, I extract my wallet, roll up the note, and post it through the grille. Lao Tzu rips it in two, and scrunches it up his nostrils to plug a nosebleed. 'So. Which way is the toilet?' I ask. Lao Tzu looks at my swelling bladder. 'I had better show you the way.' Liverpool Cathedral is a tiled rat-run maze. Lao Tzu crawls ahead on his belly. I backstroke after him. Water slides down the walls in curtains. Sometimes sprinklers erupt in my face. My bladder-baby begins to wail with the voice of a seal dragged inland against its will. 'Are we nearly there yet?' I gasp. I stand up in a grotto. Stalactites drip. A row of men in uniforms occupy the urinals. I wait. I wait. But none of the men moves.

'Colonel Sanders!' General MacArthur claps my shoulder. 'One of the natives stole my platinum lighter! Worth a fortune, dammit!

Heard anything on the grapevine?' I have been encased in the body of the chicken magnate to spy on GHQ, and to discover if they know anything about the kaiten project. How weird to be so fat. I know unseen meanings flow beneath the words, but it is hard to focus with a singing bladder. 'No?' General MacArthur sneezes a fountain. 'Lemme give you a lift to the port, anyhow.' The US Jeep drives to Kagoshima port. My bladder is now a child clinging to my waist. I am afraid she may be punctured by a sudden jolt of the Jeep, but we get to the ferry terminal without mishap. Unfortunately, the complex has been rebuilt since the war, and all the signs are in Braille. I consider pissing into a trashcan, but I am afraid of the headlines – 'Local Boy Miyake Forgets Toilet Training' – and stumble down a corridor. Urine streams in pulses from a dying beagle. My bladder is nearly too heavy to carry. 'This way,' hisses an invisible companion. I find a brand-new toilet as vast as an airport. Floor, wall, ceiling, fittings, sinks, urinals, cubicle doors – snow-blind white. The only other patron is a speck in the distance. A lawyer. I go up to the nearest urinal, hold my golden twin against the wall, and—

The lawyer hums 'Beautiful Boy' in such an offputting way my bladder corks up. I glare at him and jump with shock – he is standing right next to me, pissing away. He still has no face.

I awake with an hysterical bladder to a hideous shipwreck noise very near. The typhoon batters back the door when I shift the sack of earth. I piss through the crack. The urine flies off and probably reaches the Sea of China. I go back to my nest of tarpaulin, but nothing can sleep through this night sky violence. The god of thunder is stamping over Kagoshima, looking for me. I wonder why my dreams are so clear – usually they evaporate the moment my eyes open. When I began my serial uncle visits, post-Anju, I imagined there lived somewhere, in an advertland house and family, the Real Eiji Miyake. He dreamed of me every night. And that was who I really was – a dream of the Real Eiji Miyake. When

I went to sleep and dreamed, he woke up, and remembered my waking life as his dream. And vice versa. The typhoon catches its breath, and renews its assault as a gale. The potting shed is not going to blow away. I roll over on something hard, and find a medium-sized, flat, round stone. I put it in my backpack. When the gale subsides to a high wind, I am amazed to hear a person snoring – inside the potting shed! I get up and look behind the narrow partition. A woman, still asleep! She does not look like a gardener – she must be a visitor who somehow got trapped here by the typhoon too. Maybe she was too afraid to tell me she was here, and just fell asleep. Do I wake her? Or would that scare her to death? Her eyes open. 'Uh . . .' I begin.

'So, you found me at last.' She springs up and her kimono swings open. I am too startled to speak. For a weird moment, I mistake her for the mother of Yuki Chiyo, the girl who reported herself lost at Ueno. She dabs my nipples with her wet thumb, her other hand explores inside my boxer shorts – this is wrong, I already told Ai I love her, but her lips slide open for me and a million tiny silver fish change direction. I cannot fight this. I cannot move, look away, respond.

So I come.

Over her shoulder I glimpse Mrs Persimmon. She perches on the sack of earth and sucks dripping pulp from persimmons. She spits out shiny stones.

The bright garden lies trashed by an orgy of gods. Spilt juices from green veins scent the peaceful air. Ripped blooms, torn branches, uprooted shrubs. I find a small, flat, round stone. I put it in my backpack. I would love to stay a while and watch the pond, but I want to avoid the potting shed owner, and anyway the Yakushima ferry leaves in ninety minutes. I wade through the ripped bougainvillea and clamber over the wall, in time to surprise a schoolgirl on a passing bus. My only witness. Back among the houses, neighbours are already up, discussing the mending of fences. I stop at a Lawson's and buy a bottle of Minute Maid grapefruit juice and a cup ramen – kimchee flavour – and ask the girl to add hot water. I eat it on the sea wall. Sakurajima belches ash into the spotless sky, and the sea is ironed smooth. Typhoons wreck worlds but the following morning cleans worlds up. I phone Uncle Money to say I am still alive – I tell him I spent the night with friends in Kagoshima – then I walk the rest of the way to the port. The ferry is waiting – cars and trucks are already being herded on by harbourmen with flags and whistles. I fill in my boarding card, pay my fare, wash, brush my teeth and look for a telephone.

'Typhoon eighteen was on the news,' said Ai, 'but it didn't get much attention because of the pigeons.'

'Pigeons are grabbing headlines?'

'All day yesterday, all over Tokyo, pigeons were flying into buildings, colliding with cars. Like some freaky disaster movie. You can imagine the rumours, theories and experts cramming the TV stations. Secret government tests, avian flu, Aum cultists, magnetic-wave shifts, earthquake doom-mongers. Then the moon last night had its brightest halo for twenty-seven years. How ice crystals in the atmosphere could affect pigeons nobody knows, but it adds to the general spookiness. And this morning, I went to buy some coffee for breakfast, and the camphor tree in front of the prison was black with crows! Worse than an amateur brass orchestra warming up! Seriously, it was as if the prince of darkness was due any moment.'

'So much for my measly typhoon.'

'Let me change the subject before the beeps go. I spoke with Sachiko before she went to work yesterday evening. If you need anywhere to stay when you get back to Tokyo, you can kip here. On the sofa. If I say so. You have to clean up and cook every third day. And you mustn't answer the phone in case Sachiko's gran calls and assumes you're her live-in lover.'

'Hey . . .' I like the 'if I say so' most of all. 'Thanks.'

'Don't decide yet. Mull it over.'

Several islanders spot me as I board the ferry. Schoolmates' mothers, cousins' friends, a sugarcane and fruit wholesaler who does business with Uncle Orange. They ask about life in Tokyo, more out of politeness than interest. I say I am back to collect my winter clothes before the weather changes. Talk is of the typhoon, and how much repairs will cost, and who is likely to pay for what. I hide in the second-class flooring area, and make a sort of protective barrier with my backpack to doze behind. A Kansai ladies' ramblers' club takes up the rest of the floor around me. They are kitted out in flannel shirts, body-warmers, multi-weather trousers, silly hats and sensible footwear. They unfold maps and plot routes. You can tell the islanders apart easily – they looked bored. Because there was no sailing yesterday afternoon the boat continues to fill with passengers. I shuffle up for a man with a greyhound jawline and cheekbones who asks me what time the ferry arrives at Kamiyaku, the main port on Yakushima. He pays for this information in unshelled peanuts. I accept a few to be courteous but they are badly addictive. We munch our way through most of the bag, piling up a mound of husks. Greyhound is a publisher in Ochiai and knows Ueno lost property office – he met Mrs Sasaki's sister at a literary dinner once. The engines groooaaarrrrrrrr into life, the hiking ladies wooooooooo! and the porthole view rotates and slides away. The nine o'clock news bulletin is about the expected resignation of another prime minister following a coalition collapse. 'Nothing is older than this morning's news,' says Greyhound, 'and nothing is newer than Pericles.' Pretty soon the offshore reception turns the news to hiss, and the Kirishima-Yaku national park video clicks on. All islanders know the script off by heart. It lullabies us on these crossings.

All Japan has been concreted over. The last sacred forests have been cut down for chopsticks, the inland sea has been paved over and declared a national carpark, and where mountains once stood apartment buildings vanish into the clouds. When people reach the age of twenty their legs are amputated and their torsos are fitted with interfaces that plug directly into sophisticated skateboards – for use in the home or office – or into grander vehicles, for longer journeys. My twentieth birthday was back in September, so I am long overdue this rite-of-passage operation. But I want to keep my legs attached, so I joined the resistance movement. I am taken to be introduced to our three leaders, who live in Miyakonojō, a place remote beyond cars. Their bodies are amputated too, for extra camouflage. Their heads sit in a row, under the blazing sun. Their necks are trussed to the edge of a bowling pit, and I realize I have been brought before Gunzo, Nabe and Kakizaki. Fortunately, when they see me they blink excitedly – 'Messiah! Messiah! Messiah!' This perplexes me. 'Are you quite sure?' They seem to be. 'The message shall be revealed to you! You alone shall reverse the meteoric dive of humanity into endless suffering!' That sounds great. 'How?' Kakizaki's lower jaw falls off, but he says these words: 'Pull out the plug.'

At my feet is a bath plug, with a shining chain. I pull. Underneath is earth – since the asphalting laws, earth is forbidden. It stirs, and a worm wriggles upward and out of the hole. Another follows, and another, another. The last Japanese worms. They wriggle their way to a preordained position on a nine-by-nine grid. Each position on this grid is a kanji or a Japanese character, written in worm bodies instead of brush strokes. These words are the one true scripture. It is also death for the worms – the tarmac hotplates their tender bodies. As they sizzle, they smell of tuna and mayonnaise. But their sacrifice is not in vain. In the eighty-one characters I read truth – the secrets of hearts and minds, quarks and love, peace and time. The truth glows in blazing jade on my memory's retina. I shall impart this wisdom to my thirsty species, and the arid deserts will bloom.

◆

'Miyake! Miyake, you mongrel! Wake up!'

The upside-down face of Mr Ikeda, my ex-sports teacher, floats above me. A half-eaten tuna-and-mayonnaise sandwich wilts in his hand. I jerk up with a groan of annoyance. Mr Ikeda assumes I am just sleepy. I have to remember something . . . 'I saw you in the ferry terminal, but then I said to myself, "No, Miyake is in distant Edo!" What are you doing back so soon? The big city too much to handle, hey?'

I am forgetting something. What is it? 'Not really, sir. Actually, I—'

'Ah, to be young in Tokyo. I could almost envy you if I wasn't already me. I spent the first two Great Primes of my life in Tokyo. I waltzed into *the* top sports university – you wouldn't have heard of it – and a wild young thing I was, too. The days I had! The nights I had! My nickname among the ladies gives you the full story. Ace. Ace Ikeda. Then in my first teaching post I put together one of the finest high-school soccer teams Japan ever saw. Could have gone all the way to the national cup qualifiers, if the referee hadn't been a geriatric, blind, crippled, corrupt, dribbling sack of slugshit. Me and my boys – our nickname? The Invincibles! Not like' – Mr Ikeda waves his hand in disgust at the students in their 'Yakushima Junior High' track-suit tops – 'this pack of mongrels.'

'Are you coming back from a friendly, sir?'

'Nothing friendly about that bloated faggot tapeworm Kagoshima coach. During the typhoon last night I was praying a lorry of something flammable would crash into his house.'

'So, what was the score, sir?'

Mr Ikeda grimaces. 'Kagoshima Tosspots – twenty; Yakushima Mongrels – one.'

This knife I cannot resist twisting. 'One goal? A hopeful sign, sir.'

'Kagoshima Tosspots scored an own goal.' Mr Ikeda skulks off. The tourist video clicks off – we must be within broadcasting range of Yakushima. I look through the window and see the island, sliding over the horizon. The prime minister promises that under his guidance the country will become a lifestyle superpower. Greyhound cracks open a peanut. 'Politicians and sports coaches need to be smart enough to master the game, but dumb enough to think it matters.'

I remember my dream.

'Are you suffering from sea-sickness?' asks Greyhound. 'Or was it your ex-games teacher?'

'I . . . dreamed I was a sort of Sanzōhōshi carrying the Buddhist scriptures from India. I was shown the divine knowledge necessary to save humanity from itself.'

'I'll give you six per cent on the first ten thousand copies sold, nine per cent thereafter.'

'But I can only remember one word.'

'Which is?'

'"Mumps"'

'As in . . .'

'The illness that makes your neck swell up.'

'"Mumps" what?'

'Mumps . . . nothing.'

'Deal's off.' Greyhound shakes the bag. 'I ate the last peanut.'

Yakushima grows whenever you look away. Leaving a place is weird, but returning is always weirder. In eight weeks nothing has changed but nothing is the same. The Kamiyaku river bridge, the crushed-velvet mountains, the gaol-grey escarpments. A book you read is not the same book it was before you read it. Maybe a girl you sleep with is not the same girl you went to bed with. Here comes the quay – one of the rope-throwers shouts at me and waves. One of Uncle Tarmac's mah-jong boozing partners. The gangplank is lowered, and I join the big group of disembarking passengers. I should go and pay my respects to the head of the family, Uncle Pachinko. But the point of this journey is to pay my respects to Anju. Outside the ferry ticket office a van pulls up, and a wholesaler who does business with Uncle Orange offers me a lift.

'Are you going as far as Anbō?'

'Jump in.'

We drive off. 'Warm day,' I say. 'Rain soon,' he replies. Rain is always a safe bet on Yakushima. The wholesaler is a quiet man, so there are no embarrassing silences. He gestures to me to help myself to a sack of ponkan oranges, which are the island's chief export and easily the most delicious fruit product in the country, if not the whole of Asia. I must have eaten ten thousand ponkans since I came to Yakushima. Cut me open, you get ponkan juice. I watch the forgotten details of my home. The rusty oil drums up by the tourist lodges, the tiny airstrip, the dying sawmill. This far south-west, the trees are still wearing their shabby summer leaves. We pass a cluster of racing cyclists in sleek, tropical fish-colours. The road bucks here. Over the bridge, the waterfall, and here comes the village of Anbō.

The cemetery hammers and saws with insects. The trees stir and the afternoon stews. An ancient October recipe. The Miyake family corner of the enclosure is one of the best tended – my grandmother still comes, every morning, to clean, weed, sweep, and change the wildflowers. I bow before the main grey gravestone, and walk around the side to the smaller black stone erected for Anju. It is inscribed with the death-name the priest chose for her, but I think that is just a way for them to palm more money from grieving mourners. My sister is still Anju Miyake. I pour mineral water over her. I put the bunch of flowers in the holder, together with those our grandmother arranged there. I wish I knew the names of flowers. Clustered white stars, pink comet-tails, crimson semiquaver berries. I offer her a champagne bomb, and unwrap one for myself. Then I light the incense. 'This,' I tell her, 'is a present from our mother. She gave me the money, and I bought it from a temple near Miyazaki station.' I take out my three flat stones and build her a pyramid. Then I sit on the step and press my ear against the polished stone, tight, to see if I can hear anything. The sea breathes peacefully over the edge of the land.

I want to kiss the tombstone, so I do, and only a dark bird with rose eyes witnesses. I lean back and think about nothing in particular until the champagne bomb explodes. So little lasts. Mountains, classic songs, real friendship. Mist rolls down from Mt Miyanoura, dimming the sun, turning the blue sea beery. I brought our great-uncle's kaiten journal to read parts to Anju, because they both died under the sea. But I think Anju will hear clearly if I just read quietly to myself, here or wherever. I don't have to say anything about what happened in Tokyo. Being is louder than saying, for her, for me, for us. Ants have discovered Anju's champagne bomb. 'Hey, Anju. Guess who I'm going to go see now?'

The last time I walked up this valley path I was carrying my man-of-the-match trophy, kicking a stone. I was about a third shorter than I am now. I half-expect to meet my eleven-year-old self. Weeds colonize the middle of the track. Not a soul is around. A nightingale sings about another world and a monkey screams about this one. I pass the torī gate and the stone lions. I never went back to the shrine of the thunder god. A famous craftsman came from Kyoto to replace the missing head, and the tourist department printed his new face on pamphlets. I see the forest has nearly smothered the steep path. Every winter his believers become fewer. So gods do die, just like pop stars and sisters. The hanging bridge no longer looks so safe. My footfalls thud rather than boom, as if the planking could crumble any day now. The river below is swollen from last night's rain. Over half the rice fields in the valley have fallen into disuse. Farmers die too, and their sons are making money in Kagoshima or Kitakyūshū or Osaka. Rice field terraces and old barns are allowed to collapse – typhoons are cheaper than builders. The valley belongs to insects, now. I kick stones. Unkempt shrubs grow from the eaves of my grandmother's house. I watch the old place, as mist thickens into rain. She is a sour lady – but she loved Anju too, in her fierce way. Leaving a picture lets you see the whole frame. The worst that can happen is that she screams at me to go away, and after the last seven weeks that no longer seems so bad.

'Gran?'

I wade through the grass into the courtyard, and think of an old tale of a spinning-wheel sorceress awaiting her philandering husband's return, in which the house goes to rot and ruin, but the wife never ages a day. I see a pearly movement between mossy stones – the coils of a snake! Neither its head nor tail are visible, but its coils are as thick as my arm. Snake disappears behind a rusting rotovator. Did Anju talk about a pale snake once? Or did I dream it? I vaguely recall our grandmother talking about a snake that lived in the storehouse when she was a girl, and was supposed to be the harbinger of a death in the family. That must be superstition. Snakes never live for seventy years. I think. I knock on the doorframe, and force open the stubborn door. I hear the radio. 'Gran? It's Eiji.'

I slide the insect screen aside, step into the cool, and breathe in deep. Cooking sake, damp wood, the chemical toilet. Incense from the tatami room. Old people have a particular odour – I guess they say the same about young people. A mouse disappears. The radio means that my grandmother is probably not at home. She was in the habit of leaving it on for the dog, and when the dog died she left the radio on for the house. 'Gran?' I peer into the tatami room, ignoring a weird feeling that somebody has just this moment died. A feather duster is propped against the foot of the family altar. Hanging scrolls of autumn scenes, the vase of flowers, a cabinet filled with the trinkets and baubles of an island lifetime. She has never left Yakushima. The rain is splashing through the mosquito netting, so I slide the glass across. I used to be afraid of this room. Not Anju. During O-bon she used to lie in wait outside, and burst in to catch the spirits eating cherries our grandmother left out for them. I look at the dead in the black lacquer cabinet. Dressed in oilskins, suits, uniforms, costumes hired from photographers. And here is my sister, toothy on her first day at elementary school.

'Gran?'

I go into the kitchen, help myself to a glass of water, and sit down on the sofa that me and Anju tried – and failed – to levitate. She blamed my puny ESP powers, because she could bend spoons with hers. I believed her for years. The sofa boingggggggggs, but after a long walk on a sticky day it is comfortable, way too comfortable . . .

I dream all dreamers, all of you.

I dream the frost patterns on the temple bell.

I dream the bright water dripping from the spear of Izanagi.

I dream the drips solidifying into these islands we call Japan.

I dream the flying fish and the Pleiades.

I dream the skin flakes in the keyboard gullies.

I dream the cities and the ovaries.

I dream a mind in eight parts.

I dream a girl, drowning, alone without a word of complaint. I dream her young body, passed between waves and currents, until it dissolves into blue and nothing remains.

I dream the stone whale, wrapped in seaweed and barnacles, watching.

I dream the message bubbling from its blow-hole.

'We interrupt this programme to bring an emergency bulletin . . .'

'A massive earthquake has struck the Tokyo metropolitan region within the last sixty seconds. The National Bureau of Seismology reports a quake of 7.3 intensity on the Richter scale, which exceeds the Great Kansai Earthquake of 1995, and indicates extreme structural damage throughout the Kanto basin. Members of the public listening in the Tokyo region are requested to remain calm, and if possible, leave the building for open space away from the danger of falling masonry, and be prepared for aftershocks. Do not use elevators. Turn off gas and electrical appliances. If possible, stay away from windows. The Rapid Earthquake Response Unit is assessing the tsunami risk. All programmes are cancelled until further notice. We will be broadcasting emergency updates non-stop, as we receive more news. I repeat . . .'

The room is cold. I turn the radio right down, and pick up the antique telephone. I try three times, but Ai's number is dead. So is Buntarō's. So is Nero's. No reply from Ueno. Nothing from the Tokyo operator.

I would give anything to be dreaming right now. Anything. Are the airwaves and cables jammed because half the phone users in the country are trying to call the capital, or because Tokyo is now a landscape of rubble under clouds of cement dust? Outside, a century of quiet rain is falling on all the leaves, stones and pine needles of the valley. Inside, the radio man announces that a state of emergency has been declared. I imagine a pane of glass exploding next to Ai's face, or a steel girder crashing through her piano. I imagine a thousand things. I grab my bag, slide down the hallway, scrunch my feet into my trainers, and scrape open the stubborn door. And I begin running.

Nine

DAVID MITCHELL

Ghostwritten

Winner of the *Mail on Sunday*/John Llewellyn Rhys Prize

'The best first novel I have read in ages . . . it beguiles, informs, shocks and captivates.'
William Boyd, *Daily Telegraph* Books of the Year

Cloud Atlas

Shortlisted for the Man Booker Prize and winner of the Richard & Judy Best Read of the Year

'An impeccable dance of genres . . . an elegiac, radiant festival of prescience, meditation and entertainment'
Neel Mukherjee, *The Times*

Black Swan Green

Shortlisted for the Costa Novel Award

'Spry, disconcerting and moving. It is also extremely funny even – or especially – at the blackest of moments.'
Kate Kellaway, *Observer*

The Thousand Autumns of Jacob de Zoet

Shortlisted for the James Tait Black Memorial and Commonwealth Writers' Prizes

'Spectacularly accomplished and thrillingly suspenseful . . . it brims with rich, involving and affecting humanity'
Peter Kemp, *The Sunday Times*

SCEPTRE